Acclaim for C.D. Payne's

Youth in Revolt:

The Journals of Nick Twisp

"This American cult 'Adrian Mole' is an altogether rougher, sexier, and funnier tale. . . A rollercoaster ride through the nemesis of adolescent angst." —*London Mail*

"A sussed, silly and energetic account which literally bulges with Nick Twisp's hormonal excitations. . . Faster and funnier than 14 ever felt before." —*The Punter* [UK]

"In the course of 499 pages, Nick falls in and out of favor with his divorced parents; he looks for love in all the wrong places; he invents; he schemes. He even burns down half of Berkeley. But throughout, this novel—or three novels—is extremely readable. For while Nick searches for the joys of sex, he finds a great deal more—a general *joie de vivre* and compassion that prove addictive." —*L.A. Reader*

"A hilarious six month journey through the thorny underbrush of sexual desire, frustration, and (occasionally painful) discovery. . . Payne does not offer up his characters to the altar of hackneyed change or growth. He gives us instead a wonderfully original refugee from parental cynicism and the 'gulag of the public schools' whose scorn, bad attitude, and unflagging horniness persist in a way that is engagingly real. . . There is a refreshing frankness and celebration in the writing that elevates it above the mere silliness of much of today's comic fiction." —*New Haven Advocate*

"*Youth in Revolt*. . . [is] a hefty coming-of-age novel which actually lives up to the publisher's comparisons to *A Confederacy of Dunces* and *Portnoy's Complaint*, and in many ways surpasses them... One of the funniest novels I've ever read." —*Hypno Magazine*

"Payne's ability to constantly introduce new characters and new plots while interweaving the old ones is like watching an aerialist interrupt his highwire act to take out a lawn chair, then do a headstand on it and start juggling with his feet. And then just as you're wondering how he can get out of that predicament, he sets fire to the juggling balls. It's hard to say which are more satisfying: the twists you can tell are coming or the ones that take you by surprise." —*Berkeley Express*

"It's a high honor and distinct privilege, then, to introduce C.D. Payne's totally unsentimental and extremely funny first novel, *Youth in Revolt: The Journals of Nick Twisp*. It's the antidote to Salinger's tale of the teenage saint Holden Caulfield." —*The Oregonian*

"*Youth in Revolt* is an unstintingly hilarious black comedy, almost certainly the funniest book you'll read this year... Nick is irresistible, for his first encounters with adult phenomena always seem to bring out an appropriately warped response or an almost-brilliant insight. . . Nick's voice is unique and indelible, Payne's language rich and inventive. C.D. Payne has set a high standard for himself." —*Los Angeles Times*

"A genuinely funny book, one that will have many readers laughing out loud. . . Nick is an inspired chronicler of his inner life and philosophy . . . Payne captures the trials of adolescence in these perilous times, dealing with far more than just the pangs of hormonal upheavals." —*Sonoma County Bohemian*

Young and Revolting

The Continental Journals of Nick Twisp

Also by C.D. Payne

Youth in Revolt: The Journals of Nick Twisp

Revolting Youth: The Further Journals of Nick Twisp

Revoltingly Young: The Journals
of Nick Twisp's Younger Brother

Cut to the Twisp

Civic Beauties

Frisco Pigeon Mambo

Queen of America

Young and Revolting

The Continental Journals of Nick Twisp

Book V: Youth in France

C.D. Payne

ISBN 0-7414-3417-2

Published by:

INFINITY
PUBLISHING.COM

1094 New DeHaven Street, Suite 100
West Conshohocken, PA 19428-2713
Info@buybooksontheweb.com
www.buybooksontheweb.com
Toll-free (877) BUY BOOK
Local Phone (610) 941-9999
Fax (610) 941-9959

Printed in the United States of America

Printed on Recycled Paper

Published July 2006

To Joy

A NOTE ON THE SERIES

Youth in Revolt contains Books 1, 2, and 3

Revolting Youth is Book 4

Young and Revolting is Book 5

Revoltingly Young is Book 6

Cut to the Twisp contains text deleted from the post-1994 U.S. and U.K. editions of *Youth in Revolt*, plus additional short pieces.

MAY

TUESDAY, May 11 — I'm married!

I'm on the lam!

I'm overseas!

Presently, I'm rolling across Belgium with a counterfeit passport in my pocket, bulky wads of hundred dollar bills secreted about my person, and The Woman Who Is Expecting (Not Happily) My Child nestled at my side. Sheeni, of course, has claimed the window seat of our extravagantly posh bus, though she seems less than transfixed by the Belgium countryside. Can't say I blame her. So far Europe looks like the American Midwest with zealously enforced anti-littering laws and extremely aggressive foreign car salesmen. Everyone on the road seems to be driving like a lunatic, including our chunky lady bus driver. If I weren't in a state of near nervous collapse, I'm sure I would be experiencing no small measure of highway terror.

Not thinking too clearly, but I calculate I've been awake nearly 40 hours—ever since we left Yazoo City, Mississippi: hallowed venue of recent Twisp-Saunders nuptials. Took a bus to Atlanta, then hopped a plane to Brussels. Didn't fly directly to Paris in case Sheeni's dad had alerted French authorities. My astute wife reasons French customs will be less vigilant at obscure Belgium crossings. I hope so! Frightfully nervous at Brussels customs, but Sheeni got us through with magnificent charm in overdrive. No luggage search or inspection of intimate bodily cavities, thank God. No language barrier so far as Belgians mostly proficient in English. Can't blame them as their own native tongue (Flemish? Martian?) sounds like complete gibberish.

Stomach is rumbling. Nothing but airline food since yesterday. Can't remember when I had my last bowel movement. Fear I may not be cut out for world traveling. Sheeni fresh as a daisy. On plane, she tucked up her legs, curled against a tiny airline pillow, and slept like she was in her own virginal bed. Don't see how she does it. After 10 minutes in that posture, my legs would be in a state of permanent crimp. After 20 minutes gangrene would be setting in. State of health not helped by two swarthy Belgians behind us smoking like chimneys. Can't believe they permit smoking in such confined quarters. Just try lighting up on a bus in California. You'd be rocketing out a window in two seconds flat. One of them, I noticed, was wearing a Wart Watch. I hope it was our authorized Taiwanese model and not some cheap Chinese knockoff.

Road sign for French border: Only 10 km to go. My next entry, diary, may be written from a French jail cell.

8:50 p.m. We're in Paris! Too tired to write much. Attracted intense interest of French customs officers. Scared shitless (I wish), but relieved to see object of their fascination was my surgically remodeled Belmondoesque physiognomy. Many queries in voluble French expertly parried by my charming wife. God knows what she told them. One even wanted my autograph for his aunt (apparently a big Jean-Paul Belmondo fan). Luckily, I remembered to sign it Rick S. Hunter, my latest pseudonym (I've had lots). Now gleaming inside each of our passports is an official full-page hologram that reads "3 month visa, one entry." Sheeni is totally legal and I'm nearly so (visa is genuine; only passport is fake).

Our crazed Paris taxi driver was even more of a road menace than Belgian bus driver. Paris a blur of lights, honking horns, and screeching tires. At last reached our semi-decrepit two-star hotel, reserved miraculously by Sheeni via pay phone in Yazoo City. No trouble from fawning desk clerk, another Belmondo fan.

I'm officially honeymooning in Paris, France!

That reminds me: must get voltage converter for laptop. This stupid country has entirely different plugs.

Excited wife wants to go out and explore the town. No way, Jose. This guy is going to bed.

WEDNESDAY, May 12 — I spent the first 45 minutes this morning holed up in our tiny unventilated bathroom. All too obviously it had begun its life several centuries earlier as a closet. Not much had changed except for the introduction of a coffin-sized metal shower, micro sink, and peculiar Frenchified toilet.

When I emerged, treading lighter, My Love was seated on the windowsill and gazing out across the city. She wrinkled her nose. "What were you doing in there?"

"Making a very special gift to the people of France. How's the weather?"

"Glorious. I can't believe I'm actually in Paris."

I sat on the rumpled bed to put on my shoes. "Well, just remember, if it weren't for me, darling, you'd still be solving algebra problems back in Ukiah."

"If it weren't for you, Nick Twisp, I wouldn't feel like throwing up right now."

"Hey, you were the guy who said let's skip the condom."

"I wish I *were* a guy, Nickie. The only time they experience nausea is when they write out the paternity support checks. I can't believe how unfair the human reproduction process is to females."

She's correct, of course. In the immortal words of Barbra Streisand having a baby is like shoving a piano through a transom. Thankfully, we males (mostly) dodge the whole messy business.

I strolled over, gave her a kiss, and looked out the window. Many genuinely antique stone buildings and in the distance a patch of shimmering aqua.

"What's that water feature?" I asked.

"It's the Seine, you twit. And over there are the spires of Notre-Dame."

"Do they have a football team too?"

"Nickie, you are *so* retarded."

"Call me Rick. Hey, let's go eat."

7:25 p.m. I'm bushed. Must have walked 900 miles. God knows what the hour is in real American time. My head is buzzing; my eyes feel like French intellectuals have been using them for ashtrays. Sheeni, of course, is her usual indefatigable self. You'd think our hungry zygote would be slowing her down. My theory on sightseeing: if you've read all the guidebooks, why bother visiting the actual places? Hell, you already know what you're going to see. As usual, Sheeni not persuaded by flawless Twispian logic. Has been boning up on the City of Light since Day One. Knows every significant landmark and its history back to 508 A.D. Intends to inspect each one THOROUGHLY. Dogs are barking angrily. Must acquire more comfortable shoes if crippling foot crisis to be averted.

First stop after breakfast was hotel tourist kiosk for voltage converter and oversized sunglasses. Seems Jean-Paul Belmondo has a *much* higher profile in Europe than Ukiah, California. While masticating complimentary croissant in dank hotel dining room, accosted twice by eager film buffs. Both German-speaking so could only smile and nod as they chattered enthusiastically in unintelligible grunts. Sheeni no help as she exhibits the usual Francophilian contempt for German Culture.

Strolling the boulevards, felt like a glamorous celebrity behind dark glasses, though visually handicapped when stumbling through dim historic interiors. Viewed mucho masterpieces at the Louvre, including the *Mona Lisa*. Yeah, I'd have to rate it marginally more polished than the paint-by-number version my old Oakland pal Lefty attempted in the fourth grade. One drawback of Growing Up Fast: youthful Sheeni gets into French museums for free, while even more youthful Rick S. Hunter (whose passport identifies him as 18) has to stand in long lines to pay full-fare for the overpriced adult tickets.

All in all, I'd rate the Louvre a real eye-dazzler, but that silly glass pyramid in the courtyard has got to go. Very steamy when the sun hits it. Now I know how those ants felt that I used to fry with my magnifying glass when I was a kid. Also overdue for demolition: Pompidou Centre, a hideous eyesore across the piazza from an outdoor café where we ate dinner.

Sheeni claims Paris is the greatest creation of the human race: "The jewel of the Earth." She makes a cogent case, but why for the past half-century have armies of builders been doing their best to uglify the place? Personally, I think those arrogant architects should be strung up by their thumbs and beaten soundly with their T-squares. Even Sheeni had to concede all those monstrous high-rises glimpsed in the distance are a blot on the landscape.

Twenty-four hours in romantic Paris and have not been laid once. Made blatant overtures toward lovely bride, but she insists on an evening *café au lait* first. Spending great wads of euros. Must find out current exchange rate. It appears they're worth about 10 cents US. Thank God we came here with mighty American dollars.

THURSDAY, May 13 — Three times, diary. Twice last night and once again this morning. Yet despite all those prolonged feet soaks, blistered dogs are still snarling. Meanwhile, on the sex front, Sheeni continuing to rebuff my advances. Now says she is having her period, although it was my understanding that chicks who were preggers didn't get those. She scoffed and said that was an old wives' tale. I reminded her that we were here on our honeymoon and that guys brought certain expectations to these occasions. She replied that there was far too much to see and do in Paris to linger in bed with some 14-year-old sex maniac. "I'm nearly 15," growled François Dillinger, my trigger-happy and lately sex-starved alter ego. We withdrew with our T.E. (Thunderous Erection) to the midget bathroom and dealt with it in a manner not covered by the Napoleonic Code.

5:20 p.m. Dogs now happily appeased. François spotted smart shoe store on Boulevard St. Germain and insisted on brief interruption in Sheeni's rigorous tourism program. Removed sunglasses and received doting service from giggling shopgirls. Rejected modish Italian loafers in favor of unusual Rumanian import with spongy rubber soles a full three inches thick. Apparently popular with miners of Eastern Europe. Like walking on clouds! Dogs in heaven. Sheeni appalled. Said shoes must have been exported to France by mistake. Said I looked like a hobbit on vacation from Middle Earth.

Salesgirls not too complimentary either, if Sheeni translations to be believed. Protests ignored. Shoes a bargain: only *E*180. Additional footwear bonus: thick soles augment stature. Now nearly as tall as Sheeni's erstwhile boyfriend Trent Preston. Wife so disgusted she bought two pairs for herself—considerably more expensive than mine and untouched by Rumanians.

Exiting with our purchases, I noticed a McDanolds right next door. François was jonesing for a burger, but Sheeni insisted on lunching at another authentic Parisian café—complete with unintelligible menu, snotty waiters, and lofty prices. Believe it or not, restaurants in France have the nerve to tack on a compulsory 15 percent tip. It's no wonder the waiters treat you like dogs. This place had a busy lunch crowd puffing away madly on Gauloises and Marlboros. Helpful for American trade deficit, but hell on health-minded tourists. I ordered the excellent-looking grilled sausages, which turned out to have been made from parts of the animal normally discarded by civilized persons. At least the accompanying French fries and salad were edible. Sheeni said her mussels were "delicious in the extreme." Leonine young waiter flirted outrageously throughout lunch with my wife. Wish I understood French. For all I know he may have been asking for her phone number. I had to sit there and seethe while he chatted her up. Then she made me leave the twit an *additional* tip. Talk about adding insult to injury. Later, she admitted that she was disappointed that he had detected she was an American.

"It's so distressing to discover one speaks French with an accent," she lamented, as we strolled through the Luxembourg Gardens, which confusingly are not in Luxembourg but right in the middle of Paris.

"Your French is superb," I reassured her.

"How would you know?" she demanded. "Let's face it, Nick or Rick or whatever your name is, in this country your language skills rank at the sub-toddler level. I think you should acquire some French. And fast."

"But why? We're only here on 90-day tourist visas."

"Well, I'm not going back. And need I remind you that you are a fugitive from justice? Overstaying your visa is hardly going to make much of an additional dent in your criminal rap sheet."

Damn. Stuck in a country where I can't even converse with preschoolers. I didn't dare tell her that I had already been tested scientifically and judged incapable of learning a second language.

Oui, I'm in a pickle.

11:35 p.m. Relaxing in hotel room in warm postcoital glow. Sipping mock champagne and nibbling bonbons. Sheeni, getting over period fast, decided to pretend she was realizing a girlish dream: losing her virginity to handsome Frenchman in sumptuous suite at Paris Ritz. Kept her eyes closed the whole time and whispered endearments in French to some Frog named Philippe. I didn't mind. Philippe may have been winning the maidenly sighs, but I was the Yank getting his ashes hauled.

FRIDAY, May 14 — Rude shock at breakfast. While dining on my usual complimentary croissant (bacon and eggs apparently being unknown in this country), I happened to glance at the *International Herald-Tribune*, a newspaper legible to English speakers. The headline read: "U.S. Dollar Sinks to New Low against Euro." It turns out that my bargain $18 Rumanian miners' shoes actually cost over $200. And that *tarte aux pommes* I snacked on yesterday set me back nearly $10. Ten bucks for a goddam piece of apple pie!

"Well, Rick," commented Sheeni, sipping her complimentary canned o.j., "no one said Europe was a bargain. That's why we need to find an apartment. Do you have any idea what this hotel is costing us?"

"Don't tell me. I don't want to know!"

"It won't be easy," she continued. "I can put up my hair and pass for 20, but even in your rare mature moments you barely look your age. I suppose I could try to pass you off as my younger brother."

"Nothing doing. We're Mr. and Mrs. Rick S. Hunter and that's what it's going to say on our door."

"Oh, dear. I seem to have married a Neanderthal. Well, at least try not to smile so much. The French don't understand gratuitous smiling. They tend to assume you're either insane or retarded."

"I feel the same way about them."

"Naturally there are only certain *arrondissements* in which I'm willing to live."

"What's that?" I asked.

"Those are the various districts of Paris. To compare it to the Bay Area, there are certain preferred districts like San Francisco and others like Oakland."

"Hey, I was born and raised in Oakland."

"Yes. That was precisely my point."

2:15 p.m. Back at the hotel to change into our most "mature" outfits. We may have a lead on a possible apartment. Sheeni had the idea to go to the Sorbonne and check for rental notices on campus bulletin boards. If your concept of college is pretty coeds sauntering across leafy quadrangles toward ivy-covered halls, France's oldest university will come as a jolt. It's more like a soot-begrimed medieval urban slum. Not a frat house or football stadium in sight. Lots of pretty girls though, and more than a few that François would rate as strikingly beautiful. This may explain all those outdoor cafes. There are worse ways to pass your time than sipping a cognac on a Parisian boulevard while the cream of Gallic pulchritude passes by. I'd certainly rate it higher than watching 22 helmeted brutes pummel each other on a gridiron.

Improbably, we did locate a notice board and while Sheeni was jotting down some addresses, she was affably addressed by a tall Frog in a cashmere sweater who was only slightly better looking than Trent Preston. His aquiline nose shrieked of aristocratic forbears. It was complemented by one of those chins that appear to have been chiseled from granite. They had an interminable conversation in French that involved much eyelash fluttering, unconscious hair smoothing, and gratuitous smiling. All in all, I'd say it was a provocative case of blatant flirting. Nor was any effort made to involve or even acknowledge the scowling American in the sunglasses and unusual shoes. The upshot of all of this, I found out when at last the fellow tore himself away from my wife, was that "Alphonse" had revealed that a friend of his was soon to vacate his digs in the Montparnasse district.

"You mean this Alphonse creep wants us to move in with him?" I asked, shocked. Did the French have no respect at all for the institution of marriage?

"No, silly," Sheeni replied. "His friend has a furnished flat in Alphonse's building. He's moving out on Sunday. Alphonse says the rents are affordable and his *aubergiste* is very liberal minded."

"Is that his mistress?"

"Nickie, your incomprehension continues to astound. *Aubergiste* means landlady. And this one is willing to rent to students, Algerians, even Americans. It could be a wonderful break for us."

Yeah, ruminated François darkly, and not a bad opportunity for Alphonse either.

5:17 p.m. The "flat" turned out to be a one-room attic apartment with an alcove for a bed and an open-air tin bathtub in the adjoining kitchenette. The elusive toilet we discovered in the skimpy clothes closet. The scarred walls and slanted low ceiling appeared not to have felt the lash of a paintbrush since Jean Gabin was in diapers. Up five long flights of stairs with no elevator in sight. At least there was an expansive view across the chimneypots (and satellite dishes) of Paris. The rent is *E*900 a month, which Sheeni thought was reasonable for a convenient location on a picturesque street off the avenue du Maine. But Madame Ruzicka, the "liberal-minded" elderly landlady, regarded us with a skeptical eye. After a long interrogation of Sheeni in her stuffy old lady's apartment, she directed My Love to step out into the hall so she could have a private chat with the silent male. She looked me over as a disheveled green parrot grumbled in French on its messy iron stand.

"Now, young man, why are you wearing those glasses?" she inquired in excellent English. Her accent was from somewhere east of France. "Are you a drug addict?"

I removed my sunglasses.

"Ah, you bear a superficial resemblance to a certain movie actor. No doubt an inconvenience for you, though perhaps useful for attracting pretty young things. She is not your sister, of course."

"No, she's my wife."

"Well, that is slightly more plausible than her story. And what age do you claim to be?"

"I claim to be 18."

"Most extravagant. And your parents?"

"All deceased."

"You should inform your wife. She is not aware of their passing. You were married where?"

"In Mississippi last week. It was perfectly legal. We could show you the license, if you like."

"Legally married in Mississippi. How extraordinary. But I believe your South is quite an eccentric region. And why have you come to France?"

"Sheeni—my wife—desires to live in Paris. She is a great enthusiast for all things French."

"Well, perhaps she will outgrow that delusion. Do your parents know where you are?"

"Our parents have thrown up their hands. They are very narrow-minded. They kicked us out."

"I have heard American parents do that. Extraordinary. And how will you support yourselves? It's most difficult to be employed legally in France."

"I invented a novelty watch that is very popular with teenagers. For this I have received royalties approaching one million dollars. It's called a Wart Watch. Perhaps you've heard of it?"

"I may have seen such a timepiece disfiguring the wrist of one of my tenants. Its appeal eludes me. And now the proud creator stands before me to boast of his accomplishment."

"Well, you asked how I was going to pay the rent," I replied, offended. It wasn't like I was dying to climb five flights every time I went out for a magazine. At these prices you'd think they could afford to put in an elevator.

"Thank you, young man. This has been most enlightening. You may go now. I will call you if I decide in your favor."

9:47 p.m. No message from the nosy *aubergiste*. For a change of pace we had dinner in one of the numerous Vietnamese restaurants to be found in Paris—a legacy, says Sheeni, of past colonial misadventures in Indochina. The food was great, the prices were reasonable, and for a change we didn't have to get down on our hands and knees to beg the waiter for the check.

My fourth day in Paris and I've yet to spot the Eiffel Tower. Must not be as imposing as popularly supposed or perhaps they've taken it out for cleaning.

SATURDAY, May 15 — I have been married for exactly one week. And who said teen marriages never last?

"I've decided what you need is total immersion," announced my anniversary bride at breakfast this morning. Perhaps in honor of the occasion the ubiquitous croissants had been replaced with complimentary mini baguettes. These were served with tabs of butter and tiny packets of Israeli jam. No costly protein as usual. All around us restive Germans were grumbling for sausages.

"Total immersion," I repeated hopefully. "In what—your nubile young body?"

"In French," she replied. "I can see now that is the only way you are going to learn. From this moment forth, I shall speak to you only in French. It's for the best, darling."

She said more, but—not surprisingly—the balance of her remarks was unintelligible. Yes, it's a bit disconcerting for a fellow when the only person he knows within 10,000 miles decides to withdraw unilaterally from their common language. *Merde!*

My new all-French wife and I took the subway to today's museum: the Orsay. This one, in a converted railroad station, was not as jammed with mossy antiquities as the ostentatious Louvre across the river. Room after room of stunning Impressionist paintings stuck away as an afterthought on the second floor. Those guys really knew how to paint, even if they couldn't stay between the lines. I liked the Cézannes; Sheeni appeared to prefer the Renoirs, though perhaps she was admiring the sheen on the gilded frames. And what a shock to turn a corner and come face to face with *Whistler's Mother,* enduring forever her maternal disappointments.

We had lunch under the immense fin de siècle murals in the ritzy upstairs restaurant. Mobbed with tourists, but somehow the French manage to make institutional food quite palatable. Sheeni nodded approvingly while commenting on her trout. Or perhaps she was inviting me to employ her braised filet in some bizarre sexual rite. I hadn't a clue. I hope she tires of this charade soon, as I feel it is not conducive to a placid marital life.

10:47 p.m. Back from a perusal of the bookstores on Boulevard St. Michel. A warm, pleasant evening, though relations with incommunicado spouse getting frostier. One of the shops had an English-language section, so at least I could reacquaint myself with my mother tongue. Not for long. Sheeni yanked the computer magazine from my hand and replaced it with the latest issue of *Paris Match*. Enjoyed the rampant nudity in French ads, though doubt it contributed much toward vocabulary building.

Still no message from Madame Ruzicka, nor sightings of E.T. (Eiffel Tower). Annoyed wife just removed my probing hand from her delectable body while making forceful declarative statements. François prays she has not resorted to the ultimate linguistic weapon: no sex until I learn French!

SUNDAY, May 16 — The buzzing telephone rudely awakened us at 6:14 a.m. Fearing it might be the FBI, I grunted a disguised "bonjour." It was Madame Ruzicka calling to say the apartment was ours if we still wanted it. We did. But not even this good news broke the language barrier. Excited wife leaped out of bed and, throwing on her clothes, harangued me to: hurry? stand on my head? leap naked from the window? Every toddler in France could understand her, but I was clueless as usual.

2:48 p.m. We're moved! Already, I have climbed those marble stairs nine times—four while hefting weighty suitcases. *Extremely* aerobic. In a few weeks I may have the lungs and leg muscles of a Swiss mountain goat. Thank God for my deep-cushioning Rumanian shoes. I expect even Sheeni may be sporting them soon. Madame Ruzicka admitted natural selection at work in winnowing tenants for top-floor apartments. Only the very young in prime physical condition can make the grade. Seems like a pretty lively floor from what I've seen so far of our neighbors.

Three muscular young guys live across the hall. Next door is a swarthy dwarf with a Clark Gable moustache and Norma Shearer head scarf. I wouldn't want to climb all those stairs with legs that short. Our building is all 19th Century carved stone on the outside, but the interior is a letdown: narrow stairs, pinched corridors, crumbling plaster, and gloomy lighting. A wig shop occupies the ground-floor storefront. No budget "miracle fiber" styles like Carlotta used to wear. According to Madame Ruzicka, they sell only hand-sewn human hair wigs fashioned on the premises. Each one can take a month or more to make. Sounds like even more tedious work than some of my former mind-numbing wage-slave jobs. And a mere three centuries late for the big fashion boom in wigs.

Extortionate rent and deposits made a scary dent in diminishing stash of hundred dollar bills. Then the vacating tenant showed up and demanded *E*500 for the decrepit kitchen gear and appliances. Seems all the landlady provides is the dripping sink. He settled for $300 in U.S. greenbacks as I could sense he was not anxious to haul the midget stove and refrigerator down all those stairs. Must get cash infusion soon from Sheeni's clandestine accounts!

Rudimentary furnishings are included with the apartment, but Sheeni has gone off with Alphonse's cute girlfriend Babette to buy towels and sheets. Despite her French-sounding name, Babette is a rosy-cheeked English girl—speaking that most welcome language with a charming Welsh accent. I suspect one or both of them is rolling in euros. They live in a swanky third-floor apartment down the hall from our landlady. (Note: Sheeni informs me that the French refer to the third floor as the second floor, and the second floor as the first floor. Can an entire nation not count?)

I should talk. Previous stair count in error. We're *six* flights up, though God only knows what floor we're on.

4:35 p.m. We're swaddled in Egyptian cotton. Our apartment may not be much, but we've got linens worthy of a Rothschild. While Sheeni was out, I took the bare mattress for a mid-afternoon test snooze (and lonely wank), finding both moderately satisfactory. We also have a couple of tables, a fake pine bureau, some non-designer lamps, and a threadbare sofa no worse than old Mrs. DeFalco's in Ukiah. No radio or TV—how *will* we fill those silent hours?

While our domestic arrangements are coming together, our marriage seems to be falling apart. Wife just handed me this alarming note:

> Nick/Rick,
> If anyone asks, tell them you're 18. And please don't mention that we're married. Why are you speaking Spanish???
> —Sheeni

Why? Because two can play those games, kiddo. Yep, I have dredged up my primitive schoolyard Spanish. Every time Sheeni speaks to me, I reply: *Habla Ingles, por favor*. This ploy, though, may be backfiring. I just noticed that she has removed her wedding ring. Talk about blatant "don't exist" messages. And this one from my loving wife!

MONDAY, May 17 — Middle of the night. Awakened by a mystery noise. Traced annoying sounds to our closet, where I discovered my forgotten cellular phone chirping away in a suitcase. I closed the door, sat on the toilet, and answered the call. It was Connie Krusinowski, my ally in amours, stuck in desperate traffic on the 405 Freeway in Los Angeles.

"Rick, why haven't you been keeping in touch?"

"Sorry, Connie. I didn't think my phone would work over here."

"That's obvious. But thoughtful Connie just paid your bill and had the service switched over to international."

"Thanks, Connie. What's happening with Sheeni's parents?"

"You can relax for the time being, Rick. They are presently scouring Mexico for their runaway daughter."

"Mexico! Why there?"

"Simple, amigo. I sent my maid Benecia down to Tijuana with some bribe money. She got a suspicious Hunter-Saunders marriage entered there on the public records."

"Connie, that's brilliant."

"Yeah, it was pretty devious even for me. So, where are you, guy?"

I filled in my friend on the events of the past week. She was not pleased to hear that Sheeni was no longer wearing her wedding ring.

"Jesus, Nick, it's hard enough to drag a Saunders to the altar. Don't tell me now I have to worry about poor Paulo backsliding on me." Connie has been conspiring to wed Paul, Sheeni's jazz-playing incarcerated older brother.

"They can be pretty skittish, Connie. Kind of like adopting a feral cat. I'm thinking of getting Sheeni 10 wedding rings—one for each finger. So what's happening with you?"

Connie reported that things were going so well it was almost scary. Her parents' lawyers were thrashing out the divorce settlement, her dad was now engaged to Lacey (glamorous erstwhile girlfriend of both Paul and my father), and Paul was getting friendlier every time she visited him in jail (where he's confined on a marijuana rap).

"Has he asked you to marry him?"

"Not yet. But it's only a matter of time. I am resolved on that point. You are my inspiration, Rick."

"Thanks, Connie. I appreciate all your help in springing Sheeni from that prison camp for unwed mothers."

"My pleasure, guy. So, how many hours a day are you spending with her?"

"Well, approximately 24. We're on our honeymoon, you know."

"Too many, Rick. That's obviously your problem. You can't crowd a Saunders. Remember, Rick, everyone wants what they cannot have. You have to be more unavailable."

"OK, Connie. I'll try." Promising to stay in touch, we rang off.

Mulling it over, I decided to bone up on my Spanish. Latin men, François reminds me, are notorious for their unavailability—especially to their wives.

7:48 p.m. Another day in language hell. No museum-hopping as most such venues closed on Mondays. Sheeni buried lovely nose in heavy French tome. Hope it's a book on baby rearing and not a guide to do-it-yourself divorce. To boost my unavailability, I went grocery shopping and did the laundry. No Safeways in Paris? Bought necessities in little specialized shops, where you allegedly receive personalized service and certainly pay through the nose. Lugged ten days' worth of laundry and two bags of groceries up six flights.

Made dinner with our antique pots and pans. Surprised they weren't melted down for cannon during the Napoleonic wars. Must upgrade soon to Teflon. Wife had seconds of pot roast and commented, I hope, approvingly on the cuisine. She apparently never heard of the rule that the person who doesn't cook does the washing up. Should have worked out the division of labor back when we were still speaking English. Since I didn't know the Spanish for "Look, the dishes are stacking up," I washed them myself.

Lots to learn about being married, I can see that now. Not just uninhibited sexual congress 24 hours a day. Wonder who started that myth? The need to remain aloof now in fundamental conflict with desire for sex. I must deny my need for what Sheeni isn't willing to give so that she will want what she cannot have. I'm beginning to understand now why married men seek out prostitutes. Paying for it in cash is just so much less complicated.

TUESDAY, May 18 — Fixed my darling a big plate of bacon and eggs this morning. Miraculously, this culinary return to our Anglo-Saxon roots restored her facility with English.

"Nickie, this isn't working out."

I froze, fork stalled in mid-air. "What isn't?" I gasped.

"Full immersion in French. And do you know why?"

"Why, darling?"

"Because you're not making an effort. And I'd like to know why not!"

Pushed to the linguistic wall and just aced out on the last piece of bacon, I confessed. Science had determined, I informed her, that I was incapable of learning a second language.

"That's awful!" she exclaimed. "But why didn't you tell me?"

I sipped my coffee. "I don't know. It's, uh, a guy thing."

"OK, Nick, I admit it. I'm not a guy. So please explain."

"Darling, when a fellow gets married, he wants to be . . . the hero. He wants his wife to admire him, to be proud of him. He doesn't like to admit to, well, any weakness."

"But speaking infuriatingly crummy Spanish in France is OK?"

"Well, it's not great," I admitted.

"But, Nickie, what are you going to do if you can't learn French?

How will you get by?"

"Search me, Sheeni. That's why I suggested we conserve our money by living in Topeka."

Sheeni sighed and slumped down in her chair. "Nickie, this is terrible."

"I know," I admitted. "If Hemingway had had my problem, he would never have met Gertrude Stein."

6:15 p.m. Distressed wife, at least, was cheered by the news that her parents were off combing Mexico on a fruitless quest. Perhaps they'll turn up Ambrose Bierce instead. To get reacquainted, we only toured one museum (Musee de Cluny: more medieval detritus—from moth-eaten tapestries to Charlemagne's jockstrap) and spent the rest of the afternoon in bed. After sloppy seconds, I dared to broach the subject of my love's naked ring finger.

"Nickie, marriage is a very private affair."

"Really? I thought it was a rather public statement of one's mutual and loving commitment."

Sheeni thought this over while I fondled an area once off-limits by statute to anyone except lawful husbands. What a travesty this modern age has made of those customs!

"Nickie, we're residing in one of the world's most sophisticated cities. Even you will have to admit that being knocked up and married at age 15 is rather déclassé."

"Lots of great people got married young, darling."

"Please, Nick, I'd rather not hear any more about your Mr. Gandhi and his child bride. I think we should keep our marital status a secret until we're older."

"And if other guys ask you out?"

"Nick, I'm in France to learn, not for the opportunity to date a slew of attractive and fascinating Frenchmen."

Somehow I was not entirely reassured by that statement.

TUESDAY, May 18 — Another middle-of-the-night phone call. I can see I'll have to send Connie a Rolex set to Paris time.

"Freeway backed up again, Connie?" I yawned.

"The pits, Rick. There was another police chase. What some people won't do to get on TV. You know somebody named Joan Twisp?"

"Sure, she's my sister," I replied, suddenly alert.

"I thought maybe there was a connection. There can't be that many Twisps around. I mean it's kind of a funny name."

"Connie, were the cops chasing her?"

"What? No, there was an article about her in the *L.A. Times*. She had a kid."

"Oh, right. She was due about now as I recall." More yawning.

"Well, Rick, your sister made the front page."

Another familiar quiver at the base of my scrotum. Why was news of my family always so dire?

"Why, Connie? What happened?!"

"Ms. Twisp delivered a gorilla. She dropped an 18 pounder."

"You're kidding, Connie."

I thought my sister looked more than usually blimp-like the last time I saw her.

"No, they had a photo of the bruiser. It's quite a monster. She named it Tyler Twisp. You could tell the hospital P.R. people wanted to make a big deal out of it, but they were kind of embarrassed because she wasn't married."

"I know, Connie. It's another shocking Twisp scandal."

"The father is a guy named Dimby. Some married rocket scientist. He refused to comment on camera. You want me to break up his marriage?"

"Don't bother, Connie. The guy's a creep. My sister is well rid of him."

"Apparently his other kids were all on the small side. So they figure it must have been the mother's genes responsible for Tyler being so tubby."

"Eighteen pounds! Is that a new world record, Connie?"

"Not even close, Rick. She missed it by about five pounds. Still, I wouldn't want to pass a watermelon that size."

You can say that again. Wow, the Twisps carry a gene for gigantism. Too bad it hasn't affected my penile development. You'd think by now all those years of incessant masturbation would have triggered some cataclysmic genetic event.

"Who was it?" drawled Sheeni sleepily when I crawled back into bed.

"Connie," I reported. "I'm an uncle."

"That's nice," she sighed, dozing off.

The other part of the story I think I'll keep to myself. I don't think Sheeni needs to know that Twisps have a predisposition toward awe-inspiring birth weights.

11:22 a.m. Woke to the drone of rain on the lead-sheathed roof. Heavy clouds rolling in from the west. Just a few hours before, those same clouds had rained on English-speaking London, where I could have unfurled my umbrella and ordered beans on toast with admirable fluency. Instead, I joined Sheeni in our tin tub, where I soaped her exquisite curves and she drilled me in French numbers. She says at least I should learn these so in shops I don't just hold up a fistful of bills and have the clerk pick out what I owe.

"Not everyone in France is honest, you know, Nickie," she pointed out.

I know. I didn't mention that the last wedge of Camembert I lugged up the stairs from our local *alimentation* appeared to have cost me over *E*40.

3:40 p.m. No tourism today. Too wet. Sheeni read her book; I practiced my numbers and studied the view out our rain-splattered garret window. Lots of Parisian pigeons waiting out the storm. Seemingly quite at home, yet they have no more French than I do. The buildings across the street looking grandly immutable in the gray light. All the work of long-dead builders who somehow got it right. Rising in the distance: a lone skyscraper—the tallest in the city—truncated today by low clouds. Locals, I am informed by my wife, refer to it as the box that the Eiffel Tower came in. So now I've seen the ugly box, but its famous contents still elude me.

Much noise continues to emanate from apartment of muscular dudes across the hall. Loud bangs, deep thumps, lusty shouts. Could be vigorous group sex (they dress flamboyantly), but from the way they mentally undress my wife every time we pass in the hall, I think not. Sheeni speculates they are Italian stonecutters hammering out gravestones in their living room.

Ray of sunshine. Smiling Babette just knocked on the door and invited us out for an evening at "le jazz club." Too bad Alphonse is coming along too.

11:53 p.m. Back home from musical evening. Still raining. All four of us squeezed into Alphonse's Twingo, a radically shrunken micro car. Lots of similar toy-sized cars zipping about Paris. Only practical size as they can be parked in the smallest nonexistent spots. Very scary as death is a certainty if you hit anything. Drove to bustling club scene on rue de Lappe. Don't ask me where that is. All Paris streets lurch off at crazy angles so impossible to follow any route. Left sunglasses at home to increase perceived unavailability to marriage-denying spouse. Overheard several "Belmondo" comments in line while waiting to pay exorbitant cover charge, but nightclubbing Parisians too cool for blatant celebrity toadying. Thousands of hours of acute suffering and scab picking represented by profusion of piercings flaunted by the younger jazz lovers. Damn, I should have worn an earring or two.

Trendy cellar jazz club jammed with sweaty, gyrating bodies of every race. Toxic air poisoned by 10,000 Gauloises. Powerful din generated by quartet of North Africans apparently confusing jazz with heavy metal. As usual, I was many decades too late for the golden age. Sidney Bechet and Edith Piaf where are you I thought as I bought first round of drinks from cute waitress in low-cut top. A *pichet* of red wine, plus a virgin *diablo menthe* for the expectant mother, who gave me a look of heart-shriveling reproach. I'm used to it. Excused myself to go to the men's room and discovered the "toilet" was just a smelly hole in the floor. What a culture!

Joined throngs in dancing frenetically to throbbing beat, though François fears genuine enjoyment of this activity will forever elude me. Prospect of letting myself go virtually nil. Product of thousands of years of natural selection leading to inhibited tight-ass honky in impact-cushioning shoes. Next generation of same already in the oven. Sat out some dances and attempted conversation over noise with Babette while Alphonse chatted up wife in French. Both are biology majors. Both offspring of surgeons and both planning to go into the family business.

"What are you doing in Paris?" shouted Babette.

Good question. My interrogator has sparkling blue-green eyes, kissable lips, and a slender Welsh nose that's pure nasal fascination.

"We're on our honeymoon," I replied. Someone kicked me under the table.

"How romantic!"

"Yes, it's a trial marriage," I elaborated, feeling the wine. "Very popular now in San Francisco. That's where we're from. Kids pair off in high school and get married. No more going steady. That is so déclassé."

"Extraordinary," commented Babette. "You Americans are so progressive. And when you graduate will you be getting a divorce?"

"I hope not. Especially now with the baby on the way." I dodged another kick.

At that moment a shapely redhead, apparently inebriated and perspiring heavily, grabbed me by the shirt, uttered something in a sexy whisper (all I caught was "Belmondo"), and dragged me out to the dance floor. In a cellar jammed with multi-pierced hipsters this tight-assed *imposteur* was in demand!

WEDNESDAY, May 19 — Middle of the night. Someone close by is playing an accordion. Old melodies, squeezed out softly and mournfully like a lonely whisper in the dark. I've heard it other nights too. The sad tunes creep into your being and rouse you gently, like the soundtrack to a dream. You lie there and listen, wondering about all that Deep Stuff that can worry a guy in the dark in a foreign city. Sometimes the music pauses and I imagine the player lighting a cigarette. And then it resumes with an even sadder song that really breaks your heart. So you roll over, and try not to cry, and wonder how it's all going to turn out.

When I awoke I was startled to find that I had remembered all of my French numbers from *un* to *cent*. I may not be as hopelessly ill prepared for life in this country as I imagined. I think the secret is not to try to get your mind around the vast bulk of the French language, but to carve off small bits and concentrate only on those. Today, for example, I propose to learn all the ways to say "Unhand my wife, you cad!"

For breakfast I made hot Scottish oatmeal with warm French cream, which My Love accepted coolly. She is annoyed that I refuse to remove my wedding ring and blabbed to the neighbors our most intimate secrets. Well, perhaps she shouldn't eavesdrop on private conversations, even if Babette and I were screaming at the tops of our lungs.

Since relations were already rocky, I decided I had nothing to lose by broaching yet again certain delicate financial matters.

"Darling, what are we going to do when our cash runs out? Don't you think we should take my Wart Watch funds that you are holding and open a joint account here?"

"That, Nickie, would be foolish in the extreme. French banks are not nearly as circumspect as your fugitive status requires. Do you want to have *all* your money confiscated?"

I wasn't entirely sure that wasn't an apt description of my present situation. But I realized tact was called for here.

"Then how will we pay our bills, darling? Do you have any idea what we spent last week on cheese alone?"

"Don't worry, Nickie. We'll manage. Perhaps you should think about getting a job."

Doing what? Teaching English to Parisian pigeons?

"You know, darling," I reminded her, "since we're now married all that money in your clandestine accounts is community property."

"Not exactly, darling. I believe common law defines as community property those goods and chattels which the couple acquires *after* their marriage."

Great. I would have to marry the daughter of a sleazy lawyer.

No sun again today, but the rain had stopped. Tourism has resumed. First we toured the old Opera House, a grand wedding cake of a building ornamented with a voluptuousness bordering on the obscene. I mean those guys had time on their hands for gilding cherubs. Of course, Paris also has a modern new opera house, which nobody bothers to visit as it is boring in the extreme. Next we wandered through the historic Marais district to the Place Vendôme, a classy part of town geared toward the deep-pockets crowd. Sheeni paused to admire a yellow diamond necklace in the window of Cartier that even Donald Trump would have to think about putting on layaway. No question Paris is a fun place, but having a billion or so in the bank would really open the doors to a good time.

Had kebabs for lunch from a takeout stand. Financially panicked Rick S. Hunter is now insisting on strict economies. Leaving sunglasses at home may have backfired. Stopped three times on the street by Frogs-on-the-make who had long conversations in French with Sheeni about my appearance. One guy made some suspicious notations in his Palm Pilot for which I later received no credible explanation. No E.T. in sight as usual. I'm beginning to think the whole thing is a myth.

THURSDAY, May 20 — I've got a job. Madame Ruzicka has offered to hire me as a part-time concierge slave in exchange for halving our ruinous rent. I'm to haul out the trash, sweep the endless stairs, mop the lobby, and generally tidy up the joint. Since no actual cash will be changing hands, we both avoid burdensome government red tape. She conserves euros and adds some cachet to her building by employing a janitor who looks like Jean-Paul Belmondo.

We had a nice chat in her apartment while My Love was off with Babette getting a stylish Parisian coiffure. Madame Ruzicka likes to practice her English, and I'm always ready for a gabfest with the person who stands between me and homelessness. Hard to believe, but she was once a famous Czech circus star. She had to leap off the trapeze and leave in a hurry when the Russians invaded in 1968. She used to tour with French circuses, but eventually got too old and fat for flying through the air in a tutu. Lots of her relatives are still in the business as the Ruzickas have had sawdust in their veins for generations. She showed me an old publicity still of herself in her prime. Pretty damn foxy, with nary a slack muscle on her curvaceous bod. No moustache either at that time.

Later, as I was hauling out the garbage cans in my dirty gray apron, two tenants stopped me to make earnest entreaties. I could only shrug and say "Sorry, I don't speak French." Good thing I don't either. I think maybe they wanted me to fix something in their apartments. Hey, I don't plan on being the slave of everyone in this building.

So depressed by my new employment status that Sheeni took

me out to the movies to cheer me up and flaunt her expensive new hairdo (she did look great, of course). Since French films aren't subtitled here, I insisted on seeing an American movie (the latest Nicholas Cage epic in original undubbed English). Felt a wave of homesickness for my native land despite all the explosions and car chases. Shocked to see cineastes all around us whipping out their lighters and puffing away. If they tried that in California, there would be more mayhem in the theater than on the screen.

FRIDAY, May 21 — Right after breakfast I had to don my apron and go down to deal with fresh graffiti from the latest student *manifestion*. Every time you turn around in this town herds of students are marching by bearing signs. Too bad they don't write a few in English for the benefit of us foreigners. I haven't a clue what they're complaining about. Such militancy is almost unknown in America. Perhaps if French schools imposed compulsory gym, there would be less energy for such exercises.

As I was scrubbing away Alphonse and Babette emerged from the front door. They seem surprised to see me in my new custodial capacity. Alphonse especially appeared embarrassed that he had been mixing socially with the proletariat. He was even more surprised when his girlfriend invited us to their place for dinner tonight. I accepted without hesitation. Our own larder was nearly bare and I wasn't eager to hit the shops as I seem to have forgotten all my French numbers. Bummer.

While I swept the public areas, My Love went off for solo clothes shopping and to investigate school possibilities. I can't imagine why anyone would want to think about school in May. The horrors of September will be upon us soon enough. Three more needy tenants stopped to chat—one of them, I regret to say, an American expatriate. He wanted me to look at his balky fuse box, but I declined, citing rigid union work rules. He sighed and asked me if I wanted a job walking his toy fox terrier Maurice twice a day. I agreed, but said there would be an extra fee for cleaning up after it. He pointed out that the damn dog only weighed eight pounds. I said maybe so, but they can still be big producers. So he thought it over and said OK, but I would have to show him the bags. I've marked him as a potential tightwad.

4:30 p.m. Took Maurice for a walk and got totally lost. Foolishly, I had left home without my Michelin map. Soon in despair, but gave Maurice his head and he led us right back to our street. Pretty smart dog for having a brain that couldn't be any bigger than a pecan. Tiny Maurice is also something of a babe magnet. Lots of cute French girls stop to pet him and chat up his Belmondoesque master. I just nod soberly and answer "*Oui*" to anything they say. Feel rather self-conscious though clutching baggie, since most French not into pooper-scooping. Walking very treacherous in this town as Parisian canines said to produce 16 tons a day.

10:45 p.m. Back from dining downstairs. Sheeni dressed in flattering Parisian fashions, the cost of which she divulged to anxious husband in a blur of rapid French. Most toothsome French cuisine prepared by Alphonse. Babette explained that her boyfriend hates all things English and therefore does not regard her cooking as worthy of serving to company. He nodded in agreement while spooning up the seafood soup. Apparently he understands at least some English, but does not deign to speak it. Babette likes to embarrass him with personal revelations. She said the French are so reserved they would never consider inviting people to dinner they just met, so she has to take the initiative.

"Parisians are the stuffiest of all," she said, pouring the wine but giving My Love only a symbolic splash. "They resolutely despise anyone new. You have to prove that you're worthy of their company."

Alphonse declined to disagree with that statement. Instead he launched into a breezy philosophical disquisition that lasted all the way through the next course (braised lamb, cheesy potatoes, and asparagus). Apparently, French guys like to monopolize the conversation. If the food hadn't been so good, I'm sure I would have been mildly annoyed. Somebody should write a computer program that provides instant dinner-table subtitles. I could have brought my laptop and been clued into the conversation. Only I ate the stalks of my asparagus—a blunder I suspect was regarded as yet another American gaucherie.

Next course was green salad. Since the French have a morbid fear of cutting lettuce, you have to fold the whopping big leaves onto your fork and shove them into your mouth before your garden origami comes undone. Nevertheless, François would willingly bed our hostess for the recipe for her boyfriend's savory vinaigrette.

For the cheese course we adjourned to their spacious living room, where everyone paired off by preferred language. I chewed a creamy wedge that smelled like Dwayne Crampton's sock drawer and asked Babette if she minded the attentions her boyfriend was lavishing on my wife.

"It's just the way French men are, Rick. They're programmed to flirt. No one takes it seriously. A bit obnoxious at times, but I regard it as part of the French zest for life. Of course, if the girl is presentable and doesn't offer much resistance, they're more than willing to seduce her. One must make allowances for these small transgressions."

"I wouldn't."

"No, you Americans would reach for your pistols."

I couldn't help but blush. It was true I had shot someone just recently.

"Which is not to say," she continued, "that Americans never flirt."

Oops. Had François been glancing too frequently at her well-filled-out LSU sweater?

"Do you have some interest in Louisiana?" he inquired, changing the subject.

"I love it, Rick. Alphonse took me to New Orleans this year for Mardi Gras."

A week of drunken revels in a wild party town with sweet Babette. That could relieve any guy's post-exams tension. Sudden outburst of laughter from our companions. Glancing over, I noticed our host had placed a well-manicured hand on my wife's bare knee.

"Alphonse," called Babette, "shall we serve the coffee?"

That got his mind back on business. We had tiny cups of strong espresso. No decaf in France? I may be wired for days. Oh well, it gives François more time to contemplate violently disagreeable ends for you know who.

SATURDAY, May 22 — My second week as a married stiff. We celebrated with some light pre-breakfast intercourse. I have contrived an elevated posture that applies more friction to Sheeni's vital button. She seems very appreciative. Most delightful to dispense with sensation-deadening condoms, though it is all I can do to delay my explosive climax until all parties are satisfied. I try not to think about where exactly I'm sliding my throbbing T.E. Or what my fingertips are caressing. Or what my lips are nibbling. Seems rather ironic that men have to suppress every sensory input while women are struggling to gather sufficient stimulation to make the whole business worthwhile. Bad engineering, I'd say.

Sheeni remarked that she read a magazine article that claimed women enjoy a richer sex life with uncircumcised partners. I scoffed and said I didn't see how the absence of a foreskin could make a whit of difference. Still, it gives me something new to feel insecure about—especially in a city crawling with three million intact Frogs. And why wasn't I consulted before undergoing such infantile mutilations? I'm surprised some sharp lawyer hasn't filed a class-action lawsuit on behalf of us millions of scalped pecker victims.

Since there was a chill in the air, Maurice—looking like a miniature Humphrey Bogart—set off on our morning walk in his tan trench coat. Devastatingly cute, but not as macho as one might wish. Several young fellows of questionable motives stopped us to chat. Maurice and I like to window-shop along Parisian streets. The full peculiarity of the French character is on open display in their shop windows: exotic foodstuffs, bizarre lingerie, curious antiquities, eccentric office apparatus, even an enormous eyeball in an optician's window that looked like something on loan from Godzilla. This menacing orb drew a growl and bark from my protective canine. Fortunately, his trench coat came equipped with pockets, so Maurice could lug his own baggie. Now I just have to train him to clean up after himself.

After our walk, Madame Ruzicka sent me on an emergency run for birdseed for her parrot Henri. She gave me a note so I wouldn't have to pantomime my request for the perplexed shopkeeper. Henri is a messy eater. I dragged out her wheezy old vacuum and cleaned up around his stand. Since he was a secondhand bird (abandoned by a departing tenant), Madame Ruzicka wasn't sure of his age.

"He's a tough customer," she cautioned, filling his seed bowl. "Don't get too close. He's an ear-biter."

"How long have you had him?" I asked, keeping my distance. Henri eyed me suspiciously.

"Too long. Since before you were born. A damn gypsy stuck me for a bundle of francs and this nuisance bird. I should have thrown him in the soup long ago."

Henri fluttered his feathers and picked out a likely-looking seed. If he was worried, he wasn't showing it.

I wondered if there was a Monsieur Ruzicka. "Was your husband in the circus too?" I asked.

"I had no husband."

"How come?"

She peered at me over her spectacles. "You Americans are almost as nosy as Czechs. My *cheri* already had a wife—a good Catholic one. They are both long dead. I doubt if even their children think of them these days."

"That's sad."

"And you, Rick, do you think of your parents?"

"Not if I can help it," I admitted.

"I remember mine with great fondness. I had a marvelous childhood. But then, it was a different time."

When I trudged back upstairs, I found My Love absent with no explanatory note. I downed a meager lunch and unearthed my cellular phone from the closet. Couldn't say what time it was on the other side of the world, but—like Connie—I wasn't going to let that stop me.

My old Ukiah pal Fuzzy DeFalco answered on the second ring. "Rick! Where are you?"

"Oh, I'm here. I'm there."

"Jesus, Rick, you're in tons of trouble for cutting so much school."

"That's the least of my problems, Frank."

"Gee, Rick, you're almost as big an outlaw as my friend Nick Twisp. The rumor going around school is that you busted Sheeni Saunders out of some home for expectant chicks and her parents are so pissed they put a contract out on you."

I gulped, then reminded myself that the Redwood High rumor mill is prone to gross exaggerations.

"Frank, I doubt they'd want to murder their own son-in-law."

"You mean you're married?!"

"Yep. We got married in Tijuana. The judge spoke English so it was totally legit."

"Wow, Rick, I can't believe all the kids these days getting married. I hope Lana doesn't find out. She'd want to nail me for sure."

Fuzzy then filled me in on his love life, which was torrid in the extreme. But I was more interested in another local couple: Trent Preston and his lovely wife Apurva Joshi.

"They keep the whole school talking, Rick. It's a wonder anybody gets any studying done. Sonya Klummplatz was blabbing all over school that she nailed Trent. Hard to believe, but she showed Lana a pair of jockey shorts that she claimed she scored off him as a souvenir. But she didn't get him to sign 'em or anything, so who's to say they were really Trent's? She also mentioned some pretty explicit anatomical details, if you catch my drift. Anyway, Trent asked her to button up about it, so she had a big confrontation with Apurva in the cafeteria."

"Damn, Frank. What happened?"

"Well, Sonya informed her that she'd made it with her husband and that proved that he really loved her instead of Apurva, and that she should do the honorable thing and just go the hell back to India."

"Jesus. What did Trent say?"

"Trent wasn't there. He was at the regional swim finals. I think that's why Sonya picked that day for the fight."

"Did Apurva attack her?"

"No, she just sort of cried hysterically. But Candy Pringle dumped her lunch tray over Sonya's head, and those two mixed it up pretty well. I guess Candy and Apurva are kind of buddies now since they both got screwed over by their dudes."

Head cheerleader Candy Pringle has been going through a prolonged rocky patch with star quarterback Bruno Modjaleski.

"Damn, Frank, I hope Apurva's OK."

"Well, all three got suspended. The rumor is Trent and Apurva are now seeing a marriage counselor."

Thank God. No way I could afford to fly back there now to patch things up. And I need that marriage to last!

"I hope you know what you're doing, Rick."

"Why, Frank? What do you mean?"

"If Nick Twisp ever finds out you married Sheeni, you'll be dead meat for sure."

"Relax, Frank. That guy can't touch me."

Another lie. He touches me all the time. He touched me this afternoon too, despite two sessions this morning with my lovely wife. Why do guys have only one thing on the brain?

8:13 p.m. I was making dinner and babysitting Maurice when My Love trudged up the stairs. I don't know how she's going to manage all those steps in a few months when burdened with an 18-pound fetus. This touchy topic, I've noticed, we both leave untouched. Nor has Sheeni been warming up to Maurice, even though he's about 8,000 times nicer than her own stupid dog Albert. So far, for example, he's shown no inclination toward turning me over to the gendarmes.

I got totally jealous when she revealed that she had spent the day at the Musée Rodin. Not that eyeballing dreary sculptures had much appeal, but she mentioned that on her way she saw the Eiffel Tower. She couldn't fathom my interest in that monumental erection.

"It's not like it's a magnificent work of art by a creative genius such as Rodin. It's just an exercise in engineering. Rather like the Golden Gate Bridge. I can't believe tourists come from all over the world to gawk at a highway bridge."

I felt obliged to defend my hometown landmarks. "Well, Sheeni, you do get a nice view of the city from mid-span."

"If you're lucky. Half the time it's socked in solid with fog. At least the Eiffel Tower has a nice restaurant on it."

"Really? Why don't we go sometime?"

"Are you paying? Meals at the Jules Verne start at *E*300 per person."

Jesus, and I thought San Francisco was into tourist gouging.

SUNDAY, May 23 — Today we took an ambitious subway ride out to the porte de Clignancourt to tour the Marché aux Puces—the famous Paris flea market. Since the Métro is supposed to be rife with thieves and pickpockets, I was on hyper-paranoid alert the entire way. And nobody told us that part of the journey is by foot. Changing trains to connect to another line involved trouping down endless corridors like some underground Bataan death march. At least there was plenty of unabashed billboard nudity along the way to revive one's lagging spirits.

The flea market itself is enormous—sprawling over many streets and through dozens of buildings. Quite a smorgasbord of goods—from low-life peddlers hawking junk gleaned from dumpsters to swanky antique shops with vintage Art Deco furniture that could put a big bite in Baby's milk fund. We got some nice china dishes (slightly chipped), some glasses that may be crystal, a Scrabble game, a portable radio-tape player, and a used skillet with only one nasty scratch in the Teflon. Saw several affordable TVs, but the French government makes every TV owner pay a whopping compulsory tax to support public television. In America, of course, the public TV stations just beg for money and are politely ignored.

One stall specialized in vintage French movie posters, which are much larger and more vividly printed than American versions. Featured in the front window was a mint-condition broadsheet for *A bout de souffle*—that landmark film (*Breathless*) in the history of Twisp-Saunders relations. I suggested it couldn't hurt to go in and inquire about the price, but Sheeni said "don't bother" as she has "gone off" that film.

Damn! I hope that wasn't a gratuitous "don't exist" message for Jean-Paul Belmondo.

We had spicy takeout from a couscous stand for lunch, then hit another street of sellers. Bad move. Sheeni spied an old portable typewriter with an extra row of keys for French accent marks. She exclaimed that it was even nicer than her French language typewriter back in Ukiah because this one was made in France. Big deal. I tried to convince her that investing in a typewriter these days was like buying a horse collar or an eight-track stereo, but she was unpersuaded as usual. She didn't even negotiate (she thinks haggling is uncouth), and paid the beaming vendor the full *E*50. And guess who had to lug the damn thing around the rest of the day?

Personally, I think the French should get over this pretentious fascination with accent marks. They just clutter up the page, and God knows they have to cripple your typing speed.

No pickpockets on crowded train home. And nobody swiped the typewriter, which I had left rather unattended. Have been experimenting with our new radio-tape player (no tapes, alas). Lots of unintelligible talk programs and station after station playing rap in French. Something of a revelation. Believe I have now discovered the lowest form of music on the planet.

8:47 p.m. I successfully cornered Maurice's wily papa and extracted from him all accumulated dog-walking fees. I knocked on his door and was surprised when it was opened by Miss Bette Davis—complete with flighty right hand waving about her lit cigarette.

"Ah, a tradesman," she said, removing a fleck of tobacco from her tongue. "I was expecting Paul Henreid, but I suppose you'll have to do."

Mr. Hamilton is not, as I had supposed, some dull business functionary transferred to Paris by his American employers. He is a celebrated female impersonator who performs six nights a week at a nightclub on the place Pigalle. Of course, suspicious Carlotta already had noticed that his eyebrows were rather more groomed than is typical for middle-aged men. His Carol Channing impersonation, I'm told, is the toast of five continents. He is also reputed to do a mean Joan Crawford.

MONDAY, May 24 — Much litter in building from riotous weekend. While sweeping the fifth floor hallway, I heard someone far below toiling slowly up the stairs. Some wheezing octogenarian, I thought. But when the climber at last came into view, it turned out to be a girl (not much older than me) carrying a large colorful bird in a metal cage. She looked grimly at the stairs ahead of her, then smiled when she caught sight of me.

"Bonjour. You must be my aunt's new American protégé."

"I'm Rick," I replied, dropping my broom and hurrying down toward her. "Would you like me to carry that for you?"

"Would you, Rick? That would be most kind."

The bird squawked angrily when she passed me the cage. Even relieved of her burden, she labored haltingly up the stairs and walked with a limp as she led me down the hallway toward her door. She extracted her key from her purse and turned it in the lock. This set off a cacophony of bird cries from within. In a corner of the small living room a large wire cage held four more colorful birds, all obviously pleased to see her.

"Bonjour, my babies!" she called, taking the cage from me and placing it on a table. "Thank you, Rick. Jiri! Hush now!" The squawking bird shut up when she fed it a seed from the pocket of her skirt. She smiled and held out her hand.

"I'm Reina Vesely. Forgive the mess."

We shook hands and she sniffed the air. "I hope it doesn't smell too bad. Five birds can get rather offensive. I don't even notice it myself now."

"It's fine," I lied. Monosyllables were all I could manage. She was quite overpoweringly beautiful. Pale skin like Meissen porcelain under cascades of deep bronze hair. Aristocratic cheekbones. Delicate features laid on in supernal harmony.

"So thirsty from those stairs. Would you join me in some lemon water?"

It took a moment for my dazzled brain to compute that she was not proposing a mixed-sex scented bath. "Sure."

Her kitchenette had actual cupboards, not stacked-up wooden crates like ours. She filled two tall glasses with sparkling water and handed one to me.

"Salut," she said, clinking her glass against mine and swallowing deeply. "Sometimes I think those stairs are getting steeper."

"I know the feeling. Weren't there any apartments available on lower floors?"

Her smile lit up her extraordinary gray eyes. "I'm like my birds, Rick. I like to be close to the sky. Besides, climbing stairs is good therapy for my leg."

"You have, uh, a disease?"

"No. It was an accident. Two years ago. I'm much better now.

You and your beautiful wife are quite the topic of conversation in the building."

"You've met Sheeni?"

"No, but I've passed her on the stairs."

"So you're Madame Ruzicka's niece?"

"Only spiritually. We're both Czech, but not related as far as we know. She was friends with my grandfather. And now she is my kind benefactress."

"She seems like a nice old lady."

"She is my dearest friend. She saved my life. But I won't bore you with that story. How do you like Paris, Rick?"

I filled her in on my limited Parisian experiences.

"Oh, but, Rick, you *must* see the Eiffel Tower! You must go to the top! I love it up there. But perhaps I was born for high places."

You can say that again. Anything less than a grand palace would be a crime against nature.

6:33 p.m. My Love is back from solo tourism, with several detours for more clothes shopping. She points out that a person living in Paris cannot be expected to make do with a wardrobe acquired in the boondocks of Mississippi. I suppose not, but if she buys any more clothes, we'll need a map to find the toilet in the closet. She was interested to hear that I had made the acquaintance of Ms. Vesely.

"It's a pity that someone so pretty has such an affliction," she commented.

"You think she's pretty, darling? I hadn't noticed."

I am resolved to learn from the mistakes of my idiot divorced father: one does NOT praise another woman to one's wife.

"Yes, rather attractive. I wonder what sort of accident it was?"

"She was probably run down in the street by some crazed Twingo driver. It's all poor Maurice and I can do to get across the streets in one piece."

"You have to be careful, Nickie."

My Love is concerned for my welfare!

"That dog is owned by an American," she continued. "If anything happened to it, I'm sure we'd be sued."

"Uh, right, Sheeni. I suppose tourist-flattening is a daily occurrence here. Back home drivers actually stop for pedestrians in crosswalks."

"Motorists *are* rather polite in California," she acknowledged.

A surprising admission. Is it possible that My Love is herself experiencing a twinge of homesickness for the Golden State?

TUESDAY, May 25 — A sudden tragedy yesterday in Los Angeles. At 2:33 a.m. Connie called me with the shocking news. Her father, noted industrialist Bernard H. Krusinowski, has suffered a massive cerebral thrombosis. The prognosis is not good. He's deceased. Connie was devastated.

"How did it happen, Connie? Where? When?"

"It was right after lunch, Rick. He was taking a siesta with Lacey."

"He was in bed with Lacey!?"

"That's right. Apparently, they were right in the middle of things when he suddenly reared up and went limp. I mean, his body went limp."

"Right, Connie. I understand. That's awful."

A tragic end to an eventful life. But, personally, I couldn't think of a nicer send-off to the next world.

"How's Lacey?"

"She's a mess, Rick. She's under sedation. Rita is taking it hard too."

Rita Krusinowski is Connie's mother and my father-in-law's alleged mistress.

"I think I killed my father, Rick. I think it was the strain of the divorce that pushed him over the edge."

"Don't be silly, Connie. Your father was a competitive, hard-driving executive. He was a victim of America's obsession with success, rich foods, and large smooth-riding automobiles. Did he do much walking?"

"Nobody walks in L.A., Rick. The smog would kill you."

"And how about all those cigars he smoked, Connie?"

"Dad did enjoy a nice Cuban cigar. You think maybe they hardened his arteries?"

"No question about it, Connie. They call it Castro's revenge. Your father was a walking time bomb. Have the arrangements been made?"

"Yeah, Rita's taking charge as usual. She wants to bury him in Palm Springs, but I'm against it."

"Why, Connie?"

"Palm Springs is where you go for the weekend, Rick. It's not a place to spend eternity."

I told Connie not to blame herself and to call me any time she needed emotional support. Hard to believe just a few months ago I got naked in a hot tub with a rich old guy who is now a corpse. I just hope I didn't pick up any of his cerebral thrombosis germs.

7:12 p.m. Took a leave of absence from my many jobs today for an expedition by train to the Palace at Versailles. Didn't see the whole thing because My Love's feet gave out. That will teach her to sneer at practical Rumanian footwear. Perhaps the French language offers sufficient superlatives to describe Louis XIV's suburban development, but I find English sorely lacking. It just goes to show what a guy can accomplish if he's the absolute ruler of the richest state in Europe, has millions of peasants dutifully paying their taxes, commands the finest artisans in the world, wants to invite 20,000 of his fellow aristocrats to sleep over, isn't a devotee of restrained Danish Modern, and never has to worry about zoning officials or building inspectors. Just when you think things can't get any more mind-bogglingly stupendous, you turn a corner and discover you were just in the guest quarters. The really impressive stuff is still ahead. The whole place makes Hearst's *San Simeon* (visited long ago on a tension-packed family vacation) look by comparison like a tool shed. Nor did Louis scrimp on the gardens. Offhand, I'd estimate it would take me several lifetimes to mow his grass. And just the thought of all that geometrical hedge-trimming makes my arms tired. The French may be even more rigorously anal in their landscaping than the Japanese.

Quite a shock to the system to go from such monumental gilded splendor back to our own modest hovel. I switched on the radio and instantly had an entire band singing rap in my living room. That, at least, is a luxury Louis XIV never enjoyed.

WEDNESDAY, May 26 — I introduced myself this morning to our diminutive neighbor. When we met in the corridor, he was dressed modestly for the street in a red satin cape with matching turban. A large red stone (ruby?) was flashing fire from his right earlobe. His name is Señor Alfredo Nunez, he is 53 inches tall, and he's from San Miguel de Allende, Mexico. He is employed as a clown by the most prestigious circus in Paris. Apparently, there are several year-round circuses in Paris operating in permanent premises. He informed me that the boisterous stonecutters across the hall are fellow entertainers: the Boccata brothers, a team of precision acrobats from Italy.

"And please, Rick, may I inquire what is your favorite song?"

Señor Nunez speaks a formal and rather florid English.

I admitted I was partial to Frank's version of "My One and Only Love."

"I know it well," he replied. "Often in times of adversity I have endeavored to emulate the panache of your Mr. Sinatra. But perhaps you prefer monsieur Belmondo. No?"

I assured him that Frank would always rank Number One in my pantheon of Cultural Champions.

Señor Nunez was so pleased he forked over two complimentary passes to the circus.

No tourism today. My Love is taking it easy. The perfection of her divine right foot is now marred by a painful reddish lump on her little toe. Sheeni is calling it a callus; I think it looks suspiciously like a nascent corn. Unconscionable that such an incipient carbuncle could gain a toehold upon one so genetically blessed. My Love must now weigh her inclination to explore Paris against her commitment to fashionable footwear. An aesthetic dilemma I hope she resolves soon as it has left her cranky in the extreme.

Her mood was not improved when I inquired if she'd given any thought to summer employment.

"What would you have me do?" she demanded. "Slouch against a lamppost on the rue Saint-Denis and solicit fat German businessmen?"

I suggested she check to see if the wig salon was hiring. "It might be congenial work," I pointed out. "The location is convenient. And it would give your feet a rest."

She gave me a look that could freeze off warts.

Both Maurice and I were happy to escape for a bracing walk to our favorite café on the rue Delambre. They serve a *tarte tatin* that makes your taste buds roll over and swoon. The waiter, evidently a Belmondo fan, gives me improbably fast service and in computing the bill often makes glaring errors in my favor. Not once has he added the compulsory tip. After such an artery-clogging snack, Maurice and I like to sniff around the deserted lanes of the Cimetière Montparnasse. I'm amazed the French devote so much valuable real estate to dead folks. Many of the wealthier decedents are salted away in their own miniature stone temples, encrusted with bizarre ornamentation. Artisans can really let their imaginations run riot when they're working for clients who can't complain. My favorite is a tomb for a guy named Charles Pigeon that features a full-length sculpture of him and his late wife lounging in bed. No nudity though. This macabre couple is stretched out for eternity in their best bronze pajamas.

7:10 p.m. When I returned from walking Maurice, I was surprised to discover Sheeni was not alone. She and handsome Alphonse were having a tête-à-tête in intimate proximity on the sofa. Oblivious to my presence, they chattered on in that mellifluous language whose very phonemes suggest wanton licentiousness even when discussing the weather. After the interloper finally departed, we faced off for angry words.

"Why shouldn't I have visitors during my convalescence?" Sheeni demanded.

I pointed out that she had a toe callus not brain cancer. And wives weren't supposed to entertain attractive men while their husbands were away.

"What about your private liaison with that pretty parrot fetishist?"

I replied that assisting tenants was part of my concierge duties. I said I was tired of doing all the work around here. "I'm your husband, Sheeni, not your goddam maid."

She said if I were her maid, I would have been discharged long ago. She said if I desired a "domestic queen," I should have married my "previous girlfriend" Sonya Klummplatz.

A low blow. Just because a guy takes a girl to a dance and inadvertently has sex with her doesn't mean he likes her.

The fight went on. Sheeni said she did not intend to go through life with dishpan hands.

I offered to buy her some rubber gloves.

She told me where I could put those gloves. She complained that all I cared to do was exercise some "abbreviated inbred dog," while "virtually ignoring" the world's richest cultural milieu.

I said I liked Paris, but thought we should try to get a handle on our expenses.

She said this was the opportunity of a lifetime and she intended to make the most of it—even if her body and her "so-called marriage" had to suffer.

After more ugly words and much slamming of our two available doors, we hammered out an uneasy compromise. Sheeni has agreed to do some occasional "light dusting" and to shop for "groceries and other essentials." And I will make an effort to display more enthusiasm for exploring "this magical city." No, attending circus performances via complimentary ducats does NOT qualify.

Sheeni, of course, is a tough negotiator. But François stood firm and refused all entreaties to ditch our comfortable Rumanian footwear. He informed her in no uncertain terms that one cripple in the family was enough.

THURSDAY, May 27 — The wee small hours of the morning. The lone accordionist was serenading the night with my favorite song. Even Frank would approve of this version of "My One and Only Love." I sighed and gazed across the pillow at that slumbering person, so desirable in the soft moonlight. Like Frank I was bewitched, bothered, and bewildered. Is it a bad sign, I wondered, that I love her most of all when she's asleep?

10:55 a.m. Strange happenings are afoot. My cellular phone rang during breakfast. "Hello, Connie," I said. "How's the freeway?" But it was some Frog speaking French. I passed the phone to Sheeni, who had a long animated conversation with the guy. Turns out it was the fellow with the Palm Pilot who accosted us on the street last week. We have an appointment to meet with him tomorrow. All I could get out of my suddenly Sphinx-like wife is that he might be able to assist us with "visa matters."

3:14 p.m. I have yet another job. Reina has contracted for me to help her move her birds up and down the stairs. She has a trained bird act with a small circus in a northern suburb. She can only play in intimate venues where the audience sits close to the action. In bigger, better-paying shows the birds would get lost—too far away to be seen clearly. Plus, she's only been training "her babies" for a few years and they cannot always be relied upon to perform like little troupers. Theoretically, they're supposed to shoot baskets, ride scooters, wave French flags, and do other cute tricks. But they can be temperamental and sometimes get distracted.

"And what do you do when that happens?" I asked, hoisting the travel carriers into her aging Mercedes station wagon, crowded with colorful props.

"I scold them, Rick. I pretend like it's all part of the act. Our audiences are mostly children and they don't seem to mind. The owner of the circus threatens to fire me, but he hasn't so far. He's something of a beast."

"Sexual harassment?"

"Daily, Rick. But I can handle him. I get back about 22:30. Are you sure you don't mind helping me so late?"

"No problem, Reina. That's still early afternoon on American time."

We shook hands and I watched as she drove off. Something felt amiss. Oh, right. I felt deprived. She hadn't given me a tasty seed from her pocket.

6:45 p.m. Sheeni took her tender toe for a test-walk and returned with some vital groceries, including a whole, intact, slimy, semi-smelly fish which she expected me to decapitate and clean. It really is amazing what married people can find to argue about. Somehow we never debated the uses of a guillotine as a kitchen appliance back when we were dating. Then I discovered that we had a fish but no lemon, so we had to grapple over who was going to brave all those stairs to run that errand. Needless to say, it was the guy in the sensible shoes that got elected. And should one lousy lemon cost *E*5? I really have to find some way to cram French numbers into my brain.

Ten minutes later: Puffing like a steam engine, Sheeni is back with my change. She has given that larcenous shopkeeper a piece of her mind.

11:30 p.m. Back from more bird lugging. My physique may soon rival those of the muscle-bound acrobats across the hall. Reina introduced me to her fellow performers. Big-billed Jiri is a toco toucan. Radek and Milena are blue/gold macaws. Salmon-tinged Damek is a Moluccan cockatoo. And friendly Zuza is a green-winged macaw. All raised by Reina from babyhood (I should have had it so nice).

Reina invited me to share a nightcap with her. My first experience of brandy, which I judged no worse than regular unleaded. No photographic evidence in her apartment of a loving boyfriend. Hard to believe. The place doesn't smell *that* bad. At the very least you'd think those lusty acrobats down the hall would be camped outside her door. Not to mention lonely Señor Nunez.

Sheeni was not pleased that toting five birds up six flights took nearly one hour. And I don't think she'll be thrilled to learn that François accepted an invitation from Reina to take a sunset cruise on a Seine excursion boat this Sunday. No mention was made of bringing along any extraneous spouses. Somehow I'll have to make the whole thing sound like strictly a business matter. That will take some doing, even for me. Fortunately, Sunday is a long way off.

FRIDAY, May 28 — My phone chirped in the middle of the night. For the sake of my nerves I prayed it was Connie Krusinowski. It was.

"Rick! There's been another disaster!"

"What, Connie? Is your father not buried yet?"

"Of course he's buried. Over 200 mourners showed up for his funeral at Forest Lawn, including Paulo's father comforting my mother—not that I need his services any longer. I wish the old fart would just butt out. Anyway, it was all very moving."

"You buried your dad in Glendale?"

Somehow that didn't sound like much of a step up from Palm Springs.

"It's quite a prestigious plot, Rick. It's just a few hundred yards from Marilyn Monroe's crypt. Rick, my father changed his will!"

"Oh? Bad news, Connie?"

Somehow I sensed he hadn't thought to cut me in for a tidy sum.

"He left Lacey ten million dollars!"

Wow, Lacey was now sexy, beautiful, and rich. What an attractive combination of qualities.

"Well, Connie, they *were* engaged to be married."

"And whose share of the estate do you think her pile is coming out of? Not my mother's, that I can assure you!"

"Oh, dear, Connie. Are you suddenly impoverished?"

"Not hardly, Rick. But now Lacey is a wealthy woman on the loose. I just know she's going to make a play again for my Paulo."

"But Paul isn't at all materialistic, Connie."

"I know that, Rick. But deep down even the most spiritual guy likes to know where his next meal is coming from. Rick, you've got to call your father."

"What!?"

"You've got to tell him his old girlfriend is now a millionaire and wants him back."

"But, Connie, Lacey despises my father."

As, come to think of it, do I.

"She's emotionally devastated, Rick. Former lovers are always slightly more appealing under those circumstances. But your father's window of opportunity here is very narrow. You have to insist he get on the ball immediately."

"Jesus, Connie, I don't know . . ."

"Rick, who flew you guys out of Crescent City?"

"OK, Connie," I sighed, "I'll call him."

Damn. Back to being matchmaker for that creep. What did he ever do for me, besides donate some defective sperm?

3:10 p.m. We barely made it back in time from our mystery appointment for me to help Reina carry her birds down to her car. And poor Maurice had to hold it all morning (his papa sleeps in from his late-night theatrical high jinks). We took the Métro to Belleville, an exotic, somewhat seedy Sino-African district. The address was a former clothespin factory, now converted to trendy offices. Mr. Denis Bonnet's suite was on the third floor. No, his name is not pronounced like your granny's old sun hat. His tall, anorexic secretary dresses like she recently relocated from Mars. She served us some sort of fizzy herbal beverage, then Mr. Bonnet appeared and had another earnest conversation with Sheeni. He is one intense dude. Even his sharp black suit looked like it was on an adrenaline rush. I'd guess his age as around 30.

Then three giggling schoolgirls—dressed like prostitutes—entered, squealed when they saw me, and jumped around clutching each other as if it were 1964 and they had just spotted Ringo Starr. This went on for quite some time. I wondered why they weren't in school or heavily medicated. More people entered. Very outlandishly garbed. Everyone was smoking, talking at once, and looking me over. One artsy guy in yellow silk pantaloons and muddy combat boots offered me a small cigar from a case hammered out of old East German license plates. I politely declined. You'd think people that hip would know a little English, but everyone prattled away in French. I sipped my herbal drink and listened to My Love's calm responses. God knows what she was telling them. Then, suddenly, everyone was shaking hands and kissing cheeks. The schoolgirls were led away (back to their padded cell?) and the meeting adjourned.

Mr. Bonnet introduced us to another guy in a suit, a Mr. Petit, who escorted us back to his office, where we had a seat while he inspected our passports. I noticed that he exclaimed and slapped his forehead several times while interrogating Sheeni about my documents. This I took as a bad sign. He also made several phone calls that appeared to be urgent in nature. Hey, I never wanted to come to his damn country in the first place.

Eventually, that meeting concluded as well, and we returned to the reception area, where I was photographed from every angle by the secretary. Then, at last, we were trooping down the stairs to the street. The whole thing had been only slightly worse than root canal surgery gone awry.

My Love is still clammed up about what's going on. She says there's no need for a long speculative discussion since at this point things are still "so tentative."

I informed her that I was keeping an open mind, but wished to go on record that as far as I was concerned "total nudity" was off the table.

"I'm not taking my clothes off, darling," I insisted. "Especially not around those wacky girls."

"You are one sick individual," was her only comment.

9:30 p.m. Couldn't procrastinate any longer. Called my father at his lumber company office in Ukiah. I figured he'd be back from lunch—poised at his keyboard for more public relations dissimulations.

"Hiya," I squeaked, "this is Nick."

"Nick who?" he demanded.

Another profound parental "don't exist" message. I'm used to them.

"Nick Twisp. Remember? Your son?"

"Nick! Where the hell are you? Are you calling from some jail? Hey, buddy, I'm not bailing you out!"

"I'm not in jail, Dad. I'm doing fine. I'm OK."

"Oh, yeah? I suppose you're on the streets somewhere, peddling your ass for drug money."

"No, Dad. I've got three jobs. I'm not on drugs. I'm doing great."

"Jesus, Nick, I never thought you'd turn out so bad. I should have slapped you down hard after that first smart remark."

Leave it to my father to belt a three-year-old.

For Connie's sake I soldiered on. "Dad, I've got some interesting news. Lacey's boyfriend just died and left her ten million dollars."

"I'm not falling for your lies, Nick. No way that drug-addict horn player had that kind of dough."

"I'm not talking about Paul Saunders, Dad. Lacey dumped him when he got arrested. She was engaged to an older man who manufactured truck springs in L.A. He just had a stroke and left her a fortune. You can read about it in the *L.A. Times*. His name was Bernard Krusinowski."

"Ten million, huh? That's a lot of lettuce."

"Yes, Dad, Lacey's *extremely* distraught. You might think about calling her to offer some solace."

"You've talked to her? Does she want to hear from me?"

"Of course, Dad. I heard her tell a girlfriend that you were the love of her life."

Why I wasn't struck dead for telling that lie I'll never know.

"Yeah, Nick, lots of my old girlfriends feel that way."

What a stuck-up creep. I gave him Lacey's phone number and wished him luck. He didn't ask me to keep in touch. I didn't ask him to eat shit and die. I'd call it a draw.

SATURDAY, May 29 — My third week as a married person. Well, they say the first year of marriage is the toughest. I did knock a piece off my old lady, though I'm not sure a 15-year-old really qualifies. We've both found that energetic intercourse is a good way to work off one's frustrations. Were this not the case, I'm sure the divorce rate would be about 99.5 percent. The murder rate, no doubt, would be similarly elevated. Since Sheeni dislikes clingy guys, I don't tell her that I love her, though I'm willing to admit it when asked. She doesn't. Nor does she mention that she loves me. There seem to be so many topics married people don't discuss. For example, this morning when we were doing it for the third time I was wondering what was going through Sheeni's mind. Was she really into it or was she thinking about breakfast? I often feel oddly strange on third go-arounds. Like I'm trespassing in some way on my bodily functions. I climaxed again, but I could tell my prostate was resentful.

An extravagantly warm and beautiful day. Paris certainly knows how to do spring. Frisky Maurice led me all over the neighborhood. We stopped at the intersection of boulevard Raspail to inspect a large statue, which turned out to be of Honoré de Balzac, the notable dead author. I expect when I'm a celebrated writer, the city of Oakland will be erecting statues of me. I only hope they're a bit more flattering. As captured in pigeon-flecked bronze, Mr. Balzac appeared to be undergoing an especially agonizing case of writer's block. Or perhaps he'd just received a particularly groin-pummeling critical review.

When I returned, My Love was serving coffee and snacks to the

Boccata brothers. She made the introductions. In turn, I had my limp hand crushed by Baldo, Bartolo, and Bernardo Boccata. Such muscles! With all that sinew concentrated in one small room, things soon felt quite claustrophobic—especially with their compulsion to juggle everything at hand. I never imagined so many of our possessions could be circulating in space all at once. Communication was difficult because their English is rudimentary and apparently their French is even worse. My Love gave it a stab.

"Where are you from?" she asked.

Although she was too polite to mention it, I could sense she was troubled by the airborne gyrations of her precious French typewriter.

Baldo, the eldest, was elected to respond. He pointed out the open door toward their apartment across the hall.

"I mean in Italy?" added Sheeni.

"Pisa!" announced Bartolo, the hairiest, as all three inclined sideways at a dramatic angle while continuing to juggle.

Enchanted, Sheeni burst into applause; I managed a grudging smile.

"You are Americans?" queried Bernardo, wearing the tightest t-shirt and pants. He appeared to be extremely well developed all over.

"Yes," replied my wife. "From San Francisco."

"San Francisco!" exclaimed Baldo. "North bitch! North bitch!"

I bristled. If these cretins thought they were going to insult my wife in our own home, they had another thing. . .

"Yes, North Beach," nodded Sheeni. "We often go there. Don't we, Nickie?"

"Er, not lately that I recall."

"Nickie, these nice fellows have given us free tickets to their circus. We're going tomorrow evening."

Uh-oh, I seem to recall a previous engagement. Damn!

"Make like ball," said Bernardo, flopping on the floor. "We tumble you."

"Sorry, some other time," I replied, as the other brothers dropped down and poised with their legs thrust obscenely in the air.

"Really," I insisted. "I just had a heavy breakfast."

But the brothers and my once loving wife would not be denied. I gripped my knees tightly, tucked in my head with its delicate brain, and was twirled about in the air and tossed back and forth by my sadistic neighbors.

Just another sunny day in Paris, France!

SUNDAY, May 30 — Another beautiful morning. No wonder tourists are descending on this burg in unstoppable hordes. As a harried resident, I can't help but wish they'd go someplace else. I hear Vienna is nice. Since no one was up for church, we decided to go to our local flea market, the Puces de Vanves. Sheeni declared she "couldn't live one more day" without a cheese grater. An odd craving, I thought, since I do 98 percent of the cooking and have yet to feel the need to pulverize cheese. Madame Ruzicka requested we keep our eyes peeled for a "parrot muzzle." A jest? It's hard to tell with brusque old ladies.

Alphonse drove us all in his Twingo. Since I invited Señor Nunez to accompany me as my designated haggler and change checker, we were more than usually cramped. My Love claimed the front seat to coddle her toe. Although height challenged, Señor Nunez is more than a little broad in the beam. To accommodate him, Babette was obliged to sit almost in François's lap. This enforced propinquity to her concentrated Welsh femininity I did not find at all objectionable. She smelled wonderfully enticing and her lovely neck, just inches from François's famished lips, cried out for nuzzling. Quite stimulating, but I was spared an embarrassing T.E. as my prostate is still prostrate from yesterday's exertions.

One good thing about shopping with a dwarf is that you could look like Elvis himself and no one would notice. All eyes are on the short guy. This despite the fact that Señor Nunez was dressing conservatively today in a rugby shirt and blue bermudas. He and Alphonse competed for the title of most outrageous flirt in our party. They chatted up all the pretty sellers, while single-minded François concentrated on the winsome Babette. We had a fine time feigning excitement over the many peculiar items offered for sale.

"Ooh, a framed photo of Charles de Gaulle," she cooed. "I can't tell you how long I've been needing one of these."

"Very nice," I agreed. "And here's a rusty carpet beater for you. Just the thing to use on poor Alphonse."

I bought a frighteningly sharp German-made butcher knife for future fish decapitations. My Love unearthed a passable cheese grater, which the elderly vendor priced at a hefty *E7*. Señor Nunez came to the rescue and negotiated the price down dramatically. He persuaded the seller to toss it in as a bonus when he bought an old tambourine. The shrewd negotiator scored both for a mere *E5*, which he celebrated by performing an impromptu dance with his tambourine. The guy does know how to attract a crowd. According to Reina, he's quite famous in his profession.

A display of used baby clothes brought a serious aside from Babette.

"Rick, if your wife *is* having a baby, she ought to go to a clinic for prenatal checkups."

"I wish you'd tell her that, Babette. She won't listen to me."

Later I noticed those two engaged in earnest conversation while trying on shoes at a booth that sold fashionable designer surplus. Sheeni bought a pair that verged on the sensible and wore them the rest of the day with positive results. She had me carry her old pair, which I "accidentally" misplaced. I accepted the subsequent angry reprimand as another sacrifice for love.

On the ride home we had to drive around forever to find a place to park. All that bouncing around with bonny Babette revived my dormant prostate with predictable results. If she noticed, she was too polite to mention it. Really, she shouldn't lean over a guy so familiarly to scan out the window for parking spots. I won't mention where her right breast wound up.

5:15 p.m. My Love just left with the Boccata brothers for the circus. The men have to get there early to change into their costumes, adjust their jockstraps, and tape up. I expect even brawny guys risk sprains or hernias tossing each other about like that. Pleading a debilitating headache brought on by excessive brain whirling the day before, I was reluctantly excused. They went by Métro, so I expect there will be some sibling competition to see who gets to sit next to my wife. Not too apprehensive as three beefy Italians seem somehow less threatening than one intellectual Frog.

10:45 p.m. Back from my "business" social outing with Reina. For the first half hour or so I regressed again to monosyllables. Such overpowering comeliness can be intimidating even to François. Instead of the many tourist boats that ply the Seine, we opted for a city public transit boat. Less expensive, and according to Reina, this choice spared us the "obnoxious amplified commentary." We embarked on the quay opposite Notre-Dame and cruised sedately downriver. Disneyland should offer a ride so enchanting. Afloat on a river of green under the bluest of skies through the heart of Paris. The quays, trees, and grand buildings washed in gold by the setting sun. Then plunging momentarily into an echoing coolness as we sailed under the arch of a bridge. The quays alive with families, joggers, and lovers enjoying the warm evening. Tourists waving from passing Bateaux-Mouches boats. And then looming suddenly over the southern rooftops: the Eiffel Tower! Immensely tall, ablaze in lights. Wow!

"Can you imagine the effect when it was built in 1889?" asked Reina. "Rising in a few months in the middle of Paris—the tallest structure in the world?"

"Pretty impressive," was all I could mutter. I was thinking: "Damn. Eat your heart out Golden Gate Bridge."

The ride back upriver in the deepening twilight was just as enthralling: the indigo Seine now outlined on both sides by ribbons of lamps. The ornate facades of riverside structures illuminated from below to stand out against the darkening sky. Passing cruise boats, lit up like Christmas morning, sweeping the quays with inquisitive searchlights. And at my side, the exciting, unsettling, nerve-roiling presence of Reina Vesely.

We had dinner at a small untouristy bistro near the Pont Neuf and quais des Augustins. I was beginning to appreciate the French fondness for leisurely meals. Hey, what's the rush? Who cares if the waiter is bogarting the check and your neighbors are puffing out toxic clouds of nicotine vapors? Don't be so uptight, you Type-A Americans. And candlelight, we must remember always to pause and light the candles. Did anyone in the history of public dining ever look more ravishing illuminated by candlelight than Reina Vesely? I doubt it.

She told me the story of her accident. In keeping with family tradition, from girlhood she had been a trapeze artiste. She performed all over Europe with her father and older brother. (Her mother died of meningitis when she was nine.) Several years before, the circus was making a jump from Toulouse to Arles in bad weather.

"We usually performed in public halls," she said, stirring her *café creme*, "but in Arles we would be under canvas. There were delays. Everything was rushed. My father checked the rigging as he always did, but he did not have much time. The tension on the cables was not balanced. When my brother swung onto the platform where I was standing, a shackle snapped. For some reason there was no redundancy. The platform collapsed. Dusan was killed. He broke his neck. I was not expected to walk again."

"Didn't you have a net?" I asked.

"Of course, Rick. But it did not extend completely under the platform. It partially broke my fall and flipped me backwards so that I landed on my right leg."

"That's awful, Reina."

"I was in a bad state. I grieved for my brother terribly and my poor father was inconsolable. My leg was so shattered I was—how you say?—immobilized for over seven months. My aunt graciously took me in—hospital bed and all."

"What did you do all those months?"

"At first, not much. I couldn't read or sew. I was too distraught. I stared at the walls. Then my aunt had the wisdom to present me with my baby Jiri. He and my other darlings gave me a reason to live, and to try to walk again."

"And your father?"

"He quit the circus. Papa blames himself for the accident. But these eventualities are not so uncommon in our profession. That is why people come to see us. To confront their fears. They watch a man in a cage with tigers, or a woman dancing with a bear, or us performing stunts high in the air. For a moment they feel, uh, vicariously . . . That is the correct word?"

"Yes, vicariously."

"They feel vicariously those terrors they would not wish to face in real life."

"Where is your father now?"

"Back in Prague, Rick. He got a job painting the poles of highway signs. He does not mind the heights!"

She laughed and looked at her watch.

"Oh my, it's late, Rick. We don't want to alarm your patient wife."

Amazingly, she extracted the check from the waiter in less than 30 seconds, then embarrassed me by insisting on paying. Riding home on the Métro, she confessed that in her 17 years she has never had a serious boyfriend—just a "platonic" beau a few years before. That twit was a Czech horn player. I was flabbergasted. Yes, she's had numerous volunteers for that position from our building, her circus acquaintances, fellow parrot enthusiasts, and the Czech expatriate crowd, but nobody's quite made the grade.

"I have a hard enough time getting my birds to do what I want," she laughed. "Can you imagine how much trouble a boy could be? Your wife—does she cause you difficulties?"

"Endless ones," I confessed.

"I thought so. That will teach you to marry a beautiful woman. They never give anyone a moment's peace."

Somehow I knew she was including herself in that statement.

When I trudged up the stairs to our apartment, My Love was already flossing her exquisite teeth.

"Nickie, where were you? I was beginning to worry."

"Er, how so?" I asked, cautiously.

"I feared your headache had progressed to something more serious."

My Love does care about my welfare!

"Since we don't have health insurance," she added, "that would be an expense we could ill afford."

Revising my previous mental note, I replied, "I was downstairs vacuuming our landlady's apartment. How was the circus?"

"Rather overlong. I saw only one outstanding performer."

"Not Bernardo Boccata, I trust."

"Very acrobatic, but I feel that if you've seen one human pyramid, you've seen them all. No, I was most impressed with another neighbor. That Señor Nunez is a man of genius. He had me nearly hysterical with laughter."

Try as I might I could not imagine my coolly rational wife giving way to uproarious hilarity. It was all she could do merely to tolerate my jests. Perhaps I should add some riotous clown antics to my repertoire.

"Nickie, your hair smells like perfume and cigarettes. Where have you been?"

"Uh," I said, my mind whirling, "it was poker night at Madame Ruzicka's. She gets a pretty lively crowd—for a bunch of old ladies."

Damn. Sheeni's off carousing with three hunky Italians, and I'm the guy who gets the third degree.

MONDAY, May 31 — Another post-weekend morning of industrious stair sweeping and trash hauling. Boy, people in this building sure booze it up with the wine bottles. And how come we're not invited to any of the parties? When I returned from a groceries run for Madame Ruzicka, I alerted her that should my wife inquire, she had hosted a lively poker gathering the night before.

"Of course," she replied, tipping me *E*5 to boot. What a pal.

While I was swabbing down the lobby, Mr. Hamilton (Maurice's dad) invited me into the wig salon to meet the staff. It seems he has commissioned a re-creation of Judy Garland's henna tresses from *Meet Me in St. Louis* to augment his show-stopping rendition of precocious Tootie Smith's Christmas Eve crying jag from that film. His weepy, doe-eyed Margaret O'Brien, apparently, has never been surpassed.

Stout Madame Lefèbvre and her aging all-chick crew seemed extraordinarily pleased to make my acquaintance, considering the unbridgeable language chasm and my lowly janitorial status. The ancient proprietress directed her most youthful underling to serve us all *cafes* from a battered and blackened espresso maker. I smiled and gazed about the cluttered workroom. It was a hair fetishist's paradise. Shelves clear to the ceiling were stacked with old woven baskets piled high with hair of every hue. More hair-laden baskets crowded the worktables where tall ovoid heads of lacquered oak modeled wigs in various stages of production. The entire scene was rather unsettling, as if stirring deep-seated hair loss fears. A few grimy windows and a couple of buzzing fluorescent tubes provided the only illumination. I wondered if the ladies realized they were all going to go blind sewing zillions of strands of hair in such crummy light.

I sipped my coffee and turned scarlet as compliment after compliment was showered upon me—all translated by Mr. Hamilton. The lobby had never been so clean. Such neatness in arranging the trash cans. My wife was quite the beauty. And so young! I was so helpful to poor Mademoiselle Vesely. Not to mention little Maurice. My shoes looked very comfortable. And doubtless were well made. My struggles with French were so endearing. And on and on and on. Quite the boost to a guy's flagging self-esteem, even if the source of my popularity remained obscure.

Then it occurred to me that sitting around this dim room month after month, year after year, sewing their fingers to the bone, these ladies must run short of conversational topics. So lately a new subject has diverted them: the young American janitor. Jesus, they probably know all about my date with Reina. And have already debated whether in fact I have the hots for Babette. Apparently, to the wigmakers of this quarter my life was an open book.

Giggling, the matronly coffee server made a remark, which everyone boisterously seconded. Mr. Hamilton translated: "Rick, before you go back to work, they want a kiss."

No time to bolt for the door. I was grabbed, pressed enthusiastically to corseted bosoms, and showered with kisses. In his nearly 15 years on the planet Nick Twisp had never been so popular. And who says the French are reserved?

1:30 p.m. I was opening a tuna can for lunch when My Love stormed in with a newspaper. She thrust the copy of *Libèration* in my face and pointed to a small box at the bottom of page one.

"Read that!" she demanded.

"Sorry, darling. I have not spontaneously acquired the ability to read French."

Sheeni was obliged to translate. The headline read: "A ghost in Montparnasse?" It seems that visitors to the Cimetière du Montparnasse in recent days have reported witnessing a young man who resembles Jean-Paul Belmondo lurking in the vicinity of the grave of Jean Seberg.

"Who the hell is Jean Seberg?" I asked.

"Don't play dumb, Nickie. You know Jean Seberg was Belmondo's romantic co-star in *A bout de souffle.*"

"Sorry. Never heard of the chick. Or seen the movie. She's buried there, I take it?"

"Yes, of course. Hounded to an early grave by the FBI for her association with the Black Panthers. Nickie, we're supposed to be keeping a low profile here!"

"Well, pardon me for living. I assumed the graveyard was a safe place to hang out. Any mention of Maurice?"

"Yes. Witnesses have reported the man is accompanied by a small dog in a trench coat, which may symbolize the detectives who pursued Belmondo throughout the film."

Leave it to the French to over-intellectualize impish Maurice. I mixed the tuna salad and explained to my suspicious wife why I again reeked of someone else's perfume.

4:12 p.m. As I was helping Reina carry down her birds, we encountered my lovely wife on the stairs. I made the mumbled introductions. Why is it when guys are introduced, they shake hands, say "hi," and that's that? But bring two attractive women together, and even a guy can sense that only about one percent of the subsequent human discourse is at the verbal level.

"It's so nice to meet you," said Reina, "Your husband is such a dear to assist me."

"Yes," replied Sheeni, smiling just as affably. "Rick . . . does have his uses at times."

"He's very popular with everyone in the building," added Reina. "But you particularly, I think. I like your perfume, Ms. Vesely."

"Call me Reina. You must give me the name of your *coiffeuse*. That cut is so flattering."

"Of course. Rick tells me you've trained your pets to do extraordinary things."

"Parrots are quite intelligent. They respond to love and patient guidance."

"A useful strategy in many endeavors, I should think," smiled My Love. "We must come and see you perform."

"I'd love that," agreed Reina.

"Well, I won't hold you two up," said Sheeni. "I'm sure you have a busy agenda. *Au revoir*, Reina."

"*Au revoir*, Sheeni."

Not bad. Call me a cockeyed optimist, but I think those two hit it off rather well.

6:45 p.m. Dynamic Mr. Bonnet just called. We are scheduled tomorrow for health exams at a hospital in Ménilmontant, wherever that is. Can it be that the French also require prenatal checkups for expectant fathers? Perhaps they'll demand a post-conception sperm sample to probe for genetic anomalies. I think I prefer the old days when you just went at it like rabbits and took potluck on whatever came out.

JUNE

TUESDAY, June 1 — Sometime before dawn. My Love just poked me in the ribs.

"Nickie, are you awake? I hear music."

"When you think of me?"

"What?"

"Sorry. Still asleep." I listened. A nearby accordion was conjuring from the ether of memory the evanescent notes of "Time after Time."

"It's an accordion, darling."

"I can tell that, Nickie. Who do you suppose it is?"

"My guess is Señor Nunez. He often plays in the lonely hours of the night."

"You've heard him before?"

"Many times."

"Why didn't you waken me?"

"You had not indicated a prior interest in late-night accordion recitals."

"It's so sad . . . so beautiful."

"So romantic?"

It was. We went at it like rabbits. Then lay entwined, still joined in our own secretions, as the birds of Paris got it together to greet another dawn. My Love was contemplating perhaps the solitary accordionist; I was brooding over the rent that was due today.

2:15 p.m. I now have an official certificate, signed by a French-licensed physician, attesting to the soundness of my health. Unlike many of my papers, it is an entirely genuine document. Oddly, the curt Ménilmontant doctor seemed not to care one whit that we were expecting a new citizen of the *Republique*. He only inquired if I had been in an accident to have undergone such extensive facial reconstruction. I mentioned a mishap with a skateboard as he was thrusting a gloved finger where few except Dwayne Crampton had dared to venture. Not pleasant. If intercourse for women feels that intrusive, it's no wonder they take such a jaundiced view of men. If I were a chick, I'm sure I'd be committed to thoroughly inhibited lesbianism.

4:30 p.m. No cemeteries and their controversial inhabitants for us today. Maurice and I took a long stroll to the Parc Montsouris, a pleasant hilly park with a lake, artificial waterfall, and winding paths leading to quaint grottos. Lots of apartment-sized dogs like Maurice attached to attractive females. One elegantly dressed woman who stopped to chat as heinies were sniffed was perhaps only slightly more beautiful than Fanny Ardant. I stood there suddenly incredulous that I could not respond in her own tongue. I feel I have a natural affinity for French. It's just the vocabulary that is giving me trouble.

We got back in time to share a pre-bird-lugging lemon water with lovely Reina. She has been offered a position with a small but highly regarded circus touring the provinces this summer. I might not see her for months!

"I love the life of the road," she admitted. "And it would be a good test for my babies."

"I don't know," I said, skeptically. "Parrots are very territorial. They may not like being dragged around from town to town."

"But, Rick, many birds fly thousands of miles. They enjoy new places."

As we were conversing in her odoriferous abode, I took a quick survey of my feelings—always well buried in Twisps. It was true: I longed to take her in my arms and kiss her delicious lips. Such censurable desires I could not even lay at the door of lusty François. They appeared to be coming straight from the heart.

5:52 p.m. Every one is abandoning me. When I returned from

vigorous bird-hauling, I found a note from my absent wife. She has gone to the Musée d'Art Moderne de la Ville de Paris with Señor Nunez. I should *not* expect her home for dinner. Damn, I wish that woman would cultivate some female friends. Now I have to feel jealous of a dwarf.

10:10 p.m. No sign of my wayward spouse. I took the rent money down to Madame Ruzicka, who invited me in to watch TV with her and Henri. Tonight's entertainment was an old movie starring Catherine Deneuve—with my hostess providing sporadic translations and commentary. Since bored newlywed Catherine couldn't get it on with her handsome and respectable husband, she took a day job as a prostitute specializing in grotesquely repulsive clients. The worst was a degenerate with a mouthful of metal teeth. Maidenly Catherine really seemed to dig that dude. Very creepy and disturbing. Not a film designed to calm the anxieties of a fellow whose wife was out on the town with another man. Especially since the long-suffering husband wound up in a wheelchair—paralyzed for life!

WEDNESDAY, June 2 — My wife arrived home at 1:42 a.m. Rather late, I thought, for a 15-year-old. Señor Nunez took me aside and apologized man-to-man for the lateness of their arrival. Although he was too polite to say so, I gathered that it was his companion who wished to remain out so late. Apparently, they had dinner at a noted restaurant on the place Saint-Germain-des-Prés and then went to a club on a barge on the Seine that caters to dwarves and midgets. Paris truly is a town with something for everyone.

While Sheeni was flossing her teeth, she casually let it drop that she had kissed her companion on the stairs.

"Well," I replied, keeping my cool, "I suppose that is an appropriate venue for kissing a dwarf in comfort."

"He's quite an extraordinary man, Nickie. He's lived an incredible life. Did you know he's a marvelous flamenco dancer?"

That was an image I did not care to ponder in the middle of the night. I turned out the lights and we went to bed. For the first time since our wedding, I did not kiss the lips that kissed you know who.

10:12 a.m. Truly miserable morning. My parents, of course, often had it this bad, but somehow I had supposed my own marriage would be different. We ate our breakfast in sullen silence. Lately, I've noticed, Sheeni hasn't been throwing up quite as much. I suppose that's good news for our struggling zygote. I'm beginning to understand the source of domestic violence. Usually when I look at her I experience a surge of affection, but today I just wanted to smack her a good one. Hard to believe this alteration in feelings. Can't write any more. Too anguished.

9:35 p.m. Talked to Connie. My father is in L.A. She's met him. Very discouraged that her hopes now pinned on Lacey warming up again to such a "total creepy loser." Expressed hope that balding George Twisp not as bad as his negative first impression. I said "don't count on it." One piece of good news: L.A. County in major budget crisis. Contemplating early release for some nonviolent petty criminals. Paul to be sprung soon from jail?

Connie not distressed by Sheeni dwarf-kissing. Deemed it an obvious power ploy. Said I must have been succeeding in appearing unavailable. Dismissed my fears that Sheeni on some kind of sick amatory down slope: from tall Trent Preston, to me, to dwarf. What will she be kissing next, I asked, a hamster? Connie sanguine. Said I should keep my cool and resist all impulses to get whiney or clingy.

Not the sort of impulse I'm worried about. Wife and Alphonse off somewhere in his Twingo. Wish now I hadn't bought that big German knife.

THURSDAY, June 3 — Another conference with Mr. Bonnet in Belleville. Apparently, I have passed muster. The contract is almost ready for me to sign. Riding home on the Métro, Sheeni at last clued me in. They want me to appear in a music video. With those giggling schoolgirls!

"Hey, I thought we were keeping a low profile?"

"We are, Nickie. Don't worry. The whole thing is merely a vanity enterprise. No one's going to see it."

"What do you mean?"

"Those three girls are Dutch. They have an act called De Drie Magdas—you know The Three Magdas. It seems they're all named

Magda and they sing some sort of tiresome novelty songs. So their star-struck parents, having more money than sense, have hired Monsieur Bonnet to produce a music video, for which they require a young Belmondo look-alike."

"But I can't sing."

"Not a problem. The girls will do the singing."

"I don't know, Sheeni . . ."

"Nickie, this is a wonderful opportunity. Monsieur Bonnet and his lawyers can help us get a Carte de Sejour."

"What the hell is that?"

"It's a residency permit that would let us remain here legally."

"Why?" I demanded. "So you can go out with Alphonse and that genius Señor Nunez? Not to mention the Boccata brothers!"

"You shouldn't get so jealous, Nickie. I don't object when you go out with Ms. Vesely. At least I don't lie about where I've been."

Remarkably well informed, as usual. I wondered if the wig-makers had ratted on me.

"I never kissed her," I volunteered.

"Glad to hear it," she said, taking my hand and giving it a squeeze. "Will you do the video, darling?"

"Give me one more reason why I should."

"Well, for one day's work they'll pay you *E*3,000."

A pretty good reason. I agreed, but specified that all dwarf-osculation must cease immediately.

"I guess that leaves you off the menu, short guy," she winked.

She paid for that remark. For more than an hour. This afternoon in bed.

FRIDAY, June 4 — Rick S. Hunter is soon to be an obscure video star. I signed the contract this morning in Mr. Bonnet's office. Then we went to Mr. Petit's office where we filled out our health insurance enrollment forms. France, it seems, does not want any medical deadbeats on its hands. Mr. Petit is still working on a solution for my suspect passport. He asked me if I had any strong objections to becoming a citizen of Estonia. I said not unless I was expected to speak Estonian. Then he drove us to the Prefecture of Police, where we filled out more forms and submitted our health certificates and other documents. Very nervous as the place was crawling with gendarmes. Kept my sunglasses on the entire time, arousing suspicions of harried bureaucrats. Good thing we were accompanied by our own high-priced lawyer. We have an appointment in two months for a final decision on our applications. Getting into France is certainly more complicated than entering the U.S. Back home you just have to be willing to swim the Rio Grande.

As MTV seldom showcases my sort of music, I'm not a devotee of that channel. Therefore, I'm not entirely sure what being in a music video entails. All I can recall is Michael Jackson shuffling backwards in an oversized glove and grabbing his crotch. Call me Mr. Inhibited, but I think I'd be rather embarrassed doing that. I hope pre-camera anxiety does not cause massive facial eruptions. I'm sure Mr. Bonnet would not be thrilled to pay *E*3,000 to some wannabe teen heartthrob with a mugful of zits. Have been practicing some Sinatra hits just in case. Surgically altered voice prone to sudden eructations far off the musical scale. Rather distressing to my ear. Of course, these days an inability to sing is no hindrance to a meteoric ascent of the pop music charts.

To celebrate my new career and the end of our marital estrangement, I took my loving wife out to dinner at a famous boulevard du Montparnasse restaurant that was once the haunt of Hemingway, Picasso, and other notables willing to pay tall francs for butter-laden cuisine. A vast, swanky place with grand chandeliers, velvet booths, and acres of polished brass trim. Very condescending waiter as you'd expect at those prices. Not taking any chances, I ordered a steak, while My Love had the *petit-gris*, which turned out to be a plate of disgusting snails. She claimed to enjoy them, but I say you have to be nuts to pay *E*35 to eat bugs out of the weed patch. No famous film stars in attendance, but Sheeni thought she spotted Roman Polanski, a fellow artist on the lam.

10:45 p.m. Reina invited me in for a post-bird-lugging brandy, but I politely declined. I'm reminding myself now that I'm a married man, and there's no point in associating heavily with attractive neighbors if it's just going to drive my wife into the arms of the nearest dwarf. I know guys are genetically programmed to scatter their seeds widely, but François will just have to stifle those impulses—especially since we have one bun in the oven already.

SATURDAY, June 5 — My fourth week as a wedded person. I've been successfully married for nearly a month! That's considerably longer than many Hollywood celebrities manage, even with all their fame and money.

Piroque, the director, dropped by this morning for wardrobe fittings. I'm not sure if that's his first name or his last name. He was wearing burgundy silk pantaloons today and the same muddy combat boots. He must do a lot of slogging through bogs. Today he was packing his little cigars in a purse made from the spare tire of a Vespa scooter. It's a good thing Piroque is a music video director, since, considering the way he dresses, he'd have a tough time landing a normal job.

Yvette, the attractive wardrobe mistress, made me strip and proceeded to dress my near-naked torso without embarrassment. Thankfully, I'd had debilitating anniversary intercourse barely an hour before, which took the edge off my erectile response when she was doing up my pants buttons. Very stimulating as you can imagine. My costume was that of an old-time French sailor: striped shirt, bell bottoms, and squashed little cap that looks like someone stepped on it. The ponytail of my brown wig was tied with a gay red ribbon that matched my shirt. And for defense against bashers, I was issued a bejeweled cutlass for my belt.

After a great deal of intrusive poking and prodding, Piroque pronounced himself satisfied with my look. Sheeni translated his acting instructions. The main thing I was to remember was to appear aloof from the proceedings. He didn't want me to look like I was getting excessively into the music. I said I didn't think that would be a problem.

After finishing with me, they went next door to dress Señor Nunez. It seems they were in desperate need of a dwarf as well, so Sheeni recommended our neighbor. I wasn't too pleased to hear of this, but at least my fast-thinking wife has cut herself in for ten percent of his fee.

Taking it easy for the rest of the day. Must rest up so as to be fresh for my video debut. The studio is sending a car for us tomorrow morning. Early. Our makeup call is at 4:00 a.m.!

SUNDAY, June 6 — It was still dark when we motored off in the big chauffeur-driven Citroën. I could get used to this lifestyle, but probably won't have the opportunity. Señor Nunez was doing his gracious best to put certain ugly incidents behind us. He greeted me warmly and only nodded toward my wife. He also resisted Sheeni's efforts to engage him in conversation, and pretended not to notice when she elbowed me hard after I inquired politely if she had "felt the baby kick" during the night.

The right bank of the Seine was alive with activity when we pulled up in front of the Hôtel de Sens, an ancient turreted pile that appeared to be a relic of the middle ages. (Note: to keep the tourists on their toes, in France a hôtel is seldom actually a hotel.) Pulling strings with civic authorities, Mr. Bonnet had succeeded in having portions of the posh rue du Figuier and neighboring quai des Célestins closed off to traffic. These blocks were now crowded with equipment vans, catering trucks, trailers loaded with lights, mobile wardrobe vans, and a large caravan providing every creature comfort for the pampered female stars. Groups of technicians were bustling about with gear as Piroque blew on a police whistle and pitched what sounded to me like major fits. Señor Nunez and I were quickly nabbed by Yvette, who hustled us into a wardrobe van, while My Love wandered off to score breakfast from the catering truck.

Evidently, Piroque had had second thoughts about my wardrobe. Tireless Yvette had labored all through the night to sew thousands of shimmering red sequins to my shirt. And she had altered it so that when I slipped it on, my bare midriff was exposed. I couldn't imagine why anyone would wish to see a skinny stark-white Twispian abdomen, but there it was on public view. Soon it received the professional attentions of Josette, France's sexiest makeup artist. She applied a tanning base, then brushed on subtle shadows to suggest taut muscles where none had ever rippled. This was after she had transformed my face. Never again, I suspect, will I ever look quite so godlike. Eyeliner, subtly highlighted cheekbones, lipstick, mascara, the works. If only Carlotta had had access to her services, I'm sure even more guys would have been inviting me to the Christmas dance.

Meanwhile, in the adjoining chair, Señor Nunez was undergoing a transformation from shortish civilian to admiral of the French fleet. The guy was ablaze with gold braid and glittering buttons. The velvet eye patch was a nice touch too. Then Piroque peered in to survey his cast and whispered a suggestion to Yvette. She took me aside and discreetly stuffed a rolled-up sock down my pants. These French gals are certainly comfortable working around a guy's crotch.

Dawn was nearly breaking as I found My Love sipping coffee and flirting with the sound engineer. She frowned and looked me over.

"How do I look, Sheeni?"

"Like a refugee from some sultan's harem. And what's that bulge in your pants?"

"It's all me, darling."

"I doubt that very much. Did you get some breakfast? The Magda elders are spending a fortune on catering."

"I've been forbidden to eat or drink. I can't muss my makeup under pain of death. God, I'm so nervous!"

I got even more jittery a moment later when the vivacious Magdas emerged squealing from their trailer. They were dressed alike in form-hugging silver lamé sheath-type uniforms, suggesting carhops of the year 2809. Of course, none of them had the meagerest of forms worthy of hugging. They spotted me, shrieked loudly enough to jolt awake every tourist in Paris, and thundered over in their shiny mylar clogs.

"Hi, Rick," giggled the designated spokesMadga.

"Good morning, ladies. You look nice," I lied.

More giggling.

"Hi, Rick," said another Magda, in makeup that could frighten the dead.

"Hi."

"Hello, Rick," called the final Madga. "What's up, hey?"

"Not much," I admitted.

I suspected we had exhausted their reservoir of English. They smirked and looked me over with what I could only interpret as preteen lust. It's a good thing girls are not always as ghastly and repellent as they are at age 12. Otherwise, I'm sure the human race would have died out eons ago.

As Piroque was resolved to capture his precious Parisian dawn, the fog machines were activated and taping was soon underway. My job was to heave away on the oars of a rowboat as the iridescent Magdas, standing in the prow, lip-synced to the loudly amplified playback of "*Heee, Lekker Ding,*" their obnoxious song. Our wooden dory was elevated above the street on a wheeled platform to which a long plate-glass mirror was mounted at a 45 degree angle to the pavement. This hid the wheels and had the effect of making the boat appear to float on a layer of fog several feet above the roadway. While I "rowed" in one direction, Admiral Nunez labored to pull the boat in the opposite direction by tugging on a shimmery silk rope. Meanwhile, assorted extras—garbed in 18th century clothing and powdered wigs—cavorted about in front of the medieval buildings as we proceeded along. This went on endlessly take after take. A Magda would giggle, I would cough from a stray wisp of suffocating fog, Señor Nunez would take a tumble on the oil-slicked pavement, a curious pigeon would fly down to check things out, etc. My shoulders began to ache from lifting the heavy oars as the song lyric "*Hij het niet leuk vindt als een meisje het van hem wint*" drilled its way deep into my brain along with its insipid melody.

Eventually, Piroque was satisfied and we moved on to the second scene. This involved my pretending to rescue the warbling Magdas from the doorway of the Hôtel de Sens by "wrestling" with Admiral Nunez. Of course, my adversary was a professional clown, who knew how to tumble about on the hard stone without getting injured. Too bad I wasn't similarly adept. And I thought the guy was altogether rougher than he had to be, considering the fix was in and the bold sailor was expected to triumph in the end. I was about to yank off his eye patch and knife him with my cutlass when the director signaled that that was the final take. The cast and crew broke into applause, the fog machines ceased emitting their oleaginous vapors, the Magdas clutched each other and jumped up and down, and Señor Nunez shook my hand warmly. Perhaps it had all been in fun after all. At least, with any luck, I would never again have to hear that inane song.

"How was I, darling?" I asked as my dear wife emerged from the oily artificial murk.

"Well, let's put it this way. Steve McQueen can rest easy in his grave."

I took that as a sincere compliment.

After I changed back into my street clothes and wiped off most of my makeup, Sheeni and I tracked down Mr. Bonnet to extract my payment as specified in cash. All those colorful euros made quite an attractive pile as he counted them out. My employer seemed elated by the day's shooting, or perhaps he was just relieved that the "music" had at last been silenced. At his insistence, we pushed our way into the jammed caravan for the cast party. All too soon I was pinned in a corner by the three Magdas, all chattering away in excited Dutch and force-feeding me exotic low-country snacks. I could only wave forlornly as across the length of the trailer my wife slipped out the door with our neighbor. This caused me some concern. Aside from the issue of dwarfish entanglements, Sheeni as usual was packing all my money.

MONDAY, June 7 — I woke up with a hacking cough from breathing all that aerosol oil the smog machines were belching yesterday. Even Sheeni's exquisite lungs were slightly impaired. What's worse, that damn song keeps ricocheting through my head like some endless loop tape employed by Nazi torturers to drive their victims insane. Not a problem for my wife as she had been warned in advance by the sound engineer, who loaned her a pair of earplugs. Considering the extremely negligible contribution of the Dutch to the pop music scene, it hardly seems fair that they have to clog both my lungs and brain with such rubbish. At least I have chiseled my video euros from the clutches of my rapacious wife. We are "banking" them jointly in the closet with our dwindling stash of Yankee greenbacks.

9:15 a.m. Bernardo Boccata just burst in with a copy of today's *Libèration*. At the bottom of page one was a photo of a sequin-bedecked sailor wrestling a downsized admiral. It seems that Mr. Bonnet's overzealous P.R. staff scored some press coverage of yesterday's shoot. Sheeni translated the lurid headline: "Ghost of Montparnasse Now a Video Star?" No article this time. Just a caption that reported the bare facts of young American Rick S. Hunter's video debut.

"You famous guy," said Bernardo, slapping me on the back.

"This is most unfortunate," said Sheeni.

"It's a disaster," I replied. "I'm going to strangle that idiot Bonnet!"

My Love sighed and studied the photo.

"I'm surprised they published such a homoerotic image," she added.

"What do you mean?" I demanded.

"Check it out yourself, darling."

I grabbed the paper and inspected it closely. An unfortunate lighting flare had highlighted Piroque's requested padding. I appeared to be sporting a fairly spectacular T.E., presumably induced by homosexual dwarf grappling. How acutely embarrassing. Now all of Paris thinks I'm some kind of deviate dwarfophile.

3:46 p.m. My life as celebrity janitor goes on. Many tenants smiled and waved as I carried down their trash. Babette winked at me as she strolled off with Alphonse. The ladies of the wig salon gathered in the lobby and gave me a spontaneous ovation. Gratifying, but couldn't they have waited until my newly mopped floor had dried? Señor Nunez thanked me for the free publicity, but complained that the caption hadn't mentioned his name or profession. I said I had nothing to do with it and thought he had a legitimate beef. When I returned from walking Maurice, Mr. Hamilton looked at me with new respect and excused me from further baggie inspections. Exploiting my new prestige, Madame Ruzicka sent me on errands throughout the neighborhood. Only her lovely niece seemed suddenly restrained in her amiability. Lugging down Reina's birdcages, I realized there was no way I could attempt to explain that bizarre photo without sounding like a complete degenerate. One simply does not broach the subject of theatrical crotch padding with France's comeliest virgin.

"I look forward to seeing your video," she said softly, when we finished loading her car.

"It's awful," I sighed, not looking at her. "I only did it for the money."

She gently touched my arm. "Take care, my friend."

"You too," I replied.

She does get under a guy's skin. Even her birds are warming up to me. No one's tried to bite me lately and this afternoon Zuza said, "Hi, Rick! You're *cu-u-ute*!" I wonder who taught her that?

TUESDAY, June 8 — Another middle-of-the-night phone call from a distraught Connie Krusinowski. She has met my sister Joanie and nephew Tyler. She encountered the new mother and Brobdingnagian infant at the county jail. They were visiting Sheeni's brother Paul.

"What!" I exclaimed. "My sister doesn't even know the guy."

"She does now, Rick. Paulo saw the article about her in the *Times* and sent her a congratulatory card, signed 'your brother-in-law Paul Saunders.' So she looked him up. Christ, Rick, your sister's throwing herself at my Paulo!"

"Now, Connie, don't jump to conclusions. You don't know that."

"I saw all the obvious signs, guy."

"Relax, Connie. My sister's not that attractive. Paul would never go for her."

"Don't bet on it, Rick. All men subconsciously seek women capable of bearing children to perpetuate their genes. That's why they're attracted to wide hips and big boobs. So there she is flaunting her fecundity by showing off that monstrous baby. She's single, available, and has already proven she can deliver the big genetic package. I could sense Paulo was smitten. And God knows she's in desperate need of a husband."

"Connie, you're making a mountain out of a molehill."

"That Tyler is no molehill, Rick. He's a giant fucking freak! Besides, all women are attracted to guys who are incarcerated."

"They are?"

"It's a proven fact, Rick. Why else do you suppose all those murderers on death row receive so many marriage proposals? That's why you need to call your sister and tell her to lay off my Paulo."

"Connie, be reasonable."

"Listen, Rick, I've always been on your side. I stuck my neck out for you. But if your relatives start butting into my life, I can turn on you—fast."

"Connie! You'd dime me to the feds?!"

"I don't want to, guy. That's why you have to get your damn sister to back off."

I never got back to bed. I sat there cursing on the toilet in the closet, then dialed my sister's number in L.A. She answered on the third ring and seemed reasonably pleased to hear from me.

"Joanie, what's that disgusting slurping sound?"

"I'm breast-feeding Tyler, Nick. He's got a big appetite."

Total telephonic gross-out. Still, I persevered. I conveyed, in no uncertain terms, Connie's message. My sister was not impressed.

"So that rich bitch doesn't like me visiting her boyfriend, huh? Too bad for her. Nickie, why didn't you tell me your girlfriend had such a cute brother? And what's this I hear about your getting married?"

"Yeah, we got hitched in Tijuana. We're living down in Mexico now. I'm having tacos every meal. Joanie, you've got to forget about Paul. He's not the marrying kind, and he doesn't dig chicks with children."

"So what's the real reason you want me to give him a pass?"

As usual, my sister could see through me like a fluoroscope.

"Joanie, Connie is threatening to squeal on me to the feds."

"You have the nicest friends, Nick. Not to mention you married a girl who already ratted on you once to the cops."

"How did you know about that?"

"Paul told me."

"Well, it was all a misunderstanding. She didn't mean to."

Joanie sighed. "OK, Nick, we might be able to work out some kind of a deal."

Foolishly, I hadn't anticipated sibling extortion.

"What sort of a deal, Joanie?"

"Not that you're interested, Nick, but our mother goes on trial next month."

Unwisely entrusted with a gun by Lance Wescott (my repulsive cop stepfather), my homicidal mother was under arrest in Oakland for plugging him in the groin.

Joanie continued, "Things are looking bad, Nick. Lance's reconstructive surgery has failed. The guy's pretty irate."

I could see where he might be, what with now being more capon than cop. That will teach the guy to cross Nick Twisp. I healed from the beating he gave me, but now he's facing a lifetime of sitting down to pee. Serves him right.

"What's Lance doing, Connie?"

"He's put Mother's nice new house on the market. And his nasty old mother just got custody of little Noel."

Noel Lance Wescott is my baby brother, who I recently dropped on the floor.

"But Lance isn't even the father!"

"His name's on the birth certificate. That's proof enough for the stupid judge. I pity poor Noel being in the clutches of that family. So we need more money for Mother's lawyers. You have to send us another $25,000."

"What!"

"I know you've got the money, Nick. At least your wife does. So send me a check and I'll lay off her charming brother. And have fun in Paris."

"Did Paul tell you we were here?"

"Paul doesn't have to tell me a damn thing. Send me the money!"

I said I would see what I could do and rang off. Damn, why are Twisps such treacherous weasels? It's no wonder I try to steer clear of my family as much as possible. Now I have to extract 25 grand from my loving wife. I might as well try to raise the *Titanic*!

11:25 a.m. After Sheeni left on a cultural mission to the Musée Marmottan Monet, I subjected our apartment to an intensive Power Snoop. More thorough than a normal snoop, it demands great exactitude in returning every article to its original undisturbed state. One bra strap slightly misaligned in her lingerie drawer is enough to arouse the suspicions of my vigilant spouse.

In an internal pocket of her French typewriter case, I discovered this recent letter from Trent Preston:

Dear Sheeni,

It was so nice to hear from you at last. Thanks for having the foresight to send your letter to my place of employment. You were correct in supposing Apurva might misconstrue any correspondence between us. I'm pleased to hear you made it at last to Paris. I envy your opportunities for cultural enrichment there as I load concrete bags on trucks and deal with the petty annoyances of high school in Ukiah. Still, Apurva is doing her best to make me happy and we are struggling to make a go of it. We've had a setback lately from an incident involving another woman and some unfortunate missteps on my part while under the influence of marijuana.

Sorry, but I must respectively disagree with you re: your marriage. Even if your documents were not in order and some deception was involved, you stood before a judge and exchanged vows with another person. This cannot be dismissed as lightly as you suppose. I say this even as I must confess that I heartily disapprove of your choice in marriage partners.

Forgive me if I overstep the bounds of friendship here, but I think you should consider that any child you might bring into this world would doubtless be an exceptional person. I believe this to be true even if the father was indeed that disreputable N. Twisp.

[Thanks a pantsful, Trent!]

In the long run (perhaps the *very* long run) the choice for you that might entail the least regrets would be to have the baby and give it up for adoption. I'm sure a worthy couple in France would be delighted to love and raise your beautiful child. I know that in the short term this choice would involve considerable hardship and sacrifice for you. Naturally, I will support and respect any decision you choose.

I have heard from your parents and know they believe you to be somewhere in Mexico. They are frantic with worry, but were somewhat relieved by the information they received from Tijuana of your marriage. Although it is not in my nature to deceive people, I will do as you request and further in any way I can the general impression that you are residing south of the border.

Apurva's doing well and our baby's development is right on track. It really is thrilling to watch his little heart beating on the scope. Such a miracle. Perhaps someday he'll have a chance to meet your daughter. I think that would be wonderful.

Do keep me posted on your experiences in that great city so far away. We think of you often.

Love,
Trent

An alarming missive. Not only has Sheeni removed her wedding ring, apparently she's been dissing our union to Trent as a sham. Can her prejudice against Mississippi run that deep? Is it my fault that it's the only state that sanctions teen marriage? Hard to believe, but I hope she takes Trent's advice to heart. For a change that muscle-bound poet was making considerable sense. Not that I'm about to let some grasping Frogs adopt our kid. Very distressing that she's writing him behind my back. And why such low regard for the institution of marriage—hers and Trent's?

Prolonged Power Snoop failed to turn up any bankbooks, statements, or account registers. Only one thing to do. Must search Sheeni's cavernous purse—always an enterprise fraught with peril.

WEDNESDAY, June 9 — A tumultuous morning. Several oblique allusions in bed to "Parisian heat" and "sweaty hair" propelled my offended wife into the kitchenette to bathe in our tin tub. Just the chance I was waiting for. I grabbed her purse, dumped its contents on the bed, and was immediately assaulted by a nerve-wrenching electronic wailing. My heart zoomed past coronary alert phase as my wife—naked and dripping—dashed in, exclaimed in surprise, and fished a small pen-like device from the pile. She pressed something on it, and the wailing ceased.

"Just what do you think you're doing!?"

"Uh, sorry, Sheeni, your purse spilled."

"Liar! Snoop! Asshole!"

"Darling, I can't believe you've booby-trapped your purse."

"Don't call me darling. Alphonse gave me this alarm-pen to guard against gypsies on the Métro. Just what were you looking for, slimebag?"

"Sheeni, honey, I need $25,000 from my Wart Watch funds."

"What for? And stop ogling me, you pervert."

It was true she looked even more alluring than usual garbed only in moist goose bumps.

"Sheeni, love, I talked to my sister yesterday. She's uh, been in contact with Mario and Kimberly, my Wart Watch partners."

"They owe us more royalties."

"Well, yes they do. But they've had some cash flow problems because of all the knockoffs. Anyway, they have a new concept ready for marketing and they need some tooling-up funds."

"What's the concept?"

"The concept? Uh, right. Well, it's pretty confidential."

"I'm not investing anything until I hear the concept."

"Of course not. I understand. OK, the concept is, uh . . . metallic teeth."

"What?"

"Well, they're not real teeth. They're kind of fake teeth. Kids just put them in for decoration. The effect is quite startling."

"I don't get it."

"That's the beauty of the concept, darling. They're way ahead of the curve here. It seems their marketing research has shown that the oral cavity is the last great untapped region for bodily ornamentation. Teeth bleaching and tongue piercing are just the first harbingers of the coming wave of total mouth embellishment."

"They really think this will sell?"

"The focus groups have been going nuts. We all stand to make millions. And this time they're nailing down worldwide design patents to keep the knockoffs at bay."

"As if *that* will deter those despicable pirates. They only want $25,000?"

"Well, they asked for 40, but I didn't think you'd go for that much."

My Love was delayed in getting back to her tub. After she wrote out a check for $35,000, we took advantage of her impromptu nudity to go well beyond mere ogling. No, I don't know where she hides her checkbook. It wasn't in her purse, and she made me suffocate under the blankets while she went and retrieved it. Obviously, my Power Snoop had not been as exhaustive as I had supposed.

3:26 p.m. I overnighted the check to Joanie and left a message for Connie that Paul was safely off-limits from my sister. I wrote Joanie that she should immediately send me an international money order for $10,000 or I would put a voodoo curse on young Tyler. I hope she buys that threat. When dealing with Twisps, strong-arm tactics are a must. I also enclosed a summary of the metallic teeth concept for her to forward to Kimberly in Malibu. Upon reflection, it doesn't seem any more farfetched than my Wart Watch idea. And we all know how big that one hit.

THURSDAY, June 10 — Another late night phone conversation with Connie. Maybe I should just set the alarm for 2:00 a.m. and sit there with my coffee while awaiting her call. She thanked me for paying off Joanie and inquired if, when I was growing up, we'd owned many champion chihuahuas.

"We never had any dogs, Connie. Not even mutts. My parents were too cheap to spring for dog crunchies. I had a gerbil once, but it had an unfortunate encounter with the vacuum cleaner."

"Just as I thought," commented Connie. "Nick, your father is a pathological liar."

"That's hardly news, Connie. What's he up to now?"

"The jerk's been comforting the wrong rich widow. He's been throwing himself at my mother. They've been going on long walks together on the beach with Anna and Vronsky."

Anna and Vronsky were Rita Krusinowski's yap-prone chihuahuas.

"I suppose he's been claiming to be a big-time chihuahua expert?"

"You guessed it, Rick. Dogo is livid. He's ready to murder him."

Dogo Dimondo is Mrs. Krusinowski's one-armed factotum.

"What's it to Dogo, Connie?"

"Well, now that father's out of the picture, I think Dogo may have serious designs on my mother. Not that I mind. They live together practically as man and wife anyway."

"You mean they're having sex?"

"Of course not, Rick. People that age rarely do. No, they're just together all the time."

I knew all about that syndrome.

"So, Connie, what's happening with Lacey?"

"Your damn father's been neglecting her terribly. She asked me yesterday if I thought it would be inappropriate for her to visit my Paulo."

"Uh-oh. What did you say?"

"What do you think I said? I said I thought it would hurt my father terribly if she did. But I can't go on guilt-tripping her forever."

"Connie, I know my dad. He only gave up on Lacey if it's over for good. She must have rejected him again in some massive ego-bruising way. You'll have to find someone else for her."

"Damn, I was afraid of that."

"How about Dogo for Lacey?"

"That's a thought. He's old, but he's younger than my father was. He's certainly attractive in an offbeat way."

Extremely offbeat, if you ask me. Connie promised to keep me up-to-date and we said our good-byes. I crawled back into bed and lay there as a solo accordionist squeezed out the corrosive notes of "*Heee, Lekker Ding.*" I will have to have a chat with Señor Nunez. Kissing my wife was one thing, but playing that damn tune really crosses the line.

If my dad marries Rita, Connie becomes my sister-in-law. And if Connie marries Paul, she becomes my sister-in-law twice over. With all those connections, you'd think some of those Krusinowski millions would rub off on me. I didn't mention to Connie the other thought that had crossed my mind. If my first marriage doesn't work out, *I* could marry Lacey. She may not be my soul mate like Sheeni, but I'm beginning to think there's something to be said for a relationship based solely on large dollars and spectacular sex.

6:28 p.m. Mr. Bonnet messengered over a rough-edit of the "*Heee, Lekker Ding*" video. Since we didn't have a VCR or TV, we went next door to watch it at Señor Nunez's. Sheeni and I felt like visitors from the Land of the Giants. Our neighbor has decorated his flat entirely in dwarf-scale furnishings of a vaguely Spanish "old hacienda" style. Lots of ornately carved dark wood, ponderous wrought iron, and festive weavings. Of course, with furniture that small you can cram quite a lot of it into a garret studio. We perched on the tiny sofa as our host prepared tea and warmed up the VCR. Since he politely declined to play the tape with the sound switched off, we hastily tore up strips of tissue and stuffed them in our ears.

Although he may dress like a fop, Piroque the director knows his stuff. The production values were most impressive. He wonderfully captured the atmospheric look of medieval Paris, and, improbably, our boat did appear to be floating magically above the fog. The extras were suitably of the period and engagingly picturesque. Darkly mysterious Señor Nunez was menacingly grotesque. The glittering Magdas certainly seemed to have been beamed down from a different time and perhaps planet. And the young sailor? Forgive me for being so candid, but he was pretty fabulous. Even Sheeni had to admit he was "not uncharismatic." An understatement, I think. Connie's right. Our plastic surgeon Dr. Rudolpho *is* a genius. What he has fashioned from the rude clay of Nick Twisp is nothing less than the Second Coming of James Dean. I smoldered on that screen!

Of course, as Sheeni points out, "Too bad no one's going to see it."

Yeah, right. My balloon thoroughly deflated, we thanked our neighbor and returned to our dingy hovel. Then I was called down to the cellar to swab up a major sewage backup. This happens not infrequently when too many tenants flush at once. From high amid the stars to deep in shit in under ten minutes. That's the story of my life.

FRIDAY, June 11 — Another possible disaster. It all started when I got excused from my concierge duties to go on a tourism excursion to Montmartre. This is a hill in northern Paris surmounted by a big white church, the Sacré-Cœur Basilica. It looks like something from the middle ages, but actually was completed in 1919. Maybe they used an old set of plans. Lots of impoverished artists used to hang out in the neighborhood, but now it's inundated with tourists seeking Vestiges of Bohemian Life. I also wanted to check out the nearby place Pigalle, where Mr. Hamilton does his nightly female impersonation gig. Sheeni's genteel guidebook cautioned this district was tawdry and risqué, so, of course, it was tops on my must-visit list.

I thought it would be fun to ride the funicular up to the church, but as the line was obscenely daunting, we hoofed it instead. Hardly broke into a sweat from being in such great shape from living six flights up. As it was a clear day, the view from the plaza in front of the church was most awe-inspiring. The whole of Paris was at our feet, not excluding the distant Eiffel Tower and its ugly box on the fringe of our neighborhood. We went inside the basilica, which was most impressive if you're into disturbing anatomical mosaics of Christ displaying His sacred heart. Kind of spooky, if you ask me, but then I've never been the most pious kid on the block. We paid *E*5 each to hike up narrow spiral stairs with a lot of panting tourists to the top of one of the domes. An even more amazing view. I'm sure Reina would love it if she could manage those steps. But as we were trooping back down, whom should we suddenly meet going up, but Apurva's vile brother Vijay Joshi! Everyone was too thunderstruck to speak, but there's no doubt he recognized us. We continued on hastily, and a deeply shaken Sheeni insisted on returning at once to our apartment. I never got to the place Pigalle, and my wife continues to pace the floor in a state of extreme nervous agitation. She said she knew Vijay was coming to Paris for the same summer program that she'd been enrolled in, and we should have been more cautious. I replied Paris is a big place and how were we supposed to know we'd run into the bum? And what, I wanted to know, was a Hindu doing in a Catholic church?

"He's going to tell my parents, Nickie. I know he is! He's betrayed me before. What are we going to do?"

I gave it some thought.

"I guess we'll just have to murder him. I've been wanting to for quite some time."

"Oh, you're no help! This is no time for jokes!"

François wasn't aware that anyone was joking.

4:38 p.m. Sheeni has tracked down Vijay's dorm and has gone off to see if she can find the twit. I'm not sure what that is supposed to accomplish, but any rendezvous of those two always makes me nervous.

Reina reports she attended a showing of my video with other interested neighbors in the wig salon. I was a big hit, though the three Magdas and their Dutch novelty tune were a consensus pick for immediate showbiz oblivion.

"Rick, I thought your performance was excellent," she said, as I once again carted her birds down the endless stairs.

I decided to make a stab at clarifying an issue.

"Thanks, Reina. It was fun, though I felt a little silly in those ridiculous padded pants. It was a little joke of the director."

"I thought your costume was very flattering."

What was that supposed to mean? I didn't have the nerve to ask.

9:52 p.m. No sign of Sheeni. Getting rather agitated myself. Should have hired a skinhead long ago to deal with Vijay when I had full access to my Wart Watch fortune. I'd much rather pay $25,000 for that deed than throw it away on lawyers for my tempestuous mother. I sensed she was destined for future legal skirmishes the first time she walloped me with the hairbrush at the tender age of two.

11:45 p.m. My wife still not back. Not even a damn phone call! Who needs this grief? I'm going to bed.

SATURDAY, June 12 — Five weeks, diary. More than a month of wedded bliss. Alas, we may have entered another rocky patch. Wife arrived home late and gave me no goodnight kiss when she crawled into bed. Always a bad sign.

10:47 a.m. Lovely wife off on a cultural expedition. WITH VIJAY JOSHI! Husband not invited, as anniversary breakfast chat revealed he has fallen under suspicion of treachery.

"Vijay was very happy to see me," she announced, coldly decapitating a baguette with her bare hands. "We had a lovely dinner together. He has no intention of reporting my whereabouts to my parents."

"Hah! You believe that liar?"

"We'll see who the liar is," she announced ominously. "Do you recall the circumstances under which my mother intercepted my passport at the Ukiah post office?"

"Of course, darling. Don't forget I'm the guy who had to shoot your father to get it back."

"I had always supposed that it was Vijay who tipped off my parents to my plans, but he assured me yesterday that I was mistaken."

"Why would he admit it? He ratted on you to your parents because he didn't want you to leave Ukiah."

"That was doubtless the motive of the guilty party," she replied. "The only other person to whom I had confided my plans was Rick S. Hunter."

"I was all for your running away, darling. I wanted to go with you!"

"So it seemed to me at the time. And, of course, I had no reason then to doubt Mr. Hunter's sincerity."

"And still don't, darling!"

"But the seemingly straightforward Rick S. Hunter turned out to be the devious Nick Twisp—a person who knew he was incapable of learning French. A linguistically impaired person not likely to want to spend much time abroad in a non-English-speaking country."

"That's pure paranoia, darling. Vijay has poisoned you against me. What disproves your thesis is my very presence here, in France, with you—the woman I love. Have I said anything about leaving? Aren't I the guy working three jobs to try to make a go of it here?"

A flicker of doubt in her azure eyes.

"You deny betraying me?"

"I certainly do, Sheeni. I may be devious at times, but Vijay is the true schemer. He's the Quisling in our midst. Don't forget that forged letter he sent you—purported to be from me in India. The guy has no scruples. He's in love with you and will do and say anything to be with you. He knows his time in Paris is limited. When he returns to Ukiah, he will have every incentive in the world to rat on you again to your parents."

Sheeni viciously buttered her bread.

"Somebody here is lying," she replied, pointing her knife at me. "And I intend to find out who."

6:42 p.m. No sign of my absent wife. Had a lonely dinner for one at the local crêpe stand. You'd be amazed at what the French are willing to roll up in a pancake. François ruminated throughout meal on increasingly violent terminations of home-wrecking Indian philanderer.

8:15 p.m. Saturday night alone in Paris with no date, no TV, no book to read, no spouse—nada, zip, the Big Zero. Life now at the bottom of a very deep and smelly septic pit. Can't write any more. Too depressed.

SUNDAY, June 13 — Wife arrived home late last night. No kiss again. She slept late, then took a bath with her back to me. To keep up my image, François feigned indifference to these slights. When I returned from walking Maurice, she was eating a cheese omelet and reading some Frog newspaper.

"How's your omelet?" I asked, pouring myself a cup of coffee.

"Very good. The cheese grater is working well."

"Glad to hear it."

Sheeni went back to reading her paper.

"How was your museum hopping yesterday?" I inquired.

"Very informative. We went to the Musée Carnavalet. Vijay has a true appreciation for the history and culture of France."

Yeah, I thought, and so did the victims of the guillotine—right before the blade came hurtling down.

"That's nice," I replied. "Any news from home?"

"Like what?"

"I don't know. How's his sister?"

"Not good. Apparently Trent had an affair with your Sonya

Klummplatz. Things must be very bad between them if Apurva can't even offer enough distractions to keep Trent away from your old girlfriend."

A low blow. In fact, Trent only met with Sonya in order to extract from her the location of Sheeni's prison-camp unwed mothers' home. This truth I had to withhold lest Sheeni interpret his valiant sacrifice as proof of Trent's continuing regard for her. I decided on a different tack.

"Well, Trent's had the hots for Sonya for some time."

"Since when?" she demanded.

"I don't know. A long time. That's what he told me."

"I don't believe it."

"Then why did he dance with her so many times at the Christmas dance? And why was Sonya so upset when she found him alone in that hot tub with Apurva? The guy betrayed her."

"Trent Preston is *not* a chubby chaser!"

"Hey, whatever. Facts are facts. The interpretation I leave up to you. What shall we do today, darling?"

"You can do whatever you like. I'm meeting Vijay at one."

Married life. Some days it's no worse than a little mechanized scrotum-squeezing by the Spanish Inquisition.

9:15 p.m. Instead of staying home and feeling suicidal, I went with Reina to help prepare her circus caravan for her summer tour. We packed her station wagon with cleaning supplies, a picnic lunch, and her talkative babies, then drove south through heavy weekend traffic to Vitry-sur-Seine, a nondescript suburb. Her caravan was stored in the fenced yard of a trucking company. Fairly big (about 25 feet long), but more lightly constructed than American trailers, it featured flamboyant European curves and a tasteful interior done in a light-grained fake wood. There was a dining lounge in front, then a compact kitchen, followed by the usual midget bathroom with large closet opposite, and a cozy bedroom in back. Modestly sized for full-time living, but Reina had toured happily in it for many years with her father and late brother.

"Wherever did you all sleep?" I asked.

"Papa and Dusan shared the bedroom; I slept up front here on the convertible sofa. Circus people don't expect much privacy. We were quite comfortable, though sometimes I dreamed of having my own room in a real house. We've been storing it here since the accident, and I'm afraid I've rather neglected it."

While I pumped up the four flat tires with a hand pump, Reina got to work cleaning the dusty interior. Her chatty birds watched us from their cages on the tailgate of the Mercedes. Alas, no hose was available, so I filled a bucket from a hose bib near the loading dock and gave a sponge bath to the caravan's dingy exterior. Paris may be the City of Light, but there's plenty of industrial grit in its air.

We ate our lunch of salad, savory mushroom tart, and red wine inside at the small dining table. The wine went to my head and I soon unloaded on Reina all my marital woes. She listened with concern and mulled over my predicament.

"Well, it doesn't sound like she has a romantic interest in this fellow," Reina remarked.

"You don't think so?"

"Not from what you've told me, Rick. It may be she was feeling lonely and is enjoying the company of a familiar person from home. But she's not being very considerate of you."

"Well, that's sort of typical."

"I don't know your wife, Rick, but I imagine that moving to a new country, and being newly married, and expecting a baby can be quite stressful."

"You think I should cut her some slack?"

"I think there's too much cheap advice being offered in this world, Rick. When I was ill from my accident, everyone kept telling me what I should do. It became quite tiresome. People should do what feels right to them. But I'm sure your wife loves and values you. How could she not?"

A welcome affirmation that seemed to apply equally well to my companion. In a dusty apron and with her hair tied up in an old scarf, she was still infinitely desirable. The trucking yard was deserted on Sunday; we were profoundly alone together; the cozy bed in the back bedroom beckoned from only a few steps away. I reined in François's alcohol-inflamed impulses and wondered morosely if Sheeni was in similar proximity to a tempting bed. Would Vijay stoop to seducing the pregnant wife of his worst enemy? Do Republicans vote for tax cuts?

I spent the afternoon in even closer proximity to the bedroom and my employer. I helped Reina assemble and mount shelves in the hallway closet to hold her birdcages. She held, I drilled and screwed. Very tight quarters, very close bodily contact, very enticing bodily scents. Couples have gone on entire honeymoons and not experienced such intimacy. The shelf system had been engineered in France, so naturally its assembly defied all notions of logic. Exasperated by the mystery hardware, silly from the wine, we gave way to fits of giggling. It's very hard to gauge the location of a bracket when you're laughing like an idiot just one-half centimeter from someone who smelled that good.

10:15 p.m. For a change, my wife got home before I did. She looked up from her book when I entered.

"Where have you been?" she inquired coldly.

"Out. What's this?"

Something new had been tacked up on the wall by the door. It was a document, written by hand in some blotchy brown ink, and signed in a bold script by one Vijay Joshi.

"As you can see," said Sheeni, "it's Vijay's signed declaration that he has never betrayed me. He wrote it in his own blood."

Yuck. Leave it to the vegetarian pacifists to start the bloodletting.

"It was an act of magnificent courage," added Sheeni.

"But rather poor taste," I replied. "I hope he sliced deeply into his jugular."

My wife was not amused. She gave me the cold shoulder. Fortunately for all concerned, François did not grab any large German knives and reply in kind to these provocations.

MONDAY, June 14 — No check from my sister! The $10,000 extortion rebate should have arrived by now. Meanwhile, my so-called wife is off again with you know who. How much longer can life go on kicking Rick S. Hunter in the balls? Nick Twisp I could understand, but suave Rick's not the sort of guy to take this grief lying down. Performed my slave concierge duties today with notable lack of enthusiasm. Fellows in my emotional state should not be asked to haul out the debris from other people's weekend frolics. Snarled at several tenants, dumped trash cans on curb in disorderly row, neglected to mop lobby, and directed offensive French gesture at passerby who pointed indignantly at fresh Maurice deposit on sidewalk. Today's language project: learn the French for "Up yours!"

TUESDAY, June 15 — At last, a friendly female voice. Too bad it had to be Connie Krusinowski phoning at 2:00 a.m. with momentous news. Trustworthy, nonviolent felon Paul Saunders has been sprung from jail. To recover from the traumas of imprisonment, he has accepted her invitation to accompany her on a luxury getaway.

"That's nice," I yawned from my closet toilet perch. "Are you two off to Palm Springs?"

"Hardly, Rick. I have to get Paulo to an extremely romantic location far away from Lacey and your lousy sister. We're coming to Paris."

"You're what!?"

"We're arriving on Friday. I think when Paulo sees how happily married his sister is, he'll pop the question for sure."

Quickly disabusing Connie of that notion, I filled her in on the whole ugly story.

"This is awful, Rick. She hasn't spoken to you for days?"

"Not much. The last thing she said to me this evening was: 'Don't touch me, you repulsive degenerate'."

"Oh dear. And you have no proof that you didn't betray her?"

"Well, no."

"Why not? Oh, I see."

"At the time it seemed like the best course for all parties, Connie. And I did disguise my voice to sound like Vijay."

"I understand perfectly, Rick. Well, we'll have to get her away from that interfering Indian."

"I've been thinking of nudging him off the Eiffel Tower—the uppermost platform."

"Why don't you wait on that, Rick? I'll see what I can do from my end."

"OK, Connie. How's the Dogo-Lacey matchmaking going?"

"Not good, Rick. I've contrived to bring them together, but Dogo isn't rising to the bait. That guy always has his own agenda. He's furious because my mother is considering becoming a patron to your father. Why didn't you mention that the creep was a novelist?"

"He's not. His one and only magnum opus is stalled permanently on page 12."

"Well, my mother is thinking of underwriting his latest project. It's to be the definitive chihuahua novel. He's already moved into her guest room and produced some sort of outline."

At least one Twisp was getting ahead in his writing career. Go Dad!

4:45 p.m. No check from my sister! If it doesn't arrive by tomorrow, I'll be forced to call her and whisper anonymous voodoo baby curses into the phone. After I rudely snubbed Alphonse's pidgin-English request to wash his Twingo (for a measly *E*2!), his girlfriend came out and invited me on an afternoon stroll. While we walked arm-in-arm down the boulevard Raspail in the warm sunshine, I explained to Babette why everybody's favorite janitor suddenly has evolved into the Grouch that Spurned Paris. She was most sympathetic and assured me that it is universally agreed that the first year of marriage is the toughest. I said I would be thrilled just to make it through the first two months without a major homicide.

To place my marital woes in perspective, Babette suggested a visit to one of our district's more unusual tourist attractions. We paid our *E*5, walked down spiral steps into deep subterranean gloom, switched on our rented flashlights, and took an extended amble through the Catacombs of Paris. These are ancient limestone quarries piled high with the bleached bones (and scary skulls) of six million long-deceased Parisians. Even in François's most sadistic Vijay reveries, I had never conceived of death on such a massive scale. Gallery after gallery of skeletal remains heaped in great mounds—creatively fenced in by pickets of long thighbones. Quite overwhelming. Our fellow tourists, I noticed, spoke in hushed tones. Only a few dared to chuckle at the macabre signs offering quotations such as "Happy is he who always has the hour of his death in front of his eyes, and readies himself every day to die." My companion seemed to take these sentiments to heart.

"When the daily annoyances build up, this is my refuge," commented Babette. "I suppose you find that rather ghoulish?"

"Not unless you bring home souvenirs."

"You can't, Rick. Everyone is searched upon leaving."

Damn. There went my plan to swipe a rib bone, bloody it up, and present it to my wife as a self-amputated gesture of sincerity.

"All these people had problems," she added. "They loved, they suffered, and now look where they are."

"You are advocating suicide?"

"Not at all, Rick. Just the opposite in fact. Life is a gift, and we must treasure our time here. In the end, as all those around us discovered, our days here are all too short."

A comforting philosophy, I suppose. But one inconsistency troubled me. Why was she wasting her precious time keeping company with that cad Alphonse?

WEDNESDAY, June 16 — Another unsettling breakfast table chat. Sometimes I think I was better off when my wife only spoke to me in French. According to Sheeni, Vijay has divulged that a contract has been placed on my life.

"Oh, that's just a silly rumor," I scoffed. "Your father is not that criminally inclined."

"I think I know my father," she replied. "He is not a man of reason. You have crossed him many times. You have stolen his only daughter."

"Well, he can have her back."

This jest drew no laugh. My Love studied me coldly.

I coughed and went on. "You have some reason to believe this allegation?"

"I can tell you what Vijay told me. My father recently visited Dominic DeFalco at his concrete plant. A dispatcher there named Mertice Palmquist listened in on their conversation over the desk intercom. They were discussing how to locate and cause great bodily injury to someone named Rick S. Hunter. She relayed the details of this conversation to Trent, who told Apurva, who told Vijay."

"And you guys think Fuzzy's dad has some connection to the Mafia?"

"Have you ever met Mr. DeFalco?" she asked.

I had, unfortunately. As I recall, he was one intimidating dude, who had already made a serious attempt on the life of one Twisp (the near crushing of my father under tons of gravel).

I couldn't tell if Sheeni was exaggerating this threat to mess further with my head or she really believed there were paid sociopaths on my tail. In any case, I was more than a little disturbed that Vijay knew both that people were looking for me and where I lived. This is not the type of sword one likes to hand to your mortal enemy.

After My Love left for yet another day of alleged culture-mining with vile aliens, I made an emergency call to Fuzzy DeFalco in Ukiah. The hirsute teen was winding down from a hot date by watching late-night TV in his bedroom.

"I did it with Lana four times tonight, Rick. It's my new record. I'm a little sore inside down there now. You think I busted something?"

"It's just a strained prostate," I said, conscious that my own once-energetic gland was shriveling now from disuse. "Nothing to worry about, guy. Where were you doing the deed?"

"My parents were out, so we went at it in my bedroom. Lana likes it better here than in the back seat of my Falcon."

"Better watch you don't stain the upholstery, guy. That's a valuable classic car."

"I'd still rather have a Camaro, but we always do it on a blanket. How's the action on your end, Rick?"

"Great. We're going at it night and day," I lied. "Fuzzy, mind if I ask you a personal question?"

"Shoot, buddy."

"Does your father have some connection to the underworld?"

"You mean like the Mob? No way, Rick."

"Glad to hear it. So you never had any FBI guys snooping around?"

"No way. You must be thinking of my uncle Sal."

"Who's he?" I asked, alarmed.

"Well, he's actually my father's uncle. He owns a laundry in Vegas."

"That sounds pretty harmless."

"Well, it's a pretty big laundry. They do the sheets and towels for lots of casinos. The FBI got interested because they had a few stiffs turn up in their hampers. But they never pinned a thing on my uncle. He's a great guy. He always sends me very expensive Christmas presents."

I didn't like the sound of this Uncle Sal. I asked my pal to make a few discreet inquiries and promised to check back with him in a few days.

Damn. I hate to sound bloodthirsty here, but François should have bumped off Vijay and aimed more carefully when he was plugging our father-in-law.

4:48 p.m. At last, a money order arrived from my sister. For a measly $4,500! She enclosed a note explaining she had to buy a bigger bassinet for Tyler, and our father put the bite on her for an additional three grand. He's quit his job! She wasn't going to lend him a dime, but he convinced her that he will soon be marrying into a large truck-springs fortune. She says unless she wins the lottery, that's her only hope for college education funds for Tyler. If that's the case, I think my jumbo nephew better get ready for a lifetime as an undereducated blue-collar slave. One positive note: Joanie reports that Kimberly and Mario liked my flashy metal teeth idea, although Mario is thinking more along the lines of hygienic molded plastic with rhinestone inserts. Still, the concept is mine, so royalties must be paid.

THURSDAY, June 17 — Continuing silent treatment from my devoted spouse. Just to refresh my memory of what her voice sounds like, I let it slip that her brother was arriving tomorrow. She kept her enthusiasm in check. These Saunders can be a cold bunch. After she left I hurried to the local American Express office, where I cashed in my money order for euros. These I have cached separately from our communal funds in an envelope I taped under the bottom drawer of the dresser.

12:47 p.m. A curious development. My Love arrived home in a huff. A certain Vile Alien stood her up. They were supposed to rendezvous at the Musée des Arts et Métiers, but the twit never showed. (You'd think they'd eventually run out of musées, but apparently the supply is inexhaustible. If the French despise tourists so much, why do they provide so many attractions?)

Since a hole had been shot in her social calendar, I invited Sheeni out to lunch, but she scrounged up a better offer from Babette. I'm hoping my Welsh friend puts in a good word for the beleaguered husband.

7:35 p.m. Vijay is nowhere to be found. My wife made some inquiries at his dorm and discovered that he was taken away this morning. By the French state police! Naturally, My Love relayed this news to me in her most accusatory tone.

"Yeah, right, Sheeni. Like I have some clout with the gendarmes? Get real."

"You know nothing about this?"

"Only what you just told me, darling. I'm totally in the dark and I'm totally pleased. It couldn't have happened to a more deserving cretin."

My Love's response I shall not record here, lest—by the act of writing down each inflammatory syllable—the stinging emotional torment which they inflicted shall be unnecessarily prolonged.

FRIDAY, June 18 — A day of high anxiety. Even getting all that exercise walking Maurice and lugging birds, I know my stress levels are off the chart. I really should be smoking some major mind-calming hallucinogen. Perhaps I could get Fuzzy to airmail me some of Lana's soothing homegrown reefer.

My Love returned from her morning investigations with the news that Vijay won't be coming back. The guy's been deported! So much for his summer plans. For this "monstrous injustice" she continues to blame me. Personally, I think it's bad enough that she has to excoriate me for acts which I did commit, let alone for swinish misdeeds for which I'm blameless. I told her if she didn't get off my back, I would be forced to do something we'd both regret.

"Like what?" she demanded, her fine nostrils flaring.

"Like . . . like, heave your damn typewriter out the window!"

She directed at me what could only be termed a sneer.

"And what if it struck some innocent person on the sidewalk? And killed them!"

A valid point; I gave the matter some thought.

"Well, I'd make sure I donned gloves before tossing it."

"You don't own any gloves, you idiot. And it would be just like you to try and pin your nefarious crimes on me."

"Not just you, darling. You forget: Bernardo Boccata also handled that typewriter."

"And what about the innocent vendor who sold it to me?"

"I'd send him to the guillotine too!"

Marital spats. They do ramble off topic sometimes.

5:38 p.m. A call from Connie. They have arrived. Even though they flew first class and received 19 hours of nonstop privileged pampering, they're both feeling tired and jet-lagged. So they've decided to crash at their sumptuous five-star hotel and connect up with us tomorrow. I wished her well and confided that the climate at Chez Hunter was still bitterly sub zero.

10:31 p.m. A uniformed hotel bellhop arrived around dinner time with a small package from Ms. Krusinowski. I tipped him *E*.50 and eagerly opened the box. It contained a cassette tape and a note from Connie saying I should listen to it with my wife. I found that person next door chatting up a certain talented dwarf. She reluctantly excused herself and returned. I slipped the cassette into our radio-tape player, and we found ourselves in the middle of this extraordinary recorded phone conversation:

Sheeni's mother: "But why don't you come to Ukiah and see us, Paul?"

Paul: "I told you, mother, I'll visit you when I get back. Connie and I want to go to Mexico to see if we can find Sheeni."

Sheeni's mother: "I've given up on that godforsaken country. We've looked everywhere, and the authorities don't do anything even if you bribe them. And why are you going with that awful Polish-Asian girl?"

Paul: "Would you rather I got back together with Lacey?"

Sheeni's mother: "Heavens no! She's worse!"

Paul: "Mother, I've been meaning to ask you. How did you find out that Sheeni was trying to get a passport to run away?"

Sheeni's Mother: "I'm not as stupid as she thinks. I made friends with that boy Vijay and he told me. I was hoping he'd persuade his tramp of a sister to give up darling Trent, but he proved just as untrustworthy as the rest of his family. I say send the lot of them back to India!"

I clicked off the player and looked at My Love. She sighed and wiped away a tear.

"I didn't forge the tape," I said, "if that's what you're thinking."

My Love got up from the sofa, ripped Vijay's bloody declaration off the wall, and tore it into bits. Very small bits. Then she fell into my arms.

A very satisfying triumph, I must say.

SATURDAY, June 19 — Six solid weeks of marital rapture. These gala anniversaries really pile up. I awoke as I used to do: thoroughly entwined among the limbs of my beloved. We really get ourselves tangled during the night. Thrown together by forces beyond our control, we acquiesced to the inevitable and went at it again like frenzied rabbits. My dormant prostate rose to the challenge, and Sheeni's female equivalent also performed admirably. Hard to believe someone so (intermittently) hot in bed can be so icily distant when provoked. I am resolved to remain on her good side from now on.

After a leisurely communal bath, we made it just in time to Connie and Paul's swanky Art Nouveau hotel not far away (except financially) on the boulevard Raspail. One step inside the palatial lobby and I immediately felt like a trespassing peasant. I was even more unnerved when My Love disclosed that during World War II this hotel had been the Paris headquarters of Hitler's feared Gestapo. Riding up to the top floor in the ornate elevator, I wondered how many brave resistance fighters had been given manicures with pliers in this very building

A smiling Paul answered our knock. He shook my hand and gave his baby sister a perfunctory hug. Their lavish love nest was like a 1930s movie-set fantasy of flowing Art Deco curves and extravagantly streamlined furnishings. Gleaming cascades of silvery satin engulfed the great round bed—now in strenuous disarray. One could only speculate what affluent celebrities had gone at it on that richly sprung mattress.

"You're looking thin, Paul," said Sheeni.

"Hmm, you're not," he replied.

It was true. My Love has begun to thicken perceptibly around the middle.

"Don't remind me!" she exclaimed.

Connie hugged us both. She was dressed to high Parisian standards and looked like Serious Money on the Hoof. No colored contacts since Paul prefers her eyes in their natural Polish blue—always a startling contrast with her artfully sculpted Asian physiognomy. (In private Sheeni terms their torrid affair "artificial miscegenation.")

Polite conversation was made as Connie finished her elaborate toilette.

"Tell me, Paul," said My Love, "how was jail?"

"Certainly not pleasant, but rather educational. How's married life?"

"Very much the same," she replied.

Connie glanced at me questioningly. I smiled and gave her a discreet thumbs-up sign. This was noticed by my ever-observant spouse, who scowled and stuck out her tongue at me.

We breakfasted sumptuously downstairs in the hotel's ritzy dining room. Such elegance! Such refinement! Such prices! Fortunately, Connie nonchalantly signed the check, which no doubt will be added to her humongous tab. Resourceful François made this mental note: If you're down and out in a foreign city, just check into the best hotel, sample their finest in-house cuisine, sign the check, then casually saunter out.

Since this was Paul's first visit to Paris, his sister was full of suggestions for Must-Be-Seen Sights. Connie inventoried the activities she had planned for today. For a broad overview of the French capital, they would begin with a guided limousine tour. Next up was a cruise down the Seine on a private yacht, during which a catered lunch would be served. Then a return to their hotel for rest and refreshments. Dinner was at sunset at the Jules Verne on the Eiffel Tower, followed by an excursion to Paris's most exclusive jazz club.

"Sounds like fun," I admitted.

"And what's on your agenda for today?" Connie inquired.

"I'm scrubbing fresh graffiti off the front of our building," I replied.

"I'm shopping for groceries," added My Love. "Then I'm doing my laundry."

Connie gave me a sour look. Damn, she's right. I was supposed to be making marriage sound inviting.

Before we departed, I managed to take Paul aside to inquire if he thought I was the target of any paid assassins. He pondered this and said "so many" people were in pursuit of me that it was "hard to sort them all out." Hardly the comforting words of reassurance I'd been hoping for!

5:25 p.m. Had another small tiff with My Love. She did her laundry, but wouldn't take mine—even though I always drag hers along when I go to the launderette. She said forcing her to handle my soiled briefs and socks would be the "final nail in the coffin of romance." I don't think she should be so uptight. Personally, I always get a minor erotic thrill while handling her panties and bras—the funkier the better.

8:47 p.m. Another call to Fuzzy DeFalco. God knows what these international calls must be costing. I requested an update.

"Yeah, I asked my dad if he ever heard of some dude named Rick S. Hunter. Jesus, I hate talking to my dad."

"Every kid your age does, Fuzzy. I hardly ever talk to mine. What did he say?"

"He told me to keep my big Dago nose out of his business. Then he asked if I knew where you were."

Damn! "What did you say?"

"I said I didn't, but I'm not sure he believed me."

Very scrotum-wrenching. Desperate, I implored my friend to call his Uncle Sal directly.

"I don't know, Rick. I never phoned him before. I always write him little notes to thank him for his presents. Mom makes me."

"Just give him a call, Fuzzy. Tell him Rick S. Hunter is a personal friend of yours and you'd hate it if anything happened to him."

"I don't know, Rick. Say, don't you owe me some money?"

Americans are turning into such greedheads. I told my pal if he got his uncle off my back, I'd send him a check for a thousand.

"I want that in dollars, Rick. Don't be sending me no thousand pesos."

I agreed and he asked me if I'd heard the latest rumor. It seems Vijay's been deported.

"You mean from France, Fuzzy? Yeah, I heard that."

"Not just from France, Rick. They wouldn't let him back into the good ol' U.S. of A."

"They wouldn't!? What happened to him?"

"Bounced his skinny ass right back. Airline dumped him on a plane to India. Guess he's there now. His family went totally ballistic. They even got their picture in the Santa Rosa paper. Trent too. I guess he was trying to calm down Apurva, who was holding up this really bad photo of her bro'. Man, he didn't look like anyone I'd want back in my country."

Vijay is marooned in India! Nicely far away, though I have no illusions that the viper has been de-fanged. And doubtless he is now pissed off big time.

SUNDAY, June 19 — We kept our social calendars open for outings with well-heeled visitors, but no call came. I guess when you're intent on a romantic pre-proposal holiday in Paris, two is company and four is a major distraction. Sheeni moped around the sixth floor and chatted up various neighbors (not Reina though). I rearranged the furniture so the bed was no longer in the immediate line of fire of any gunmen bursting through the door. At 7:00 p.m. we said "to hell with those guys" and went out for dinner. This time I had my crêpe wrapped around chunks of roasted goat cheese. Not bad, but personally I'd have preferred a real cheeseburger and fries. No, I haven't disclosed to Sheeni what befell her deported buddy. And I'm resolved to be alert for any attempts by that vile alien at communicating with her. I still don't know how her letter from Trent slipped past me. Censoring his wife's mail— I can see now that this is a duty every sensible husband must embrace.

MONDAY, June 20 — My Love has rashly invited her brother and Connie to dinner. Worse, she has extended the invitation to Señor Nunez, even though we have only four rickety chairs. He is bringing the wine, his own preferred seating, and his accordion. God knows what I'm supposed to serve. Not a cookbook in the place, plus my endless janitorial chores are backing up. And our kitchenette is a joke. The only thing I'm well equipped to do in there is slash my wrists. I hope that Mafia hit man shows up this morning. He could save me a great deal of bother.

11:48 p.m. It's over! The stove didn't explode. The chef didn't slice off anything major. No guests keeled over from salmonella poisoning. All in all, you'd have to call our first dinner party a success. I made a nice *plat du jour*, which certainly sounds French even if it was spaghetti and meatballs (you were expecting *blanquette de veau*?). We switched off all the lamps and lit a dozen candles—a lighting effect My Love termed "gilding the squalor." Pillows were fluffed, mounds of stuff were shifted away from the closeted toilet, and the radio-tape player was tuned to the least offensive available music.

Señor Nunez arrived first. He was dressed in a green velvet suit—a fashion statement, I thought, that veered very close to the leprechaunesque. He tasted my sauce and made a few adjustments to the seasonings to great effect. I'm beginning to think the only thing that guy can't do is dunk a basketball.

A moment later Connie and Paul staggered in from their long march up the stairs. They soon revived when Señor Nunez poured the wine, and Sheeni circulated with the cheesy appetizers. Paul remarked that our apartment was much nicer than his cell at the L.A. County Jail, and Connie said the view out our window was "positively alpine." Both got on famously with Señor Nunez, who for being a lonely guy can really mix it up socially. Paul got him talking about life as a circus clown, and soon he had my guests falling out of their chairs from laughter. As usual, My Love seemed transfixed, hanging on the guy's every word (something she never does with me).

Later, when Sheeni was mixing the salad, I got a few minutes alone with Connie to discuss the absent Vijay.

"I made a few calls," she said. "They took care of the matter."

"Calls to whom?" I asked, impressed.

"Associates of my father, Rick. How do you think we got so rich making truck springs?"

"I don't know, Connie. How?"

"By making springs for military vehicles. That's about 80 percent of our business. So naturally, we have quite a few contacts in the government. Just mention 'radical Islamic activist' and their ears perk right up."

"But Vijay is a Hindu."

"Is he? Well, if he tries hard enough, he may find some immigration official who cares about that distinction. In the meantime, he's not getting back into France."

"Or America, Connie. The U.S. deported him to India."

"Well, he can brush up on his home culture. Want some advice, Rick?"

"Sure."

"Keep that sexy dwarf away from your wife."

"I'm trying to!"

After dinner Señor Nunez brought over a spare saxophone, and he and Paul played duets.

They sounded so marvelous the Boccata brothers invited themselves over to listen, flirt with the ladies, and help finish off the wine. In between numbers, Connie put on her Chinese accent and chatted up Bernardo, who was obviously enthralled. Watching her I observed that she was sipping wine, enjoying the music, charming a genuine Italian, and appearing unavailable to the guy she desperately wants—all at the same time. What a pleasure to watch a pro at work.

TUESDAY, June 21 — My phone chirped in the middle of the night. It was Connie calling from across the neighborhood.

"Hi, Rick. Thanks for the nice dinner."

"No problem," I yawned. "Is there more to this conversation?"

"Rick, if you look under your sofa cushion you'll find two *E*100 bills."

That's a trend that should be encouraged—dinner guests hiding money on the premises.

"Gee, thanks, Connie."

"I want you to take Paulo out to lunch tomorrow, I mean today."

"OK. A little brother-in-law bonding?"

"Right. Order a nice meal and some expensive wine. I want you to talk him into popping the question. Now that I've finally slept with him, I'm even more convinced that he's the man for me."

"You think I have some influence over the guy?"

"I'm counting on it, Rick. And my unborn children are counting on it too."

Damn. What a genetic burden to have dumped on you at 2:00 in the morning. And all that wine wasn't going down too well either.

3:12 p.m. As instructed by Connie, I took my brother-in-law out to lunch at yet another famous Hemingway haunt on the place St.-Germain-des-Prés. It's a wonder the guy found the time to write what with all his high-profile café hopping. I expect when I become a Revered Author, throngs of tourists will descend on the Golden Carp in Ukiah to soak up the budget Cantonese atmosphere that catapulted me toward Literary Greatness. I must remember to negotiate a kickback from Steve the waiter for the boost in business.

Although the name of today's eatery suggested unappetizing fly larvae, Paul explained it was inspired by two statues of Chinese salesmen mounted high on an interior wall. We sat outside even though French restaurants have the gall to charge *more* for al fresco grub that's exactly the same hash they're slinging inside. Infuriatingly unAmerican, if you ask me. Living dangerously, I closed my eyes and pointed at something on the menu, which turned out to be a tasty array of tiny chops carved off something the size of a squirrel. My guest had the non-mysterious scallops with mushrooms.

Chewing my midget chop, I got down to brass tacks.

"Paul, you have to get married—to Connie."

"Oh, really? And what if I'm not the marrying kind, Rick?"

"Everyone gets married, Paul. And at 25 you're way past due. It's time to perpetuate your genes."

"You think so? I'm not sure I'm ready for that. Perhaps I should start with something less demanding like a cat."

"Connie's rich, Paul. You'll have a whole staff to mind the kiddies. They won't be a burden. Just a few minutes every night in the nursery to tuck them in and remind them how lucky they are to have rich parents. Really, it's not that much of a bother."

"You paint an attractive vision of fatherhood, Rick. But I think there's more to it than that."

"It's the most rewarding thing a guy can do," I lied. "And Connie loves you very much."

"She's a cute kid. But so young and rather spoiled."

"Maturity isn't measured in years, Paul. Connie knows what she wants and she's out to get it."

"And if I resist?"

"Here's the situation as I see it, Paul. You're a piece of steel: an unbending, rigid, strong, independent-minded hunk of jazz-playing ferrous metal. Connie is a powerful and wealthy magnet. You may not be particularly interested in that magnet, but like it or not it's adhering to you. And you can't repeal the laws of physics."

"I'm stuck, Rick?"

"You're stuck, Paul. It's time to pop the question."

He speared a scallop and thought it over.

"And if the marriage doesn't work out?"

"No big deal. Connie gets her wish. You get handsome Polish-American progeny. You may not want them, but your genes will thank you. Then the magnet comes unstuck. And you're free to enjoy your big divorce settlement. No hard feelings."

"You make it sound so simple, Rick."

"It is simple, Paul. You're stuck. It's time to face the music."

"Handel's Wedding March?"

"Precisely."

"You can honestly recommend marriage?"

"Not to worry, Paul. It's always harder on the other party than it is on a Saunders. Just take it one day at a time. And don't leave any sharp instruments lying around."

On our journey home on the Métro the topic of conversation proceeded naturally from marriage to prison. Paul said jail was simultaneously tedious from the enforced idleness and anxiety-producing from the all-pervasive atmosphere of violence. Since jail tended to attract the mentally unstable and the overly aggressive, you never knew when an inadvertent slight could lead to a punch in the nose or a shank in your gut. I gulped and asked Paul if he thought I was destined to serve much time.

"Hard to say, Rick," he replied. "I think your best bet is to become so famous no judge would dare sentence you to jail. Celebrities generally get just a slap on the wrist and maybe a fine. Otherwise, our prisons would be filled with musicians and actors—all busted for drug possession, spousal abuse, drunk driving, seducing minors—you name it."

A valid point, I thought.

"And how do I become famous, Paul?"

"Just keep at it, Rick. You may be doing better than you think."

We got back to my place in time to assist Reina with her bird lugging. Just my luck, those two gave immediate evidence of finding each other fascinating. While we were loading the cages into her car, Paul explained to Reina that the reason Damek has been plucking out his feathers lately is that he is in love with Milena.

"No, Damek likes Zuza," she pointed out.

"Maybe he used to," said Paul, "but he's thrown her over for Milena, who prefers Jiri. She's told him to drop dead and he's now a mess."

That much was indisputable. Damek really had let himself go. Do birds have rocky relationships just like people?

"Milena can be something of a tease," Reina admitted. "But how can you be certain that she's the one who's upsetting Damek?"

Paul shrugged. "I don't know. It just seems obvious."

"Paul's very intuitive," I noted.

"Really?" she laughed. "And what can your friend tell about me?"

"Quite a bit," he replied, flashing that enigmatic Saunders' grin I knew so well.

I had no doubt that he did. And I didn't like it one bit.

7:38 p.m. My Love came home depressed from a day of school scouting. She's narrowed it down to three possibilities (all pricey private academies), but the nosy administrators are insisting on personal interviews with at least one living, breathing parent.

"How about Paul?" I suggested. "He's your living, breathing elder brother."

"Hah! As if I'd trust my brother anywhere near an authority figure. He'd probably light up a joint and we'd all be expelled from France. I was thinking of Señor Nunez."

I stifled an impulse toward sarcasm. No, I would not inquire if he was on her short list. My Love bristled anyway.

"You have something to say about that?" she demanded.

"Merely that I don't see much family resemblance between a chestnut-haired American girl and a swarthy Mexican dwarf. I think even trying to pass him off as an adoptive parent is likely to raise suspicions. School administrators are programmed to suspect the worst and sniff out dirt. Why else would they pursue a career that involves bossing around hostile teenagers?"

"Then what would you suggest? Some of us are not content to let our education lapse at grade nine."

"Hire a professional, darling. Find a motherly actress and pay her for a morning of her time. Mr. Bonnet could probably suggest someone."

"Hmmph."

I recognized that snort. It was how my wife acknowledged perceptive and valuable advice.

WEDNESDAY, June 22 — A comparatively early late-night phone call. It was barely past midnight and I was deep in my favorite sort of dream: abduction by aliens for purposes of experimental sex. A phone chirp halted the proceedings in mid-probe. Connie was livid.

"Rick, are you not my friend? Do you have some hidden agenda that requires you to sabotage every aspect of my life?"

"Not at all, Connie. I talked to Paul and convinced him that marriage to you was inevitable. He's resigned to his fate."

"I wish! Tonight he dragged me way out of town to see some crummy little circus. I hate circuses! He wanted to watch some crippled bird freak that he said you introduced him to."

Uh-oh. Why hadn't Reina mentioned their attendance tonight when I helped her carry up her birds? A bad sign.

Connie raged on. "Then we had to talk to her after the show and see a bunch more dumb tricks. I know what kind of tricks that girl is planning."

"It's not Reina, Connie. Paul has some weird affinity for birds. He can tell what they're thinking."

"And I can tell what *he's* thinking. He wants to see that girl again."

"Well, we won't let him, Connie. That's all there is to it. You guys had better leave."

"What?"

"Cancel the rest of your trip. Tell him your lawyers need you back in L.A. for estate issues. But tell him you need to stop on the way back in Vegas to get married."

"Don't wait for him to propose?"

"You can't, Connie. The guy's just not equipped for it. But he's ready to pop. It's time to lance that boil."

"God, Rick, can't you think of a more romantic metaphor?"

"You can be married by this weekend, Connie. If he wavers just remind him that you're stuck on him for good. He'll understand."

"OK, Rick. If this works, I'll be eternally grateful."

"Thanks, Connie."

"And if it doesn't, I'll be extremely vengeful."

Yeah, I didn't expect anything less.

I went back to bed, but the sexy space aliens had vanished.

10:45 a.m. More disturbing phone calls. Some days I think I would be better off if I heaved my cellphone (not to mention myself) out a window. My first call was to Fuzzy in Ukiah. The guy seemed strangely eager to talk with me. He assured me that his Uncle Sal in Vegas had absolutely no interest in Rick S. Hunter or his whereabouts.

"He hasn't put any major muscle on my trail?" I asked.

"No way, Rick. My uncle's up to his ears in dirty linen. People go to Vegas to cut loose. We're talking round-the-clock orgies. All that partying can be hell on sheets. Uncle Sal doesn't have the time to send trigger-happy gunmen after some kid in Mexico."

"Well, that's a relief, Fuzzy."

"Yeah, don't be so paranoid, Rick. So, where exactly are you in Mexico?"

"Well, we move around a lot."

"Around where? You mean like in the Mexico City area?"

"Sometimes."

"Well, what's your address?"

"Why do you want to know, Fuzzy?"

"Hey, Rick, we're pals. I'd like to write to you sometimes. Share my thoughts and feelings."

Instant paranoia. My pal Fuzzy was no more inclined toward heartfelt correspondence than Dwayne Crampton.

"Sorry, bad connection, Fuzzy. I gotta go." *Click*.

Damn. Uncle Sal must be putting the screws to his nephew to cough up my address. I knew something was amiss when the fur-laden teen didn't immediately demand the thousand bucks I promised him for phoning his uncle. *Merde* and double *merde*.

My next call was to Ukiah's weightiest gossip queen. I discovered Sonya Klummplatz enjoying a late-night tub soak.

"I'm annoyed at you, Rick Hunter," she announced, splashing about like some exhibit at Marine World.

"Whatever for, Sonya?" I cooed. "Didn't I get you a date with Trent Preston?"

"Yes, and a memorable time was had by all. But then you went and married that bitch Sheeni Saunders."

"You should thank me, Sonya. I eliminated some of your competition. You know Trent was always stuck on her."

"That's true, I suppose. Hey, I had my first driving lesson today. I sure hope I don't run down Apurva in the street anytime soon."

"Please, Sonya, don't do anything rash. Say, are you still buddies with Lana?"

"She's my dearest friend, even if she is spending 99 percent of her free time this summer balling that jerk Fuzzy DeFalco."

"That's what I wanted to talk to you about." I filled in Sonya on my recent exchange with Fuzzy and asked if she could find out what was going on through Lana.

"I'll give it a shot, Rick. I'd hate to see my first lover riddled with hot lead in a hail of gunfire. By the way, I just saw somebody on TV who looked a lot like you."

"Oh, who was that?"

"I don't know. Some weird video. Three lame-looking girls were singing some stupid song while this cute sailor was molesting a midget."

Instant testicle-dribbling panic!

"Where did you see it!?"

"I don't know. I was cruising the channels. It might have been MTV. So, how do I get in touch with you, Rick honey?"

"Uh, I'll call you. Goodbye." *Click*.

Could they actually be showing that inane video on American TV? Does no one in this world have any standards?

1:37 p.m. Still no sign of Sheeni. God knows where my wife has got to or what expensive frock she is presently trying on. For a woman dedicated to the life of the mind, she certainly devotes a lot of her time and my money to dressing up her exterior. Too on edge to hang out in our apartment, so I ducked into the wig salon to take potluck for lunch. No one seems to mind when I show up uninvited at mealtime. Madame Lefèbvre clutched me to her bosom and kissed me on both cheeks as Antoinette, her youngest minion, grilled sausages for all in an ancient electric fry pan. These, I'm happy to report, contained none of those objectionable parts that the French seem so fond of.

None of the ladies possesses a word of English, but I gathered from their enthusiastic expostulations that they were congratulating me on the brilliance of my recent dinner party. I gulped down a second glass of wine and promised to invite them all up soon for a wild evening of American-style debauchery. They cheered, got rather giggly, and insisted on having me try on Mr. Hamilton's nearly completed commission. They dragged me in front of the grandly ornate mirror whose golden-hued glass has flattered generations of picky clients. Staring back at me was a sun-kissed Prince Valiant striking Napoleonic poses for an adoring audience of beaming wig-makers as Madame Lefèbvre fed him cake from a silver plate. Call me a pampered lapdog, but I came away with my mood much improved.

4:12 p.m. I fear My Love has gone off the fashion deep end. She returned this afternoon with the frumpiest dress in Christendom—all ruffles and jumbo polka dots. At least this purple and puce monstrosity was modestly priced; she had unearthed it in a secondhand shop. I'm amazed my wife even frequents such stores.

My latest alarming news caused nary a ripple in her calm demeanor. She said she had spoken just that morning with Mr. Bonnet and had learned of the video's unexpected popularity in Holland.

"Rick, just because the Dutch manifest bizarre tastes in music doesn't mean we have to panic."

"But, Sheeni, Sonya saw it in Ukiah! It was on American TV!"

"I repeat, Rick, there is no American distributor for that wretched song. If Sonya saw it on TV, it must have been featured on some European news program carried on public television. And those shows have minuscule audiences. So why are you calling your former girlfriends?"

"She never was my girlfriend, Sheeni. I need her to spy on Fuzzy and his murderous relatives. Darling, you have to call up your father and persuade him to cancel that contract on my life."

"I'll do no such thing," she replied, ironing her budget dress. Cheap perfume aromas rose in nauseating waves from its artificial fibers. "If I called my parents, they'd trace the call and find out we're in France."

"And what will you do when the hoodlums burst in with guns blazing? Do you imagine they'll spare you?"

"I expect my father has given them explicit instructions to do exactly that. I imagine you'll be taken out when alone. A discreet shot to the back of the head while sweeping the lobby or walking Maurice in the park. No fuss. No witnesses."

"My God, Sheeni! Don't you care!?"

"Of course, I care, darling. That's why we have to keep a low profile. That's why we can't do anything foolish like telephone my parents."

6:15 p.m. We are getting dolled up. Connie has invited us out for a farewell dinner. She and Paul are leaving tomorrow afternoon for Las Vegas, home of that sudsy assassin Uncle Sal. I wonder if I could persuade her to drop by his office and make him an offer he can't refuse.

Sheeni's miffed at me again. Why I don't know. All I did was inquire if she was going to wear her nice new dress.

THURSDAY, June 23 — A gray weary morning after a very late evening. Don't ask me the time. Don't ask me if the lobby has been swept. Don't ask me if Maurice has relieved his tiny bladder.

Dinner last night was a lavish affair at a flashy restaurant on the rue Boissy d'Anglas. Perhaps to appeal to Paul's spiritual side, the dining room was dominated by an enormous gold Buddha. And complementing Connie's devotion to chinoiserie was a sinuous bar in the form of a carved dragon. Diamonds sparkled, champagne corks popped all around us, waiters bustled about with artfully labored-over creations. My toothsome smoked duck had been more elaborately laid out than Tutankhamen's aunt. I hope I look that good when I'm stretched out for viewing after my Mafia hit. Alas, the meager conversation was as morose as my mood. Paul seemed preoccupied by the imminent termination of his swinging bachelorhood. My lovely wife mostly stared at her plate and picked at her shrimp. I watched my back for snub-nosed revolvers. Only cheerful Connie endeavored to keep the conversational ball afloat. She revealed that her mother has agreed to fly to Vegas for the wedding. The bad news is that she is bringing along my father!

"Didn't you have a fight with that guy once?" inquired Sheeni.

"Yeah," sighed Paul. "I had to deck him. And now he's signed up to be the best man at my wedding."

We Twisps do get around.

"It wasn't my idea, darling," said Connie, glaring at me. "I don't know what my mother can be thinking."

"She's probably not thinking at all," remarked my spouse. "She's enmeshed with a Twisp—not a state conducive to rational thought."

"We Twisps can be devastatingly attractive," I admitted.

"Oh?" said Sheeni. "When do you start?"

In a desperate attempt to enliven her party Connie ordered a second bottle of champagne and decadent chocolate desserts all around. Mine contained the concentrated essence of an entire bag of Halloween treats. It worked. By the time our gay foursome went on to the place Pigalle, even the groom-to-be was virtually bubbly.

Señor Nunez is not the only genius in our midst. The mild-mannered Mr. Hamilton, papa to Maurice, puts on a phenomenal show. True, his place of employment is something of a dive: painted entirely black, dimly lit, with sticky floors and air that would choke a Louisiana refinery worker. The boyishly flirtatious, heavily spangled wait staff delivers the overpriced drinks with carefree indifference to the undulations of their plunging necklines. Envious Carlotta has no idea how they are able to flaunt such seemingly genuine curves.

Mr. Hamilton made his dramatic entrance as Jeanette MacDonald belting out "San Francisco" on a red velvet swing. This, of course, drew a great roar of approval from the crowd and pangs of homesickness from at least one exile from the Bay. Accompanying the star was an elderly pianist poured into a bulging cocktail dress. That person I believed to be an actual woman since it seemed unlikely that anyone would wish to simulate such an appearance. She pounded out each song with an immense grin on her face and laughed at every joke as if she hadn't heard them 10,000 times before. Mr. Hamilton was a master—contorting his seemingly bland features into picture-perfect evocations of Hollywood and Broadway greats: Garbo, Joan Crawford, Ethel Merman, Lucy, Garland, Streisand, Diana Ross, Liza, Carol Channing, Bette Davis, and countless others. The voices were spot on too—especially his winsome Edith Piaf and rousing, scat-singing Ella. His time-tested patter, delivered half in French and half in English, never missed a laugh. He owned that audience and, ever greedy for more, we stomped and whistled and howled until he gave us three encores. Even Sheeni applauded lustily and conceded in the taxi on the ride home that our talented neighbor—high-kicking across the stage in his spike heels—displayed the nicest pair of legs in the joint.

And now it is the morning after, and all I want to do is lie in bed and nurse my throbbing head.

11:05 a.m. Sheeni just brought me two aspirins, kissed me ardently, and made a "small request" (her words). Somehow I am powerless to refuse her. Yes, diary, in this time of need Carlotta must answer the call.

3:47 p.m. We're back. I have removed that monstrous polka dotted dress. Improbably, Sheeni has volunteered to make dinner. Of course, I was skeptical this morning that I could fool anyone into thinking I was that lovely person's mother.

"Sheeni," I demanded, "why did you pick such an ugly dress? This thing is an abomination!"

"Yes, it is rather," she conceded, helping me into one of her own delightful bras, "but it was the closest thing I could find to my mother's own tastes. We must strive for verisimilitude, darling."

It's true that Sheeni's 5,000-year-old mother does favor eye-pummeling prints in nausea-inducing color combinations. This dress would be right up her alley. Carlotta shuddered and put it on. Alas, it fit like a glove—once I had stuffed in sufficient bra padding to inflate the matronly bosom. Next on was a pair of opaque tights to conceal my long lapse in leg shaving. Then a pair of sensible shoes produced from where I know not. Finally, Sheeni removed a ratty gray wig from her cavernous purse and plopped it on my head. We surveyed the results in our castoff mirror.

"I look horrible," complained Carlotta. "Just awful. And not nearly old enough to be anyone's mother."

"We'll take care of that," she replied. "I picked up this cream at a theatrical makeup store."

Sheeni scooped out a great dollop from the jar and smeared it on my face. As it dried a film formed on my skin that gradually crinkled. The effect was fascinating and more than a little disquieting to observe. In five minutes my face was a mass of wrinkles. Carlotta looked like one of those leathery Nepalese sherpas who had spent a lifetime in the merciless Himalayan sun.

"I think you better introduce me as your great-grandmother," cackled Carlotta. "I don't look a day under 112."

"A little makeup should fix that, Mother dear."

Foundation, rouge, powder, eyeliner, mascara, lipstick. Soon, My Love managed to bring down Carlotta's apparent age to a brisk, well-preserved 72. She stood back and pondered her handiwork.

"A bit mannish from the Belmondo overtones, but it will have to do," Sheeni commented.

Unfortunately true. My facelift had burdened the once semicomely Carlotta with yet another obstacle to beauty. And my surgically altered voice, rumbling in the lower registers, could never aspire to its former lilting loveliness. Sheeni handed me a pack of Marlboros.

"Light up when we get there. We'll try to pass you off as a heavy smoker. But don't say any more than you have to."

"Don't worry, darling. Your mumsey will be the essence of maternal solicitation and regard."

"She better be," replied My Love. "If she ever wants to get laid again."

Not a very daughterly remark.

Of course, on our way out we ran into Mr. Hamilton and his ward on the stairs. He accepted our enthusiastic praise with quiet thanks. Out of his evening gowns and mesh stockings the guy is modesty personified. He complimented Carlotta on her transformation and insisted on lending her a pair of brassy earrings from his Joan Crawford collection. They did add that Hollywood and Vine finishing touch. He also lent me his frisky little dog, much to my daughter's annoyance.

"Maybe I should have asked Mr. Hamilton instead," grumbled Sheeni on the Métro. "At least I know he's credible as a woman."

"Don't be silly," replied Carlotta, offended. "You forget how many fellows asked me to the Christmas dance. And didn't I have that brute Bruno Modjaleski wrapped around my little pinky?"

"What else was he wrapped around?" she replied. "That's what I'd like to know."

"We never went beyond a few passionate kisses, did we, Maurice?

And thank God for that."

Completely in accord as usual, Maurice licked my face—getting a tongue-full of rouge and necessitating an emergency makeup correction.

Sheeni's preferred school rose like an ivy-entangled relic of the late Napoleonic period behind a high stone wall in a ritzy neighborhood. Visions of onerous tuition bills danced in my head as we were led down the bleak halls to the headmaster's office. Things got off to a rocky start. I reached out to shake Dr. Emile Annick's hand and gave the portly white-haired scholar a nasty burn with my lit Marlboro. How do cigarette smokers shake hands I wondered as he wrapped his paw in a dampened handkerchief and Mother and Daughter apologized profusely.

I snuffed out my cigarette in what Sheeni later informed me was a porcelain saucer of great antiquity and nervously lit another. We all sat down—excepting only curious Maurice who stretched to the limits of his leash to sniff out all the corners—and the interview commenced.

"Your daughter has greatly impressed the admissions committee," Dr. Annick boomed in English. "She is a remarkably intelligent girl."

"Yes, fortunately she takes after me in that respect. Her father was something of an idiot. All he could do was amass great piles of money."

Sheeni grimaced, but Dr. Annick beamed through his pain. I knew I had struck a nerve.

"That reminds me, Mrs. Saunders," he continued, "should your daughter be accepted, we shall require a bank reference."

"No problem," Carlotta exclaimed. "I am personal friends with J.P. Morgan."

"I believe Mr. Morgan died in 1913," he replied.

"Uh, I was referring to his son."

"That gentleman passed on in 1943."

These French intellectuals do know their American financiers.

"Junior was my godfather when I was a child," Carlotta elaborated. "I used to frolic on his lap and play with his gold watch."

More grimaces from My Love. I prayed for a change of subject. Fortunately, ever-empathic Maurice came to the rescue. Intrigued by Dr. Annick's flannel-clad leg, he began to hump it vigorously. Odd, he had never exhibited such behavior before. Perhaps it was the stimulating academic atmosphere. More embarrassed apologies as I struggled to rein in the panting canine. To his credit, Maurice may have been a toy fox terrier, but when stimulated there was nothing toy-like about his equipment. For all I know he may be impregnating mastiffs in his spare time.

The interview lurched on and eventually got around to my expectations for my daughter's academic program.

"Uh, gee," Carlotta stammered. Why hadn't I been prepared for these sorts of trick questions? "Uhmm, philosophy—I expect every girl should have a good foundation in that. And history of the Bourbons, that's a must. French, I suppose, though personally I think you can overdo it. Maybe some biology with an emphasis on the human gestation cycle. And cooking, of course."

"Cooking?" inquired Dr. Annick.

"Cooking and homemaking skills," confirmed Carlotta. "Those are a must. My daughter must be prepared for her future life as a loving wife and mother."

"My mother is making a jest," laughed Sheeni. "It's her wonderful American sense of humor. Aren't you joking, Mother dearest?"

I knew better than to trod any further down that road. Lamentably, I had been born too late for the Era of Good Housekeeping. I laughed, crossed my legs athletically, and knocked a crystal decanter off the chuckling pedagogue's desk.

I expect it will be added to our first tuition bill. Despite his reservations about her eccentric mother, Dr. Annick has accepted my dear child and spouse for the fall term.

5:28 p.m. Before changing clothes I decided to waltz my alter ego through the wig salon. Carlotta was pleased to see Madame Lefèbvre required several minutes to realize that the strange old lady in the deplorable synthetic wig was their favorite American janitor in disguise. Of course, I also threw her off the scent by replying to her polite inquiries in mock Swedish. Carlotta's eventual unveiling sent the entire staff into hysterics. When at last they regained their composure, the ladies crowded around to exclaim over Carlotta's aged skin and amply padded bust. I endeavored to explain through pantomime how the wrinkles were achieved chemically, but I fear I left them clueless. Perplexed but charmed, they showered Carlotta with kisses in a great wave of mock Gallic lesbianism. I left secure in the knowledge that Carlotta had provided them with many more days of conversational fodder.

I wasn't so pleased to encounter Reina hauling Damek down the stairs. My first impulse was to turn my head and march right past her, but I knew this was her last performance before she left on tour and I felt terrible for forgetting my afternoon duties. She was shocked when the elderly stranger addressed her by name and took the heavy cage from her.

"Rick, is that you?" she exclaimed.

"It's me," I said, trooping back down the stairs with the cage. "Sorry I'm late." I gave her a greatly abbreviated account of Carlotta's afternoon activities.

"You're so cute in that dress, Rick, I feel an irresistible urge to kiss you."

Carlotta does seem to have that effect on people. I paused on a landing and put down the cage.

"Well," said Carlotta, "don't let me stop you."

She smiled, we embraced, and our lips met.

Like plugging into the main power line from Boulder Dam.

Eventually, she pulled away. I could have gone on forever.

We both seemed a little stunned.

"I, I never kissed a woman before," she said, not looking at me.

I wiped a smudge of Carlotta's lipstick off her lower lip.

"I'll miss you," I said at last.

"I'll miss you too," she replied.

When I returned to our apartment, I found a cheese omelet burning on the stove and Sheeni engrossed in a phone conversation. I flipped off the gas and dumped the smoking pan in the sink.

"That was your friend Connie," she announced, clicking off the phone. "My brother went for a magazine three hours ago at the airport and hasn't been seen since."

FRIDAY, June 24 — Can't write much. Too tired. Virtually no sleep. Four middle-of-the-night phone calls from you know who. Needless to say, she never got on the plane. No, Connie Krusinowski is not an easy person to ditch. Most energized by Paul crisis. Has alerted French police. Has retained expensive firm of international private detectives. Has sicced her lawyers on Paul's credit card company. If he charges so much as a soupcon of soup, he'll be nailed within four minutes. She estimates he had only a few hundred dollars in euros on him. Can't get far in pricey France on that. Also he is sans saxophone, so no means of gainful employment, though she is not overlooking his pool-cleaning expertise. Occupational opportunities for pool cleaners in France? Connie's minions checking that out.

At 1:45 a.m. Connie rang up and demanded I waken Sheeni to ask if she surreptitiously slipped cash to brother. I did so (reluctantly). Wife greatly pissed off. Vigorously denied any funds transfers. Inclined to believe her, as I know she is not overly generous with my money. Tried to reassure Connie on that score, but met with usual dire threats. Sometimes wish I had never met the Krusinowski clan. Of course, would not mind terribly if Dad marries Connie's rich mother, though doubt much baksheesh will trickle down to wayward son. Still, the guy can't live forever, especially with his nicotine habit and drinking problem—not to mention menacing Dogo lurking in the shadows.

Another phone call at 3:17 a.m. Connie now convinced Paul in contact with Lacey. Believes he has received cash infusion from her from ill-gotten Krusinowski millions. I attempt to dismiss such conjecture as pure bridal anxiety and paranoia. Connie somewhat mollified, though intends to have detectives investigate her buxom rival.

Another call at 4:22 a.m. Connie now speculating that my treacherous sister Joanie diverted cash from Mother's lawyers to Paul Saunders' liberation fund. I tell her to take a sedative and get some sleep.

Last call at 5:06 a.m. Connie in panic recalls she has given Paul expensive Rolex Perpetual Oyster wristwatch. Solid gold case and precision Swiss movement. Real diamonds in lieu of numerals. We agree all pawnshops in Paris must be watched.

The bad news is Paul must report to his probation officer in Los Angeles in ten days or he'll be in violation of his parole. Back to jail if he misses that date. The good news is the wrinkle cream washed off with no problem. Carlotta once again retired. The bad news is that I'm in total turmoil over Reina. Possible to love two people at once? I thought True Love caused a circuit to fuse in your brain, rendering you entirely indifferent to other females. Apparently not.

11:12 a.m. All in all, it was a pleasure to escape the building this sunny morning to take Maurice on his walk. More like he took me. I merely hung onto the leash and ruminated on my problems while he navigated his preferred course. Call me callous, but it seems to me that Connie should just accept that Paul has dumped her and get over it. Let's face it, getting a Saunders to commit is always a long shot. She gave it a yeoman's try. And why am I so irked that Sheeni burned up our only Teflon pan? It's amazing the toll these petty annoyances take on a marriage. Before in Ukiah all I wanted to do was hold Sheeni. Now half the time I just want to hold her neck—and squeeze.

Maurice and I enjoy the smells of our neighborhood. We may be living in the world's most glamorous city, but after a while it's just home—the neighborhood. Not that much different in essentials from Oakland. Considerate Maurice led me down a new street where I discovered the lonely outpost of an American donut chain. I went in and ordered my usual assortment. Just like home except the coffee was better, the clerk was cuter, dogs were welcome, and the tally was three times higher. There may be some truth to Sheeni's total immersion theory. Sipping my coffee, I realized I had greeted the clerk, answered the obligatory Belmondo queries, ordered my donuts, paid the requested total, and thanked her—all without resorting once to my mother tongue. Plus, I'm married but would like to take a mistress. Jesus, am I evolving into a Frog?

Loud bellowing and fierce squawks were resounding through the halls when I trudged wearily back up to the sixth floor. My heart sank. I hurried down the corridor and found Connie angrily confronting an alarmed Reina, who was trying to calm her agitated birds.

"There you are, Rick," said Connie. "You will please inform this person that I am no one to be trifled with."

"I don't know what she wants, Rick," cried Reina. "I haven't seen her boyfriend! I don't know where he is. I've asked her to leave, but she refuses to go. She's disturbing my babies."

"That woman is lying, Rick. I know it. I know that my dear Paulo has been in this apartment."

Instant alarm. François was insanely jealous.

"How do you know that, Connie?" he demanded.

"I can sense Paulo's lingering aura. You know how intuitive I am."

Alarm canceled. François merely had a nut case on his hands.

"Reina," I said calmly, "if you happen to see Paul, could you let us know right away?"

"Of course, Rick. I'm sorry he's disappeared."

"Connie," I said, taking her arm and steering her toward the door, "there is no way Paul can go in or out of this building without my seeing him."

"Are you sure, Rick?" she asked.

"I'm positive. Plus, Sheeni and I have alerted the ladies in the wig salon on the ground floor. Believe me, they are all-seeing and all-knowing. A flea couldn't sneak into this building without their spotting it—let alone a good-looking American guy."

I led my distraught friend back to our apartment, where we discovered a concealed Sheeni speaking animatedly into my cellphone. She rang off when I opened the closet door.

"She was talking to Paulo!" screamed Connie.

"Don't be an idiot," replied my wife, rising from her toilet perch. "That was Mr. Bonnet, Rick. They're releasing your video in France."

Now it was my turn to scream. "Why?!!!!!"

Sheeni shrugged. "Money talks. Improbably, it seems to be exhibiting all the signs of an international mega-hit. Apparently, it's the biggest thing to strike Denmark since salted cod. The Finns are going wild too, if you can believe it."

"This is awful!" I cried. (International mega exposure being the last thing I needed at the moment.)

"Fuck your stupid video," interjected Connie. "We have to find my fiancé! Paulo may be in danger!"

"In danger of dumping you," muttered Sheeni.

"What did you say?!!" demanded Connie.

François had to referee his second brawl of the day. What a morning!

1:38 p.m. During lunch I asked my sullen wife if there was anything about her brother's disappearance that she was concealing from me.

"Don't be ridiculous, Rick," she snapped. "My brother does not confide in me. Your arrogant friend assumed she could force him to marry her. So of course he left. I just hope her spoiled rich girl's presumption doesn't result in Paul becoming a fugitive. My brother's an irresponsible fool, but he doesn't belong in jail—unlike some people I could mention."

I didn't like the sound of that. Not one bit.

4:05 p.m. After lunch Sheeni departed for parts unknown and I collapsed on the bed for a tension-packed nap. I slept fitfully and woke feeling only moderately suicidal. Then I helped Reina haul her birds, boxes, and baggage down to her car. Countless trips up and down those monumental stairs. Each armload impressing on my psyche the impending distance between us. I also felt bad that I had never made it out to that distant suburb to see her perform. Some friend I am. Just farewell pecks on the cheek because Madame Ruzicka and the wig salon ladies also there to see her off. We waved goodbye from the curb as she drove off in her packed station wagon. Three months! God knows where I'll be when she comes back in September.

5:38 p.m. Sheeni returned with a brand new Teflon pan. I kissed her in the kitchenette and expressed the wish that everything would remain non-stick in our home except our marriage. She kissed me back and volunteered to vacuum. Stunned, I pointed out that we lacked such an appliance. She proposed to borrow Señor Nunez's wheezing Hoover. I fondled a breast and mentioned that Connie had phoned to invite us out to dinner. She nibbled my lip and politely declined. No, she did not mind if I went without her. I nuzzled her neck and reminded her not to miss the dust bunnies under the bed. She removed my hand and reminded me to run up the tab on Connie.

9:05 p.m. I returned from a memorable five-star dining experience and got another severe shock. Sitting on my sofa in our atypically neat and spotless apartment, sipping tea from *my* cup and conversing in French with *my* wife was François's tanned and muscular arch-nemesis: Trent Preston.

"Hello, Rick," he said. "Or should I call you Nick?"

SATURDAY, June 25 — Seven weeks, diary. Seven long, rather trying weeks. Needless to say, we greeted this day with no anniversary intercourse. In fact, last night Sheeni dragged me out to the corridor to insist that it would be a "needless affront" to her old boyfriend for us to sleep in the same bed "while he was visiting." Another dire shock. She's invited the twit to stay with us. In our privacy-impaired one-room apartment! François was all for grabbing the razor-sharp German blade, but I somehow kept him restrained. Eventually, bedtime rolled around and Sheeni sorted us out. She took the bed, Trent occupied the sofa, and the man of the house slept (attempted to sleep) on the sofa's removable back cushions on the cruel though clean floor. In the middle of the night I heard Trent rise for a manly and vigorous piss in our sequestered toilet. I suppose it was too much to expect the clod to relieve himself discreetly out a window. At least he returned to the sofa. One step closer to the bed and he would have faced immediate defenestration.

Can't write much more. Too stressed out. Somehow I seem to forget how good-looking that ungifted poet is. How transparent is the profound effect he has on My Love. How seemingly inconsequential to her is his status as a married man and father-to-be. Ostensibly, the jerk is here as an emissary of the beleaguered Joshi family. He proposes to plead Vijay's case with French immigration officials in hopes they can call off the I.N.S. dogs back home. I wonder if that isn't just an excuse to get away from the stresses of married life. God knows I could use a break right now. Maybe a few weeks back in Ukiah with sexy Apurva. Yes, I'm beginning to appreciate the therapeutic benefits of wife-swapping. Where do I sign up, François asks?

And *why* did Sheeni reveal to Trent the actual identity of Rick S. Hunter?!! What *could* she have been thinking of?

SUNDAY, June 26 — Didn't see much of my "roommates" yesterday. They were off on daylong tourism expeditions, while I remained at home paralyzed by a black depression. Today got off to an early start when Connie bustled in unannounced at 6:45 a.m. Perhaps she's still on American time. Seemed surprised by peculiar sleeping arrangements and handsome stranger lounging on sofa in t-shirt and boxers. They introduced themselves, as we couldn't be bothered. Connie excited by news at last of absent love. Paul still in France. Yesterday he cashed in his ticket at an Air France office in Vitry-sur-Seine. I was familiar with that burg. Ominously, it was the gritty suburb where Reina stored her caravan. If she has gone off with Paul, that's it. The last straw. More grief I cannot take.

Connie insisted on dragging me back to her hotel for breakfast consultations, even though my companions had not yet roused themselves from bed. I tried not to imagine how they might be exploiting this privacy windfall. I was so stressed by these disquieting ruminations I could barely choke down my princely breakfast. Connie, as usual, did most of the talking.

"God, Rick, I can't believe Sheeni dumped that fellow to go out with you."

Another ego boost. I'm used to them.

"As I recall, Connie, I did tell you that Trent was good-looking."

"Yes, but you didn't tell me he was better looking than Brad Pitt. What does he do?"

"He goes to high school in Ukiah, writes truly wretched poetry, and works part time heaving around bags of concrete."

"What a waste. My mother has lots of contacts in the film industry through her charitable work. I know she can do something for him."

"Forget it, Connie. We want Trent to be *less* attractive to my wife, not more so. Now you see why I had to get him married off."

"Right, Rick. Well, the jury's still out on that ploy. And what are you doing sleeping on the floor? Can't you see what that says about your rank in the hierarchy?"

I explained Sheeni's reservations about our sharing a bed in front of her guest.

"You get right back in that bed, Rick. You have to declare yourself the alpha male here or you're doomed. You must establish your dominance over the female. This is primitive, old-brain stuff, Rick. It's social dynamics at the lizard level, but cannot be ignored."

"You're right, Connie. I have to show them who's boss."

"That was my mistake with Paulo. We got overeager, Rick. We pushed him too hard. I have to find him to reassure him that he's in charge. We don't have to get married—not right away. We can just live together."

"Uh, right, Connie."

"You're a guy, Rick. What do you suppose my Paulo was doing in Vitry-sur-Seine? I mean I went there yesterday. The place is a dump. The cultural opportunities are nil."

I didn't feel it wise to reveal just yet my suspicions to Connie.

"Well, it's pretty far from the city center. I imagine hotels are cheaper out there."

"My detectives checked all the hotels in the area. Paulo hadn't been at any of them."

"It's a mystery, Connie. Of course, he disappeared before. He only came back to his family last summer. They hadn't seen him for years."

"Paulo was finding himself, Rick. Now he's got that out of his system. And now he's got me."

Boy, does he ever.

11:27 a.m. When I returned to the apartment, my wife and houseguest were absent. Would it kill her to leave me a note? No telltale moist spot in the bed, but there were two damp towels draped over our open-air tub. How do you suppose they managed that? Did each person wait out in the hall while the other guy bathed? Damn, I should have concealed a video camera in here weeks ago.

Still depressed but no longer paralyzed, I snooped through Trent's stuff. No condoms in evidence, which could be interpreted as a positive sign. Except he knows Sheeni is pregnant, so why bother? But then Trent seems like the kind to worry about catching diseases. No return ticket either. How long does that freeloading creep think he can impose upon our gracious hospitality? Some possibly positive signs: A murky Polaroid of a fetus-like swirl (sonogram of Trent Jr.?). And a 5x7 color photo of Apurva looking most alluring in a gold and purple silk sari. What a dish. Such beautiful children they'll have together, and they owe it all to me.

An inside pocket of his grip coughed up this troubling letter:

> Dearest Trent,
>
> How exciting that you may be visiting Paris soon. Do try to persuade your "in-laws" to lend you the airfare. We can have a fantastic time exploring together—just as we always planned. Most places are free, so your only expense would be the daily Métro fare. We can take meals at my place; Nick's cooking is not absolutely inedible. And don't worry about my "husband." I have him under my thumb. Do come, darling!
>
> Love,
> Sheeni
>
> P.S. I agree it's a disgrace what happened to poor Vijay. I have a well-connected lawyer here who may be able to assist us with this matter.

Under her thumb, huh? Well, we'll see about that. And why, I wonder, are all of her "marital" references in quotes?

3:48 p.m. Wife and pal not back yet. Must have lunched out. While walking Maurice, two cars boom-boomed by with "*Heee, Lekker Ding*" blaring on their radios. I sensed that somewhere three Magdas were bouncing up and down with joy.

7:12 p.m. I timed it perfectly. Just as I was serving up my one savory braised pork chop, solo baked potato, and individual salad (with leaves torn limb-from-limb American style), in trooped you know who.

"That smells delicious," exclaimed Sheeni. "We're starved!"

I smiled graciously. "Gee, darling, I wish you'd let me know your schedule. I assumed you were dining out. But you're welcome to see what you can dredge up in the fridge."

They opted instead to go down the block for budget crepes. Most satisfying (for me), though I suppose a hollow triumph, since Sheeni probably picked up the tab with my money.

10:45 p.m. Trent and I cope with our intolerable proximity by ignoring each other as much as possible. But after his sixth extravagant jet-lagged yawn, I decided it was time to put my foot down and claim my rightful place in my own bed. Sheeni was incensed.

"And I suppose you'd consign the person expecting your child to sleep on the floor!"

"No one has to sleep on the floor," I replied calmly. "Reina's apartment is empty. Your guest can bunk there."

"Oh, so you have a key to that woman's apartment," she sneered. "How cozy!"

I replied that I didn't have a key, but explained that having assisted several tenants who had locked themselves out, I knew that the cheesy door locks could be pried easily with a credit card.

"Hah!" scoffed my wife. "You don't have a credit card!"

True enough. But I said a piece of stiff cardboard works just as well.

"This is terrible," she replied. "What if someone breaks in and steals my French-language typewriter."

"Don't worry," I said. "No junkie in France is that desperate."

Five minutes later my enemy was bedding down in Reina's odorous apartment. Jesus, she could have at least left a window open to air the place out.

After we returned, I raised the matter of this morning's public bathing.

"Well, how do you suppose we managed?" demanded Sheeni. "Trent took a quick bath while I went down to buy some croissants. After breakfast I had a bath while he took a stroll through the neighborhood."

"Oh."

"Though I don't see why we bothered, since I am intimately

familiar with his magnificent body. And he with mine!"

"Sheeni, you might have informed me that he was coming. This is my home too."

"I didn't want to have another fight, Nickie. All we do is fight."

I put my arm around her and kissed her.

"I don't want to fight with you, darling."

She kissed me back.

"You're right, Nickie. Finding another place for Trent to sleep was a brilliant solution. It's bad enough having one guy invading my privacy—let alone two."

She leaned in for an even more intimate nuzzle.

"Nickie, darling, Trent doesn't have much money. You know I'm hopeless in the kitchen. If I let you know when we're coming back, can you make us dinner?"

"Oh, all right. I suppose it won't kill me."

We kissed, then Sheeni excused herself to go floss.

Alas, diary, it's true. She does have me under her thumb.

MONDAY, June 27 — No belated anniversary intercourse last night either. Wife too tired. Said they had walked all over Paris in summer heat with just low-protein budget meals to sustain them. Hope excessive culture seeking not injurious to developing fetus. And how come we don't have any sonograms of incipient Twispette?

Major setback in houseguest relocation scheme. Unbeknownst to me, thrifty Reina had sublet her apartment. New tenant arrived late last night and discovered handsome guy asleep in the buff on moonlit bed. Mystery sleeper not disturbed by bustle of suitcases nor rightful occupant's preparations for slumber. Trent awoke this morning to find himself embracing negligee-clad female. Several snuggles and caresses ensued before reviving mental faculties recalled that Apurva on distant continent. Startled inspection confirmed sexy bedmate unknown to him. Woman opened eyes, smiled, and inquired if he was included with apartment. Trent dove for sheet and clutched it to his naked torso. Hasty introductions were made. Trent apologized for trespass on room and her person, threw on clothes, and departed.

Boy, those Prestons lead charmed lives. If it were me discovered naked in that bed, I'm sure I would have been arrested immediately and tossed into jail with the other sex deviates.

No baths this morning, nor eagerly anticipated roll in hay. Trent arrived just as preliminaries underway. Sheeni unclinched instantly and I had to lie there contemplating violent Trent disembowelings until T.E. faded away. After breakfast wife and enemy left for Belleville to meet crafty lawyer Mr. Petit. Needless to say, I hope their mission fails.

10:52 a.m. Just met the new tenant. Very pleasant and chatty English girl in late teens or early twenties. Not beautiful, but cute and shapely with bobbed brown hair and lopsided smile. A few inches shorter than me and incredibly toned. Name is Violet Barnes. Has never met Reina, but heard about sublet on circus grapevine. Native of Birmingham, lives in south London, and has summer gig with same circus that employs Señor Nunez and the Boccatas. She is a bender with a box act.

"What's that?" I asked, sipping the tea she kindly prepared.

"What's a bender, Rick? Oh, you *have* lived a sheltered life."

Amazingly, she then bent forward at the waist until her head, arms, and shoulders were not only between but beyond her legs, and she was staring up at her own muscular backside. A handy posture for scanning your butt for pimples or checking your bumhole for lint.

"My God, does that hurt?"

"Not at all," she replied, unwinding. "Of course, it would probably kill you. Hyperextension of the spine, Rick. Takes years to achieve."

"You're a contortionist!"

"That's right. I fold myself up like a pretzel and squeeze into wee boxes."

"Are you double jointed?"

"No such thing, Rick. Just endless stretching and training. You could be a bender, Rick. You've got the right build: slender and skinny. Here, have a biscuit. You look like you could use one."

I nibbled my cookie-like biscuit while Violet unpacked and I explained my connections to Trent.

"Wife's former boyfriend, huh? How the hell old are you, Rick?"

"I'm older than I look," I lied.

"That's good, I suppose. Well, it was quite a shock. I hoisted a few on the train from London. Then had a few more with some bender blokes. So they drop me off here, I stumble up 8,000 steps, the place smells like somebody died, I switch on the light, and there's this naked Adonis snozzing away on the bed."

"What did you think?"

"Want the truth, Rick? I felt this very deep conviction that there was the man I was going to marry. It was destiny, I was sure of it."

"Oops, you're a little late."

"So I found out. Most annoying. All the great men get taken early. Especially you Yanks, it seems. Say, don't you look like somebody?"

"Jean-Paul Belmondo."

"That's it. Be a great gimmick for your bender act. Everybody needs a gimmick, Rick."

"Is yours squeezing into little boxes?"

"I wish. That's as common as houses. I'm working on this routine with a unicycle, but there's a slight problem."

"What's that?"

"I keep falling on my ass."

As I was leaving Violet gave me one of her souvenir t-shirts. Under a photo of Violet squeezed into a transparent plastic chest the size of a breadbox, painfully twisted letters spelled out: "I Got Bent in London."

4:12 p.m. Endless dog-walking, janitorial, and shopping chores. Finally, I took a break, gulped down a ham sandwich, and dialed Sonya's number in distant Ukiah. It was morning there and she was still working on winching herself out of bed. She sounded depressed.

"Have you heard the news, Rick? My boy Trent's in Paris."

"Really? Do you know how long he's planning to stay?"

"Long enough I hope for me to dispose of Apurva's body."

"Sonya, you have to stop saying things like that. Did you talk to Lana?"

"I talk to her all the time. I think you're in trouble, Rick."

"Why, Sonya?!"

"According to Lana, Fuzzy's uncle has promised to drop a four-barrel 429, whatever that is, into Fuzzy's Falcon if he finds out where you are. Or was it a 942? Anyway, Lana says Fuzzy is suffering from severe anxiety about his dumb car. He's desperate for a bigger motor."

Some friend Fuzzy turned out to be. He'd stab a pal in the back for more horsepower.

"You know what I think, Rick?"

"What, Sonya?"

"I don't think you guys are in Mexico at all. I think you're in Paris too. I think that's why Trent went to France. To find Sheeni."

"*Usted es muy loco, Sonya,*" I insisted. "*¡Yo estoy en Mexico!*"

"You're not fooling me, Rick. So here's my deal. You get Trent to break up with Apurva, or I squeal to Fuzzy."

"Sonya! Be reasonable!"

"Yep, Rick, in a few weeks ol' Fuzzy may be peeling rubber with the best of them. Think it over, dude!" *Click.*

Damn! Why did I ever call that maniac? That chick is toxic waste on the hoof. I should have learned my lesson by now.

8:17 p.m. Despite being tormented by anxiety, I managed to have dinner ready by the time Sheeni and T.P. (twisted poet) returned. I made a simple but hearty beef stew, which they set upon like hungry cannibals. It appears Apurva's commitment to vegetarianism has made no lasting impression on her husband. Sheeni reports they were encouraged by their interview with Mr. Petit, who has promised to employ his contacts within the French Police to discover why Vijay was blackballed from the First World. On a more positive note, she said Mr. Bonnet soon will be sending us our first residuals check. I hope it's a hefty one; it can help with my funeral expenses.

Connie showed up while T.P. was doing the washing up. Though devastated by Paul's continued absence, she managed to do quite a bit of casual flirting with our houseguest—much to my wife's annoyance. She also offered to let Trent bunk in her spacious hotel suite—a generous offer that seemed agreeable to him.

"And if Apurva calls here for you, Trent?" Sheeni asked. "Shall we give her the phone number of Connie's room?"

The twit opted to stay put.

To pass the time, My Love dragged out the Scrabble board. Seldom in the history of the world has that game been played at such a cutthroat level. The competition only could have been more intense if all sides possessed nuclear weapons. I put my foot down and insisted we limit the play to English words. The biggest surprise was Connie's mastery of the game. I had no idea her vocabulary embraced so many obscure, high-scoring words. She and Sheeni battled it out for victory, while T.P. and I grappled to escape the testicular-bruising embarrassment of last place. No doubt about it, our manhood was on the line with each letter we placed on that accursed board. The ladies seemed to be staking their ovaries as well.

And who was languishing in the cellar at the end?

Trent Preston.

If only one did not have to bring complete candor to one's diary. Who made up that rule?

OK. The cad beat me by two lousy, stinking points.

Even worse for the tranquility of my home life, Sheeni finished a shocking 16 points behind her wannabe sister-in-law. Nor was she first in line for the good sportsmanship medal.

Glad that's over. All I have to worry about now is being arrested by the FBI and assassinated by the Mafia. Much less stressful.

TUESDAY, June 28 — Unbelievably explosive climax this morning, diary. Well, all that accumulated tension had to be discharged some way. Better through sex than via a massive coronary thrombosis. My Love was accommodating this a.m. because our privacy has been restored. Friendly Violet dropped by at bedtime last night and volunteered Reina's lumpy sofa to T.P. for the duration. He accepted since Sheeni was on the warpath and he'd be within hailing distance should Apurva phone. (And why hasn't she, by the way?) Violet may not be able to wed her Man of Destiny, but at least she can (sort of) sleep with him. Personally, I think a pretty contortionist might have a lot to contribute in that department, though I fear such sexual stereotyping will shock the sober academics destined to read my future published journals. I say anyone who *hasn't* speculated about contortionists in that way can cast the first stone. Hell, it probably even crossed T.P.'s upright mind as he bedded down not 15 feet away from that Siren of Suppleness.

9:05 a.m. Lots of Prestonian yawns at the breakfast table. He mentioned that he had stayed up half the night conversing with Violet and found her "quite an interesting person." She has promised to show him some of the preliminary bender stretches. (He already has the necessary gimmick; he could recite bad poetry while tying himself in knots.) I encouraged him to chat on as I knew these sorts of revelations are poison to other females. Why should I be the only guy getting in the doghouse with Sheeni? It worked like a charm. Her tone was distinctly arctic when she told him to get lost so she could take a bath.

10:17 a.m. More proof that the Celebrity Lifestyle is not all great sex in luxurious settings. Such annoyances! I was squeezing a nascent zit when the door suddenly burst open and in stormed a French television crew with lights glaring and camera rolling. A cute chick in a black beret and tight sweater stuck a microphone in my face and addressed me in rapid French. I stood there stupefied while Sheeni screamed, rose up in the tub like an angry goddess of the bath, and nailed the cameraman on the nose with a bar of soap. He grunted but continued taping. I ducked behind my wife's moist pink torso—calculating that unless French TV broadcast full-frontal nudity they wouldn't be getting much useful footage. Switching to English, the crazed reporter doggedly pursued her victim.

"Did you come to France to become the 'American Belmondo?' Are you planning more videos with the Three Magdas? Who is this girl? Are you lovers? How long have you . . ."

"No comment!" I chanted, grabbing a towel and draping it over my head. "No comment!"

"Get out!" screamed Sheeni, hurling herself at the inquisitive newsperson and wrestling for the microphone. "Get out of here!"

I didn't see much of what happened after that, being under the towel, but I gather the Boccata brothers burst in and quickly ejected the intruders. No doubt they lingered on the scene to ogle my wife, who yanked the towel from my head, clutched it to her exquisite body, and ordered everyone to leave. I pray our next apartment has a private bath. And a burly doorman to halt trespassers at the lobby.

Sheeni just informed me the TV invaders were Dutch not French. How she knows this I haven't a clue.

11:28 a.m. I ran into Señor Nunez on the stairs. He has purchased his own 38 triple-short admiral's uniform, which he is adding to his act. He for one is thrilled that our first music video is such a runaway success, and expects it will do wonders for his career. He believes the appeal of the song lies in its very simplicity, as "any moron" can appreciate it. I agreed that profound mental impairment was certainly an asset for digging The Three Magdas.

3:37 p.m. After a lonely lunch (my wife being off as usual with another man), I dragged out the full complement of toxic chemicals and tried to catch up on my graffiti abatement. I've been talking up portable sandblasters and anti-graffiti coatings to Madame Ruzicka, but she seems to prefer corrosive solvents and my free labor. No doubt in 30 years when I come down with multiple cancers she will be too dead to sue. As usual my labors attracted a small crowd of kibitzers, and I had the opportunity of introducing Babette and Violet. They have a lot in common, each being one of approximately 30 million UK females. I'm hoping Violet can show Babette some contortionist maneuvers for escaping the vile clutches of randy Alphonse.

Babette lingered long enough to serve as interpreter when Madame Lefèbvre bustled out from the wig salon to inquire about the handsome young American seen so frequently these days with my lovely wife. I explained the circumstances and reassured her that he was both married and sleeping with Violet. This, I'm sure, will raise a few eyebrows in the salon. I also asked her to be on the lookout for invading news crews, paparazzi, and Mafia hoodlums. She promised her staff's full cooperation and gave me my daily quota of hugs and cheek kisses. Even better, Babette caught the bug and felt compelled to throw herself at me for quite a stimulating squeeze.

Later, the postman brought me this welcome missive:

> Dear Rick,
>
> Somehow everything got packed away and we are on

the road at last. Thank you again for your assistance in loading my car. My babies went on strike! Our first performance was a disaster. But their issues have been sorted out and they are adjusting to the traveling routine. Of course, they miss the nice young American who has been so kind to us these past months. I'm enclosing a program with our scheduled route. It can change, of course, from unforeseen delays and disasters. As you can see, our direction is generally south.

A Miss Barnes should be arriving soon to occupy my apartment for the summer. Thank you very much for helping her if she has any problems.

It is pleasant to be traveling again, though I find I am missing my father and brother very much. I will write again when I can. If you wish to write to me, please address your letter to the circus's Paris office and they will forward it. (Sorry, I don't have e-mail yet.)

I think of you often and look forward to seeing you both again in the autumn.

Fondly,
Reina

No mention of Paul. That could be good news, or he may have asked her to keep mum about his presence. Rereading the letter, I could perceive no hint at all of whirlwind romances with passionate American jazz musicians. And such excitements, it seems to me, would have to leave some imprint on her prose.

5:45 p.m. Connie just called in a state while I was cooking dinner. My miserable in-laws have been leaving alarmed messages for Paul on Connie's phone. Because of the upcoming July 4 holiday, Paul's probation officer has had to move up his appointment. To this coming Friday! That's only three days from today.

"Damn," I said, "Paul's going to miss it for sure."

"You have to call up Paulo's parents, Rick."

"What?!"

"I have it all figured out, Rick. You can call them tonight from my hotel. You can pretend to be Paulo. You can tell them you're delayed here and ask them to call the damn probation officer to reschedule."

"But, Connie, I don't sound anything like Paul!"

"Just speak with a hoarse voice. And say you've got a cold. We have to buy some time. I'm sure my detectives are homing in on Paulo. I have a jet standing by. We'll fly straight to L.A. as soon as he's captured, I mean found."

Somehow, Connie got me to agree to her plan. I think it was the prospect of her leaving the country that did it. That and her usual threats.

7:18 p.m. For dinner I made my version of Mrs. Crampton's world-famous chop suey. Authentic bean sprouts and real water chestnuts from the can. About 98 percent of the latter remained uneaten on the plates, leading me to wonder how much longer those professional chestnut divers will have jobs. I imagine it is rather perilous work too.

While T.P. was doing the washing up in the kitchenette, Sheeni took me aside to confide that the cad hasn't spoken to his wife since he got here. Apparently, they'd had "words" just before Trent's departure. About what Sheeni did not know, though as any husband can tell you, when it comes to marital squabbles there is an entire universe of topics to choose from. It wouldn't surprise me if my own alluring wife figured prominently in the Prestons' airport wrangle. And now Trent is playing Mr. Passive-Aggressive, a tactic I would have thought beneath him. So I ducked into our closet, dialed my old number in Ukiah, said "Hi, Apurva, could you hold, please?" when she answered, and handed the phone to her startled husband. He was still deep in conversation when I left for Connie's hotel. To Sheeni I merely stated that I was going for a walk—trusting that the indeterminacy of my return would discourage extramarital trespasses upon her person. Helpful to my peace of mind, though for all I know they may have been going at it like adulterous rabbits all afternoon in some tawdry hotel. They *were* rather vague at dinner about the day's cultural activities.

10:32 p.m. Well, another of Connie's wacky schemes blew up in my face. Sheeni's old man, crafty lawyer that he is, wasn't fooled for long by his putative son's claims of a virus-induced throat frog.

"Who is this?" he demanded.

"It's me, Dad. Paul." I croaked. "I'm too sick to travel. Just a bad cold. Can you ask my probation officer to reschedule? Say, in another month?"

"At what age did you acquire your first saxophone?"

"Er, what?"

"Name three of your best buddies in high school."

"Well, let's see, uh, there was John. Uh . . . Mike . . . uh, bye-bye."

Totally panicked, I bailed on the call. Connie was not pleased.

"I can't believe that my own mother chose to sleep with that man," she snarled. "I'm putting my foot down with Paulo. Sorry, but I am *not* inviting his father to my wedding."

"His mother certainly added a great deal to my wedding through her absence," I pointed out.

"Neither will be invited," she declared. "I hate to say this, Rick, but I wish my Paulo had been born an orphan."

"Me too," I admitted.

How much simpler life would be if Sheeni and I had met in some home for orphaned teens. Some progressive, sexually enlightened institution far away from Trent, Vijay, Connie, Mr. DeFalco, Uncle Sal, Señor Nunez, The Three Magdas, and all things French.

WEDNESDAY, June 29 — Another beautiful day; the tourists have descended in force. Everywhere you go you hear obese, sweaty people complaining in Midwestern twangs about the exorbitant prices. Alphonse for one despises the Americans even more than the UK and German tourists. He says if we showed a little discipline and didn't buy all that needless made-in-China junk and run up record budget deficits, the dollar might still be worth a dime. True, my countrymen may be profligate in their ways, but at least we're not driving around in Twingos.

My despondent pal Violet accompanied Maurice and me on our morning walk. She is quite bent out of shape over T.P.

"Not only is he gorgeous beyond belief," she declared, "but we connect on every level. I feel like I've known him forever."

Me too, but I don't find the sensation at all pleasant.

"He's rather young," I pointed out.

"But very mature for his age, Rick. I want him so. I can barely stand it."

"What do you mean you want him?" I asked, ever eager for insights into the female mind.

"I mean I want him," she insisted.

"How exactly?" I persisted.

"Well, if you must know, I want him inside me."

An extraordinary admission. Women actually experience sexual desire. Sheeni practically has to be dragged kicking and screaming to bed, and then she treats it like she's just doing you a favor.

"Men are pretty weak," I replied. "You could have him if you made an effort."

"Possibly, Rick. But what would that accomplish? It would just make things worse. Like taking that first big hit of heroin. Sure, it's great while it lasts, but then you want more. And your friend loves his wife. I know he'd wind up despising me."

We walked on in silence while Maurice sniffed the lampposts. Odd, he's taken a vow to sniff every post, yet rarely displays much interest when he encounters an actual dog. Violet took advantage of these pauses to stretch into improbable configurations while blasé Parisians passed us by without a glance.

I was still a bit unclear on the concept. "Why exactly, Violet, do you want a guy inside you? I mean, what's the appeal? Isn't it rather, uh, uncomfortably intrusive?"

"Rick, are you entirely deranged? You claim to be married. Why don't you ask your wife?"

I knew I wouldn't get a straight answer on that topic. I never do.

1:42 p.m. Unexpected guests for lunch. Sheeni and T.P. returned early with a discouraging report from Belleville. According to Mr. Petit's spies, the dirt on Vijay came from high up in U.S. military intelligence. Lunch was rather discouraging as well. All I could scrounge up was a dented can of bouillabaisse left behind by the previous tenant. This I hastily stretched with some flat Pepsi found in the back of the frig. Fortunately, T.P. volunteered to make a run for an emergency baguette.

"There must be a mix-up," commented Trent, recoiling from his first sip. "Joshi is a pretty common Indian name. There could be thousands of Vijay Joshis out there. The authorities must have him confused with someone else."

"Or Vijay could be a deep-cover radical extremist," I speculated, "sent by his masters to infiltrate the West under the guise of an obnoxious high school student."

"Rick, your soup tastes like bilge water," commented My Love.

"Why do you call him Rick when he's really Nick?" inquired T.P.

A rather impertinent question, I thought.

Sheeni gave the matter some thought. "He's a person with multiple personalities—all rather tiresome. I suppose at some level I must prefer Rick to Nick."

"And how is one preferable to the other?" he asked, persisting in his impertinence.

"Rick is I believe—though here I may be deluding myself—slightly less devious than Nick. I like to think he is imbued with a certain Gallic . . ." Here followed a phrase in French, which brought a snort of derision from my adversary. The balance of their discussion re: my character and its flaws continued in French. It grew quite lively and rather heated at times. I didn't mind. I enjoy being the center of attention even when my many shortcomings are being dissected in an unintelligible tongue.

Exhausted by his encounter with my cuisine, T.P. excused himself to take a nap at Violet's. After he departed, Sheeni dropped her bombshell. Mr. Bonnet is most impressed with Trent. He wants him for his next music video. Since T.P. desperately needs money for baby bassinets, etc., he has agreed to delay his departure and go before the cameras next week.

Rick S. Hunter, for one, was put out by this news.

"Hey, I thought I was supposed to be their big new video star!"

"Rick, that was a serious miscalculation. I can see that now. You can never rely on horrible acts to bomb deservedly. We have to keep a low profile."

"Yeah, I suppose so. But shouldn't Trent be keeping one too?"

"Not at all. If he became famous, he could speak out publicly against the injustice done to Vijay. He could put pressure on the U.S. government. Plus, Trent is fluent in French. And he's a great singer!"

Big deal. I found the whole thing very unsettling. True, I didn't really want to be in the center of a massive media spotlight. But I sure as hell didn't want to share it with that twit either.

4:26 p.m. Spent most of the afternoon composing a letter to Reina. Despite Rick S. Hunter's best efforts to project a cool Gallic reserve, I'm afraid it emerged as something of a mash note. Dropped it into the post with a sense of guilty anticipation. Adultery, I find, is even more unnerving a prospect than marriage was.

11:47 p.m. Sheeni opened her purse strings—something she does even less often than her thighs. Can't believe I just wrote something that catty about My One and Only Love. Oh well, I'm a bit drunk. She took us out to dinner (a double date with Trent and Violet), and then we went to see Maurice's Dad. That guy is so great. If writing doesn't work out as a career, perhaps Carlotta could apprentice herself to Mr. Hamilton. I can see myself prancing nightly across the stage as a buxom Liz Taylor, fingering my faux beauty spot and flaunting bogus diamonds the size of stalactites. Uh-oh, head is swimming, room is spinning. Must stop now. And so to bed, perhaps to snare a piece . . .

THURSDAY, June 30 — No nooky last night. Sheeni objected to sharing her ravishing body with objectionable drunks. But sex, glorious sex was on the menu this a.m. I've decided to take Violet at her word and accept that chicks desire and enjoy sex as much as guys—even if 98 percent of the fun takes place within their persons. It was time to put my traumatic rape behind me and acknowledge that females embrace another aesthetic in bed. No more tentative or apologetic approaches. To overuse some common agricultural metaphors, I plowed that familiar furrow until the rooster crowed, the cows came home, and the silo was emptied of its last groat.

11:17 a.m. Must always wear my sunglasses now when I go out, even on days like today when rain threatens. Even so disguised I was stopped by several people on the street this morning while walking Maurice. Three ominous words stood out in their unintelligible inquiries: *"Heee, Lekker Ding."* Naturally, I shook my head and kept on walking. Had to drag poor Maurice past several enticingly aromatic trees too. How difficult life must be for the dogs of celebrities.

1:33 p.m. Yesterday's excruciating lunch seems to have scared off all my customers. Just as well. I'm not running a restaurant here. I grabbed a quick takeout crepe from my favorite discount stand, then forced myself to check in again with loathsome, treacherous Sonya back in Ukiah. Somehow, she always seems to be loitering beside the phone. Naturally, she demanded to know what steps I'd taken to render T.P. single and available. Before replying, I made her promise that anything I divulged would go no further than her big fat ear.

"Well, Sonya, I got him to extend his trip here. He won't be going back to Apurva anytime soon."

"Nor to me from the sound of it," she replied sourly. "What else have you done?"

"Well, he's now sleeping in the rooms of a female contortionist."

"What!"

"Don't worry, Sonya. He's not stuck on her. But you can't wean a guy away from his wife without reintroducing him to the concept of attractive, available females."

"Contortionist, huh? I suppose they're having great sex in impossible positions."

See, it's a very common train of thought.

"Not at all, Sonya. Violet won't sleep with him because he's married."

"Is she nuts?"

"No, she's English. They're very reserved. I've also lined up a starring role for Trent in a new music video."

"Accomplishing what?"

"You know how people who are successful in the entertainment field always ditch their spouses. It's practically a given."

"OK, Rick, I guess you're making an effort. I won't snitch to

Fuzzy for the time being. But you better check in regularly. I was about to dial his number when you called."

A cold shiver ran down my spine.

"OK, Sonya. Anything happening in Ukiah?"

"Like what, Rick? You know this town. The place is as dead as my love life. I started a new quilt project as a summer alternative to bingeing, insanity, and suicide."

"That sounds nice, Sonya. Have fun."

"Hey, drop dead."

The only pleasant part of that conversation was hanging up. Gee, and bubbly Sonya seemed so upbeat back in sewing class. Of course, it goes without saying that I'm not really trying to break up Trent and Apurva. In fact, I hope someday to be invited to their gala fiftieth wedding anniversary party.

6:28 p.m. The phone rang as I was stirring cornstarch into tonight's dinner. It was Connie calling with dire news. Mr. and Mrs. Saunders, the in-laws from hell, have just checked into her hotel.

"Oh, no!" I exclaimed.

"They're here. And they're pissed," she confirmed. "I'll get back to you when I can." *Click*.

"Who was that?" demanded Sheeni, clearly alarmed. "What is it? Is it about my brother?"

My mind raced. "Uh, that was . . ."

"Don't lie to me, Nick Twisp!"

I capitulated. "That was Connie. Your parents have, uh, arrived. They're at her hotel."

My Love turned pale and sat down on the bed.

"Well, that's just fine and dandy. That's just what I need!"

"It'll be OK, darling," I reassured her. "Paris is a big place. They don't know we're here."

"I think you should go see them," volunteered T.P., who I had never before taken for a complete idiot. "I think you should make an effort to work things out."

Sheeni fired off the blackest look I have ever seen. And miracle of miracles, she wasn't looking at me.

10:48 p.m. No call from Connie. Though she left untouched

tonight's goulash (one of my better culinary efforts), My Love has calmed down. She's agreed that if we lie low while her parents are here, there's no reason to fear we might run into them. They will be distracted anyway by their search for Paul. And T.P. has been told in no uncertain terms to stuff his parental reconciliation proposals. He's also been obliged to cancel his evening stroll with Violet. Sheeni wants all familiar Ukiahan faces banished from the boulevards. And tomorrow I have to make Connie remove herself and the ogre duo to some other swanky hotel in a faraway *arrondissement*.

It was rather like Ann Frank's family hiding out from the Gestapo. The hours crawled by. I tried to read my computer magazine, Sheeni paced up and down the floor, and T.P. stared wistfully out the window until Violet arrived to drag him back to her celibate pad.

JULY

FRIDAY, July 1 — Sheeni is missing! Can't write much. Too distraught. She sent us out this morning under hats and behind sunglasses. Me to run errands for Madame Ruzicka. T.P. to Belleville for wardrobe fittings and consultations with Piroque, the director. When I returned, Sheeni was gone, as were her bags, her clothes, and her French language typewriter. No note, of course. According to Madame Lefèbvre (interpreted by Violet), the ladies in the wig salon saw her enter a taxi around 10:15. They assumed that she was going away for the weekend and that her husband would be joining her for a romantic getaway in the country if his video stardom and janitorial duties permitted. I wish.

T.P. denies knowing where she went. Nor has her lawyer Mr. Petit heard from her. Connie speculates that she may have gone to join her brother. My friend is approaching despair. The Saunders are driving her nuts and Paul is proving unexpectedly elusive.

"The guy doesn't stay in hotels," Connie complained when I phoned her with my alarming news. "He doesn't charge things. He hasn't pawned his fucking Rolex. How the hell am I supposed to find him?"

"We'll find them," I reassured her. "We've got to."

"I hope so, Rick. I think it's a very bad sign that Sheeni bolted too. A very bad sign."

2:26 p.m. No one in the building has seen Señor Nunez. He doesn't answer at his door either. Could My Love have run away with a dwarf?

10:52 p.m. No word from Sheeni. No phone call, no letter. I divided up the city with T.P. and we spent most of the day searching. No luck. Rather futile. We know Sheeni is hiding from her parents, so it isn't likely that she would be lingering conspicuously in public venues. Still, we had to try. T.P. thinks she'll return when she knows her parents have left the country. God, I hope he's right.

Can't write any more. Have to go pace the floor and wring my hands.

SATURDAY, July 2 — Eight weeks, diary. Very scary to wake on this anniversary day alone in bed. Even worse, T.P. chose to spend the night on our sofa. Said he wanted to be here in case Sheeni called and sleeping with Violet becoming too stressful. Sexual attraction too powerful. Nightly demonstration of bender moves leading to excessive physical contact, triggering anguished desires. Know the feeling.

Mood not improved this a.m. by naked Trent bathing not five feet away from where I was attempting dispirited croissant ingestion. It really is obscene what that guy looks like with his clothes off.

One piece of good news. Wife not cohabitating with dwarf. Awakened in middle of night by poignant chords of "My One and Only Love." Roommate and I threw on clothes and pounded on Señor Nunez's door. He opened door in disheveled admiral's uniform. Offered us swigs from his tequila bottle. We stayed until bottle empty. He hadn't seen my wife, but extended his sincere commiserations. Said women can torment your soul, but each one builds a new room in your heart. Not sure what that meant, but T.P. seemed to think it was profound. Our host squeezed out a few more sad songs and T.P. sang along. Sounded no better than a youthful Frank Sinatra. He had to desist when the open window brought the sounds of nearby sobbing (Violet?). Wish Señor Nunez knew a few upbeat tunes.

SUNDAY, July 3 — No news. T.P. and Violet spent the day together searching, but I was too paralyzed by despair. Regret all the fights, all the unkind words, all the clashes of wills. Sheeni had followed her dream to Paris, and I had tagged along to bitch about who was going to take out the garbage.

If last summer you had told me that someday I would be residing in a one-room garret apartment in Paris with Trent Preston, I would have said you were out of your mind. The pompous self-righteous bastard does not improve upon close association. Acute lack of privacy too. Have to wait until he leaves to take baths. No way I'm going to give him the satisfaction of comparing our physiques. He continues to insist Sheeni will return, but her missing typewriter gnaws at my soul. Why lug along that boat anchor if you're planning to come back? Is she holed up in some backwater hotel typing up a critique of our marriage?

MONDAY, July 4 — Independence Day back home. Just another day of heartbreak and despair in Paris. Accompanied T.P. and Violet to Belleville for videotaping in case runaway wife chose to lurk in vicinity. Piroque decided to throw Violet into the mix as an additional visual distraction from the star, a Madame Roux, billed without shame by Mr. Bonnet as "France's Oldest Rapping Grandmother." A true abomination. Makes The Three Magdas seem positively semi-talented. Incredibly ancient skinny old lady (must use the same wrinkle creme as Carlotta) with big flashy guitar.

Location was an abandoned sewer pipe factory. While the white-haired star rapped, T.P. strolled about the decrepit machinery in a skimpy loincloth and adjusted various bolts with an enormous rusty wrench. He also worked up a great oily sweat (professionally applied by Josette, the makeup artist) rapping along on what I assumed was the refrain. Meanwhile, Violet—in faux leopard-skin bikini—twisted herself up to slither painfully through assorted sections of grungy pipe, getting rather grotty in the process. No atmospheric fog this time, but lots of flashing lights and bursts of brightly colored flame. Another feast for the eyes, though a severe bastinado on the ears. At least the stupid tune didn't drill its way into your brain for all eternity.

After the grisly confection was in the can, Mr. Bonnet counted out the big piles of euros. He wasn't sure what to do with Sheeni's commission, but finally slapped the *E*200 onto her husband's itchy palm. The cash infusion was welcome, though most unsettling that my wife didn't show up to collect. Very unlike Sheeni to miss out on her share of anything. Gratifying at least that Rick S. Hunter earned 50% more for his video debut than T.P. Of course, that guy didn't have to wrestle a dwarf.

Skipped the rap wrap party. Too depressed.

9:12 p.m. Taking direct action at last. Went to local print shop and commissioned rush job. Four hours later took delivery of 10,000 fluorescent orange stickers reading "S.S. CALL R.S.H." Have distributed stacks to various building tenants and Madame Lefèbvre's staff. They've agreed to adhere them in highly visible locations as they journey about the city. I already plastered our neighborhood, though I doubt My Love in immediate vicinity. Still, feeling optimistic that she will spot one soon, decipher the message, and check in. Hoping she remembers my current name is Rick S. Hunter, since I've mentioned it frequently enough and we are married after all.

TUESDAY, July 5 — Woke with a start in the middle of the night. I forgot to pay the rent! Damn. Then at breakfast T.P. refused to fork over his rightful share of the housing tab. Insisted he was a guest, not a tenant. In that case I informed him I was officially revoking his guest invitation. I told him to scram, he told me to get out of his face. The twit had the nerve to declare that he was here as a guest of Sheeni, not me. OK, but with provocations like that it won't be my fault if he winds up with a large German blade buried in his liver.

Madame Ruzicka was understanding about the late rent payment. Said in her experience domestic turmoil was the number three cause of non-payment of rent. Too depressed to inquire about other causes. I knew over-tipping the janitor wasn't one of them. She speculated that Sheeni no longer in the city and inquired if we had investigated the railway stations. I said no, but that sounded like a good idea.

4:45 p.m. French still in dark that passenger trains are obsolete.

Paris, it turns out, is lousy with railway stations. T.P. and I flashed Sheeni's photo around in all of them—some, I was pleased to see, already bearing orange stickers. Nobody remembered seeing her, but many expressed a desire to date her. Even François is appalled by the indefatigable sexism of the French male. Why can't those Frogs give it a rest sometimes?

9:28 p.m. Connie escaped briefly from Saunders' manic clutches to take me out to dinner. Naturally, I tried to sticker the restaurant ladies' room, but was ejected by the irate attendant. Countless millions employed in French restrooms to panhandle patrons for the privilege of taking a piss. Have all the decent jobs here gone to China?

Unaccountably, Connie also invited T.P.—perhaps to keep her flirting skills in tone. Had to hear all about T.P.'s exciting video breakthrough. Wants a copy for her mother to circulate among Hollywood's elite star-makers. Gag me with a spoon—though in a pinch pricey French mystery cuisine will do. Don't ask me which part of what animal I was masticating tonight; I'd rather not think about it. Connie reports Mr. Saunders has filed some sort of legal notification with Los Angeles County that an AWOL parolee has been kidnapped to France (not "in" France, as that would imply Paul illegally left the country of his own volition). Wonder how often Paul's probation officer hears that excuse? More creative, at least, than "I overslept and missed the bus."

Connie also divulged that Sheeni's father openly boasts that he is offering $40,000 to have me killed. Not unexpected news, but scrotum-jangling nonetheless.

"Must have gone up," commented T.P., sucking the marrow out of a lamb bone. "The figure I heard was $25,000."

WEDNESDAY, July 6 — When I returned from my morning canine constitutional, T.P. informed me that he had just heard from Mr. Petit. The lawyer reported that his snitches here learned from their mole within the U.S. military that the source of the alert on Vijay had been an official of the Krusinowski Spring Company.

"I had nothing to do with it," I announced. "It was all Connie's idea."

"I look forward to relaying this report to Sheeni the next time I see her," he replied.

Time to shake off my lethargy and knife my houseguest. Or go to Plan B.

2:26 p.m. On the train to Blois (pronounced "blwah," like I feel). At least I hope that's my destination. French transit system rather daunting to confused Americans. Feeling semi-confident I was on the right platform in the right station and boarded the correct train. Conductor did not seem perturbed when he inspected my ticket. Our car is pretty plush even though I bought the cheapest seats. No peasants with bleating goats or squalling children. Just bored-looking student types and backpacking tourists. Naturally, I have clandestinely stickered the entire train.

7:04 p.m. A short (but pricey) taxi ride from the station brought me to the grassy lot in Blois where the Cirque Coco-Poco had pitched its tents. The matinee performance was nearly over, but I bought a ticket and went in. No mammoth enterprise like the American circuses I'd been dragged to at the Oakland Coliseum on father-son bonding outings. The tricolored one-ring tent was smaller than a high school gym and sat perhaps 500 folks on folding aluminum bleachers. Lots of empty seats for this show, but the crowd of mostly kids cheered every trick and applauded with gusto at the conclusion. The most entertaining act I saw was a giant man about eight feet tall who performed with a little monkey. They were dressed alike in colorful tunics, and the joke was that the monkey was the trainer and the giant was the performer. Every time the big guy stood on his head or balanced on one leg on a milk bottle the monkey would feed him a treat and take a bow. Even I had to smile. No sign of Reina, but when the little four-piece band rose to play the exit march, I realized with a start that the mustached trumpet player in the gaudy red velvet uniform was Paul.

I made a call, stuck a few stickers, then wandered around outside to the back of the tent. I found my brother-in-law sitting on a crate and swabbing out his horn. He seemed pleased to see me, though he could tell the feeling wasn't mutual.

"Hi, Rick. Did you see Reina's act?"

"No, I came in too late. I didn't know you played the trumpet."

"Oh, I play well enough to be hired by a small circus desperate for a horn player. Connie didn't go home, huh?"

"No. And your parents arrived last week to add to the fun."

"Damn."

"Sheeni's gone, Paul. Have you seen her?"

"I'm sorry to hear that, Rick. No, I haven't seen her. When did she leave?"

"Last Friday. No note or anything. She heard your parents were here and cut out."

"That sounds like Sheeni."

"You should have talked to Connie, Paul. You should have told her you didn't want to get married."

"Connie's not an easy person to talk to—especially if you're giving her bad news. I was hoping she'd get the message and go home."

"What about your probation requirements, Paul?"

"The world is a big place, Rick. Lots of places to see. I'd be fine never going back there."

"But you could be arrested."

"Not likely, Rick. The authorities aren't going to bother extraditing someone from Europe over a petty drug offense. They have bigger fish to fry."

"It's hard to stay in France legally, Paul."

"I've never paid much attention to the rules, Rick. We're kind of alike in that respect. I wish, though, you hadn't told Connie I was here."

"She didn't answer her phone, Paul. I just left a message. You still have time to get away."

Paul sighed. "Yeah, I suppose."

"Will you rat on me, Paul?"

"That's not my style, Rick."

"Are the cops closing in on me?"

"They do seem a little closer, Rick. I'd watch your step. Want to stay and see Reina?"

"No, I have to get back."

We shook hands and wished each other well. As it turned out, I ran into Reina returning from a nearby market as I walked back toward town. She seemed delighted to see me and invited me to stay for dinner. I declined. She asked how was my wife, and I said Paul would fill her in on that story. I said I had a train to catch. She gave me a hug and said her babies missed me. I just made it to the station in time and climbed aboard in a state of abject misery. Somehow I seem to have wound up alone and friendless in a strange country thousands of miles from home—assuming I even had a home to go back to.

10:55 p.m. When I returned, I found T.P. lying in the dark in a mild catatonic state. Hard to believe, but the guy was even more depressed than me. He and Violet had had a busy afternoon.

"I've made a mockery of my marriage vows!" he exclaimed, when I prodded him to haul his tanned carcass off *my* bed.

"Well, these things happen. Nobody's perfect." I tore off a great length of unwaxed floss, handed it to him, took one for myself, then felt a fresh wave of longing for my absent love. How I loved to watch Sheeni floss at bedtime. She brought such industry to the task.

"It was rape!" T.P. confessed. "She told me no and I forced myself on her. Then she told me she loved me. I'm very confused."

"Doesn't sound much like rape to me. Violet told me she wanted you bad. She was only holding back because you're married."

"How can I ever face Apurva again? I vowed to forsake all others, and I've already slept with two other women!"

I prayed the second victim was Sonya and not Sheeni. It didn't seem polite to ask. Nor did I inquire how he enjoyed sex with a professional contortionist.

"You know what the worst part is?" he asked.

"No. What?"

"It was the best sex I ever had. Violet's just incredible!"

Well, that clears up that issue.

"Trent, it's all part of the great learning experience called life. You will go back to Apurva a better person having known Violet. And no, you will *not* blab about your affair to Apurva. Remember, she's your wife, not your confessor."

"Doesn't she have a right to know?"

"Everybody has a right to remain blissfully ignorant. It's the eleventh right they forgot to put in the Constitution. Telling her would only cause needless pain. Just keep your lips zipped."

"Why should I listen to you? I abhor everything you stand for."

"You're not my favorite person on the planet either. But at least I live in the real world. It's you zealots with your lofty principles and rigid standards who cause most of the pain and suffering in this world. Go ahead, destroy your marriage. See if I care."

We flossed on in silence.

"What should I do about Violet? I love her too."

"Violet's not expecting your child. Therefore, Violet must be, uh, put aside."

"We didn't use a condom."

"Trent! Are you a completely insane?!"

"I don't know, Nick. I think maybe it's this city. One gets . . . rather carried away."

THURSDAY, July 7 — Horrible, horrible news. Connie called me at 4:00 a.m. on her satellite phone from 32,000 feet over the Atlantic.

"You better clear out of there fast, Rick."

"Why?! What's happened?"

"Paulo's mother saw your damn video at the hotel yesterday. They've notified the French police."

"Fuck!"

"Thanks for locating Paulo, Rick. I owe you a big one."

My mind was reeling. Where will I go? What will I do?

"Are you still there, Rick?"

"Uh, yeah, Connie. I'm sorry Paul decided to stay in France."

"Don't be silly, Rick. Paulo's right here on my plane with his repulsive mother. We're flying straight to L.A."

"He changed his mind?"

"Let's just say with the help of my muscular detectives his father didn't give him much choice."

Great. They kidnapped Paul.

Another troubling thought: "Connie! Where's Paul's dad?"

"He didn't come with us, Rick. I knew something was up, and I finally got Paulo's mother to spill. Her husband's remaining in France to find their daughter and track you down."

"Shit!"

"Fly, Rick! Get the hell out of there! Now!"

9:38 p.m. Can't write much. Too fatigued. Too stressed. Registered in an elder hostel off the rue des Pyrenées in the slummy 20th *arrondissement* under the name Mrs. Morag Fulke, a Scottish pensioner. Passport of her late tenant slipped to me by Madame Ruzicka this morning, along with assorted items of surplus old-lady apparel. Landlady most sympathetic. Said my rent paid up until the end of the month. Will hold my apartment until then should I clear up matters with the gendarmes. Even with heavy application of wrinkle creme I don't look much like Mrs. Fulke's passport photo. Oh well, who looks that closely at gray-haired biddies anyway? Desk clerk at elder hostel certainly distracted by my dazzling print frock. A riot of cabbage roses tailored in the style of 1952. Topped by a big straw hat laden with artificial fruits to hold down my wig in the Paris breezes. And one of those open-mesh veils to add a sense of drama and mystery while obscuring the crow's-feet. Yes, Carlotta has returned—this time as her granny from the highlands.

Hopeful that T.P. will keep his promise not to snitch to gendarmes. He seemed slightly friendlier since our heart-to-heart last night. I think he's realized that leading an exemplary life of strict moral rectitude is a bit more challenging than he assumed.

I vacuumed up all my ready cash and cut out as dawn was breaking. Miraculously, Sheeni hadn't laid her sticky fingers on my concealed euro stash. Still, rent and other expenses had taken their toll. Only *E*2,853 stands between me and peddling an old lady's scrawny bod on the rue St. Denis. At least this hostel is clean and reasonably cheap, though they kick you out between the hours of 10 a.m. and 6 p.m. and impose a two-week limit on guests. After that I may be sleeping on the quay under a bridge.

Stickered the neighborhood, then hung out in dining room until bedtime. Read hostel's complimentary copy of *International Her-*

ald Tribune. Disturbing story about possible cryptic neo-Nazi communications appearing all over city. Speculation that someone trying to alert the "SS" about "R.S.H." which was believed by authorities "to be a reference to Adolf Hitler." What a bunch of dummkopfs. Leave it to the over-analytical French to find a fascist conspiracy in a lonely husband's desperate plea.

Now I must bed down in a small room with nine other elderly gals. Hope they all keep their clothes on and don't mind a bit of athletic snoring. A nightmare lack of privacy to be sure, but at least the toilet is private.

FRIDAY, July 8 — Boycotted the communal showers, but was still subjected to considerable geriatric nudity. Most traumatic. Not at all conducive to a healthy sexual outlook. During the worst moments I shut my eyes and tried to think about the girls' locker room back in Ukiah. Rapidly acquiring the reputation of an eccentric among my fellow hostel inmates. Rather standoffish, and I reply to polite conversational approaches in my version of an unintelligible Scottish brogue. Occasionally, I do make a little sense. One lady asked me how I kept my hands looking so young, and I blurted out "vigorous daily masturbation." Short-circuited that conversation, but, hey, it works for me.

11:08 a.m. Another alarming story splashed all over the front page of the *International Herald Tribune*. This one headlined: "'American Belmondo' Sought on Child Abduction Charges." The usual homoerotic dwarf-grappling photo of the young video star and a very flattering shot of My Love that I had never seen before, inducing fresh pangs of anguished heartache. What a beautiful girl I'm married to, even if she did look rather young and innocent and virginal in her photo. I can only imagine how she is reacting to this media exposure (we also made the front page of *Libèration*, I noticed). Of course, the article was libelous in the extreme. It said I had abducted young Miss Saunders at gunpoint from a medical facility in California. The only gun I ever used was against her lying father and now I wish I'd taken some marksmanship training before that. And let us not forget that the "victim" is nearly six months older than the alleged perpetrator, and it was she who coerced me into coming to this accursed country. If it weren't for Sheeni, I'd still be a bookish wanker back in Oakland. In short, I'm innocent!

Well, as you can imagine, I was so incensed, I fired off an immediate rejoinder to the paper, declaring that I hadn't abducted anyone, that we had been married legally in Mississippi, that my wife was expecting my child, and that we had been very happy together until her meddlesome parents arrived and began spreading those vicious lies. I also noted for the record that Mr. Saunders was a lawyer who associated openly with reputed mobsters and had been shot recently under mysterious circumstances possibly related to his Mafia entanglements. Suck on that, Father-in-law dear! I also phoned up his hotel, identified myself as Mr. Saunders' private secretary, and said he would be checking out today as he had just been indicted in California.

3:26 p.m. Rode the Métro to our old station and strolled warily down a side street that afforded a glimpse up our block. Three police cars and several news vans were double-parked in front of the wig salon. I doubt much hair was being sewn in Madame Lefèbvre's premises with all that excitement going on. Feigning disinterest, I strode resolutely on.

9:42 p.m. Need a shower most desperately. Frivolous French deodorant starting to fail and wrinkle creme beginning to itch. Am reduced to contemplating midnight nude swim in the Seine. Had dinner in a budget Chinese restaurant around the corner from hostel. No major surprises except for amputated chicken foot in watery soup. Attributed it to a slipup in the dimly lit kitchen. As I was scarfing down my combo rice plate, my ears were assaulted by the opening chords of "*Heee, Lekker Ding.*" Swiveled around in seat to watch sensationalist news report on greasy TV mounted high on wall. Flashed my photo, then cut to interview with The Three Magdas. Lots of giggling in Dutch overdubbed into French. I could be wrong, but they did not appear overly scandalized by their brush with felonious child abductor. Then cut to shocking scene of gendarmes leading T.P. out of my building and into waiting squad car. Very unsettling. Pray that twit has the fortitude to stand up to interrogation. Next watched in open-mouthed astonishment as excerpts shown of invasive bath-time video. Disturbing deer-in-headlights shot of dazed Rick S. Hunter, then much camera jostling as view shifted toward My Love. Her privates were pixelated, but bobbling pink and damp for all of France to ogle were her divine breasts. This brought a roar of approval from my fellow diners—all clearly of the degenerate, lowlife class. Then my father-in-law appeared to make a heartfelt appeal to the people of France to help track down his missing daughter and her vicious celebrity kidnapper lest this "nightmare turn into a tragedy." The ogre also declared he was offering a *E*10,000 reward for information leading to Sheeni's safe return and/or the capture of her kidnaper. I prayed this sum was coming from his Rick S. Hunter whack fund. Needless to say, it was all I could do to gag down my complimentary mango sorbet, pay the check, sticker the umbrella stand, and lurch out into the autonomous night.

SATURDAY, July 9 — A sad anniversary, diary. Nine weeks since My Love and I said "I do," and over a week since she was taken from me. Every waking minute of the day I wonder where she is, what she's doing, and why the hell she hasn't phoned. Really, I don't see how she can remain on the lam for long with all this publicity and the big reward on her head. The nagging moral question: When she is found, should I turn myself in to face the consequences with her?

Still no shower and growing ever more ripe, like a female-impersonating Camembert. I tried sneaking into the hostel bathroom at 3:00 a.m., but these gals have such twitchy bladders they are always bobbing up to take a tinkle. All I could manage was a quick face wash and wrinkle creme reapplication. This preview of old age is a real downer. I really don't see how people cope past age 40.

Since it was the weekend, I dressed a bit more casually in a lavender nylon jogging suit and my Rumanian miner's shoes. Such a relief from the matronly street shoes that Sheeni had dredged up and those aromatic cabbage roses. That frock may have to be taken out and burned as a public nuisance. My sartorial effect was rather butch, but eyebrows in the hostel dining room were raised no more than usual when I strolled in. I noticed my ostracism is now complete.

No one chose to sit at lonely Morag Fulke's table, which is just as well as I was free to bogart the complimentary *International Herald Tribune*. A big splash about the Sheeni Saunders rescue reward on page one and a nice photo of Mr. Bonnet looking even more intense than usual. He has reason to be focused. Thanks to all the Rick S. Hunter hoopla, "*Heee, Lekker Ding*" is now Number One on the French hit parade. And is doing very well in the lucrative U.S. market, where media interest has been "similarly intense." A final paragraph in the article noted that U.S. citizen Trent Preston, believed to be an associate of the "American Belmondo," was assisting the police with their inquiries. I hope that doesn't mean he's singing like a canary.

4:28 p.m. Spent the morning on the streets stickering and wracking my brain trying to figure where my wife could be holed up. Something tells me she's still in the city and I must be overlooking some obvious clue. My suspicions keep coming back to Alphonse, but I dare not approach him since I know the cad would turn me in for the reward.

After the meagerest of budget lunches, I rode the Métro to the distant suburb where Señor Nunez and pals perform. Sure enough, after loitering in the station for nearly an hour (and getting propositioned twice by decrepit and obviously desperate Frogs), I saw Violet exit a train and fell in beside her as she walked toward the circus auditorium. She seemed glad to see me, but cautioned that I should ditch my buoyant stride and adopt the halting gait of an enfeebled oldster. So I clung to her lovely arm and practiced being aged and infirm. As usual, frisky François was feeling anything but that in the presence of such an attractive chick.

Some good news at last. T.P. didn't spill. All he told the cops was I left in a hurry that morning, and, no, I hadn't said where I was going. They pumped him endlessly for details about Sheeni and me, but his responses were politely vague. When Mr. Saunders arrived, Trent told him flat out that he was making a bad situation worse and should just go back to Ukiah. Not something the ogre wanted to hear. He informed T.P. that his presumption would cost him his part-time concrete slave job with Mr. DeFalco. How vile.

Doesn't my callous father-in-law care if Trent's poor baby starves?

The further good news (from Violet's perspective): the detectives told Trent not to leave the country. He's stuck here until the case is resolved.

"Doubtless, Rick, you think I'm a terrible person for seducing a married man."

"Call me Morag. I'm a little confused, Violet. Last I heard Trent was beating himself up for raping you."

"How sweet. Oh, God, Morag, I really am quite frightfully gone on the bloke. It's all I can do to tear myself away from him to go to work. Is his wife as beautiful as her picture?"

"Well, she's, uh, not unattractive."

"Does she really love him?"

"She always conveyed that impression."

Violet defiantly gripped my infirm arm. "Trent loves me, Morag! He told me so this morning."

What a mess. I didn't know what to say. What I am sure of is if news of her husband's Parisian philandering somehow gets back to Apurva, the blame will be dumped squarely on Nick Twisp's gray-wigged head.

Since one has many lonely hours to fill when one is on the lam, I attended the circus via a complimentary ducat from Violet. Much more lavish than Reina's humble show. Plush seats, full orchestra, glittering costumes, lumbering elephants, death-defying stunts, scantily clad beauties spinning by their teeth, and a troupe of raucous clowns led by an acclaimed dwarf. Amusing I suppose, but does antic slapstick really qualify as genius? I thought my other former neighbors were just as accomplished and drew equal applause. The Boccata brothers defied gravity while hazarding hernias with their energetic acrobatics. And Violet bent herself up like a pretzel to the gasps and winces of the awed spectators.

Entertaining to be sure, but I left feeling more depressed than when I entered. I suppose performing in a circus beats toiling in some office, but it seems to me there's something sad about risking your neck eight times a week for the delectation of strangers. And doesn't prodding the same costumed bear through the same flaming hoops day after day become rather tedious? Of course, being an impoverished and homeless fugitive can give one a jaundiced view of any show business enterprise. Sour Morag Fulke may be every entertainer's worst audience nightmare.

SUNDAY, July 10 — More bad news. Mrs. Fulke has lost her happy home. I've been bounced from the elder hostel. Apparently, complaints were received. The manager ejected me this morning for "inadequate personal hygiene." Incensed, I told him the fault lay with his facilities, not with me. "We Scots invented the bathtub!" I ranted, "But we canno' be expected to disrobe in front of peeping strangers!" He wasn't sympathetic and refused my demand for a full refund. So I packed in a hurry and swiped the latest *International Herald-Tribune* on my way out.

Never noticed it before, but this country is crawling with cops. Everywhere I go there are black-caped gendarmes giving me the hairy-eyeballed once over. Parked well out of sight in a derelict café, I was happy to see that Rick S. Hunter's clandestinely submitted Protestations of Innocence were given prominent play on page one. A gratifying sidebar, featuring comments from neighbors, led off with Madame Lefèbvre declaring the fugitive youth was "the finest, most attentive husband any woman could desire" and stating that my persecution was the "gravest injury to justice" since the notorious "Dreyfus Affair." I wasn't aware that Richard Dreyfuss had had legal difficulties in France. Other supportive neighbors praised my devotion to animals, willingness to assist the handicapped, and diligence in graffiti removal. All very inspiring for a guy stranded in the rain without even a storm drain for shelter. Trudging along later with my grip, laptop, and purse, I tried not to glance at my reflection in shop windows. I looked just like one of those bag ladies I used to see mumbling curses to unseen companions in downtown Oakland.

Then I got really morbid and thought about my homicidal mother. I wondered if her trial for assault with a deadly weapon was over yet. Perhaps it was, and she was already driving nuts her new cellmate in some maximum-security prison. Unfortunate, I suppose, but at least she had a roof over her head.

5:37 p.m. Still raining. Thanks a pantsful, God. Mrs. Fulke's bouffant wig has lost all of its pouf. I look like something the tide washed up. And I wish the damn wrinkle creme was less soluble in water. Now I look like a drowned old lady with peculiar streaks of blooming youth. I made a call to Babette, but Alphonse answered. So I asked him point-blank where he was hiding my wife. He replied in French, but François was in no mood for that *merde* and told him so. In halting English he said he was completely in sympathy with me, had no idea where Sheeni was, and hoped very much that I located her soon. Sounded quite sincere too. Damn. I suppose it's nice to know that guy isn't as big a jerk as I thought he was, but there goes my one best hope of getting a bead on My Love. Unless the treacherous bastard was lying through his teeth.

Question of the moment: Shall I scrounge up a budget dinner or throw myself into the Seine? I could hardly get much wetter.

MONDAY, July 11 — Not dead yet, though it was close. In fact, I'm freshly showered and more than a little cozy. My benefactor is Mr. Hamilton, whom I appealed to in desperation in his austere dressing room after his second performance last night.

"Who are you supposed to be?" he inquired, wiping off his makeup. "Edna May Oliver? Marie Dressler? Or perhaps Ruth Gordon as the sexy octogenarian in *Harold and Maude*?"

At least he didn't guess Elsa Lanchester from *Bride of Frankenstein*. I explained my predicament and threw myself on his mercies.

"Kicked out of your elder hostel and rejected by three hotels," he sighed. "How ungracious of them."

"I'm not looking my freshest," I conceded, "but I don't see how anyone could mistake me for a prostitute."

"You'd be surprised at some of the ladies making a living off tourists in this town. Well, Rick, you can't go back to my place. I expect the building is being watched. But my accompanist has a spare room. She may be able to put you up for a few nights."

"Is she to be trusted?"

"I certainly hope so, Rick. After all, she is my mother."

For some reason Mrs. Hamilton goes by the name of Madame Zyxlenska, even though she's an American widow from Scranton,

Pennsylvania. Perhaps she always wanted to have the last name in the phone book. She and her two chubby cats occupy one of Paris's odder apartments in a secret garden behind a high stucco wall in the once slummy, now swanky Marais district. This vine-covered dwelling consists of two retired streetcars stacked one atop the other and remodeled into a warren of tiny rooms. Jammed with exotic clutter, but still visible here and there are some of the original iron scroll-work and ornately carved wood. Tired Mrs. Fulke took a quick shower, then crashed under the lantern roof in the second-floor guest room. I didn't even wake up when a 25-pound feline bedded down on my face.

2:27 p.m. More itchy bra strap irritation. Turns out if you wear such undergarments, daily showering is a must. Unfortunately, I have to remain dressed as the Scottish pensioner lest I be spotted by a nosy neighbor through one of the innumerable streetcar windows. Madame Zyxlenska, though, lent me a nicer wig to replace Mrs. Fulke's drowned one and gave me the run of her cosmetics-laden vanity table. To thank her I made brunch (she formally retired from the kitchen some years ago) and got the score on her son. After a stint in the Navy as a pharmacist's mate, he went on to study pharmacy in college on the G.I. Bill.

"All that talent," she sighed, "and the guy was headed for a career as a pill pusher."

"Did you try to talk him out it?" I asked.

"Never, Morag. I always told him it sounded like a wonderful career with loads of security."

"Why did you do that?"

"Reverse psychology. If I told him he was wasting his life, he would have gone on doing it for sure. Do you ever listen to your mother?"

"Very rarely," I admitted.

"Fortunately, Gene took a few music and theater classes as required electives. Then he was offered a role in a touring company of "Hair" and that was it for pharmacy school."

Mr. Hamilton's first name is Eugene, which may explain why he is known to all as "Mr. Hamilton."

"Did he have to take off his clothes on-stage?" I asked, trying not to imagine a long-haired Mr. Hamilton cavorting in the buff.

"Sure, but he didn't mind. We performers are all exhibitionists at heart. Did you ever consider a career as an actor?"

"Not really. Why?"

"Well, your Mrs. Fulke is a treat. It seems to me, though, if they can make a salve to give you unsightly wrinkles, they ought to be able to make one for me to take them away."

She had a point there. Might be a worthwhile marketing opportunity for Mario and Kimberly to explore.

8:12 p.m. Weighed down by heavy dinners (grilled by me) and gigantic lap cats, we were vegging in front of the TV (the nightclub is closed on Mondays), when what should come on but T.P.'s new rapping granny video. Madame Zyxlenska said it was introduced as starring the notorious American Belmondo's "closest friend" Trent Preston. Another shocking media untruth. The editing was peculiar too. Just a few cutaway shots of the old lady, while Piroque's camera focused lovingly on the scantily clad American with the big wrench. Madame Z, for one, was smitten.

"Who is that gorgeous boy?" she asked. "Do you really know him?"

"I suppose," I replied with ill-concealed boredom. "He used to go out with my wife until she dumped him for me."

High-fives were then exchanged. Yes, it's nice to have someone on my side for a change. Even if she is a fat old lady.

TUESDAY, July 12 — Madame Zyxlenska took Mrs. Fulke to her favorite gypsy fortune teller. I was skeptical, but she claimed that four years ago Madame Gulumba correctly predicted her son would break up with his boyfriend and that she would inherit their cats and streetcar apartment. A long Métro ride to the south brought us to Madame Gulumba's office, which was the back half of an old van up on blocks in an alley behind a tenement. The seer was a tiny brown crone with far more wrinkles than her two supplicants put together. Since Mrs. Fulke couldn't very well say she was looking for her absent wife, I let Madame Z do the talking. She handed over one of Sheeni's anklet socks (this precious artifact was the only article of her clothing retained by me), and said we were seeking a young woman who had been missing nearly two weeks. Madame Gulumba lit a tab of incense, chewed something intently (her gum?), and pondered the sock.

"She is with someone," croaked the ancient gypsy.

"A woman?" I asked hopefully.

"A man!"

"Where are they?" inquired Madame Z.

"Mountains! I see mountains."

"What mountains?" I demanded.

"Mountains. Green mountains."

Could My Love actually be holed up in Vermont?

Try as we might, we couldn't get the fortune-teller to nail down anything more specific—a not-unexpected copout. Sure, be vague about the details, but be very explicit about collecting your fee. I had to fork over *E*35 I could ill afford to find out my wife was off somewhere mountaineering with some stud.

1:15 p.m. In such a funk, I could barely make lunch. Not one of my better efforts either. Most of the mélange went to the two cats, who only picked at it. Their names are Jeeves and Ruggles, though it is clear that it is we who serve them. Phoned Babette, who said Alphonse had not been out of the city and barely out of her sight for many weeks. Definitely not off on any mountain expeditions. Damn. Who could Sheeni be with? I keep drawing a blank—unless she's off trekking in Nepal with Vijay.

8:48 p.m. Just had a call from Connie in a most excited state. Paul's probation lapses have been cleared up and they're engaged to be married.

"You should see the size of the rock on my finger," she bubbled.

Impressed I was not. "But, Connie, didn't you buy it yourself?"

"Well, yes. But Paulo helped me pick it out. He has exquisite taste, you know."

I asked Connie why the wedding wasn't until next week.

"My Paulo needs a little time to recover from his surgery."

"Is he sick?"

"No, but I was. I found out the silly dear had had a vasectomy. You can imagine the shock to my unborn children."

"Aren't those kind of hard to reverse?"

"Not if you get the right surgeon. I've lined up the best tube and tickle guy in the West. Paulo goes under the knife tomorrow morning."

"I hope it works out, Connie. Aren't you worried about him bolting again?"

"All taken care of, Rick. I had a private chat with his surgeon. He's going to slip in a GPS chip."

"What's that?"

"It's a little chip that ties into the Global Positioning Satellites. I'll be able to track Paulo's movements anywhere on the globe in real time with an accuracy of two feet."

"You're putting it in his balls?!"

"We have to, Rick. He'd notice the incision if we put it anywhere else."

Looks like Connie finally will have her guy by the short hairs.

"If Sheeni comes back, Rick, and has her baby by caesarian, I recommend you slip one in too. These Saunders just can't be relied on to remain on the porch."

You can say that again. After Connie thanked me again for helping track down Paul, I told her she could return the favor by yanking our father-in-law out of France.

"I don't know, Rick. I suppose I could invite him to the wedding, but that's asking a lot."

"You've got to, Connie. I know Sheeni won't return until he's left the country."

"OK, Rick. I'll see what I can do. Perhaps I can get him interested in my mother again. Even he would be an improvement on your father."

"What's my dad doing now?"

"He just got himself elected president of the American Chihuahua Society. The guy is such an obnoxious little climber. I really do detest him."

Welcome to the club. It's a big club with an active and evergrowing membership.

10:47 p.m. All alone by the telephone. No calls from Sheeni, alas. Madame Zyxlenska off performing. So as not to attract undue attention on the Métro, she commutes in her usual shapeless housedress, then dolls herself up at the club. She has an entire wardrobe there of sequin-strewn gowns—like a time capsule of Ethel Merman's closet.

Cats and I trying to watch TV, but the networks here do irritating things like dub "The Simpsons" into French. Too depressed to remain conscious a minute longer. Time for bed.

WEDNESDAY, July 13 — Another restless night of psychological self-abuse. Unlike the physical kind, this can go on endlessly with no pleasurable sensations whatsoever. Why has my life so seriously derailed? First, I have parents who are thrilled to see the back of me. Then I fall in love with a girl who takes all my money and abandons me. For my best pal I choose a kid (Lefty) who finks on me to the cops and another (Fuzzy) who would see me dead for enhanced zero-to-60 performance. Trying to look on the bright side though. For example, the wrinkle creme is doing wonders for my skin. Not a zit in sight—helpful when you're an adolescent trying to pass for 74.

2:17 p.m. Went shopping in the neighborhood with Madame Zyxlenska. More proof that Paris is trying to copy San Francisco. The Marais is like our gay Castro District, only with more historic buildings and not as rigid Levis-and-moustache dress code. Lots of trendy shops, though we stuck to our local *boulangerie*, *fromagerie*, and *épicerie*, where Madame Z was well known and received friendly service, even though to my ears her "French" sounded like an outrageous parody. Affable welcome also extended to her silent houseguest in the bilious dress and ridiculous hat. A typically warm Parisian experience, though I think I would have preferred the faceless anonymity of grocery shopping at Safeway in America.

Over lunch Madame Z told me how she came to leave suburban Scranton in her late sixties for a nightclub career in Paris. It seems that her son's elaborate act, timed down to the second, requires a skilled accompanist who can mind all the cues and stay on the beat. Yet this is just the sort of profession that attracts unreliable artsy types prone to on-the-job abuse of mind-altering substances.

"Want to know how to get ahead in this world, Morag?" she asked.

"OK."

"Show up on time and do your job. That's all there is to it."

Good advice, I suppose, though she didn't mention that it helps to be related to the person doing the hiring. Considering my relatives, I'll probably wind up grooming chihuahuas for my father or guarding my jumbo nephew Tyler in his carnival sideshow exhibit.

THURSDAY, July 14, Bastille Day — Does it surprise you that the most important national holiday in France commemorates a riot? Rather like California celebrating Watts Day or New York sending all the school kids home for Attica Day. Woke up to the sounds of jet fighters screaming by overhead. Not as I feared air cover for the SWAT team sent to arrest me. These planes spewed red, blue, and white plumes to dress up the sky for the big military parade on the Champs-Elysées. Watched a little of it on TV, but saw no rose-covered floats or giant pneumatic figures of Napoleon—just a bunch of military types marching in formation. Pretty boring, but intimidating, I suppose, to the Belgians or other hostile neighbors.

Not easy being depressed, on the run, and cross-dressing as a senior in a city filled with millions dancing and partying in the streets. Mrs. Fulke took a lonely hike through the throngs of celebrants along the Seine. Lots of bands, food booths, strolling entertainers, and marginally clad chicks gyrating to the music. Kept my eyes peeled for Sheeni, but saw not a hair of her. Many orange stickers in evidence though. Comforting to think that my minions are everywhere. Ran into T.P. and Violet walking along arm-in-arm. Must be great being young and in love in swinging Paris. I'll have to try it sometime. Trent in dark glasses to escape crazed groupies mad about his new video. Violet reported that Mr. Bonnet has been deluged with requests for TV and radio appearances by the hot new American star. T.P. set to record his first solo song next week. Possible movie deal also in the works. With luck, he may get back to Ukiah in time for his kid's high school graduation. Didn't linger long in case T.P. being followed by undercover gendarmes. He did report, however, that Sheeni hasn't contacted him either.

Rick S. Hunter still has one leg up on his handsome rival. Passing a newsstand, Mrs. Fulke was startled to see I'd made the cover of *Paris Match* magazine. Didn't dare buy a copy, but will send Madame Z out for one later. A very gratifying addition to my scrapbook, and a magazine cover sure to be reprinted frequently in future Twisp-Hunter biographies.

11:47 p.m. Stolid Mrs. Fulke among the millions crowded on the Champ-de-Mars to observe the fireworks at the Trocadéro light up the Eiffel Tower. Wild electric colors, especially that rare, intense purple seen only at the fiery center of a rocket's blast. With every "ooh" and "aah" rising from that great crowd I pretended they were admiring me. Only a tepid boost to the ego, but a cheap form of do-it-yourself therapy. All in all, the show was pretty awesomely spectacular—even if someone did try to pick my purse—a fashion accessory I devote exclusively to used Kleenex. Get my germs and die, you filthy thief!

FRIDAY, July 15 — Invited Mr. Hamilton and Maurice over for a late lunch. The latter has worked out a nervous truce with Ruggles and Jeeves, who leave him unmolested as long as he stays off *their* furniture and doesn't nibble from *their* bowls. All spilled food items are off-limits to dogs as well. I made my version of Mrs. Crampton's celebrated Hash 'd Ham, which was well received by all. So far I've been subjected to nine years of formal education, but it seems to me the few months spent at Mrs. Crampton's bulky knee have proven far more valuable in equipping me for Adult Life.

Considering she is his mother, Mr. Hamilton seems to have quite a cordial relationship with Madame Zyxlenska. She doesn't criticize him or boss him around, and he doesn't tell her to flake off or drop dead. They listen with apparent interest when the other talks, and respond as you would to a friend or colleague. Needless to say, it was a whole new paradigm of parent-child communication for me.

Mr. Hamilton is working up some younger gals, since he feels his "Tallulahs and Dinahs and Sophies" are starting to "sail right over the heads" of contemporary audiences. He did his Madonna-in-progress for us. Very good, I suppose, though I'm not really qualified to say, not being tuned in to the post-Woodstock pop music scene. Hell, I'm still annoyed that Frank had to share the 1950s with Elvis.

Both mother and son expressed amazement that Sheeni still at large despite massive media attention. Mr. Hamilton suggested that, like me, she might be disguising her identity.

"Disguising it as what?" I asked.

"Well, perhaps as a male," he speculated.

I tried to contemplate Sheeni metamorphosed into a young dude. The request did not compute.

"Does she have a theatrical bent like you?" inquired Madame Z.

"Possibly," I admitted.

"If she's as intelligent as Morag says," Mr. Hamilton said, "I'm sure the thought has occurred to her."

"But she's an awfully pretty girl to make herself over into a boy," Madame Z pointed out.

"Well, let's see," replied her son. "Do you still have that newspaper with her photo?"

With a few deft strokes of his pen, Mr. Hamilton gave My Love a boy's haircut. The effect was decidedly unmasculine. Then he drew in a trim moustache. Slightly more plausible. Then he added a small goatee.

"There," he said. "A handsome youth."

"You don't think she'd have a full beard?" asked Madame Z.

"Not likely," he replied. "Too much work and they always look fake. What do you think, Morag?"

"She looks a bit like her brother," I conceded.

"She'd need a passport or identity card," said Madame Z. "Does she have much money?"

"Lots," I replied. "All mine, unfortunately."

"Of course, she could be adopting some other disguise," Mr. Hamilton pointed out.

"Perhaps an older woman like you, Morag," suggested his mother.

"Not likely," I replied. "If Sheeni changed her identity, it would be to something attractive and fashionable. A bag lady she's not."

While the Hamiltons rehearsed some new numbers, I took

Maurice for a walk for old time's sake. I brought along my Michelin map since neither of us were familiar with that neighborhood. We discovered a fancy street called rue de Rivoli that was crowded with affluent shoppers. While Maurice sniffed the lampposts, I stared intently at every passing young man sporting facial hair. I think I spooked a few, who detoured from their paths to give me a wide berth. One semi-Sheeniesque youth—transfixed by my gaze—halted in his tracks, fished a one-euro coin from his jeans, and pressed it into my startled palm. From that act alone I knew he couldn't be my missing wife.

Sheeni as a guy? I don't know, it seems like such a stretch. She would have to cut her lovely chestnut hair and somehow bind her increasingly prominent bosom. (Girls, I've noticed, seem to get bigger upstairs when they're preggers, perhaps anticipating looming cafeteria duties.) Nor could I see her swaggering up to some smelly urinal to let fly. Still, she did have that manly, take-charge attitude toward life. As I recall during our marriage there was a fairly constant struggle over who was going to wear the pants in the family. And she did prefer the female superior position during sex. One comforting thought: Perhaps it was Sheeni himself whom the gypsy saw accompanying my wife in the mountains.

When we returned, Mr. Hamilton took me aside for a few words before departing.

"You know, Morag, Frank loved Ava, but they didn't stay married for long. It just didn't work out between them."

"I know. He tried to commit suicide over her."

"Sometimes great love, great passion isn't enough."

"Yeah, I suppose not."

I could tell Mr. Hamilton was well-meaning and spoke from experience. Except for his oddly pruned eyebrows, he was the blandest of men in appearance. Average height, average build, average paunch, average bald spot. A complete nonentity, if you judged only by his looks. Yet he was unquestionably a man of distinction—a great artist who was the master of a difficult craft. He had known momentous love and had suffered for it. On the other hand, I'm not like him and Frank. I don't fucking give up.

I have the greatest admiration for Mr. Hamilton. Yet am I the only one who thinks that dressing up as assorted gals six nights a week to parade in front of your mom is a bit peculiar?

SATURDAY, July 16 — Ten weeks, diary. Ten short weeks since I applied the marital brand to my mate-for-life. Yes, we have faced some adversity. Yes, we shall be together again.

Large scary eruption on my forehead. I don't think it's a zit. I think it's a goddam fleabite from Ruggles. I wish he'd use somebody else's face for a mattress. Can't write much. Have to go out and search Paris for goateed young men. Also need some more wrinkle creme. Mrs. Fulke getting dangerously low on her Transylvanian beauty formula.

10:24 p.m. Even in cloud-like Rumanian shoes, dogs barking again. Must have walked 30 miles in summer heat under hot, airless wig. Most enervating. Seems to be sudden revival of facial hair among Parisian men. Inspected thousands of hirsute faces—many indignant at being stared at, more than a few obviously repulsed by appearance of starer. Forehead boil now the size of an angry red golf ball. Madame Zyxlenska all for making emergency visit to local clinic, but vetoed by me as too dangerous. Madame Z now heating up large intimidating needle for proposed lancing operation. Lance: frightening procedure that can scar one for life. Lance: evil cop stepfather who can scar one for life. Just a coincidence? I think not.

SUNDAY, July 17 — Had to stay inside today as I have a feminine sanitary napkin fastened over my draining facial boil. Does wonders for Mrs. Fulke's already severely impaired looks. Hard to believe all that ghastly pus produced by my innocent teen body. Enough to gag a goat, but brave Madame Z has not yet run screaming from her home. Women, I think, have a higher nausea threshold for these sorts of horrors. It's so they won't be repulsed by the numerous foul discharges expelled daily by their disgusting babies.

Madame Z kindly translated the *Paris Match* article for me. Hard to believe all the errors of fact the French press can cram into 800 words. Still, it's often said that for media personalities there is no such thing as bad publicity. Rick S. Hunter has realized his dream of international mega-fame, even if he does (temporarily, I hope) have to hide out from the cops.

Inspired by Clyde Barrow and John Dillinger (other misunderstood fugitives), I have composed another missive to the press. This one treats in greater detail the events leading up to my marriage to my alleged abductee, Sheeni Saunders, and details in full our loving regard for one another. It was previewed approvingly by Madame Z, who thought it was just the sort of heart-wrenching saga to appeal to the French public's romantic side.

"It's just like the story of Abelard and Héloïse," she commented.

"Oh? Who are they?"

"He was a great poet and philosopher in 12th Century Paris. He wrote beautiful letters to Héloïse, but things didn't work out and he wound up being castrated."

A sudden scrotal spasm. That was not the sort of reassurance I had in mind.

MONDAY, July 18 — Another anniversary. One year ago today I commenced writing this modest journal. Back then I was a lonely miserable kid in Oakland. Now I'm a lonely miserable married person in France. No longer a kid, not yet a man, and detoured temporarily (I hope) into female senescence. All in all, not the sort of year I expected when I journeyed to the shores of Clear Lake last summer for that fateful first meeting with you know who.

Back to mundane life. Purulent boil from hell mostly drained, but forehead now looks like I've been igniting cherry bombs on it. Have discarded sanitary pad, and Mrs. Fulke combing gray locks down low in front. Look like Alice B. Toklas on an especially bad day. Have banished Ruggles from my room, though he has figured out that by heaving his furry bulk against the door he can spring open the lock. Very smart for a cat. Wonder if he could extricate himself from a mailbag at the bottom of the Seine?

4:12 p.m. Just had a phone call from Connie. The news started off fairly good. She interrogated Paul in the hospital while he was coming out of the ether. She did this because she'd read that modern anesthetics work just like truth serum. People in a groggy, post-operational state do not have the mental perspicacity to lie.

"Did you ask him if he loves you?"

"Don't be silly, Rick. I had more important fish to fry. As it was

I had to bribe the nurse, and she only gave me five minutes."

"What did you find out?"

"You know that wacky bird girl you tried to fix him up with? My Paulo never slept with her!"

"He didn't?!"

"Definitely not. He tried, of course. Well, Paulo is a virile guy and will be even more so when his stitches come out—so his surgeon assures me. But that girl turned him down."

"She did?!"

"Indisputably so. Not even heavy petting. Paulo was sleeping in one of the equipment vans. The trumpet was on loan from the circus. My Paulo never betrayed me!"

"That's great, Connie. How's his chip working?"

"Flawless. I can tell every time he gets up to use the john from clear across town."

"That should be very helpful, I suppose. Is Mr. Saunders coming to your wedding?"

"That's what I called to warn you about, Rick. There's been a hitch in our plans."

Instant alarm.

"What kind of hitch?"

"Paulo's odious father refuses to come home. He claims the police there are close to making an arrest."

"An arrest of whom?!"

"Well, they wouldn't be arresting Sheeni. I think you better take another powder, Rick. And quick! The cops may be closing in on you."

Fuck! And double fuck!

7:38 p.m. On the train to Amboise. I've had to say farewell to Madame Zyxlenska and her Streetcar Named Sanctuary. She seemed sad to see me go. She said Mrs. Fulke was a model houseguest and was welcome back anytime. She assured me that France has mountainous regions galore to the south. Since that is the direction Reina's circus is heading, I thought I'd team up with her. Mrs. Fulke can lay low with her and keep her eyes peeled for goateed young men. Since Sheeni was so taken with Señor Nunez, the Boccata Brothers, and other such types, I feel it is likely that she will be drawn to any circuses visiting her area. Naturally, Reina's private life is her own, and it is no concern of mine whether she had an affair with Paul. The fact that he threw himself at her and was rejected does not imply that the object of her heart's affection lies elsewhere. Still, that smoldering kiss on the stairs must have counted for something. Really, I should not feel so excited at the thought of seeing her again. After all, as I keep reminding myself, Mrs. Fulke is a married woman.

TUESDAY, July 19 — I've decided lovely Reina is a bit like her birds: friendly, but not appreciative of surprises. She was certainly taken aback last night when an elderly Scottish pensioner showed up at her caravan door. She'd been following the press reports with interest, so there were numerous misconceptions to clear up. No, I was not a sexual predator and kidnaper. Yes, I was wanted by the police, hence the funky disguise. No, I did not really enjoy dressing up like old ladies. No, I had not been in a terrible accident. It was just an unfortunate reaction to a fleabite, possibly exacerbated by excessive use of wrinkle creme. No, I was not interested in turning myself in to the gendarmes. Yes, my hunt for my missing wife had turned south and could I possibly accompany her in that direction?

This request brought the conversation to a dead stop. I had never seen gracious Reina look so stricken. She explained all the reasons why this would be impossible. Her birds would not tolerate another person in the caravan. Circus people are very close-knit and most suspicious of strangers. She could get in trouble for harboring a fugitive and be expelled from France. My wife would find such an arrangement most objectionable. And so on. Very disheartening. Soon we were both weeping over our cups of tea as her empathetic birds fluttered restlessly on their perches. She did consent to let me crash that evening in her station wagon, where I passed a most uncomfortable night and woke at dawn. Where to now? God only knows. I seem to have come to the end of the road.

8:45 a.m. Walked into town to scrounge up some breakfast. Must be some ugly towns in France, but I've yet to see one. This one looked like it was posing for scenic postcards in every direction.

Picturesque bridge over Loire, quaint river promenade lined with dazzling flowers, fairytale buildings nestled under great fortified château. Found a café and wolfed down three croissants. No dinner last night, so semi-famished despite profound despair. Should I jump off bridge? Be an inspiring final view. Very romantic location for suicide of modern-day Abelard. Might become a tourist destination over time. Boon to local economy. Sheeni could move here when she got old to write a wistfully regretful memoir of our days together. She could open a little shop and sell her book along with postcards of the two fabled lovers in younger and happier days.

1:26 p.m. Suicide on hold. Mrs. Fulke spruced herself up as best she could and submitted an employment application to circus boss Madame Marie Poco. Small, tough-talking broad, but not bad looking for being so old—at least 40, I'd say. In need of honest Ticket Seller, but Mrs. Fulke not qualified due to near-total ignorance of French language. Also out as Diesel Generator Technician. Deemed too old and slight for Roustabout. Perfect for Trumpet Player opening, except can't play trumpet. Only one other vacancy: Assistant Animal Attendant. Managed to talk myself into that job on a trial basis. Off the books, of course, since lacking proper sanction from Government of France to sweep up monkey shit. Therefore, I'm to stay out of sight if the gendarmes come around. "No problem with that," I assured her. Starting wage an astonishingly meager *E*65 a week. I'd earn more if I had a commercial license and could drive a truck. Will be permitted to sleep on bales of hay in camel van. Hoping "camel van" is circus slang and vehicle does not contain actual camels. No drugs permitted or wanton promiscuity with townies. No overtime pay, no weekends off, and no bitching about the long hours.

"It's a great life," said Madame Poco, welcoming me aboard. "If you fit in, you'll love it."

"I'm sure I will," Mrs. Fulke lied.

10:58 p.m. Very fatigued. Can't write much. Have bear scat in my wig and down my jogging suit (bored bear named Beez gets frisky when introduced to new attendant). My supervisor even older than Mrs. Fulke. Wiry Italian guy named Captain Lapo with ill-fitting false teeth and wine on breath. Seems friendly enough. Unclear what he is captain of besides my fate. Circus like traveling U.N.; many nationalities represented, so de facto lingua franca is English. Captain Lapo introduced me to my rake, shovel, and wheelbarrow. Showed me around the cages. No lions or tigers, thank God. Bear pretty scary, but said to be a sweetheart. Monkeys will bite unless you show them who's boss. Ditto the mild-looking ponies. Boa constrictors must not be permitted to grab you around the neck. Fortunately, they eat infrequently and defecate minimally. The same cannot be said for the camels (Ajax and Omar), who will spit their foul-smelling juice or kick you in the ass. Alas, they do occupy the eponymous camel van, but fortunately hay (and Mrs. Fulke) stored in a separate compartment, redolent with authentic camel aromas.

Have made myself at home as best as I can in my tiny metal cell. One lonely window for ventilation and one light in the center of the ceiling. Assorted hay bales that can be arranged creatively to suit one's furniture needs. No storage at all. Clothes I'm keeping in Mrs. Fulke's ratty suitcase. Under a steel plate in the floor is a compartment holding the van battery. Here I've stashed my money, jars of wrinkle creme, Rick S. Hunter's passport, photos of Sheeni, and her plastic-wrapped keepsake sock. A hay bale over the plate keeps it concealed from prying eyes. Thankfully, the door to my new home has a fairly substantial lock. So far no bugs except angry horseflies. Perhaps they're angry at finding only camels and *moi*.

Sneaked away this evening to watch Reina perform. Most charming and entertaining act. Diverting clowns haul out the cart containing birds and props, so most in audience don't notice that the pretty trainer in the sexy dress walks with a limp. Parrots pass balls back and forth, drive toy tractor around pylons, climb fire truck ladder for daring rescue, perform stunts on "high wire," and more. Big applause at end led by elderly animal attendant. She really is quite a wonder. And such a beacon of loveliness in a lonely guy's life.

WEDNESDAY, July 20 — Nothing like spending the night in a camel van to make a person nostalgic for his garret apartment in

Paris. Hay bales not as resilient to the spine as a city person might assume. Nor are cud-chewing camels on other side of thin metal partition ideal companions for restful sleep. Have been given long list of camel care requirements by their swarthy owner, a Mr. Iyad Maymun. He and his younger (and prettier) wife Nuzhah do handstands and somersaults on top of their sauntering beasts, believe it or not.

Asked Captain Lapo this morning where I was to shower. He looked at me blankly and said he used a bucket in the pony van (his residence). I said that would not do for me as I was "a woman," causing him to check me out brazenly. Had he not noticed my alleged sex before? He suggested I use the shower in the roustabout's caravan. I had inspected that loutish lot at dinner in the cookhouse the night before and suspected that any female who crossed their threshold would be in for a stimulating time. So I knocked on Reina's door, and she (reluctantly) let me in.

After my shower, we had a quick chat while I prepared Mrs. Fulke's face for public view. Forehead getting better. No longer looks like a relief map of Mars. Reina is not enthusiastic about my hiring myself on as assistant animal flunky. She says it is the lowest job in the circus, that they will work me like a dog even if I am supposed to be an old lady, and that few last more than a few weeks in that position. I said I didn't think it was that much of a comedown from unpaid janitor and had to be better than my alternative, which was jail.

She sighed and said we mustn't appear too friendly lest it raise suspicions. She had already lost face with Madame Poco over Paul's sudden defection.

"Do you miss him that much?" I couldn't help but ask.

"Well, I thought he was my friend. He could have at least given notice and said goodbye."

I decided not to tell her why his departure had been so unexpectedly abrupt.

"He went back to America with Connie. They're getting married this week."

"Is that so? Well, he must have changed his mind."

We brooded silently over our gloomy thoughts until Damek

screamed. You have not known the full dimension of human hearing until you experience a cockatoo's cry in a confined space. I nearly jumped out of my skin.

2:12 p.m. Shit. This is the new metaphor for my life. I rake it, I shovel it, I haul it, I dump it. I sprinkle fresh straw and refill water buckets. By the time I finish the last cage, it is time to begin anew on the first cage. And where does all that diverse and exotic excrement go? I dump it in a corner of the lot, and eager French gardeners of both sexes roll up with their wheelbarrows to trundle it away. At least some of us, I feel, should get a life.

Cookhouse tent remarkably like high school cafeteria. No one extends much of a welcome to the new guy. I've been sitting by default at the old folks' table. Captain Lapo, the grizzled band members, Madame Poco's elderly bookkeeper, a superannuated clown, etc. Only desultory conversation and most of it in French. Mrs. Fulke the object of some envious glances though. She appears to be the only diner at the table with her own native teeth.

After lunch I sneaked into town to augment Mrs. Fulke's work wardrobe. You can't clean a monkey cage in a garden frock. Also got some scarves to tie down her wig as monkeys extraordinarily grabby little creatures. Their master is an English gent named Granley or Granola something, who takes such a scientific approach to animal training he gives his monkeys numbers instead of names. I have already decided the twit must be killed. He wears the most pretentious khaki bush suit like he's just leaving on safari for Big Game. Also sports the silliest red moustache and a coiled bullwhip on his snakeskin belt that I would very much like to apply to his freckled hide. Did I mention that in the cookhouse he likes to monopolize the seat beside Reina? Of course, he hasn't deigned to say two words to the new monkey attendant. Nor have many of the others. Reina's right. In the circus hierarchy I'm the lowest of the low. It probably doesn't help that I exude an all-pervasive odor of ripe camel dung.

11:35 p.m. We're on the move. The air of permanence about our encampment was all a sham. After the evening performance, everyone set to work packing up. I would like to have helped Reina hitch up her caravan, but had to assist Captain Lapo in securing the animals for transport. Last to be packed away were Ajax and Omar, who assisted with taking down the main and cookhouse tents. This task is normally handled by elephants, but our circus (thank God) travels sans pachyderms. I can just imagine how much those beasts produce. Hitched to a common chain, my roommates dragged down the poles and pulled up the stakes, but you could sense they felt the whole business was a big imposition on them.

I traveled in the cab of the camel van, piloted by Mr. Maymun. His wife of the shy smile and 10,000 gold bangles rode in their lavish caravan, which was hitched to the bumper. Don't ask me if that's legal in France. Behind it was attached another smaller trailer containing a washer and dryer. Many of the circus people tow these mobile laundry facilities. Don't know what us peons do. I expect I'll be washing Mrs. Fulke's clothes in the river.

Iyad drove at an excruciatingly torpid pace so as not to disturb his camels and/or wife. He's from Tunisia and was very pleased to hear that Mrs. Fulke was not as he feared a Jew. We crawled through the large city of Tours, then tiptoed down the road to Chinon, where 98 percent of the circus had already pulled onto the lot and was fast asleep. Sounds like a good idea. I shall now turn out the light and hit the hay bale hard.

THURSDAY, July 21 — Barely light outside when I was roused from my fragrant bed. Luckily, I hadn't washed off my makeup. Madame Poco employs a curious incentive plan. No breakfast until all tents up and everything squared away for next show. I hardly had time to use the doniker (circus lingo for w.c.). Amazing how much work involved in moving the entire agglomeration, and this is just a small show. Fortunate that circus traditions go back to Roman times. If somebody came up with the concept today, I'm sure it'd be dismissed as an impractical folly.

True medieval serfdom for all, but at least the grub not bad. Good thing eats are provided. Otherwise, on my salary I'd be reduced to filching bananas from the monkeys. Have observed that the little people in the company seem to pack away as much as the normal-sized folks. This is not true of the giant Donk, who is quietly but methodically decimating the barnyards of France. His pampered monkey Dink dines at his side and displays better table manners than many of the roustabouts. I don't provide maid service for that ape. Donk and Dink reside in the giant's modest caravan (which I would guess to be rather dank).

Chinon is another storybook river town dominated by a vast ruined castle atop a rocky bluff. In case anyone hadn't heard that the circus was in town, at noon our ornate bandwagon was cranked up, waking the dead from here to the Swiss border.

4:20 p.m. Camel herding on a remote corner of the lot. Iyad likes to supplement his camels' diet of pricey hay, oats, and dates with free grass from the field. So far Ajax and Omar pretty docile about being dragged out here to graze. Gives me a little free time to relax and obsess about my personal problems. Have decided that getting plastic surgery was the dumbest thing I ever did, next to burning down half of Berkeley. Never should have let Connie talk me into it. OK, maybe it helped a little in dragooning Sheeni to the altar, but it certainly complicates trying to hide out in France. I think Reina is completely turned off by the Mrs. Fulke routine. Let's face it: has any woman in history ever been successfully wooed by a guy dressed like a chick—especially an old ugly one? Not even a randy lesbian would find Mrs. Fulke appealing. Plus, I'm so busy shoveling shit I barely have time to scan the audiences for my goateed wife. I'm trying to maintain a positive outlook though. At least the countryside is spectacular. Some people pay big bucks to vacation in this beauty spot; I get to enjoy it with all expenses paid.

Have you ever noticed how camels walk? Pretty funny. First they move both feet on one side of their body, then swing along both feet on the other side. You could get seasick just watching them. Hey! Where are those guys going?

7:46 p.m. Ajax and Omar are back. Iyad is furious. How was I to know they'd want to spend Happy Hour in the Vienne River? I don't see how a 132-pound old lady can be expected to control a ton-and-a-half of rampaging dromedaries. Iyad says I should hit their legs with a stick. Right. I can just imagine how they'd react to that. I'd rather hit Iyad with a stick. Running after his camels made me miss out on dinner, always the high point of a serf's day. I was reduced to buying a bag of salted nuts from Carlos, one of our ever-hustling snack vendors. He had the nerve to charge me full price too.

10:05 p.m. Stepped out of the camel van for a breath of air and beheld an awesome sight. The vast castle on the hill is illuminated at night. It floated above the twinkling lights of Chinon like some immense relic of a grander age. Princes and kings probably hung out up there centuries ago. Knights in armor may have fought and died on its crumbling battlements. Now the Age of Chivalry was long past and I am alone in the dark with my head in the stars and my feet ankle-deep in you know what.

FRIDAY, July 22 — Another day, another 16 tons dumped on the pile. All this exercise is reviving my depressed hormones. I'm finding I very much miss the physical aspect of married life. Let's face it: once you've intimately known Sheeni Saunders on a semi-regular basis, it's hard to return to those lonely dates with your palm. I go at it anyway, though on the other side of the partition Omar and Ajax moan in protest. Those dudes aren't getting any either (unlike the debauched monkeys), but maybe all that cud chewing keeps them pacified. Sorry if my journal is beginning to read like "Doctor Doolittle," but I do spend a lot of my time talking to the animals. Well, cursing them at any rate.

During lunch a delivery van pulled onto the lot with a package for Morag Fulke. Very gratifying for the lowliest serf to be singled out in this way. The box contained a shiny new cellphone and this note from Connie:

> Dear Morag,
>
> Forgive me for assuming that you will be just like Paulo and run after that crippled parrot girl. I don't know what she's peddling, but my guess is it's attracting a crowd. I've figured out that the police must have discovered your cellphone and were trying to triangulate your location every time you used it. So you must toss it in the river and use this one instead.
>
> Our wedding is set for Saturday. I can't wait. My Paulo made one last run for it, but we intercepted him near San

Bernardino. I think he was trying to reach Mexico via secondary roads, the silly dear. Hope he is capable of functioning on our honeymoon, since I want a little Saunders on the way as soon as possible.

Hope you find his sister soon. I hear you are doing a good job building sympathy for your side in the French press. I know our father-in-law is furious at this turn of affairs. Good work!

Your loving sister-in-law,
Connie

It's a shame I have to miss Connie's wedding. I'm sure it will be a gala affair, even with my mother-in-law in attendance. Nice of Connie to send me a new phone, but there's no way I can ditch the old one. I'm expecting a call on it any minute now from Sheeni. She just has to call me soon. She has to!

4:48 p.m. Spotting Reina leaving the lot, I tossed down my shovel and caught up with her. She was walking into town to buy fresh produce for her babies and consented to have Mrs. Fulke tag along.

"Your forehead's looking better, Rick," she commented.

"Call me Morag. I saw your act, Reina. I think it's great."

"Thank you. I think we're improving. I'm sorry, uh, Morag, that we can't sit together at meals."

"Your Mr. Granley seems rather attentive."

"He's very nice. He's nearly twice my age and has a wife back in England. Madame Poco alerted me to that fact. Men rarely volunteer such information, I've found."

"We should all be shot," I conceded.

"Rick, I know you think you're married, but it really is a crime having sex with an underage girl."

Her glance, so full of hurt and reproach, took me aback. Frankly, I'd been hoping for a little more continental sophistication here. I could see no recourse except the truth.

"Sheeni's older than I am," I blurted out.

Reina halted in her tracks. "What! How old *are* you, Rick?"

"I'll be 15 next week."

"My God, Rick! You're just a baby! You should be home with

your parents."

"My parents don't want me. Nobody wants me."

Not a bad ploy. Reina put her arm around my shoulder and kissed me on my withered cheek. I tried to kiss her lips, but she drew back.

"None of that, Rick," she said. "In your country I could be arrested for kissing you. Your lawyers could sue me for corrupting a minor."

Damn, I knew it was a mistake telling the truth. It almost always is.

Didn't find the *Herald Tribune* in Chinon, but Reina picked up the Tours paper. No mention of me, but the entertainment page featured a large photo of T.P. with his hair slicked back and dressed in an oddly tailored, rather punkish orange suit. Image-molding by Mr. Bonnet? That would be my guess. The breathless article, translated by Reina, said he had finished recording his sensational new song and was rumored to be "a bad boy" with a certain Magda of the famed Three Magdas. I didn't point out that that would certainly be illegal, but when Reina commented "He's cute," I informed her that he was both married and going steady (a morally precarious dilemma I wouldn't mind grappling with myself).

SATURDAY, July 23 — Another anniversary of my wedding day. Another morning without soft caresses, without the touch of warm arms about me, without the tingle of excitement as I slide my engorged . . . well, never mind. A gloomy day in more ways than one. Rain threatens. Circus people hate rain, Iyad informs me. It can cut attendance by one-half or more. Everything gets soggy. Animals get restless. Acrobats and aerialists resort more often to the rosin bag, but still hands can slip, tricks don't work, people can get hurt. Townies sit on their mitts and don't applaud. Who needs it?

11:45 a.m. As I was wheelbarrowing my way past the office caravan in a chilly downpour, Madame Poco waved me over. She said if Captain Lapo delegated any more of his work to me, he could just retire and collect his old-age pension. I noticed he seemed to have considerable leisure to loiter about the coffee urn and chat up the midgets. So Mrs. Fulke put her excrement-caked foot down and told him she would not be feeding any more of those cute little live bunnies to the snakes. That was his job.

"And what'dya thinka you wassa eatin' for dinner lasta night?" he demanded.

"We had grilled lapin. It was delicious."

"That'sa rabbit!"

I trust the ignorant old fool was misinformed. Mrs. Fulke has adopted an ethical stand and for once is sticking to it.

3:18 p.m. Still raining. What a mess. Madame Poco had another truckload of sawdust delivered, which we serfs swarmed over with rakes and shovels. Dispersed it about the public areas in a futile effort to keep the mud at bay. I found a wide sombrero-type hat in the camel van to shield Mrs. Fulke's delicate face from the rain. Toiling away, I looked like the world's oldest peasant, but was rarely given as much as a glance by the passing townies. Fortunate for them we aren't living two centuries before. One word from me and those candy-munching aristocrats would be off to the guillotine.

7:05 p.m. I slipped in out of the rain and caught Mr. Granola's act, which I'd characterize as the lazy man's acrobatics. He stands there blowing his police whistle while his monkeys work out on a miniature trampoline. They perform back-flips, link up by tail in mid-air, leap onto the next guy's shoulders until they're stacked four high, etc. A real crowd-pleaser, since who isn't charmed by the antics of our little primate cousins? Few would suspect that behind closed doors the monkey van is the scene of near nonstop total depravity. And what's our genetic overlap with these crazed sex fiends? Over 96 percent, I'm told. It's no wonder a healthy young primate like me is so on edge all the time. Let's face it: I'm not getting my rightful share. And what about Mr. Granola? That British twit associates professionally with lecherous monkeys, yet stashes his wife in a distant country. I must remind Reina to bolt her door at all times.

SUNDAY, July 24 — Question: When do circus people get a day off?

Answer: In winter or when they die—whichever comes first.

Today we have three shows scheduled, plus we move again tonight. And it's still raining buckets. I wonder what suicide by letting yourself be sucked down into French mud would feel like?

Well, Connie must be married and on her honeymoon by now. I'm sure I would have heard from her if things hadn't gone as planned. Another Saunders successfully hog-tied. I hope the news gets back to Sheeni, and she is inspired by her brother's example to come forward and resume her rightful place in my bed. I miss her dreadfully, and I'm sure she must feel the same way at least somewhat. Besides, a fetus should be at its father's side if proper bonding is to take place. I'm not making that up. I read it somewhere in a magazine. Something to do with the timbre of the male voice resonating through the amniotic fluids. Too bad I hadn't thought to cut out the article. I'd send it to Trent.

2:26 p.m. Since Mrs. Fulke has ceased to be his doormat, Captain Lapo is manifesting new respect toward my alter ego. Carving up horsemeat for the bear, he mentioned that one can earn considerably more money in the circus if you work up some kind of act. For example, if there's a glitch in the program, he runs out to do a little fire-eating. In a pinch he can also pull out the loose skin under his chin and pound a nail through it. Very helpful in keeping the townies appeased until the next act gets ready.

He offered to teach me fire-eating, which he demonstrated after lunch. He tears narrow strips of cloth and wraps them tightly around the ends of his slim metal torches. These he dips in ordinary gasoline siphoned from the tank of the pony van. No, he doesn't coat his lips or mouth with anything. He just lights a torch and straight in it goes, then he blows out great plumes of billowing fire. The trick, he says, is to exhale steadily while the torch is in your mouth. If you forget and inhale, gas fumes can be drawn down into your lungs and ignite with explosive consequences. He offered to let me try, but Mrs. Fulke shuddered and politely declined. Nor was she interested in the piercing routine when informed that no trick nails were employed. They are standard hardware-store nails pounded through living flesh. Do this daily and after a while you cease to bleed much. All very fascinating, but not for me.

I could tell Captain Lapo was pegging me for a mere shit-shoveling circus dilettante. Jugglers, he declared, always had a place in the circus. Same for stilt-walkers. But Mrs. Fulke, he sneered, was "too old" to learn those arts.

"Ever throw a knife?" he demanded.

"No," I admitted. "But I shot a man recently."

That impressed him, but sharpshooters, he said, were seldom employed by circuses these days. Too much trouble from the "damn insurance leeches."

11:48 p.m. On the road at last. I'm riding back with the camels this time as it is too hard on the nerves to watch the scenery crawl by at Iyad's anemic pace. Has the guy no testosterone at all? He gets passed by nuns on scooters, for God's sake. Rain stopped, but it was still murder packing up. Everyone and everything slipping and sliding in the mud. Roustabouts wrestling with dripping tents that can weigh double or triple their dry weight. Everyone short-tempered from fatigue. Ajax and Omar not happy about being asked to haul heavily loaded trucks out of deep muck. Sure those guys smell bad, but I'm beginning to see things from their point of view. What this circus really needs is an elephant or two. Can't write any more. Somebody just passed the mother of all camel farts.

MONDAY, July 25 — We're in Poiters, one of the larger towns on our route. Could be good for Sheeni-spotting. Not exactly mountainous, but we're atop a fair-sized hill. Seems well off the beaten path—where goateed young men might lay low to foster internal growth.

Managed to cadge another shower from Reina after our usual erection-delayed breakfast. (I am speaking here of tent erections, although I cannot say I remained entirely flaccid within her sexy shower. Too bad she wasn't in there with me.) She's much friendlier these days since she found out I was just a kid and not a depraved virgin despoiler. Somehow, though, I have to subvert the new and ghastly sisterly feelings she is now manifesting toward me. I have a sister already. They are of limited usefulness, though Joanie usually can be counted on for a decent gift of birthday cash. That reminds me, I must think of a way to sneak her my address.

After nearly a week of observation I can now categorize the men who are romantically interested in Reina. They are many and varied, but I'm dismissing from consideration all the roustabouts who strip her mentally every time she walks by. These oafs do not discriminate, sometimes even letting their lascivious glances linger on Mrs. Fulke's knobby bod. No, I'm concerned here only with potential contenders.

Most forward of the lot is the safari-garbed, monkey-manipulating Mr. Granley. Reina told me without embarrassment that she admires his "dry English wit," no evidence of which I've seen. Fortunately, she thinks less of his clandestine wife. Then there is the tall clown Marcel Fazy, who paints his face as if someone just goosed him. He's always watching her and occasionally dines at her table, though he doesn't say much. I recognize all the subtle signs though. He's got it bad. Next is the affable Spanish engineering student Carlos, who sells tickets and hawks snacks. Fairly good-looking and dangerously close to her age. Claims to be a bird lover, though I know the sort of birds he likes to love. She's actually been in his caravan for drinks. Runaway camels may trample his prostrate body if he tries that again. Then there's Iyad, whose incessant flirting may just be a cultural thing. My guess is his wife keeps him on a fairly short chain and must nightly drain dry his testosterone reserve. Finally, there's Tarkan, the eldest son of the Batur clan. This is an entire family of crazed riders who fling themselves off their stampeding ponies to gyrate improbably in mid-air. Tarkan is a muscular lad from the Omar Sharif school of dark smoldering eyes. They smolder especially when he talks to Reina, which he does with alarming frequency. Hers sparkle a bit in return, I've noticed. We don't see much of ol' Tarkan socially since Mrs. Batur does all the cooking for her brood. He only drops by the cookhouse tent for the occasional coffee to go. Madame Poco tolerates this brazen pilferage despite the fact that the Batur compensation plan is said not to include free eats.

2:12 p.m. Mrs. Fulke snubbed all three decrepit band members at lunch today, though I don't think they noticed. They've been rehearsing a new addition to their repertoire: *"Heee, Lekker Ding."* Is there no escape from the torment? More proof of Frank's musical smarts: he always refused to record novelty numbers.

Before heading back to the shit mines, Mrs. Fulke swiped a few oranges and eased into the seat beside Marcel. She smiled warmly and asked him if he would kindly show her how to juggle.

The clown recoiled and looked at me as if I had just asked him to suck a few of my intimate appendages.

"Who the hell are you?" he demanded.

From my dealings with Señor Nunez I knew that clowns can be crotchety, morose, and aloof. I also knew Marcel knew who the hell I was. His accent I couldn't quite place. Rumor had it he was from Montreal.

"You make juggling look so easy," I enthused. "Is there some trick to it you can show me?"

"Why should I show you anything? If you're lonely, you're wasting your time with me."

"Show me how to juggle," I hissed. "And I'll tell you something interesting about Reina."

Marcel took my oranges and demonstrated the basics of two-ball juggling, then the more challenging three-ball cascade. The secret, he said, was to practice making consistent tosses up to about eye level. Do that right, and the catches take care of themselves. Also, keep your eyes forward and don't look at your hands.

"So what do you know about Reina?" he demanded.

"She's in love with that missing American horn player."

Marcel sighed. "You are misinformed, Mrs. Fulke. Reina loves only her damn parrots."

"What about Tarkan?"

"Tarkan is an ignorant peasant."

"Perhaps. But he's a handsome ignorant peasant."

"Such gossip does not interest me," announced the clown, getting up. "Good luck with your juggling."

An illuminating conversation. Clearly, Tarkan is the main threat here.

6:28 p.m. Then again, I could be wrong. Both Reina and Carlos absent from the cookhouse tent at dinner time. Slipping out for some emergency sleuthing, I spied Reina ladling up soup in her caravan. Seated opposite her at the intimate dinette: the grinning Spaniard. The twit had brought along his guitar!

7:28 p.m. Tormented heart assuaged slightly by envelope slipped to me by Madame Poco. Payday at last. Thin wad of crisp euros. Works out to less than a euro per ton. The question of the hour: Where in rural France does one purchase a handgun?

11:10 p.m. Fortunate that circus people such workaholics. Spanish seduction interrupted by evening performance, then Mrs. Fulke showed up requesting use of Reina's sewing machine. Grateful finally for those tedious hours in Redwood High sewing class. While I patched nonexistent holes, Spanish interloper sang away in a mellow tenor. Bad news: Reina's birds very musical. They obviously dig guitar music and Catalan love songs. Reina not exhibiting any violent revulsion either. Hope she realizes it would just be a cheap fling. That guy's going back to college in September. At 11:00 she kicked us both out, citing need for sleep. Carlos made it back to his caravan alive; not conked on head by own guitar. François was willing, but victim judged too in shape for precipitous assault.

11:58 p.m. Someone just called. On my old cellphone!

I dropped my oranges and debated whether to answer it. Finally did after the third ring.

"Hello," I whispered. "Sheeni, is that you?"

No answer. Just the sound of someone breathing.

"Sheeni, if it's you, please say something. Are you OK? Where are you, darling?"

Still no reply.

"Sheeni, if you don't say something, I'm going to hang up. This could be the cops trying to trace my phone. Please talk to me, baby."

Once again, no reply. I reluctantly terminated the call. Can't practice juggling any more. Too upset. Even François laid low by double whammy of girl trouble.

TUESDAY, July 26 — An unfamiliar fanfare woke me in the middle of the night. Not a visitation from God or the good camel fairy. It was my new cellphone chirping away. I fumbled for its elusive "Talk" button.

"Hello?" I gasped.

"Greetings! This is Mrs. Saunders."

My heart seized, then I realized it was not Sheeni's 5,000-year-old mother. It was Connie trying out her new name.

"I am visualizing the sperm swimming toward the welcoming egg," she announced.

Well, at least someone I knew was having a sex life. I congratulated her on a mission well done. She and her new hubby were honeymooning on Kauai, a small island chosen for its remoteness, restricted transportation options, and solo airport.

"How's your new husband adjusting?" I inquired.

"Very well, Rick. I think he's getting into it. He's certainly getting into me often enough. Nothing like the tropics to bring out the animal in a guy. Any news from Sheeni?"

I told her about my phantom phone call; Connie was not encouraging.

"Rick, you've got to ditch that phone. It was probably the police!"

"I don't think so, Connie. It was feminine breathing I heard."

"Breathing is breathing, Rick. There is no discernible sex difference, except in the cases of dirty old men. And then only if they're playing with themselves."

I was surprised by her expertise in this area. "You get calls like that, Connie?"

"Of course. All attractive young women do. Rick, you're much too desperate as usual. Don't answer that phone again. Speaking of desperate, have you made it with Paulo's bird chick yet?"

I enumerated the many obstacles in the way of that golden dream. She replied with her customary advice.

"Don't be too needy, Rick. Make her come to you."

I said I didn't think that was too likely as I was living in a filthy van with two smelly camels. Connie passed on one last piece of advice.

"Here's a tip from Paulo, Rick. He says to watch out for the littlest monkey."

Made no sense to me, but I thanked her and wished them both well. Paul Saunders is married at last. Encouraging progress has been made.

10:18 a.m. Unwary Carlos does not lock his caravan door, a discovery Mrs. Fulke made while its occupant and the rest of the company were having breakfast. There are two kinds of engineering types: total slobs and neat freaks. Our Carlos belonged to the latter category. His caravan looked like he was anticipating an inspection by the President of France. All pencils sharpened to a point and lined up in order of length. How anal can you get? Very nice laptop the paranoid twit protects with a password. I typed in "asshole," but that didn't work His guitar he stores under the rear bed. I considered snipping its strings, but instead loosened the tuning pegs. He'll be in for a surprise if he tries any emergency serenades. His sock drawer turned up a framed photo of an attractive chick. I doubt she is his sister. Also some perfumed letters (in Spanish) signed "Lucia" in a looping feminine scrawl. His bottom drawer yielded the biggest surprise: an immense stash of folded condoms. Accordioned out they'd stretch the length of an aircraft carrier. Obviously the guy was planning some serious fucking. I thought about confiscating the lot, but borrowed only a dozen for future personal needs. Call me an optimist, but I feel even Mrs. Fulke needs protection.

2:15 p.m. Back from a stroll into town. I'm hopeful I've found the confederate I was seeking. Can't write more. Shit backing up and monkeys are jonesing for postcoital snacks.

6:32 p.m. A shocking incident, diary. A few of us were lingering in the cookhouse after dinner when we were startled by piercing female screams. Everyone within earshot ran toward the source, which turned out to be Carlos's caravan. The door flew open and out leaped a distraught young girl clutching her torn clothing, followed by the red-faced Spaniard. Most of the screaming was in French or Spanish, but a stunned Reina managed to translate for me. The girl claimed Carlos tried to rape her, but he was denying this vigorously to Madame Poco and her burly security chief.

More screaming and shouting; I insisted Reina tell me what was happening.

"She says she tried to get away, but he was too strong. So she begged him to use a condom, but he refused—even though he told her he had some. Now Madame Poco is asking if he has any condoms. The girl is shouting, 'In his bottom drawer! In his bottom drawer! That's where he said he keeps them'."

Of course, a quick inspection confirmed her testimony, and the attempted rapist was indignantly tossed off the lot. He's lucky he wasn't lynched by a mob of angry midgets. Mrs. Fulke managed to have a few words with him as he was hastily hitching up his caravan. Yes, Madame Poco had comforted the girl (and, I noticed, slipped her some cash), but she might still tell her parents. I suggested to Carlos that he make for the Spanish border as quickly as possible. He thanked both Reina and me as he tearfully said his farewells. Hey, don't mention it, guy. Anything to help a buddy.

11:42 p.m. Another extraordinary incident. This one was not entirely planned. As arranged, Élise knocked on my door at 10 p.m. Accompanying her was a friend she introduced as Zoé. She looked even tougher than Élise, but perhaps it was just her superiority in piercings. Next to Zoé, multi-studded Élise looked practically intact.

"This place is the pigsty," announced Élise in her schoolgirl English.

"Actually it's a camel sty," I replied.

"You reside here?" inquired Zoé.

"Yes, I do."

"Cool," she replied. "I like very much."

Zoé, I sensed, was not a person of the highest standards. For example, her skimpy t-shirt, though alluring, was not entirely clean.

"You have my money?" asked Élise, sprawling on a hay bale.

I handed her the second *E*50 installment for a job well done. She slipped it into the pocket of her short shorts.

"That guy very cute," she commented. "I not scream really."

"Doesn't matter," I pointed out. "You're only 15. He would still get in trouble."

"I always in trouble," said Zoé, taking the bale beside her friend. "Trouble I like."

To my surprise the girls appeared to be settling in to stay a while. I apologized for the smell and lack of refreshments.

"So, you want to do me?" asked Élise. Her friend giggled.

Rather nonplused, I asked her to repeat the question.

More giggling. French girls are very cute when they giggle.

"You want we do sex?"

An astounding question. My heart began to pound. "But, but, I'm a woman."

Élise ran a finger down my cheek. "You forgot the shaving, Mrs. Fuck."

"That's Fulke. I'm Scottish, you know. But, dear, I'm so old!"

"Stage makeup," said Élise. "Zoé and I use it when to Paris go shoplifting."

"Store guards no watch old ladies so much," explained her pal. "How old is Mrs. Fuck?"

"Sixteen," I lied.

"Same as me," replied Zoé, tugging at my blouse.

And then, diary, we all got naked and did it like monkeys on the hay bales. Naturally, they found it amusing that Mrs. Fulke kept her wig on the entire time. My companions not in Sheeni's class in terms of physical attributes, but I wasn't complaining. And I found the little gold rings through their shaven labia most engrossing. (Pubic hair now passé in France?) I didn't last five seconds the first time, but we tied off that condom and I soon rebounded sufficiently to please both girls. In one sweaty hour I doubled the number of chicks I had slept with and, like Trent, made a complete mockery of my marriage vows. I also discovered there's a geometrical progression in sex. One is nice. But two are four times more fun. Everywhere you grope there's another soft breast or enticing ass. Very earthy and grounding. We all just completely lost our heads and wallowed in carnality like horny beasts. Do camel aromas possess aphrodisiacal powers? I have strong empirical evidence (three knotted condoms) that they do.

The girls had to do me and run. Their parents are very strict. They don't permit them to stay out late.

WEDNESDAY, July 27 — Did I dream all that? No, there are the pilfered, much abused condoms. And there is that confirming twinge in my exhausted prostate. My first orgy. Where do I sign up for encores?

Waiting for that first angry slap of guilt, but so far my conscience is clear. Do sociopaths enjoy better sex lives? Perhaps Rick S. Hunter's first novel will explore that question in depth. It always helps to start one's literary career with a torrid best-seller.

For the record I should note that Mrs. Fulke discovered Élise loitering among the disaffected youth in the car park of the French equivalent of a convenience store. Employing the well-known principle that the tendency toward juvenile delinquency is directly proportional to the thickness of the eye makeup, Mrs. Fulke honed in on sullen Élise. It was all I could do to persuade her to wash her face, remove her nose stud, and change out of her slutty clothes for our agreed-upon transaction. Even so, I don't think she impressed Madame Poco as France's most innocent virgin. That may be why Madame Poco slipped her the hush money instead of calling the gendarmes. No doubt this isn't the first time one of her employees has been caught molesting a local. The romantic lives we circus people lead make us irresistibly attractive to those stuck in conventional humdrum lives. Oops, got to go. Time to start raking out the night's accumulation.

11:43 a.m. I have made a formal request to Iyad that he provide a mirror in his camel sty for Mrs. Fulke. Clearly, I'm growing up fast. Can no longer regard shaving as an occasional task like zit squeezing or penile measuring. Now a daily necessity. Fortunate that elderly ladies often bewhiskered or I might have blown my cover through inattentive grooming. Also helpful that 98 percent of my whiskers are as blond as Jane Mansfield. Speaking of matters feminine, Mrs. Fulke's b.o. beginning to contest for olfactory supremacy with camel odors. And thin blankets (we serfs cannot aspire to sheets) rather crusty from recent tidal wave of bodily fluids.

4:12 p.m. Back from an excursion to a Poiters launderette with Reina. Just the two of us alone in her station wagon with piles of intimate apparel. Unlike Mrs. Fulke, she favors the frilliest of undergarments. How I would love to slip those lacy confections on (and off) her exquisite limbs. French laundry machines most adept at sucking two-euro coins from pockets of impoverished proletariat. At least I had the smarts to stuff my entire odorous pile into one machine. Profligate Reina, I noticed, used three.

We watched our clothes revolve and discussed the previous day's shocking events.

"I still can't believe Carlos would do such a thing," said Reina. "He seemed so committed to his fiancée back in Barcelona."

"The guy was engaged?"

"Yes, Rick, to a very lovely girl named Lucia."

"Call me Morag. Then why was he putting the moves on you?"

"Don't be silly, Morag. He was just lonely. He missed his sweetheart."

"If he missed her so much, why was he singing love songs to *you*?"

"Carlos is a very romantic boy. He sings love songs all the time. They were not necessarily directed at me. He knew how much my babies loved his singing."

"What about all those condoms? The guy obviously had sex on the brain."

"You misjudge him, Rick. Carlos volunteers with a youth group that does disease-prevention outreach work. They distribute those condoms to at-risk young people."

"Call me Morag. Then he wasn't trying to seduce you?"

"Of course not, Morag. What gave you that idea?"

Uh-oh. I planted the jailbait in the wrong guy's caravan. There's *E*100 down the drain. Damn!

Reina leaned in close to whisper in my ear. I liked it when she did that.

"Are you worried I'm going to run away with some man?"

She smelled much better than I did.

"I wouldn't be if you ran away with me," I replied.

"And what about your wife?"

"She doesn't think we're married, Reina. We might not be. To tell the truth, we lied on the marriage form."

"But your baby-to-be is very real, Rick. You can't run away from it."

"I wish it was our baby-to-be, Reina darling."

She smiled. "You are a very sweet boy, Rick. Your Sheeni is a lucky girl."

"Yeah," I sighed. "Go tell *her* that—if you can find her."

7:04 p.m. We had some sort of cabbage stew for dinner. The embattled cookhouse crew wished to clean up early because we move again tonight. Those hard-working Serbians make Mrs. Fulke look like a pampered layabout. Nonstop toil from sunup to sundown, and all they get is a lot of grousing from ungrateful midgets, etc. Fortunately, like me, they barely comprehend a word of French.

Mrs. Fulke stopped by Marcel's table for a juggling tune-up. My oranges not cooperating. What a pickle puss. Greeted me like I was another visitation by the Black Death. OK, the guy has to paint on a silly face every day and pedal around on a tiny tricycle. But that doesn't mean he's exempt from the rules of civil discourse. After all, nobody forced him to become a clown. And I thought Canadians were supposed to be excessively polite. With his sour disposition, it's no wonder he sleeps alone—assuming he does. I don't actually have his caravan under surveillance. Anyway, he told me I was tossing the second orange too soon.

"Don't throw it until your first ball has reached its highest point," he snarled.

"Thanks," I said. "Well, it looks like Carlos won't be serenading Reina again."

He gave me a look that could freeze molten lava.

"That fool was wasting his time," he sniffed.

"Why do you say that?"

"Reina has a very strong maternal drive," he observed. "What does she call her birds?"

"Her babies," I admitted.

"Correct, Mrs. Fulke. She has five babies already. That girl doesn't need a man."

"You may be right. I hadn't thought of that."

"Looks like your little drama was all for nothing," he added, getting up and walking away.

What did he mean by that?

THURSDAY, July 28 — We're in Périgueux, another hillside town overlooking a meandering river. The name is pronounced like you're snorting up a hocker. Towns were built on hills in the old days to withstand attack from whichever marauding horde was on the warpath that week. Perhaps the Russians invaded at some point, since there's a big multi-domed church in the center of town that looks like a branch of the Kremlin. Never realized France was such a nation of rivers. Every couple of kilometers you're crossing another Distinguished Waterway. Big change from California where the sparse rivers are confined behind dams or dry up to a trickle in the summer.

Iyad has presented me an old cracked mirror in a dingy frame. Mrs. Fulke thanked him warily and nailed it to the wall of my sty. A cheerful and homey touch, assuming you grew up in a Halloween haunted house. The big news is one of Mr. Granola's monkeys, Number Eight, gave birth during the night. Not entirely a man of science, he named it Number Fourteen, even though there were only 12 other monkeys. Rather adorable little guy (the baby monkey, not Mr. Granola), stuck like glue to his mother's pendulous teat. Reina said the pair looked just like a monkey version of the Madonna and Child. When this blasphemy reached my ears, I stepped back quickly, but the expected thunderbolt never struck. Mr. G has instructed me that I am to be extra attentive in keeping the cage clean, yet am not to disturb the new mother. How exactly I am to accomplish this the twit didn't say.

I suppose Number Fourteen could be the littlest monkey that Paul warned me about. Does not impress one as evil spawn of the devil, but am prepared to defend myself should the hairy little milksucker turn on me.

After breakfast I called Madame Ruzicka to give her the bad news that I wouldn't be returning to my apartment. She said I had become so famous she was thinking of leaving it just as it was and opening it as a museum for tourists. Plus, there's that additional tourist draw, T.P., living just down the hall with Violet. (I trust he has explained this arrangement somehow to Apurva.) Madame R said all her tenants are proud to have had their garbage hauled out by the notorious Rick S. Hunter, and everyone is hoping that the young lovers are reunited soon. She said that when Madame Lefèbvre of the wig salon heard that a warrant had been issued for my arrest, she and her staff led an angry *manifestion* to the Palais de Justice.

"All of Paris is behind you, Rick," she assured me. "You are the most popular young man in France."

Very gratifying to the soul as Mrs. Fulke returned to her shovel and the exigencies of life as an itinerant serf.

1:45 p.m. Mr. Granola had some more competition at lunch today for the seat beside Reina. Madame Poco at last scraped up another horn player, a young guy named Jiri Mestan. A thin chain-smoker with that artsy sophistication impoverished European men like to project in lieu of driving a Porsche. His black leather jacket is such a cliché and the fatuous fedora was mere blatant affectation. Jean Gabin he is not. Jiri is Czech like Reina, but I'm not worried. She already has her babies; she doesn't need a man. Besides, I'm almost positive she loves me.

5:03 p.m. Mrs. Fulke visited with Reina while I cleaned out the monkey cage. Reina spends a good part of her free time cooing through the cage wire at the new baby. She's had a phone call from disgraced Carlos in exile in Barcelona.

"He told me he never saw that girl before. She was waiting in his trailer when he returned from dinner. She had torn her own clothes!"

"Not likely," I sighed. "But what else do you expect the guy to say? They always try to blame the victim."

"I believe Carlos," Reina insisted. "I saw Madame Poco give that girl money. That's why she did it. For the money!"

"Could be, Reina. But it's all water over the dam now."

"No, it's not. Carlos's family is very upset. And so is Lucia."

"He told them?!" I asked, incredulous.

"Yes, Morag, he felt he had to."

What is this mania for incendiary candor? All that simpleton had to say was he returned early because he missed Lucia and he would have been home free. Back in the bosom of his family and some nice bonus pussy besides. Jesus, some people are just not equipped for Life in the Real World.

Time to change the subject.

"That Jiri is a fast worker," I observed.

"Who? Oh, Jiri's an old family friend. I've known him since I was six. My bird Jiri is named after him."

"Did you get him the job?"

"I did suggest him. I felt I had to make it up to Madame Poco for Paul leaving without notice."

"What makes you think Jiri will stick around?"

"Well, he needs the work. And he loves me very much."

"What!"

"He was kind of my boyfriend back before my accident. It was just, what do you Americans call it, puppy love?"

"I'm Scottish," Mrs. Fulke testily reminded her. "So how do you feel about him now?"

"I don't know," she said, making silly faces at the suckling baby. "We'll have to see, won't we?"

7:51 p.m. Did some snooping around the lot after dinner. Jiri drives a little Twingo-sized truck with a primitive homemade camper built onto the back. Not even a caravan to his name. Hope he's not planning to shower at Reina's. Mrs. Fulke may be monopolizing her hot water. Could he be the one Paul was warning me about? Could "littlest monkey" be some sort of jazz slang for old boyfriend? Or is Mestan Czech for "monkey?" Jiri not very little, but he is cadaverous. Too bad cigarettes take so long to kill a person. The guy must have insatiable oral needs. Never seen without a Gauloise or trumpet in his mouth. I'm amazed he can remember whether to blow or suck. Probably taken from the breast too soon. I'm a bottle baby so in total empathy. As Sheeni has pointed out, it's a miracle I never got hooked on cigarettes. Still, I hate to think of Jiri's nicotine-stained maul besmirching Reina's innocent lips. Most unfortunate that saintly celibate Carlos no longer here to keep her occupied in the evenings. Somebody should have alerted me that the guy was a eunuch. I miss his nice singing!

11:12 p.m. I was ruminating on means of introducing plastic explosives into cigarettes when my old cellphone rang. Wrenching emotional turmoil, but in the end I had to answer it.

"Hello?" I said.

No fucking reply.

"Sheeni, darling, let's not play these games. Speak to me, baby. Tell me where you are. Or at least let me know if you're coming back. It's torture not to know where we stand. This is the longest we've ever been separated. Nearly a month! Do you miss me, darling?"

No reply. Just breathing.

"Sheeni, I can't stand this. Are you trying to drive me insane? I have to hang up in case this is the cops. I'm going to hang up now. OK?"

No reply.

"Sheeni, have you been reading the papers? Everyone's on our side! We're the most popular couple in France. Your father is powerless against us now. It's safe for you to come back. I'm sure if you did, I could resume my video career. We could sign some big endorsement deals! You could buy your own private school in Paris. The teachers wouldn't dare give you a 'B,' not that they would anyway. You'd get into the Sorbonne for sure. How about it, darling?"

No reply. I screamed and flung the damn phone across my sty, breaking Mrs. Fulke's new mirror. Seven years bad luck?

Who cares? I'm totally sick at heart. I just destroyed my last tenuous link to Sheeni. The phone (and my life) are in pieces.

FRIDAY, July 29 — Life sucks. That is my new personal philosophy. Life sucks. Shit happens. And then you die. The same story for thousands of generations. Previous residents of this town hung out, made cheese, crushed grapes, and could look forward to getting sacked by Vikings, slaughtered by Huns, raped by Normans, tortured by the Inquisition, or machine-gunned by Hitler's SS. It's the same old, same old. So I sit around in my dank sty, toss oranges in the air, and await the next calamity. Finally making some progress. Can keep two on the move for nearly ten seconds.

Angry Iyad just extracted *E*5 from Mrs. Fulke for mirror breakage. I have now been shoveling shit for this outfit for almost two weeks and have less money than when I started. My new motto: Serfdom Sucks.

11:08 a.m. Beez the bear sulking because everyone over at the monkey van oohing and aahing over the new baby. I know how he feels. I showed up to shovel and there was Reina fastened rather familiarly onto Tarkan's dusky arm. Hasn't she had enough of that apish infant and Turkish pony jockey? She said hello, but naturally Tarkan barely acknowledged the lackey who cleans up after his ponies.

"Number Eight is such a good mother," remarked Reina. "I wonder who the father is?"

"Number Three most likely," said Tarkan. "He's the biggest and the strongest."

Yes, that would be that lout's criterion for reproductive success. I don't suppose he's ever even cracked a book. First time I had seen him without his hat. The guy has the hairline of a retarded gorilla. Barely an inch of forehead divides bushy eyebrows from thick black hair. There's a dude who will never have to worry about going bald, assuming he lives past next week.

Things got interesting when Mr. Granola showed up. Reina released her grip, so Tarkan let a hand rest casually on her shoulder. This obliged Mr. G to remove and re-coil his bullwhip—a phallic symbol if ever there was one. Meanwhile, as we were chatting away pleasantly like civilized adults, Number Three decided to get it on hot and heavy with Number Seven. That sort of thing does cast a pall in mixed company. Virginal Reina blushed crimson—doubtless inspired by the knowledge that this was exactly what her human companions (all three) aspired to do to her.

2:26 p.m. Dyspeptic Marcel the clown not impressed when Mrs. Fulke demonstrated her new ball facility after lunch. Said he had seen better juggling from an armless blind man. He seemed even deeper in the dumps than usual, so I decided to draw him out.

"Did you know that new horn player used to be Reina's boyfriend?" Mrs. Fulke inquired.

Marcel gave me a look the color of midnight in the dungeon.

"He thinks he still is."

"Perhaps, but Reina doesn't need a man."

"She didn't," he commented ominously.

"What, what do you mean by that?"

"Are you blind as well as stupid, Mrs. Fulke? It's the new monkey. It has changed the equation completely."

"How so?"

"Reina has seen a real baby—or a close enough approximation. Much more cuddly than a parrot."

"She wants one herself?"

"Nature cannot be denied, Mrs. Fulke. But who will be chosen? That is the question. We are about to witness an epic struggle between the man of action and the artistic personality."

"Tarkan Batur versus Jiri Mestan?"

"And perhaps other contenders," he snapped, strolling away.

Beware the littlest monkey. Paul was right!

7:17 p.m. War may have commenced. First skirmish at today's matinee? I noticed during the wild-riding Batur Family performance there were some decidedly flat notes erupting from the horn section—especially when Tarkan was attempting something particularly neck-breaking. These musical punctuations inspired the audience to laugh rather than cheer. Scowling Tarkan not amused.

No sign in the crowd of my goateed wife, alas. Much less facial hair out here in the sticks than in Paris, so she'd be easy to spot. Lots of pretty girls though. Never seen such a concentration of beauty. No wonder the Germans were always invading.

10:42 p.m. Black despair. Lovely Reina just seen strolling in the moonlight with both contenders. Noticed Marcel skulking in shadows. Wish he'd do the honorable thing and waste the competition. Aren't clowns supposed to have a dark side? I could see him laughing maniacally as he flails away with his bloody hatchet. Jesus, sometimes I even scare myself.

My problem? I think my orgy has worn off. Despite prolonged mental funk and fresh new "Life Sucks" philosophy, hormones are reasserting themselves. I need it bad and I don't particularly care where I get it. Not a very enlightened attitude, but, hey, it works for the roustabouts. Not to mention Number Three. Yes, God, for my next life, I'm praying I return as a monkey.

SATURDAY, July 30 — Why do these Saturdays roll around like clockwork to remind me of my missing wife? It's a hell of a way to start the weekend. Next time I'm going to get married on a Monday. That day already starts out depressing.

Mr. Granola showed up at breakfast with his moustache waxed and sticking straight out obscenely at the sides like hairy red dagger points. You'd think being married, over 30, and English would be handicap enough for the guy. Love propels men in strange directions, as I can attest as Mrs. Fulke's bra straps chafe ever deeper into my shoulders. She's so much less fun to be than the late, lamented Carlotta—that sprightly wannabe vamp, who was born to tease. Let's face it: Mrs. Morag Fulke is just an ugly old crone with bad b.o. and horrible clothes. *Nobody* is going to ask her to the prom.

10:45 a.m. New scandal wracking the Cirque Coco-Poco. Someone has immersed Jiri Mestan's prized trumpet in a vat of oily sludge drained from the crankcase of the diesel generator. Amazingly, this act of vandalism cannot be laid at my doorstep. I didn't do it. Honest! Now there is fear that grit has worked its way into the valves, necessitating a total rebuild. Therefore, outraged Jiri reduced to using the circus's dented loaner horn, still redolent with Paul Saunder's talented saliva. Despite this encumbrance, Madame Poco has warned him to play it straight. Further musical improvisations will not be tolerated. She asked Tarkan if he had any knowledge of the deed, but he responded as if the whole matter were beneath his contempt.

11:12 a.m. Just received a call from Violet, the sexy Brit who is bending over backwards (and forwards?) for T.P. She got my new number from Madame Ruzicka and was checking in to see how France's best-loved fugitive was getting on. I told her my life was only slightly worse than that of a deep-shaft coal miner in China. Violet was sympathetic, but had more urgent matters to discuss. Apurva has just hopped a plane in San Francisco. No, she is not going to visit her poor exiled bro in India. She arrives in Paris tonight!

"Uh-oh," I gasped. "What does Trent say?"

"Not a great deal, Rick. He just lies face down on my bed and moans. I think the poor dear is on emotional overload. Mr. Bonnet is merciless. Trent has made six media appearances in the last four days. Did you see him on TV?"

"Sorry, Violet. I don't have a TV."

"No, you wouldn't, I suppose. Well, he was marvelous, of course.

The French love that he's so charismatic and speaks their language. But now I'm afraid he's having a nervous breakdown. You're his best friend, Rick. What should I do?"

Why does everyone suppose Trent and I are pals? Just because he hasn't ratted on me (yet) to the cops doesn't mean we've stopped despising each other.

"Well, Violet, my advice would be to move Trent back into my apartment and to pretend you're just friends while Apurva's there."

"But what if she wants to sleep with my darling?"

"Well, does Trent wish to sleep with her?"

"Of course not. He loves me!"

"Then he should just tell her he's temporarily impotent from the strain of becoming a media superstar. He could tell her that Elvis had the same problem back in 1955."

"I never knew that, Rick."

"Violet, I just made it up. Elvis had girls coming out of his ears. But it always helps to have some credible facts on your side when you're telling a major whopper."

"You don't think we should tell Apurva the truth?"

"You can if you want, but it'll get ugly. Apurva is pretty formidable in her own polite way. Might be too much for Trent to cope with."

"Do you think she could get . . . violent?"

"Probably not. But when the shit's approaching the fan, my strategy is to lie early and lie often. You can buy some time, send Apurva home appeased, then figure out your long-term plan."

"Sensible advice, Rick. How did you get to be so wise?"

"A difficult childhood, Violet. It works every time."

Trent has all the luck. Not only is he sleeping nightly with his flexible mistress, but he will soon be reunited with his loving wife. Personally, I would be content to achieve even one of those pleasant states.

4:28 p.m. During today's matinee, Mrs. Fulke wandered over to the Batur encampment to chat up Tarkan's mom. Mrs. Batur not that unattractive considering she has seven kids and a moustache. The whole clan travels in a giant truck-like caravan pulled by a big semi-tractor. She was alone with just the two little ones, so she invited Mrs. Fulke in for a cup of strong Turkish coffee and some homemade sweets. Most impressed by her homemaking skills. Interior of polished dark wood neat as a pin and you could eat off any surface. Eventually, the girl chat got around to the topic of her handsome eldest son's marital prospects.

"I trust you've selected a suitable girl for him from your village," I said.

"Our home is in Istanbul, Mrs. Fuck. It's hardly a village."

"That's Fulke. I'm Scottish, you know. But certainly you wish your son to marry a Turkish girl."

"I wish him to marry a girl who will make him happy. And give us lovely grandchildren."

"But, of course, she must be of your faith."

"That would be nice, Mrs. Fulke. We are Christians, you know."

"Oh."

I thought that guy on the wall looked a lot like Jesus. Damn. Who'd have thought they'd have Christians in far-off Turkey?

"Your Tarkan is exhibiting some signs of an inclination toward Miss Vesely."

"Reina is a lovely girl. And so patient in training her dear parrots."

"She's Czech, you know."

"Her family is many generations in the circus and very well thought of. Has she sent you as her emissary to arrange the marriage details?" she asked, beaming expectantly.

Somehow our chat had gone seriously off-course.

"Er, no," I replied. "It is my understanding that Miss Vesely is engaged to Mr. Mestan."

"I do not believe that to be the case, Mrs. Fulke," she replied, still smiling but not as radiantly.

"Oh? Are you aware she named one of her parrots after Mr. Mestan?"

"That is of no consequence. It was before she met my son."

It was time, I decided, for desperate measures.

"Because of her accident, Miss Vesely is incapable of bearing children!"

No longer smiling, Mrs. Batur sipped her coffee, then spoke. "I don't know what your interest in this matter is, Mrs. Fulke. I understood you to be employed here as an animal attendant. I did not feel it was my place to inquire why someone of your age and sex would want such a job. I can tell you that my husband has made discreet inquiries with Reina's aunt in Paris. Madame Ruzicka assured him that there were no medical impediments to her niece enjoying a happy and prolific marriage. Now, if you will excuse me, I must begin our dinner preparations."

Setting down her cup and mumbling inanities, Mrs. Fulke lurched from the scene.

What a disaster. Why are parents these days so fucking progressive, enlightened, and tolerant? All parents, that is, except my own?

10:38 p.m. No TV, no radio, no book, no wife, no life. So I bought a bag of mixed nuts (no discount) and watched both evening performances. According to the law of averages, one of these days Tarkan is going to slip and be trampled by his ponies. Try as I might I could think of no scheme to hasten that tragedy. Villains in cowboy movies slip a burr under the hero's saddle, but Tarkan does his tricks bareback. Sudden noises can spook most horses, but circus ponies are inured to the loudest din. Perhaps enterprising Jiri will be more successful.

Curiously, I find I'm beginning to identify with our show. I get upbeat like the others when there's a straw house (sell-out performance), and smile proudly when the townies are enthusiastic like they were tonight. As they clapped and stomped, I found myself wishing they were applauding me. Even Omar and Ajax, I notice, step livelier when the crowd cheers. Perhaps that's what everyone needs to get out of bed in the morning: an adoring public.

SUNDAY, July 31, 1:42 a.m. — Reina just left. She unexpectedly dropped by the camel sty to discuss my conversation with Tarkan's mom. News gets around fast. All I could offer her were some well-bruised oranges, a seat on a hay bale, and Mrs. Fulke's embarrassed apologies.

"The Baturs were quite mystified by you, Rick," she commented, peeling her orange. "They asked me if I thought Jiri had bribed you to say such things."

I groaned and knocked my head against the partition, startling my roommates on the other side. A cascade of camel piss splashed against the corroded floor.

"I said I didn't think so," she continued, "and suggested that one has to make allowances for the eccentricities of the aged."

"That was nice of you, Reina dear."

"It's a good thing you're such a hard worker, Rick. Mr. Batur commented that the pony van has never been so clean. He's inclined to overlook your interference in this matter."

"That's nice of him. I guess. Are you going to marry that turkey?"

"I believe people from Turkey are called Turks, Rick. As for Tarkan and me, I don't know. I haven't made up my mind."

"The guy is totally wrong for you, Reina."

"I think I know him considerably better than you do, Rick."

"You can't marry Jiri either. He's going to live maybe another decade tops. You want to be a widow before you're 30?"

"Jiri's making an effort to cut back on his smoking, Rick."

"From what—14 packs a day to 12? What's the big rush, Reina? You're only 17."

"I'm nearly 18, Rick. And you should talk. Why did you get married so young?"

A good question. Reading back through my journal, though, it seemed like quite a sensible idea at the time.

"OK, Reina darling, here's the solution: you wait a couple of years, I get all my personal affairs straightened out, and then we get married. If Sheeni has her baby, we can adopt it. She's said many times that motherhood doesn't interest her. Then we have a few more babies of our own. No problem there. Unlike Jiri and Tarkan, I've already proven that I'm fertile."

Reina handed me an orange section, and we masticated in quiet communion. Finally, she swallowed and spoke.

"In two years, Rick, you may be back in California. You and Sheeni may be together again and happily raising your daughter. You may have forgotten all about me by then."

"Not possible, Reina. I love you. I'll always love you."

"Haven't you said those very same words to Sheeni?"

She had me there. I shrugged and silently accepted another orange wedge.

"I do like you, Rick. That's certainly true. Perhaps, in fact, from our very first meeting on the stairs. I can't help wishing, though, that you demonstrated considerably more maturity, were unmarried, weren't wanted by the police, and were at least five years older."

Sounds like conditional love to me. Fortunately, that's the kind I'm used to.

"When you're 65, Reina, I'll be 63. The age issue is no big deal. Just don't rush into things and shackle yourself to the wrong guy because you want a baby."

"Who says I want a baby?"

"Well, don't you?"

"I don't know, Rick. I don't know what I want. I'm so confused. I know I want something."

I slipped my arm around her lovely shoulders. "Well," I cooed, "there's one thing we could try."

Three seconds later I was alone and picking orange peelings off my floor. Mrs. Fulke had struck out.

10:14 a.m. I was second in line for bathing at Reina's this morning. Yes, it's true. Jiri Mestan even smokes in the shower. When I stepped in for my lukewarm ablutions, there was his disgusting butt by the grungy drain. What a slob. He may also be losing his hair, if the great hideous glob of coarse black hairs he also left behind is any indication. The good news is I caught a glance in Reina's tiny mirror of Mrs. Fulke's bod while toweling off. All that manure shoveling is starting to pay off big. I've got muscles on top of muscles like you see in those magazines. Just my luck. Finally, I achieve a body good enough to flaunt, and I have to keep it totally swaddled in old-lady duds. Too bad Reina doesn't know what she's missing.

Moments later I had the pleasure of observing Reina eject a still-damp horn player from her caravan. She told him that his second-hand smoke was bad for her birds. Then she ejected Mrs. Fulke—saying she was still mad about yesterday. Hey, what did I do?

1:45 p.m. I wish Mrs. Fulke didn't have to dine with the old folks. All they talk about is their aches and pains, and what friend of theirs was just diagnosed with terminal fill-in-the-blank. And lately Captain Lapo either has developed a twitching leg palsy or has taken to playing footsie with Mrs. Fulke. Why haven't they passed a law requiring therapeutic neutering for randy old men? Let's face it: these lingering urges serve no useful biological function.

As lunch was concluding one of the Serbian kitchen slaves brought out a nice cake ablaze with candles. How sweet of them, I thought, to surprise me a day early. Then everyone gathered 'round and sang "Happy Birthday"—to Jiri Mestan! The pushy bastard had the nerve to cut in line a few hours ahead of me. I tried to be charitable and remind myself that poor emaciated Jiri was not destined to enjoy many more birthdays. But when he blew out the candles and grabbed Reina for a grossly intimate and prolonged kiss, François made a silent resolution. That was it for the horn player. Mr. Mestan had celebrated his last birthday.

Mrs. Fulke accepted her meager slice of cake and slunk over to the clowns' table. Marcel, I could sense, had not appreciated the exhibition any more than I did. He looked up from his cake and gave me a look that could choke a camel. Mrs. Fulke returned her warmest smile.

"What do you want?" he growled.

"Have you heard the news? Tarkan's parents have been discussing wedding arrangements with Reina's aunt."

"That's nice. I hope he's very happy with her aunt."

A jest from sepulchral Marcel. Will wonders never cease?

"I think an announcement may be imminent," Mrs. Fulke insisted.

Marcel shoveled in his last hunk of cake and tossed down his fork.

"You may be wrong, as usual, Mrs. Fulke," he hissed, strolling away.

4:12 p.m. Turned into a scorching hot day. Big tent not air-conditioned. Several clammy townies dragged out in a dead faint. Most strenuous shoveling shit in such conditions. Mrs. Fulke stripped down as far as she dared go: long-sleeved jersey and pink stretch pants. Body too unfeminine and youthful to expose further. Consequently sweated like a pig. Had to tie towel around head to prevent perspiration from erasing face wrinkles. Finally, gave up and hid out in aromatic gloom under camel van. Hope today's not the day Sheeni chose to visit the circus. I'd have missed her entirely.

9:46 p.m. Just had a call from Violet, one leg of the adulterous T.P. triangle. Apurva admitted to France despite infamous brother. She and hubby have been reunited.

"God, Rick, she's so beautiful," gasped Violet. "I mean I saw her photo, but I was hardly prepared for the enchanting vision that emerged last night from Alphonse's Twingo. I felt like Cinderella's ugly stepsister."

"Was she pissed?"

"God no, Rick, she's as gracious as she could be. I mean part of me wants to hate her, but she's just so wonderfully sweet. Is it all an act, do you think?"

"Probably not, Violet. Apurva always was pretty nice."

"I'm just despising myself for trying to steal her husband. Of course, part of me wants to kill her too. I didn't sleep at all last night thinking of those two together down the hall."

"How's Trent holding up?"

"You mean is he holding out? I don't know. I only saw him alone briefly this morning and he was very noncommittal. Oh God, Rick, I think I've lost him."

"Not necessarily, Violet. Where are they now?"

"Still out seeing the town, I suppose. We did agree that he should try to tire her out through tourism."

"A good strategy. Well, try not to worry, Violet."

"Try not to worry, Rick? I don't do anything but that! I haven't been out of my room all day. I'm up here tying myself in knots."

I expect that's how contortionists relieve stress. I told her to keep in touch and rang off.

Can't write any more. Things are starting to bustle outside on the lot. The show is on the move again. Goodbye 14! Goodbye my fleeting youth!

AUGUST

MONDAY, August 1 — Fifteen at last. My birthday couldn't come a day sooner. What a change in circumstances from my last natal day with Mom and Jerry in Oakland. Back then I was a lonely virgin grimly unwrapping an official Rodney "Butch" Bolicweigski first baseman's glove. Now I'm sleeping with two camels in faraway France, a country where baseball is largely unknown. I'm in love with two beautiful girls, one of whom abandoned me exactly one month ago. Come back, Sheeni, wherever you are! I'm sure you must be thinking of me today. Probably wishing you had my address so you could send me a nice card. Send yourself instead! We now have even more in common, my absent darling. We're both 15, an age that commands no small measure of respect. Fifteen—*mon dieu!* That's halfway to 30. (Or a fifth of the way to 75, if you really want to get morbid.)

On this gala day I awoke in Brive-La-Gaillarde, a fairly nondescript burg that, not astoundingly, adjoins a river (the torpid Corréze). Lots of noisy trains chugging by our lot at all hours of the day and night. On a more pleasant note, there's been a temporary diminution in Mrs. Fulke's workload. No pony van to clean. The Batur clan had truck trouble last night and is stalled by the road somewhere in rural France. Madame Poco most concerned they won't make it here in time for the matinee. In which case, Captain Lapo will be sent out to eat a light bulb (it being too sultry for fire-eating). And Iyad will be asked to perform an extended acrobatics program atop his oppressed camels. For being the ships of the desert, those guys don't like hot weather any more than the rest of us. It was all I could do to drag them out of the van this morning, and then they launched several nasty gobs into Mrs. Fulke's sweaty wig. Even Captain Lapo, at our long-delayed breakfast, regarded me with little apparent lust in his heart.

1:43 p.m. No lunchtime birthday cake for Mrs. Fulke. I guess she doesn't rate. I *was* flattered to receive a package via overnight courier right as we were chowing down. Connie's timing is sometimes impeccable. Her gift box contained an oversized gag birthday card (also signed by her hubby) and a nifty portable satellite radio—such a thoughtful, compact gift for the fugitive on your list.

Madame Poco asked why Mrs. Fulke was receiving birthday presents in August, since—according to her passport and job application—she was born in May. I shrugged and said these overnight delivery companies are not always as reliable as one assumes.

"Who's Mrs. Paul Saunders?" inquired a nosy horn player, reading the return address on the box. I said she was my married daughter back in the States. Then I had to grab my radio back from him, which he had already soiled with his filthy cigarette ash. The creep is asking for summary dismemberment. Reina, I noticed, seemed rather downhearted by this written confirmation of Paul's new marital status. I may not yet know the full story on those two.

3:18 p.m. The Baturs made it here just in time for the afternoon show. Both caravan and pony van rolled in behind giant tow trucks. After the ponies were dropped off, the van left to join the Batur's semi-tractor in a repair shop in town. The shocking preliminary diagnosis: sugar in both gas tanks necessitating major rebuilds. We're talking tall euros—onerous bills I very much hope come out of the Tarkan Batur wedding fund. Mr. Batur obviously steamed, but no accusations have been flung so far. Innocent bystander Mrs. Fulke not displeased by these events. Again, totally blameless. Mine was not the sugary hand behind these nefarious deeds. Satisfaction without guilt. A sweet birthday surprise.

5:47 p.m. Entire circus abuzz with rumors regarding Batur sabotage and feuding swains. I overheard Madame Poco grumbling that attractive single women always cause problems for traveling shows. Some feminist she turned out to be. Baturs now dining in the cookhouse until Mom regains transportation to stores. Eating communally, but they brought their own table to minimize mixing. Many dark looks being directed toward you know who. Neither Jiri nor Tarkan appear to be shaving their upper lips. Has Mr. G sparked a moustache war?

8:45 p.m. No birthday cards in today's mail, but I don't suppose John Dillinger got many either when he was on the lam. I did receive *E*65 in cash from my employer, but she included no birthday bonus. Said if I kept up the good work I might get a *E*5 a week raise. I recognized her gesture as pie in the sky, but appreciated the praise.

My new radio is quite amazing. Somehow you don't have to aim it at any satellites, yet it tunes in hundreds of channels with remarkable fidelity. For example, there's one channel devoted exclusively to the opinionated blockheads of right-wing talk radio. Another with arcane discussions of weird hobbies like stamp collecting and bird watching. Music of every stripe, of course, but naturally I zeroed in on the channel that plays nearly nonstop Frank, interlarded with the occasional Bing (not bad), Johnny Mathis (nice), Nat King Cole (ditto), and Perry Como (yuck). Turns out Frank is the perfect accompaniment for lonely juggling practice. I can nearly keep three in the air now.

11:53 p.m. What a surprise when Reina knocked on my door with a basket containing a round of chevret, a baguette, and a bottle of wine. Somehow she had ditched all of her beaus, so I invited her in for *un petit* party: just me, Reina, Frank, and the two slumbering camels. Night still very warm, so she was dressed in the lightest of summery frocks. A creamy soft cotton that gently kissed her nubile body, just as I longed to do. I lit a few candles, opened the wine, and let Frank croon softly down from the heavens.

"Happy birthday, Rick," she said, as we clinked glasses.

"It is now," I replied.

The wine condensed the fecund beauty of France into every sip and raced straight to my head. Reina tore off a hunk of bread with her lovely hands, spread it with cheese, and handed it to me. It tasted of sunshine on green meadows. She prepared one for herself and took a greedy bite.

"I love this cheese," she said, sitting back against a hay bale. "I'll probably get fat like my aunt. Will you still love me then?"

"I'll always love you, Reina."

"How does it feel to be 15?"

"I'd rather be 25 like Paul."

"Then you'd be too old for me, Rick."

"Was he too old for you?"

"He was too, uh . . . too airy. I need someone whose head is not so far in the clouds. Who won't say sweet things and then leave without a word."

"That's how his sister left me. Not even a note."

"How sad for you, Rick."

Frank launched into "You Go to My Head."

"I can't believe you listen to this kind of music, Rick."

"My tastes are rather old-fashioned," I admitted, refilling Reina's glass. "As near as I can figure I was born about 75 years too late."

"It's different for women, Rick. These are the best times for us. Too much oppression in the past. I like your music though. Who is this singer?"

Flabbergasted by the query, I nearly spilled my wine. Somehow we got over that rocky patch and I snuggled closer. One of us, at least, smelled wonderful.

"What are you going to do when the tour ends, Rick?"

"I don't know. Go back to Paris, I guess. Get a job if I can. Would you like to live together?"

"Mrs. Fulke, me, and my babies? A curious household indeed. I don't think my husband would approve."

I looked at her in surprise. "You're going to get married?"

"I think so, Rick. I'm tired of being alone."

"Who to?!"

"I don't know, Rick. I'm having trouble making up my mind."

"I think you're just on the rebound from Paul, Reina. He hurt you more than you're letting on."

"I barely knew him, Rick. You know how little time we had together."

"Doesn't matter, Reina. These things happen quickly. It didn't take long for me."

"To decide you loved Sheeni?"

"And love you."

"Men are so much more complicated that parrots, Rick. I hardly feel equipped to deal with them. Too many emotions getting in the way of good sense. Perhaps it was better in the old days when your parents would exercise their wisdom and select someone suitable for you."

I put down my glass.

"I'm going to kiss you now, Reina. I'm giving you fair warning in case you wish to leave."

She made no move to exit or scream. Frank cooperated by launching into "This Love of Mine." We kissed. Warm bodies, mellow wine, savory goat cheese, tender ballad, a passing train, camel snufflings, Reina's perfume, Mrs. Fulke's b.o., the romance of France, the ache of love, the longing for connection. All fused into the meeting and melding of two pairs of lips.

"Why do you make me feel so happy, Rick?" she gasped, politely steering my hand away from her chest. " I must be some kind of deviate. Sitting here molesting a child."

"If it makes you feel any better, Reina, my cultural age is at least 90. A kid I am not."

We kissed again.

"I'm leaving now, Rick. If I stay any longer, I'll do something I'll regret."

"OK, but promise me you won't marry some turkey without consulting me first."

"OK, Rick. I promise."

And then she was gone. A very nice birthday. Yes, it could have been better. Blue balls are no fun. But I'm not complaining.

TUESDAY, August 2 — Connie called me at some ungodly hour

from her Hawaiian love nest. Things were still going swimmingly for the newlyweds. It turns out Connie did not rent some tacky beach condo. Their ocean-side rental manor sits on 17 manicured acres and comes complete with a cook, chauffeur, and obsequious Yale grad houseboy. She explained that she wished to impress on her husband in some dramatic way that his circumstances have now been altered radically for the better. I said that sounded like an excellent strategy, and thanked her for the cool radio and its gift of round-the-clock Frank.

"Whatever floats your coconut," she replied. "Are you ready for some good news?"

"You're pregnant?" I guessed.

"I better be for all the calluses I'm getting down there. Still too early to tell, Rick. But guess who decided he couldn't neglect his law practice any further and is now back in Ukiah?"

"Our father-in-law!"

"The very creep. And still no wedding gift yet from those cheapskates."

"Don't hold your breath, Connie. I'm still waiting for mine too. That's great news! But how do I let Sheeni know?"

"Isn't your handsome pal Trent always on TV?"

"Uh-huh. He's the Regis Philbin of France."

"Then get him to mention it during his next interview."

Another great idea from my ally in amours. I do appreciate her efforts on my behalf, especially when she remains well out of my hair on the other side of the globe.

10:12 a.m. There's been a major conflagration here, diary. It happened while Jiri Mestan was smoking in Reina's shower. Someone set a match to his *petit* Opel truck. By the time the Brive-La-Gaillarde fire department arrived, it was little more than a smoldering pile of incinerated Mestanisms. His music scores, his tacky clothes, his meager cooking items, his emergency carton of Gauloises, his wretched personal belongings, and doubtless his private condom stash—entirely devoured in flames. All the guy had left were the clothes on his back, one singed fedora, a threadbare towel (stolen from a Brno hotel), his incipient moustache, and his repulsive personality. His passport burned too, so he is now a stateless nonentity. The guy, in fact, may have ceased officially to exist.

François now acutely embarrassed by his lack of complicity in these outrages. Nonstop mayhem around here and his only crime was pilfering a few oranges from the cookhouse. It's a good thing he's such a dedicated snoop. Couldn't help but notice a suspicious character this morning loitering in the vicinity of Jiri's van. Remarkably, it was the same person I'd observed pocketing sugar cubes by the coffee urn. Yes, it's true. Clowns do have a dark side.

11:48 a.m. Talked to lonely Violet still in exile from T.P. in Paris. Not to belabor these occupational metaphors, but she was very much bent out of shape. Mr. Bonnet checked in yesterday and was furious to learn of Apurva's presence there. He said being married can be fatal to a rising teen sex symbol's career. He insisted that it was imperative that Apurva not be seen with her hubby. Therefore, she was to remain in the apartment at all times. Culture-starved Apurva not happy about this edict. Violet even less so. Now weak, tormented Trent has to resist the charms of his alluring wife 24 hours a day. Apurva determined to prove that Trent's "condition" just a transient weakness. What a trial! I'm sure I would fail miserably. Violet drops in frequently to see if they need anything, but Apurva has requested that she telephone first. And now they aren't answering their phone! Violet most distressed, but she agreed to convey news of old man Saunders' departure should Trent "take a break from his activities." She also gave me his new "mobile" (cellphone) number should I wish to call the "happy couple" myself. Bitter sarcasm, but I tried to reassure her that things were not as black as they seemed.

1:09 p.m. Big fight in the cookhouse tent at lunch today. Jiri and Tarkan going at it with assorted foodstuffs and tableware. Circus people disinclined to intervene in such fisticuffs. Everyone grabbed their plates to get out of the way, but no one rushed in to stop the battle—despite Reina's frantic entreaties. Madame Poco finally turned the hose on them when it appeared that Tarkan might be close to gouging out an eye. Not really a fair fight since Tarkan in much better shape, but it was the homeless trumpeter who jumped him. Jiri's torn lip will render him useless on the horn for many days. Happily, no kissing on the menu either. Battered Tarkan may have to take a break from death-defying pony stunts as well. Madame Poco, most disgusted, has called a meeting of the entire company after today's matinee. Heads to roll?

After the dust settled, Mrs. Fulke dropped by the clowns' table to demonstrate her new facility with three oranges. As usual, jaded Marcel most unextravagant in his praise. Said he had witnessed superior juggling by "a retarded quadriplegic." Mrs. Fulke thanked him for his encouragement, adding that these "mysterious events" certainly had triggered "a tumultuous brawl."

"I've seen better," he spat, turning his back on me. Perhaps he's annoyed that the combatants desisted before any fatalities had occurred.

6:14 p.m. A new page has been turned, diary, in the democratic tradition of equal justice and fair play among circus folk. Madame Poco's proposal at our company meeting to eject Reina and her trained birds for inciting internal strife was booed down. Donk the giant said it wasn't her fault that every man found her charming and desirable. The solution, he proposed, was that she declare her choice so that harmony might be restored.

"Who will it be, Reina?" he asked in his deep giant's voice. "We all want to know."

"Let's not be precipitous here," interjected Mr. G. "Reina should not be compelled to—."

"Shut up," counseled Mrs. Poco. "OK, Reina, which one will it be—the arsonist or the saboteur?"

Jiri and Tarkan rose as one to object to these characterizations, but Madame Poco gaveled them down. Reina pondered this distasteful choice and wisely shook her head.

"I, I can't decide," she announced meekly. "I like them both."

"Then you can't stay in the show," replied Madame Poco. "I'm running a circus here, not a training camp for gladiators."

"Howa 'bout a leetle contest?" suggested Captain Lapo. "Every fella wantsa marry Reina canna competa fair and a square-a."

"That's an excellent idea," said Donk. "I second the motion."

"We've got shows to put on," scoffed Madame Poco. "We can't

be running competitions for wives."

"Why not?" asked Marcel. "We could run it like the Tour de France—a multistage competition conducted in our free time over several weeks."

"That is completely ridiculous," declared Mr. G. "I'm sure Reina would never agree to anything so preposterous."

"Well, it might help me make up my mind," she replied. "But I'd have certain conditions."

"State your conditions," replied Madame Poco.

"Well, it would have to be conducted fairly. There couldn't be events like horn playing or pony riding. I think each contest should relate in some way to married life. And no violence. I've seen enough brawling. Also I have certain conditions for each, uh, candidate."

"State them," replied our ringmistress.

"Tarkan, darling, I love your family, but I feel if we marry, we should go off on our own—at least for the first few years."

"I was going to suggest we do precisely that, my dearest one," he replied.

His enlightened parents also nodded in agreement, the two-faced creeps.

"Very good," said Reina. "And now to you, Jiri darling. I cannot marry any man who insists on poisoning himself with cigarettes."

Jiri spat out his coffin nail and stomped on it with his foot.

"There, Reina. I smoked last one. No more cigarette I do."

A fairly reckless promise, it seemed to me.

"Do we have any other contestants?" asked Madame Poco.

Four people raised their hands: Donk, Marcel, Captain Lapo, and Mrs. Fulke.

A rumble of surprise went through the company. Everyone turned expectantly toward Mr. G., but he declined to commit.

"Any objections to broadening the field, Reina?" inquired Madame Poco.

"I'm sorry," she replied, "though I am, of course, deeply flattered, I must excuse Marcel, Donk, and Captain Lapo as I do not love them."

Bitter looks of disappointment swept the ranks of the also-rans.

"And the other, uh, nominee?" asked Madame Poco.

"I think," said Reina, "that Mrs. Fulke should explain herself."

The company turned its curious gaze upon me. I cleared my throat and rose to speak.

"I represent another interested party, thank you."

Short and to the point, that's my style.

"Are stand-ins to be permitted?" objected Tarkan's burly dad.

"No law against it," said Madame Poco. "Reina, do you have any conditions for Mrs. Fulke?"

"Yes, she must clear up all of her, uh, outstanding matters."

"The interested party shall do exactly as you wish," I replied. "And he wishes to note that he loves you very much."

"Thank you, Mrs. Fulke," she replied. "Your comments have been noted."

"OK, that's settled," announced Madame Poco. "So I don't want any more trouble. The sabotage and fights will cease. As for the contest, I appoint the three rejected suitors to be the committee in charge. Let the games commence tomorrow. And may the best, uh, person win."

8:07 p.m. My fellow contestants confronted Mrs. Fulke at dinner and demanded to know for whom I was serving as proxy. I said it was Stanley Fulke, my son the accountant back in Glasgow. I apologized for not having a photo of the lad, but said he looked a bit like the late English film star Archibold Leech. That seemed to satisfy them. They do not appear to regard Mrs. Fulke as a serious contender, the poor deluded fools. Of course, Jiri—ever fiercely jonesing for a fag—is hardly capable of the simplest rational thought.

Madame Poco is from the tough-love school of circus management. She's told Jiri "no blowing, no eating." Since his money and bankbook also burned in the fire, he had no choice but to play today. Needless to say, with Jiri's sore lip and ferocious nicotine cravings, no one was mistaking him for Miles Davis. The creep had the nerve to propose to Reina that since he "no longer smoked," he bunk temporarily in her caravan. She nixed that, so he moved into Paul's old nest in the equipment van. He's dressing in castoffs chipped in by generous crewmembers. From the way he was squirming in his seat at dinner, I'd guess his underpants were donated by a midget.

I can't help but think it's a good sign that Reina agreed to Mrs. Fulke's participation in the contest. If she weren't in my life, I don't know how I would have coped when Sheeni left. I'm sure I would be even more of a mess than I am now. Of course, if I become engaged to Reina and then Sheeni returns, I'll be in quite a pickle. My preferred solution would be to marry both and move to rural Utah. If a guy has the emotional breadth to love two chicks, why should he be artificially constrained to one? The girls shouldn't mind particularly, since it would defuse all that marital pressure, halve the housework, and give them more time to pursue their own interests. Personally, I think there's a lot to be said for sincere bigamy—especially from the feminist viewpoint.

WEDNESDAY, August 3 — I woke up feeling pretty nervous. Today I must battle against formidable competition for the woman I love. Very unsettling to have devious Marcel devising the contests. That clown looked even more jaundiced than usual yesterday. I hope we won't be asked to bite the heads off live chickens or walk barefoot across beds of flaming hot coals.

Jiri showed up at breakfast looking like something the cat dragged in. Dark circles under his eyes and he was clutching a bag of rigatoni begged off a sympathetic Serb. He sucks on the hard pasta like a cigarette until it softens, then spits it out. I suppose you could call this method of quitting smoking "cold turkey with pasta." Appears to appease the grosser oral cravings, but nothing but crazed insanity was substituting for the missing nicotine. If only vigorous, confident Tarkan could be similarly incapacitated.

9:48 a.m. Madame Poco such a little tyrant. Has no respect for the rules of gentlemanly competition. Circus was supposed to depart last night, but move delayed by Batur clan's mechanical difficulties. She fears we have exhausted Brive-La-Gaillarde's shallow pool of circus lovers. Therefore, she arbitrarily decided that for the first event, the three contestants would be sent into town to peddle color-coded tickets to today's shows. The guy who sells the most tickets wins the first leg of the Tour de Wife. The weak-kneed contest committee didn't even protest. Donk commented that it would be a good test of a husband's ability to "make it in the business world." As if any of us had such aspirations. Mrs. Fulke handed a big stack of pink ducats to match her slacks. Kind Reina loaned me her French language phrase book, but "Would you like to buy a fucking circus ticket?" not in it. Can't write any more. Our mad race into town kicks off at 10:00 a.m. sharp.

6:45 p.m. Quite exhausted. Barely capable of movement. Feel like Frog bicycle racer after particularly steep and grueling Alpine tour. Illegal steroids must be administered soon, if Mrs. Fulke to hobble over to cookhouse in time for dinner. Another hot, muggy day. Never suspected that France and Mississippi endure similar summers. French react rather coolly when oddly dressed old lady, sweating like a Yellow Fever victim, waves a circus ticket in their faces. Many assume wrongly that ticket being offered for free instead of actual price of *E*15. Difficult for non-native speaker to convey this subtle economic distinction to grasping Frog tightwads. A few took pity and coughed up the cash. Sold a total of four tickets, or one every two hours. Only *E*60 to show for Herculean effort, but I turned in another *E*405 from my fast-dwindling personal stash. That's all I could afford. Feeling fairly confident of winning because not even Joan of Arc in a thong could sell over a dozen tickets in that tight-fisted town. Committee chairman Donk to announce today's results after dinner, should I live that long.

9:12 p.m. I came in second. Jiri sold two tickets, I sold 31, and Tarkan sold 419. Either Brive-La-Gaillarde is lousy with spendthrift Turks, or old man Batur bought himself a boatload of pricey ducats. According to the committee's rules, Tarkan has been awarded five points, I have three, and Jiri has one. Tarkan also received the daily winner's kiss from the lovely Czech maiden. According to my calculations, I spent *E*405 to earn the same number of points I WOULD HAVE RECEIVED ANYWAY! More than six weeks of nonstop shit-shoveling will be required to earn it back.

Life sucks. Have I mentioned that lately?

THURSDAY, August 4 — We're in Cahors. This town not only adjoins a river (the Lot), but is nearly encircled by it. Guess the

French not too worried about floods. Quaint town does appear to have been around for centuries. Yet another medieval arched bridge in case I revisit the concept of a romantic watery death. And lots of nearby hills for my missing spouse to hide out in.

At breakfast a desperate-looking Jiri tried to renegotiate his contract with Reina so that he gives up smoking *after* he wins the contest. She said no way Jose and gave him an encouraging peck on his unshaven cheek. He's run through his bag of pasta and has no money to buy more. I'm no expert, but it appeared to me he was sucking on the inserter tube from somebody's tampon. Not a sexy look, if you ask me. I'm surprised he hasn't mugged the youngest Batur for her pacifier. His unsightly lips also swollen nastily from excessive sucking and/or horn playing. Be a shame if he had to have them surgically removed.

Next leg of the contest, "Strength and Bravery," gets underway at 10 a.m. Feeling rather strong and not unbrave, all things considered. The committee also announced that one stage of the contest will be ongoing over the next several weeks. The contestants will be observed by the members of the committee and judged whether they manifest one particular husbandly virtue. What that is they aren't saying. God, I hope it's not "Good Grooming." Mrs. Fulke wouldn't stand a chance in that category—not that the competition is all that formidable.

7:12 p.m. I did pretty well today, diary, in the "Strength and Bravery" category. The dark horse candidate is proving more formidable than many had supposed. The entire company gathered at the designated hour behind the main tent, where two steel cages had been set up about 20 feet apart. Coiled in one of them, I noted with alarm, was Panther, the larger and scarier of our two resident snakes.

A husband worthy of Reina, declaimed Donk, must possess demonstrable strength and courage. To determine which of the three contestants excelled in this category, a simple test had been devised. While Donk kept time with his stopwatch, each victim in turn was to transport the snake from one cage to the other, employing only his bare hands. The fastest finisher would be declared today's winner.

"That is, if any remain alive," smiled a sadistic clown.

While roustabouts and midgets feverishly placed their wagers, the three pale-faced contestants gathered to draw lots to see who would go first. Mrs. Fulke sensed that within at least two other scrotums, testicles were bobbling wildly.

"Wait!" shouted Reina, holding up a lovely hand. "I believe I specified no violence."

"You saida no brawlin'," Captain Lapo indignantly reminded her.

"This test entails no violence," sneered Marcel. "You'd have to be an idiot to employ violence against a six-meter boa constrictor."

"Don't worry, Reina," said Donk. "We gave him a rabbit last night. Ole Panther's not at his friskiest."

"I won't have it," Reina insisted. "It's too dangerous."

Cries of protest from the crowd.

"You want to marry some milksop?" demanded Donk.

"You will have to devise some other test," she insisted. "The snake is out."

More angry protests, led—I noticed—by Mr. Granola, but my darling remained firm. Fresh waves of love for that dear girl welled up in my heart.

"I don't mind wrestling the snake," remarked Tarkan, very brave after the fact.

"Nor I!" insisted Jiri, chewing his tampon applicator.

"Me neither," Mrs. Fulke reluctantly squeaked.

"No snakes!" declared Reina.

Clearly disgusted, the committee huddled to discuss this crisis. Finally, the two cages were taken away and Donk returned with three shovels in one massive hand and three picks in the other. These he tossed at our feet.

A husband worthy of Reina, he declared, must possess demonstrable strength and endurance. The test for these qualities would be a digging contest. The combatant who dug the *deepest* hole within one hour would be declared today's winner.

"Measured from where?" demanded Mrs. Fulke, no stranger to shovel work.

"Well, from ground level," said Donk.

"And who decides where that is after all the dirt starts flying?" I demanded.

The gamblers in the crowd agreed that was a good point. So a level line was strung across the field just above head level. Holes were to be dug directly under the line, spaced about 15 feet apart, and final depths would be measured from the line via string and plumb bob. Absolutely *no* dirt was to be flung into an opponent's hole.

"Are you satisfied, Mrs. Fulke?" asked Donk.

"Yes, thank you," I replied.

"Can we drop a snake in their holes?" inquired a roustabout.

"No snakes!" replied Reina.

Manly Tarkan and Jiri stripped to their waists, less manly Mrs. Fulke powdered her nose and donned her work gloves. Then Donk counted down from ten, clicked his stopwatch, and blew his whistle. The race was on. Dirt—and lots of it—began to fly.

Such a contest is not just grunt work. Some strategy is required. How big do you make your hole? Keep it narrow and you can dig down faster, but then your pit becomes too confined for efficient use of your tools. I decided the best compromise was a hole about one yard square. Naturally, everyone in the company gathered 'round to shout encouragement, place bets, and give advice. The consensus seemed to be that Mrs. Fulke's excavation was way too big—not that anyone cared much. All the serious money was on the muscular Turk. Only the longest odds could attract even a nibble of action on the skinny ex-smoker and the geriatric dame.

In minutes I was down two feet through loamy topsoil and banging against a concrete-like layer of viscous clay. This required preliminary dislodging by pick, then scooping out by shovel. The moist, heavy clay clung to my tools as I flailed away. Very arduous work, but I could tell my adversaries were also struggling, so at least I knew the ground strata were uniform. Fortunately, the day was a little cooler and not nearly as humid. Still, I worked up an awesome sweat. Kindly Reina and other ladies circulated with cups of water, which we gulped with the greatest of haste.

Every ten minutes Donk shouted out the time remaining. To my west, out-of-shape Jiri huffed and puffed like a steam engine. Heart attack material, it seemed to me, but at least they could bury him in his own hole. East of me, energetic Tarkan was digging away like 400 prairie dogs in heat.

At last I was through the clay and into a layer of sandy gravel. A few big rocks slowed me down, but I made good progress. And unlike my opponents, I had plenty of room to maneuver my shovel. All around my pit, the dirt rose higher and higher as I shoveled my way toward Tahiti. The buzz of excitement above me turned into a clamor of amazement as the indefatigable Pride of Scotland toiled away like a distaff John Henry. Then I heard Donk shout "One more minute!" and the entire crowd began to count down the seconds. One last furious burst of digging got me down at least another foot before the whistle blew. I dropped my shovel, wiped my brow, and felt a phalanx of powerful hands lift me bodily out of the pit.

All three diggers collapsed expectantly on the ground while the measurements were being made. Jiri had lost his oral pacifier, and his blistered hands were bleeding badly. Tarkan was one massive greaseball of soiled sweat. I had no feeling at all from my shoulders all the way down my arms. They were like two foreign appendages dangling from their sockets.

Jiri's cavity was the first measured: 3.68 meters from line to greatest depth. Then came Mrs. Fulke's: 4.26 meters. Finally, the plumb bob was lowered into Tarkan's pit, the string was marked, then hauled up and measured: 4.24 meters.

A gasp of incredulity from the crowd. Could the old lady have pulled off the upset of the century? Tarkan's father demanded an immediate re-measurement. He grabbed the plumb bob and leaped into my hole, "accidentally" triggering a small landslide. Shouts of protest as loose dirt tumbled down the sides into my excavation. Mr. Batur scooped out a token handful and repositioned the plumb bob. Product of this new measurement: 4.21 meters. Tarkan now the victor?

Explosion of vicious wrangling, as mucho euros on the line. Much shouting, swearing, name-calling, and shoving. Angry midgets seen kicking red-faced roustabouts in shins. I'd have joined in if I weren't semi-paralyzed. Finally, Madame Poco waded into the fracas, declared it too close to call, and announced it was a tie. Tarkan and Mrs. Fulke awarded four points each, hapless Jiri credited with his customary one point. Magnanimous Reina kissed us both (though only Tarkan on lips), then Madame Poco ordered everyone back to work. Since Tarkan and Jiri had to get cleaned up for the next show, guess who was ordered to refill the holes?

I thought my arms would fall off, but eventually the last shovelfull of earth was tamped back into place. All in all, I think I would have preferred wrestling the 200-pound snake.

Yeah, I was robbed.

Yeah, I'm pissed.

Yeah, implacable François is determined to even the score.

11:42 p.m. I was lounging on the rear bumper of the camel van, practicing my juggling and listening to Frank, when who should materialize out of the ether but Jiri Mestan.

"That is Frank Sinatra," he announced.

Was I supposed to be impressed?

"So it is," I grunted. "Is that an arm?"

Jiri was sucking on what appeared to be the amputated right arm of a small plastic doll. Such mislaid toys often turn up in the dusty litter under the bleachers. He looked like a cannibal in the act of swallowing an infantile snack.

Jiri removed his oral appliance and gave it a deprecating wave. "I not really need this," he replied, returning it to his mouth. "You like Frank Sinatra?"

"Sure, why not?"

"Your son, he is also musical?"

"Stanley? Oh yes, ever so."

"My playing today was very bad. Did you hear?"

"I didn't have the pleasure," I lied.

"Very bad for trumpet player to have hurting lips and stiff fingers from digging. Many painful blisters too. Why they make us digging? I am musician, not ditch digger!"

"It was a test of strength."

"I am plenty strong to be husband of Reina. Your son, he is strong?"

"Quite immensely powerful for being an accountant. He takes after his mother."

"You think Reina will marry that Turk?"

"I hope not."

"I love her too much. She always my most dearest girl. You have husband?"

"Mr. Fulke? Passed on to his reward."

"Sorry. How he died?"

"Lung cancer. He was a smoker, you know. It was quite a lingering, painful death. He had to haul around his own oxygen machine the last 12 years of his life."

Jiri chewed on his arm and mulled this over.

"We make party, Mrs. Fulke? You have some nice Scotch whiskey?"

"Sorry, no. Would you care for an orange?"

"No, thank you. I go look for party. Always parties back in Czech, but here not so much fun. Everybody tired from work and go to bed. Your son, how long does he know Reina?"

"Oh, years and years. They're always together when he goes to Paris on business."

"If he's so rich, why is his mama working like Albanian for circus?"

I looked around and lowered my voice. "Stanley is thinking of buying this circus. He sent me down here to scope it out."

"He sends his own mama to live with camels? Mrs. Fulke, your son is terrible person. He is not the right man for my Reina. That I tell you!"

"Oh, you're quite wrong, Mr. Mestan. Stanley is a wonderful man. He and Reina will be very happy together, I assure you of that."

"Then tell him to come and fight himself. Not right to have his mama digging holes. You tell him Jiri Mestan wants to see him. OK?"

"All right. I'll give him the message."

"You have any cigarettes you can borrow me, Mrs. Fulke?"

"Sorry. I don't."

"That's OK. Maybe better I keep my promise to Reina. But girls not right to control the man, right?"

"That's right. You have a perfect right to smoke if you want to. Don't let anyone try to stop you."

With that, my adversary waved his arm (the oral one) and lurched off into the night.

What a mess that guy is. If only I could get Tarkan hooked on something similarly addictive.

FRIDAY, August 5 — Madame Poco has put her foot down. Too many expensive man-hours were lost during yesterday's stage of the Tour de Wife. To minimize disruption to her serfdom program, only the committee and three contestants assembled at the usual hour (10:00 a.m.) in Cahors' bustling medieval quarter for today's competition. First, Donk made us empty our pockets of all currency and change. The sums were noted by Marcel and the cash handed over to Captain Lapo for safekeeping. Sadly, poor Jiri had only *E.27* to his name. To avoid arrest for public perversion, he was back to "smoking" feminine hygiene by-products. His lip swellings had subsided somewhat, but he still looked like someone you'd see loitering outside of a methadone clinic.

Today's event, explained Donk, would test for those essential husbandly qualities of sincerity and persuasiveness. Each of us would have one hour to waylay the citizens of Cahors and persuade them to give us money. The winner would be the guy who hauled in the most cash. To prevent cheating, each of us would be accompanied by a member of the committee. We all drew lots, and I won Donk the Giant as my panhandling buddy. The whole thing didn't seem very fair to Mrs. Fulke, and she said so.

"But I don't speak French!" I wailed. "Tarkan is practically fluent!"

"I am perfectly fluent," he sniffed, cutting me dead.

"We Czechs are not so very money-grubbing," protested Jiri, obviously hung over. The guy must have dredged up some kind of party last night.

"You may not be," snapped Marcel, "but I don't know about Reina. She has approved of this contest. And Tarkan may speak French, but don't forget he's Turkish."

True enough. The French were not known for their love of swarthy foreigners.

The committee members synchronized their watches, then Donk blew his whistle, clicked his stopwatch, and we were off. This being August, touristy Cahors was swarming with sightseeing Americans. Mrs. Fulke decided to concentrate her efforts among that affluent subgroup of English-speakers.

"Help me buy breakfast for my giant!" I called. "Help me buy some grub for the big guy."

"Hey, you can't say that!" protested Donk.

"Whatever is not prohibited, is permitted," I retorted. "Just be glad I'm not auctioning you off as someone's sex slave."

We worked our way through the narrow winding streets like the colorful beggars of antiquity. Mrs. Fulke perfected her patter and was soon hoovering up the dollars and euros. I also raked in quite a few *E*5 bills for the privilege of having one's picture taken with "Europe's most famous giant." We could have hauled in even more, but I spent a good ten minutes pursuing a goateed youth. Not my darling wife, as it turns out, but he was sufficiently intimidated when we cornered him in an alley to hand over *E*16 unbidden. Mrs. Fulke gave him back his credit cards and wristwatch. She had no use for a Rolex knockoff. I pretended not to notice as Donk slipped the cowering fellow a *E*20 bill, patted him on his back, and sent him on his way.

Both Donk and I were feeling optimistic when we returned to our starting point an hour later. I was the first to count out my haul: *E*73.12, plus $32.13 in American money and an unknown amount in miscellaneous foreign coinage. Why was I slaving for peanuts with the circus, I wondered, when I could be out here getting rich off the tourists?

Jiri confirmed his disinterest in money-grubbing. He coughed up a paltry *E*3.59. Actually, he was in minus territory for the morning, since he received a *E*10 citation for illegal panhandling from an alert Cahors gendarme.

We were both shocked when Tarkan pulled out a crisp wad of new euros still in its official bank paper wrapper. His total came to exactly *E*500. The smug creep refused to tell us how he did it, so Captain Lapo spilled the beans. Tarkan had gone directly to a meat market and had a sincere and persuasive chat with the Turkish proprietor.

"How much interest is he charging you on that loan?" Mrs. Fulke demanded.

"I don't have to tell you that," he replied.

Another bitter disappointment. Once again Tarkan got the kiss from lovely Reina and the big fat five points. Current score: Jiri - 3, Mrs. Fulke - 10, and Tarkan - 14. Thankfully, some of us got to keep our panhandling take. A nice haul for the Morag Fulke fugitive fund. I bought a bagload of spare batteries for my radio. Eager Jiri tore up his citation and took his winnings directly to a tobacconists shop. No, I didn't see him light up, but I doubt he went in there for nicotine gum.

1:12 p.m. Is it my imagination or is the entire Batur clan giving Mrs. Fulke the cold shoulder? Their ponies, though, are still producing, so I'm still shoveling. I wanted a pony badly as a tiny tot and now I've got eight. If you ever have to decide between a camel and pony as a pet, I'd recommend the horse. They're pretty friendly once they get to know you and do cute things like nuzzle your pockets for carrots or sugar cubes. Camels, though, just look at you with contempt and fart in your face or piss on your shoes. Iyad is always screaming at them, which may not be improving their attitudes.

Number 14, the baby monkey, is growing fast and starting to play. He's a little zone of adorability in that X-rated cage. Reina still visits frequently, though she has to put up with Mr. G constantly hitting on her. The cad has redoubled his attentions since getting aced out of competing legitimately in the Tour de Wife. Reina is ever polite, but if I were her, I'd grab the guy's bullwhip and start flailing away. I think he should be hung up by his moustache and poked all over with sharp sticks. After that the serious tortures could begin.

3:38 p.m. I decided to call Paris for an update. No answer at Violet's, so I called Trent's number. His lovely wife answered. She recognized Rick S. Hunter's voice and greeted me with camel-like reserve. I explained that having her brother exiled to India was not my idea.

"You cannot imagine, Nick, how much my parents have suffered."

She's right. Call me a sociopath, but I just can't conceive how being separated from Vijay could be a source of distress. Perhaps I'm lacking in empathy.

"I'm sorry, Apurva," I lied. "I'm sure this mix-up will be straightened out soon. How are you enjoying Paris?"

"It seems quite enchanting—from what I can see from the windows of this dreary apartment."

"I used to live there, you know."

"Yes, you and Sheeni. That is part of what makes it so depressing."

She sighed. I sighed.

"Is your husband there, Apurva?"

"He is out with Violet giving television interviews. Or so he says."

She sighed. I sighed.

"Do you know if he's publicizing the fact that Sheeni's father has left France?"

"I believe so. He seems especially anxious that she return. Why this is so I cannot say. I shall never understand you Americans."

"Apurva, Trent loves you. You can't give up on him."

"I do not care to discuss my private life with you, Nick. I believe that you have interfered with it enough. Nor do I trust that you have any sincere interest in my welfare."

"Apurva! I was only trying to make you happy! Didn't I help you every way I could to marry Trent?"

"Marrying Trent has not been . . . Well, enough said on that subject. Do you wish me to convey a message to him?"

"Apurva, you've got to get him to go home with you. Staying in Paris is a mistake."

"Don't you think I know that? I never wanted him to come here in the first place. But he had to come and see his precious Sheeni. And now there's this Violet woman."

"It's just an infatuation, Apurva. Trent loves you."

"Then there is something going on between them. I thought so. He denied it. Well, I see he's not to be trusted. Just like you, Nick Twisp. Goodbye!" *Click*.

Damn. I think I stuck my foot in it that time. I know I haven't always been the most guileless of friends to Apurva, but I've never wished her ill. I always liked her. And let's not forget that were it not for an unfortunate cold virus, I might have been her first lover. As far as potential wives go, she's always been penciled in on my list right under Sheeni and Reina. That should count for something.

7:22 p.m. Jiri got nailed at dinner. Reina smelled tobacco on his breath. Well, what do you expect? The fool showed up in the cookhouse tent with no visible pacifier. Naturally, Reina got suspicious. She made him produce the half-empty pack, which she tore to bits while he looked on whimpering. He's chewed up both doll arms and has had to graduate to a leg. Good thing his point total is so low. It'd be a shame if Reina had to marry a freak who walks around with what appears to be a stunted third leg growing out of his face. His moustache is turning out to be something of a joke too. Very sparse and at some angles it gives the impression of being pubic hair attached to the leg. Rather troubling to the casual observer.

11:28 p.m. Still no birthday card/gift from my sister, so I gave her a call. She was home in L.A. giving both barrels to greedy Tyler. That guy can sure slurp. She seemed happy to hear from me and said all her friends were impressed that the cute sailor in the "*Heee, Lekker Ding*" video was her fugitive brother.

"God, Nick, I never thought you'd get to be so famous. Even Mother is impressed. She's trying to find out how she can get all your royalties."

"What!"

"You know, to keep them for you."

Yeah, right.

"Isn't she in jail?"

"The prosecution made a big blunder, Nick. They put Lance on the stand. By the time Mother's lawyers finished with him, even the jury wanted to murder him. Mom was convicted of the lesser charge of aggravated assault. The judge let her off with time served and probation."

"She's not in jail? For shooting a guy's nuts off!"

"We're all terribly relieved, Nick. But you need to send us some more money."

"What!"

"That horrid Lance won't give up. Now he's suing Mother for damages in civil court—for $12 million!"

What a greedy bastard. No way his disgusting testicles were worth $6 million apiece. I groaned. The handwriting was on the wall. Evil Lance would get my video royalties too. I informed my sister I was virtually penniless and hung up.

You'd think I'd know better by now. The last person in the world to reach out to is a fellow Twisp.

SATURDAY, August 6 — Missing Sheeni terribly on this anniversary day. I've lost count of how many weeks it's been since we were blushing newlyweds in Yahoo City. Now she's gone without a word and our first French summer is passing quickly too. Back in California this is about the time I'd be bugging my miserly father for some sharp back-to-school clothes. Now I have the wardrobe of an Alzheimer's victim, and my educational career may have fizzled out to an ignominious conclusion. True, I never liked school, but I suppose it has its uses. It does toss you into a social mix with a lot of cute girls, assuming you haven't done something insane like enroll in a boys' academy. And then there are the dances, football games, debate meets, pep rallies, car cruises, etc. All in all, it sounds more appealing right now than endless shit shoveling for Third World wages. Me, nostalgic for high school? I *have* come to a new low.

11:24 a.m. Some sad news. Madame Ruzicka called Reina this

morning in tears. Her parrot Henri died. Cause of death was old age. In fact, the vet estimated he was considerably older than his owner. Might even have achieved the century mark and had three or four previous owners. The moral is if you want a lifelong companion get a parrot, not a wife. I'd consider it, but I don't imagine they look that appealing in a negligee. Scary to think if I marry Reina, her birds will be deafening me every morning for the rest of my life.

No Tour de Wife competition this a.m. The committee has scheduled it for tonight after the last performance. They announced the theme as "Balancing Your Needs." Sounds right up my alley. I have plenty of needs I'm trying to balance. Right now I'd like to balance someone pretty and compliant on top of a hay bale.

3:29 p.m. I've found my job is slightly more tolerable if I take my radio around with me. The animals too are somewhat more tractable when soothed by music. Beez the bear not a fan of Frank though. He insists I tune to the channel that plays around-the-clock, around-the-calendar Christmas music. Festive for him, but "Jingle Bells" in midsummer gives me a big dose of holiday dread. December always was an anxious month in my family—even before my mother surprised my dad one Christmas Eve with a petition for divorce. To be frank, Sinatra is also beginning to pale. Did he have to record *quite* so many sad laments of lost love? Just because Ava ditched him is no reason to keep reminding the rest of us of our marital woes.

5:24 p.m. Walked into town with Reina to buy more produce for her birds. Nice to be alone for a few minutes with my darling, though concomitant pangs of anguished longing were a trial. I tried to get her to talk about the on-going secret contest, but she refused to spill. Nor would she say how I was doing. I told her it was most unsettling to be observed constantly by Marcel, Donk, and Captain Lapo and not to know on what I was being evaluated.

"There lies the road to paranoia," I pointed out. "Is it by any chance table manners?"

"No, it's not."

Too bad. Jiri and Tarkan shovel it in like coal stokers on the *Titanic.*

Reina did confess she's had to nix as too extreme many proposed Tour de Wife events, triggering the wrath of the committee. She's also worried that Jiri's poor performance so far may be affecting his self-esteem.

"Did you hear his playing at today's matinee, Rick? It was just awful."

"Call me Morag. Yeah, but it has degenerated no more than my manure shoveling. I can barely get the stuff in the wheelbarrow now. I want you just as much as he does."

"How exactly to you want me?" she inquired.

"Well, how do you think?"

"I don't know, Morag. That's why I asked. What do men want?"

Could chicks be as confused on this issue as guys?

"Well, Reina darling, I want to be with you, to embrace you, to . . . uh, protect you."

"From what? Do you perceive me to be in some kind of danger?"

"I don't know. That's just the way men feel. They want to be protective of their sweethearts."

"Protective or possessive?"

"Both, I suppose. Guys are genetically programmed to want to be their mate's exclusive partner. We don't want to devote our precious resources to raising some other guy's spawn."

"That's rather primitive thinking, Morag."

"We're the product of millions of years of evolution, Reina. I didn't make up the rules. To give it to you straight, what guys want is to impregnate you with their seed and fight off all trespassers."

"Oh, dear. Even Jiri, do you suppose?"

"Even him, Reina. His primitive brain strives to obtain nicotine, blow the trumpet, and get you with child. He's signaling that last need by sucking on a doll leg."

"I've been wondering about that, Morag. Is it some kind of fertility symbol?"

"Yeah, he sucks on that because society does not permit him to flaunt his penis."

"Oh, he's been doing that too."

"What?!"

"When he comes over to take a shower. Lately, he's been knocking the bathroom door open accidentally while toweling off. I never realized they were such large, floppy things. Not at all like the statues in the parks. Don't you men find it rather inconvenient?"

No, but Jiri may. As he's being brutally dismembered.

SUNDAY, August 7 — Head feels like it is being stepped on by heavily laden camel. Skull may have to be trepanned soon with large-diameter drill bit to relieve pressure if six aspirins I just gulped don't bring surcease of suffering. Has tidal wave of intoxicants entirely killed off my liver? Kidneys complaining too. Fear general system failure from acute alcohol poisoning. Wasn't even drinking for amusement. It was last night's "Balancing Your Needs" test, which consisted of three contestants teetering atop overturned buckets while imbibing diverse assortment of intoxicating brews. Any guy who upchucked or whose foot touched the ground was out. Mrs. Fulke made it through beer, red wine, cognac, pastis, pear brandy, vodka, rum, and nasty French whiskey. Her downfall was a disgusting anise-flavored liqueur splashed into her cup by a drunken Greek roustabout. One swallow, and she simultaneously swooned and hurled. Not a pretty sight as I was jocularly reminded this a.m. at breakfast. Details murky after that point, but contest went on for some time. Much merriment, spirited betting, and general booze quaffing. No one missed Reina, who had been sent into town on diversion errand by crafty committee. Final drunkard left standing: the hollow-legged Czech. Probably just another night's partying for that guy. Despite alleged self-esteem issues, Mr. Mestan has come roaring back. New point totals: Jiri - 8, Mrs. Fulke 11, Tarkan - 17.

I remember from health class that binge drinking permanently destroys brain cells that you never replace. Feeling pretty stupid at the moment. Oh well, I've always thought that intelligence is overrated. If you look around, it's the stupid people who are raising hell and having all the fun. Of course, they often die young, but I suppose it's exciting to scream along on your crotch-rocket motorcycle right up until the moment you crash into that oak tree. And think how many sick people are saved annually by the donated organs.

11:26 p.m. Today's contest has been postponed as booze-impaired contenders deemed too incapacitated for any activity except plaintive moaning. Committee not in the greatest shape either. Bleary-eyed Donk just got his giant ass chewed by Reina for last night's festivities. She says committee should test for qualities that are important to chicks like honesty, openness, and willingness to listen. Skeptical giant replied that such a contest would be "extremely boring" and "unlikely to attract much wagering." Captain Lapo added that men are the best judges of what makes a good husband since we've had "way more experience at it." This would imply there was once a Mrs. Lapo. I'd pay in the low one-figures to hear the story of that unfortunate lady.

5:18 p.m. Someone may have been in my sty! I returned from an interval of camel herding on a far corner of the lot and got the distinct feeling that things were not as I left them. No sign of anything missing though. My under-floor battery safe did not appear disturbed, but it's hard to tell. No sign of forced entry, and Iyad denies using his key. Could just be hangover-induced paranoia, I suppose, but unsettling nevertheless. Getting a bit sloppy in Mrs. Fulke's persona. Her Scottish accent, for example, waxes and wanes like the moon. Must try to be more consistent, so as not to arouse suspicion.

Headache almost gone, but liver still feels like it was autopsied, critiqued by students, and sewn back in. Drinking gallons of water to flush my system. Wish the doniker weren't so far away. Sometimes I just say fuck it and piss on a hay bale. So far, Omar and Ajax have not objected to the additional flavoring.

9:37 p.m. Big scandal rocking the sports world. The Baturs have been found guilty of cheating. Marcel got suspicious when he noticed a roustabout flashing a bankroll that was way too impressive for six days past payday. He did a little detective work and discovered that Mr. Batur had bribed the booze handlers to pour less liberally into Tarkan's cup. Too many conspirators have confessed under duress (applied by Donk) to dispute the evidence. The charge stands! Therefore, Mrs. Fulke has been awarded second place, and the Turkish malefactor has received a scolding from Reina and a big fat zero points. Angry protests from the Batur camp, who claim their guy would have bested a "mere woman" even without cheating. But the committee is standing by their decision. New revised totals: Jiri - 8, Mrs. Fulke - 13, Tarkan - 14. Only one point separates the two leaders. Reina will soon be mine!

MONDAY, August 8 — A new week, a new town (Albi), a new river (the Tarn). It appears that every town in France tries to have at least one tourist attraction. Albi's is an immense red-brick structure that looks like they started out to build a fort, but decided at the last minute to make into a church. Hard to believe people travel thousands of miles to eyeball ugly old churches, but upon this twisted impulse the French have built their national economy. Albi also is famous as the birthplace of the painter Henri de Toulouse-Lautrec, a little person who made it big, but not in the circus. There's a museum in town devoted to him, which I'm sure my wife already has toured if she's hiding out here. Mrs. Fulke likely will be kept too busy for such cultural enrichments.

A very windy morning, which greatly hampered the erection of the tents. Much cursing by the roustabouts as they struggled to control the flapping canvas. Poor Omar and Ajax were getting blown all over the lot as they strained to tug the heavy tent poles into upright position. Where are the elephants when you need them? Interesting fact about that: according to Captain Lapo, our circus once employed an elephant act, but Madame Poco reluctantly let them go because elephants attract animal rights activists "like flies." By contrast, no one seems to care if camels are exploited. I believe this to be because there's absolutely nothing endearing about a camel. This is also why no one objects when unattractive poor people are exploited in mind-numbing, low-wage jobs. If you ain't cute, you don't compute—as Mrs. Fulke has learned the hard way.

3:16 p.m. I've observed there's noticeably more tonnage to shovel out after a move. Why this is so I'm not sure, since I've always found travel to be constipating. I took a break from my muck-hauling to call Violet in Paris for an update. The good news, she reports, is Apurva has gone back to Ukiah. The bad news is T.P. is even more messed up than before. Now he is no longer faking his inability to perform.

"What are his symptoms?" I asked.

"His symptoms? Oh, there's weeping, staring into space, impotence, sleeplessness, pacing the floor, impotence, refusing all food, disinclination to bathe, impotence, being surly toward TV interviewers."

"Sounds like he's depressed, Violet."

"An astute observation, Rick."

"He had words with Apurva before she left?"

"Well, I imagine he did, since you told her about us!"

"I didn't mean to, Violet. Honest. From the way she was talking I thought she knew. Is Trent pissed at me?"

"Surprisingly not, Rick. He says he admires you for having the strength to act on your convictions—unlike him—and tell the truth."

Uh-oh. The guy's even more deranged than usual.

"He's processing some difficult emotions, Violet. These things take time. My advice is to be patient and to try to distract him with cultural outings."

"But he can't leave the building, Rick. Haven't you been reading the papers? Every time we try to go anywhere he's mobbed by frenzied fans."

"You mean like teeny-boppers?"

"Some. But mostly women over 40. He seems to have struck a powerful chord with that age group."

Handsome Trent being mobbed by lovesick matrons. Why does that thought brighten my day?

"Where is he now?" I asked.

"Down in the wig salon, Rick. The ladies there take turns holding him and stroking his brow. He finds that soothing."

Madame Lefèbvre is such a rescuer. I could use a nice session on her bosom myself.

"Sounds good, Violet. That should help a lot. I predict he'll snap out of it soon."

"I hope so, Rick. He's supposed to be memorizing his lines."

"What lines?"

"You *are* out of touch, Rick. He's starring in the new remake of *Breathless*. Filming starts next week."

Truly, a low, low blow. As if it isn't obvious to all: Rick S. Hunter was born to play that part. But no, lucky Trent gets to star in the remake of Sheeni's favorite movie, and I get a one-way ticket to Manureville.

10:45 p.m. Bowing to pressure from you know who, the committee tonight staged a contest called "Willingness To Listen." This entailed the three contestants listening intently while Donk read out a list of 100 items—mostly place names, historical figures, characters from fiction, bodies of water, etc. Then followed an interval of "muddling the mix," during which raucous onlookers shouted out as many similar names as they could think of. When the combatants were deemed adequately addled, we were handed paper and pencil and told to write down as many of the items from Donk's list as we could recall. For this feverish brain dump we were allotted ten minutes. Each correct answer earned us a point, while each incorrect item caused a point to be deducted.

Not easy, but Mrs. Fulke gave it her best shot. I had 74 items on my list when Donk blew his whistle. He collected our papers and turned them over to the judges for grading. Then came the tension-filled wait for results. Much more nerve-wracking than the SATs, which only determine your college destiny. Hell, this test could affect our sex lives for years to come. Jiri sucked on his leg, Mrs. Fulke fumbled with her oranges, outwardly calm Tarkan stroked his dense lip shrubbery. Impressed I was not. If a swarthy Turk can't grow a moustache, who can?

At last Donk emerged from the cookhouse to read the mind-boggling results: Tarkan - 28, Mrs. Fulke - 47, and Jiri - 82. Another upset. This time, believe it or not, the smart money had been on the old broad. The usual storm of protest from the Batur contingent. They demanded to see Tarkan's paper and then bitterly disputed the judges' interpretation of his childlike scratchings. For example, Mr. Batur claimed that what looked to any rational person like "Prack" was actually "Freud." Sorry, guy. The browbeaten judges awarded Tarkan six additional points for having an obnoxious family, but the pony jockey still finished last.

So Jiri got the kiss from Reina and the big five points. He explained that musicians develop an ear for listening and must have a good memory to retain all those notes. Sounds reasonable. But I always heard that guys going through nicotine withdrawal have the attention span of day-old road kill. So how did Jiri rack up such an amazing score—a total that would be exceptional even if achieved by my laser-focused wife? One possible exegesis for this paradox: Mr. Mestan had a preview peek at the list.

Could somebody on the committee be playing favorites?

Here are the latest Tour de Wife rankings: Jiri - 13, Tarkan - 15, Mrs. Fulke - 16.

Yes, I'm now in first place. Yes, François is determined to stay there. If this contest is going to be conducted with all the fairness of a Russian election, count on him to be in there gouging and biting with the lowest of the low.

TUESDAY, August 9 — Had a dream involving handguns last night that was excessively violent even for me. I used my weapon to shoot two guys in the head. In glorious color with real spurting blood and exploding exit wounds. Can't say for sure if it was Jiri and Tarkan, but I remember thinking as I squeezed the trigger that I would regret this for the rest of my life. Yet at the time I found the act strangely satisfying, particularly the recoil of the weighty gun. Do you suppose actual murderers experience a similar dichotomy of feeling as they blast their victims? Anyway, I jolted awake with a pounding heart and wondered momentarily what I was doing out of my tidy Oakland bed. Then I sniffed my mattress and it all came back to me.

Everyone got paid yesterday, including Jiri Mestan, the no-longer-penniless horn player. He showed up at breakfast today with a pipe stuck in his mouth. Reina sniffed the meerschaum bowl and found it had not been smoked in. Big change in Jiri's image. He can suck on the pipe and appear almost intelligent and nearly distinguished. Even verges on the scholarly at times—a big switch from his previous aspect as dissolute baby-eating cannibal. Of course, his new affectation inspired some cuttingly sarcastic comments from Mr. G. I don't think anyone can be as jocularly malicious as the English. So amiable as they thrust the rhetorical shiv into your gut.

Jiri pretends to find Mr. G amusing, but he has stopped talking to Mrs. Fulke altogether. These days she makes it a point to get to Reina's first for her shower and then lingers about to discourage promiscuous nudity. Obstinate Jiri flashed anyway this morning. Mrs. Fulke was publicly dismissive of such exhibitions, but privately appalled. I can only hope sweet Reina doesn't come to our nuptial bed with any false expectations inspired by Jiri's pendulous example.

1:48 p.m. After lunch Mrs. Fulke dropped by the clowns' table to chat up laconic Marcel. He greeted me like I was Typhoid Mary just back from a leper colony.

"Don't you think I'm doing surprisingly well in the contest, Marcel?"

"I can't be seen talking to you. It might give the appearance of favoritism."

"You mean like sneaking the list of 100 items—that Donk informs me you composed—to a contestant prior to the event?"

"What makes you think I did that?"

"Being nobody's fool, that's what. And if you try something like that again, I'll tell Reina."

"I suggest that you are hardly in a position to threaten me, Mrs. Fulke."

"What do you mean by that?"

"Excuse me," he said, getting up. "I'm due at a committee meeting."

That devious clown has something up his jumbo satin sleeve. I can tell.

4:26 p.m. I might have seen Sheeni! A rather effeminate, strangely familiar-looking goateed youth at today's matinee. Close-cropped chestnut hair under a black beret. I noticed him from the other side of the tent because he was walking out ostentatiously on Reina's performance. He was with an older, Latin-looking man. Both dressed somewhat shabbily from what I could see. At the moment I was assisting Captain Lapo in distress after a minor fire-eating mishap (slingshot, direct hit, gasp of surprise). I broke away as soon as I could, raced outside, and just missed the pair, who were driving off in a dusty green Citroën. I ran after them, shouting and waving, but the car didn't stop. Didn't get the license number either, not that it would do me much good. I'm hardly in a position to inquire about it at the local gendarmes' office.

Was it my long-lost wife? I can't say for sure. But why would he be wrapped in such a voluminous jacket on a warm day like today? What did he have to conceal? I know it wasn't a slingshot. The security guards already tackled that juvenile offender. Madame Poco showed no mercy. She dealt out her customary summary justice: a swat on the butt, confiscation of all snacks, and ejection from the lot.

11:45 p.m. I'm back. Very fatigued. Must have walked down every crooked, winding street in Albi three times. No sign of My Love, but I stickered many buildings. If that was her today, she should spot a sticker soon. Of course, it'll be tough for her to call since my phone was destroyed. Still, she'll know I'm looking for her and am in the vicinity. They must have seen the crazed old lady running after their car today. I'm hoping she'll employ her superb mind to put these simple facts together. It seems fairly obvious to me.

To give the tourists their money's worth, Albi illuminates its monstrous church at night. Looks a bit like a prison right after the big jailbreak. One almost expects to see Jimmy Cagney shinnying down a drainpipe. Doesn't seem like the kind of burg Sheeni would favor, but she is on the lam and it is well off the beaten track.

Turns out Mrs. Fulke missed tonight's Tour de Wife contest. The committee ruled it would go on without her. The theme, I'm told, was "Openness and Communication." Each contestant was given 30 minutes to prepare a five-minute talk on "The Saddest Day of My Life." Then members of company voted on which was most revelatory, heartfelt, and pitiful. Tarkan told about the dark day his first pony died. Not a dry eye in the house. Then Jiri spoke about the day his teacher was mugged on the streets of Prague. Not only did they steal his instrument, they knocked out his two front teeth. The most esteemed Czech trumpet player of them all would never blow another decent note. So he selflessly passed on the mantle of greatness to Jiri. Open weeping in the aisles. Jiri voted Best Communicator; bummed, pony-mourning Tarkan had to settle for second place. New rankings: Mrs. Fulke - 16, Jiri - 18, Tarkan - 18.

A temporary setback, but still a close race. And somewhere out there, perhaps close by, my own darling may be jotting a few notes in her journal or flossing her exquisite teeth. I just hope to hell she's not preparing to sleep with that lowlife I saw her with today.

WEDNESDAY, August 10 — A stressful day. Shit backing up everywhere as Mrs. Fulke spent many more hours neglecting her duties to comb the town for goateed youths and/or dusty green Citroëns. No sign of either, alas. Very discouraging. Of course, I don't know for certain that it was Sheeni. But who else would walk out on lovely Reina and her charming act? The bad news is the circus moves again tonight. In a desperate quandary. Should I quit the show and stay here? If I do that I lose Reina for sure. And what if I don't find Sheeni? Or what if I find her and she tells me to get lost? Damn.

6:12 p.m. Just spoke to Connie. She couldn't talk long as she and hubby had an appointment with a realtor to go house hunting in the ritzier sections of Bel Air and Pacific Palisades. They are back from their Hawaiian sojourn and camping temporarily in her mother's house. Untenable for very long as Paul and my father chafe severely under same roof. As I recall, I had the same problem. Connie has announced publicly that she is expecting, even though—she confessed privately to me—she has not quite achieved that happy state.

"Was that entirely wise?" I asked.

"Well, Paulo is thrilled, Rick. And we like to keep Paulo happy. I believe that is every intelligent wife's duty. Besides, I expect to get pregnant any minute now."

"But what if you don't? What if Paul is still firing blanks?"

"I'm confident that he's not, Rick. I'm very intuitive, as you know. And I've had a recent sample secretly analyzed. The motility is most encouraging. Anyway, if I don't get pregnant soon, I'll just go to a sperm bank and get the closest match to Paulo I can find. They have some wonderful fellows to choose from these days."

"But, Connie, it wouldn't be a real Saunders."

"Yes, well, as you know, Rick, that could turn out to be a blessing in disguise."

She had a point there. I gave her a quick summary of my present dilemma.

"Of course, you have to stay there, Rick. It sounds like too promising a lead not to follow up on."

"But I'm competing in a contest to marry Reina. It's a multi-stage competition like the Tour de France."

"You just confirmed my worst fears, Rick. I'd always heard that circuses were cesspools of degeneracy. I'm certainly thankful I dragged my Paulo out of there when I did."

I didn't tell Connie that she was beginning to sound just like her mother-in-law. I thanked her for her advice and rang off.

9:42 p.m. Kind Reina has interceded with the committee to have today's contest postponed until tomorrow. Such a considerate, sensitive girl. She could tell Mrs. Fulke was in turmoil and dropped by my camel sty earlier tonight to inquire what the problem was. I asked if she had noticed the two men who walked out of the matinee yesterday.

"I did notice them, Morag. One doesn't like to think one is driving away the customers. I thought perhaps they had a restroom emergency brought about by excessive candy consumption. Madame Poco is so relentless in pushing the refreshments inventory. I believe that is where she makes most of her profits."

"I think one of them might have been Sheeni—the guy with the beard."

"Oh dear, Rick. Are you sure?"

"Not at all. That's my problem. I didn't get a very close look at them. And I've searched all over Albi and haven't seen them anywhere."

"Oh dear. And now we're leaving."

She gave me a stricken look.

"What are you going to do, Rick?"

"I don't know, darling. What shall I do?"

"You should stay and find your wife, Rick. You should get matters settled between you."

Perhaps, but I found it difficult to think of Sheeni when Reina was so close.

"Get ready, Reina darling. I propose to kiss you again."

No slaps. No screams. We embraced, our lips met. Have any pair in the history of the human race ever fit together so felicitously? With such intensity of contact? Such transcendence of self into cosmic fusion with another?

THURSDAY, August 11 — We're in Mende. A new location, but the river that bisects it (the Lot) we've encountered before. Yeah, against all advice, I decided to remain with the circus. Every time I thought of staying behind in Albi, I got pissed. Mostly annoyed at my inconsiderate, maddening wife. Why should I scrounge around in some crummy town where I don't even speak the language on the off chance that I'll run into her? Is she ransacking the French countryside in search of me? I think not.

Not sure what's going on with my emotions. Perhaps only girls are in touch enough to decipher their true feelings. Guys only equipped to detect the most obvious ones like blatant sexual urges? I seem to have worked through most of my sadness, and now I'm back to wanting to strangle Sheeni. Is this healthy? Probably not, but genetics could be at work. As I recall, homicidal rage appeared to be the primary emotion my father was manifesting back when he faced my mother in divorce court.

Mende a small, sleepy town in the mountains. Pretty isolated, but as Madame Poco points out there's not much competition here either. She likes to be the only entertainment game in town, which is why we generally avoid the larger cities. The rube in the sticks—that's the demographic she's targeting. Curiously, unlike our homegrown rednecks, rural Frogs are by and large quite presentable looking. This confirms my long-held suspicion that Europe exported its most debased stocks to America—there to interbreed, sport bad haircuts, buy trailer homes on the installment plan, and zoom around in souped-up pickups. Quite a few of these rejects, I fear, contributed to my own suspect gene pool.

Captain Lapo ate heartily at our erection-delayed breakfast even though his mouth is a mass of blisters. I wish I could laugh off pain like that. I know it would make my love life so much easier to bear. On a happier note, Jiri got nailed again for nicotine duplicity. It turns out he had purchased two identical pipes—one to suck publicly and another to smoke surreptitiously. The first would be kept pristine to lull Reina into complacency. But he didn't realize that the pipe tobacco he bought was so aromatic you could smell it all over the lot—and all over him. Jiri tried to bluster his way out of it by insisting that he had only promised to swear off cigarettes, not tobacco in general. But Reina said all forms were equally lethal and confiscated both pipes and his tin of tobacco. She also told him the doll leg was an embarrassment and gave him one of her birds' cuttle bones to suck. Still looks a bit odd, but I suppose the calcium is doing him some good.

2:26 p.m. Confronted by truly monstrous piles today. Talk about a high-pressure low-wage job. It's like being at the end of a mammoth conveyer belt forever discharging endless lumps of you know what. So much as pause to scratch your butt and you fall dangerously behind. Good thing I have my radio to help keep up my morale. Taking a break from lugubrious Frank, I switched to a channel that plays seventies disco music. Rather insipid, but a very good beat to swing a shovel by. Yes, I have found at last a use for the Bee Gees.

10:17 p.m. Tonight's contest theme was "Sense of Humor." Donk explained that this was one of the most essential qualities in a good husband. For once, I had to agree. Any guy who proposes to live with a chick had better be so equipped. It can function like a marital shock absorber—turning a prolonged bumpy ride into mere patches of occasional queasiness.

I prayed the committee wouldn't ask us to get up and tell jokes. I knew Tarkan was an endless font of ribald stories. Likewise, Jiri seemed to have a bottomless supply of amusing anecdotes about Growing Up under Communism. I never realized that harsh oppression by the Russians and their cronies could be such a laugh riot. Me, I have a terrible memory for jokes. My old Oakland pal Lefty, by contrast, was a true connoisseur. But of the thousands of "jokes" he subjected me to only one ever stuck: "Question: What's the difference between pussy and parsley? Answer: Nobody ever eats parsley." We both found that vastly amusing, though neither of us had sampled the former at the time. Come to think of it, I wouldn't mind a light interlabial snack right now. There's nothing like swirling your tongue around a swelling clit. But I digress.

Donk outlined the particulars of today's contest. The contestants would be given 20 minutes to prepare a five-minute comedy routine. To overcome the language barrier and assure that our alleged senses of humor possessed universal appeal we could do anything we wished except speak. No talking was permitted. Like the diabolical Marcel we would have to do our clowning without words. I contemplated this assignment and found that my mind had gone completely blank. Instant panic and flop sweat. Was it possible that I was entirely devoid of a sense of humor?

Fortunately, Tarkan was picked to go first. He played a soccer goalie who had had too much to drink. The circus company roared with delight as Tarkan wove about, nearly falling over, yet somehow always scooping up the ball and booting it back in amusing ways, or losing it in his shirt, or "accidentally" spinning it on his nose. A sympathetic critic might say he combined the lithe athleticism of Buster Keaton with the comic timing of Charlie Chaplin. Not entirely unfunny to me, but I hoped everyone could see that the hearty laughter was being led by the maniacal hysterics of the Batur clan. The whole family was overplaying its hand as usual.

Next, emaciated Jiri came out in his skimpy shorts and did a striptease in reverse. As he flounced about, leering seductively and flexing his puny muscles, he slid the occasional clothing item *on* instead of off. Rather clever idea. His articles of apparel, apparently borrowed from a midget, were all much too small for him. He convulsed the appreciative audience as he slithered into tiny shirts and squeezed his stark white legs into trousers ten sizes too small. Shrieks of merriment from everyone except Mrs. Fulke and the stony-faced Baturs. Reina, I noticed with alarm, was in stitches. At least I could take solace in the knowledge that she was applauding Jiri for the act of enclothing his unsightly body. A *Playmate* centerfold he was not.

And then it was Mrs. Fulke's time to perform. Never have I been so nervous. Not even last Christmas Eve when Sheeni chose to give me that special present. Mrs. Fulke stared out at the sea of expectant faces. They stared back and tittered. The seconds crawled by. My reeling brain tried to unlock my rigid muscles. No one was answering the phone below my neck. Then I saw my right hand, quivering with fear, rise up. Then some internal hydraulics activated my left hand. Then someone switched on a Bee Gees tape in my mind, and Mrs. Fulke found herself break dancing to a disco beat. Fairly astounding, because I had never attempted this before. Had no knowledge, in fact, of ever conceiving of the idea. I was just doing it—without apparent volition. Just goes to show what heroics the human body can rise to in times of life-threatening stress. I was gliding, I was sliding, I was swiveling on my back, I was spinning like a top on my ratty gray wig. The audience went wild and clapped along to the beat. What beat? Apparently the one Mrs. Fulke was conjuring through her rhythmic gyrations. A 74-year-old lady break dancing to some unheard melody—not even the Baturs could entirely suppress a smile.

After all the votes had been counted, Donk announced that the results were very close. Tarkan placed two votes behind the leaders, who had finished in a dead heat. It was a tie. So the committee decided to award four points to Jiri and me, and a consolation three points to the talented Turk. New rankings: Mrs. Fulke - 20, Tarkan - 21, Jiri - 22.

Thank God it turned out I have a sense of humor. I was beginning to fear the worst.

FRIDAY, August 12 — Another "wee small hours of the morning" phone call from Connie. She's in despair because they can't find a decent house in their price range.

"Well, what is your price range?" I yawned.

"I'd like to keep it under five, Rick."

"Five what?"

"Five million, of course."

I nearly dropped the phone.

"You mean to tell me, Connie, that you can't find a decent house for five fucking million dollars?!"

"Not in a neighborhood I'd care to live in, Rick. It's all fixers or tear-downs. Or some hideous eyesore that's just been redone in some decorator's wretched taste. And God forbid if it was ever owned by a movie star. Then the price is doubled. I mean would you pay $3 million extra just to say you live in a house that was once owned by Broderick Crawford?"

"Connie, you're talking to a guy who's living in a camel van. I'm having trouble relating to your problem."

Even Connie could understand that. So she spent the next 20 minutes haranguing me for not staying in Albi and looking for my elusive wife.

"Rick, did I give up when my Paulo disappeared? Did I abandon my marriage plans?"

"No, Connie," I conceded. "You didn't."

"I can't believe you're proposing to ditch Paulo's pretty sister for some Bulgarian parrot freak."

"Reina's Czech, Connie. She's a very nice person. I love her a lot."

"If she's so nice, why is little miss home wrecker accepting phone calls from married men?"

"Paul called her?!"

"Three times, Rick. Naturally, I have immediate access to his phone records. He called her yesterday in fact."

"Maybe he wanted to tell her that he was going to be a father."

"It doesn't take 48 fucking minutes to convey that news!"

"Then you should be happy I want to marry her, Connie. Paul will have to give her up."

"It doesn't work that way, Rick," Connie sighed. "Remember, we always want what we cannot have."

Boy, do we ever. Damn, now I have to find a way to eavesdrop on Reina's phone. I feel it's a bad sign that she never told me she talked to Paul. Why is it that everywhere I turn there's a Saunders busy fucking over my life?

10:18 a.m. I never got back to sleep. Just as well. I'd probably have a dream in which Sheeni was introducing me to a pack of her studly new boyfriends. At the first light of dawn I sneaked out with my towel and knocked on Reina's caravan door. She was already awake, dressed, and looking heart-renderingly beautiful. Someday soon I hope to view a sunrise through her caravan window in some capacity other than early visitor.

After Mrs. Fulke showered and shaved, we settled onto Reina's cozy dinette for coffee and croissants. By now I barely noticed the deafening parrot screeches.

"Your wig is looking nice this morning, Morag," she commented.

"Thanks, Reina. It's quite the amazing rug. You can even spin your entire body on it and it springs back into shape. Vastly superior to actual hair. Hardly shows the dirt either. And the camel spit brushes right out after you let it dry. How are my wrinkles?"

"Very uniform and authentic looking. Quite grandmotherly in fact."

"Glad to hear it."

I sipped my coffee and casually let it drop that I had heard from Mrs. Paul Saunders.

"Oh," replied Reina with equal nonchalance, "how is she?"

"Rather stressed from house-hunting and being an expectant mother."

"Yes, Paul mentioned that."

"Oh, you've talked to him?"

"A few times. He calls me. You Americans think nothing of telephoning people on the other side of the world."

"What does he, uh, call up to say? If I may be so nosy as to inquire?"

"He doesn't think I should get married. He thinks the contest is stupid."

"Really. Why's that?"

"He says if I met the right person, I would know it. That I wouldn't be troubled by these, uh, uncertainties."

"Does he say anything about his marriage?"

"He said that if he didn't marry her, she was going to have his parole revoked. You have interesting friends, Rick."

"Connie never told me that, Reina. It may not be true."

"I have no reason to disbelieve Paul, Rick."

"Does he say anything about me?"

"He says you are going to have a hard time, Rick."

"A hard time because of the littlest monkey?"

"He said nothing about that, Rick. What's this about a monkey?"

But our conversation was interrupted by the arrival of another freeloading shower cadger. Jiri entered, attempted unsuccessfully to plant one on Reina's lips, and gave Mrs. Fulke a look that could curdle cream. When, later, the bathroom door popped open, Reina and I both made a point of turning away and gazing out the front window. Someday that towel-waving exhibitionist is going to brush up against a parrot cage, and something large and floppy is going to receive a nasty bite.

5:12 p.m. The monkeys are revolting. At today's matinee Mr. Granley blew his whistle and his monkeys just looked at him like he was the Gym Teacher from Mars. No one moved a muscle. Finally, Number Three consented to do a few sprongs on the trampoline, but that was it. Their entire program of tricks was suddenly off the menu. Since Captain Lapo was in no condition to eat fire or munch light bulbs, he had to run out and pound a few nails into himself while Mr. G's act was rolled away in disgrace. No problem though with Donk's monkey Dink, who handed out his treats and took his little bows with his usual aplomb. Then Mr. G had the nerve to blame the mutiny on Mrs. Fulke. The officious twit has banned disco music in general and my radio in particular from the monkey van. Mrs. Fulke is feeling a bit smug. She's been trashing Mr. G privately to his troupe for weeks, and it finally looks like all that badmouthing has paid off. Now if only Tarkan's ponies would start paying attention.

11:42 p.m. No performances tonight for Mr. G. He's been excused for a few days of intensive act freshening. He did appear in the cookhouse along with other members of the company to observe tonight's Tour de Wife contest titled "Visions of Love." Too bad it wasn't an eye test. I always ace those, being able to spot a wart on a gnat's ass at 50 yards. No, tonight's task was to draw a portrait of Reina, who kindly posed for us in all her fully clothed pulchritude. Passing out the paper and colored pencils, Donk stated that a good husband should be artistic—a rule that was news to me. Since Reina was going to all the trouble of holding still, many non-contestants clamored to join in. At least a dozen wannabe Picassos gathered round My Sweet Love to translate her comeliness into Personal Artistic Statements.

Now I have my egotistical moments, but one thing I have never claimed to be is an artist. Never will I forget that embarrassing incident in the sixth grade when an art teacher singled me out as someone who could draw "nothing except flies." Her assessment, alas, was spot on. My artistic skills are nil, zilch, less than zero. Puling two-year-olds with soiled nappies and gum in their hair can wield a crayon with greater adroitness than any Twisp. We are not an artistic people. Nevertheless, I gazed at Reina's perfect features and tried mightily to forge a link between my eager eyeballs and my spastic hand. I've heard it's simply a matter of getting into the proper side of the brain. No such luck. Both orbs of my brain were equally inept. My portrait resembled a space alien as drawn by the traumatized victim of an intergalactic abduction and sex probe.

At last Donk blew his whistle, terminating the artistic torment. Everyone signed their drawings on the back, and Donk pinned them to the walls of the tent for judging.

Two, everyone agreed, stood out. One was no worse than the mature work of Johannes Vermeer of Delft. The other was a competent likeness. The rest were more or less pathetic, though one outshone all the others in incompetence. Once again a Twisp had achieved absolute artistic nadir.

Surprisingly, the competent likeness was by Donk. The masterpiece—Reina was amazed to discover—was by the gifted hand of Marcel Fazy. Whoever would have supposed the atrabilious clown was such an artist? He graciously signed it again on the front and presented it to Reina with his compliments. She thanked him warmly and promised to have it framed. She also kissed Donk for his commendable effort.

"But what about my drawing?" pouted Tarkan, pointing to a portrait of an ugly horse-faced girl. "Is it not clearly superior to all the others?"

No, was the unanimous verdict. The three contestants were judged equally untalented and awarded one point each. (New rankings: Mrs. Fulke - 21, Tarkan - 22, Jiri - 23.) Fervid but ultimately futile protests by the Baturs against consignment to the same category as Mrs. Fulke. As for Jiri, he merely shrugged and tore up his muddled effort, which to my eyes looked more like Omar than Reina.

Considering the slew of drunkards, adulterers, and wife-abusers who've made it big in the art world, I wonder if "artistic temperament" is a quality one should seek in a husband. Sure, Trent Preston can paint like Cézanne, but would you really want to marry the twit? That reminds me, I must get an update soon on his marital woes.

SATURDAY, August 13 — Can you believe it's been over three months since Sheeni and I were wed in distant Mississippi? And nearly half that interval has passed since our tragic parting. I marked the occasion with a somber memorial wank. For a change I mentally undressed Sheeni rather than Reina while flailing away. The usual thunderous climax followed almost immediately by a black depression. Those feel-good serotonins never linger in my brain when I contemplate my departed wife.

Wish I had an American tape measure. It seems to me my T.E. is looking more impressive these days. Who knows? I soon may be nudging Reina's bathroom door open myself to flash a Notable Specimen.

This morning's contest theme was "Judicious Thrift." The contestants and committee adjourned to Mende, whose main street hosts a regular Saturday morning flea market. Lots of rustic natives peddling items from the backs of their cars or from small makeshift trailers. As specified, each contestant arrived with exactly *E*10 in cash. As instructed by Donk, we were to wander about and purchase those items best exemplifying "judicious thrift." The guy who returned with what was judged (by Reina) the most bang for his bucks would win. (This presupposes she desires to marry a cheap tightwad.) All items had to be purchased outright and could not be obtained through loans or other devious means. To prevent cheating, each of us would be accompanied by a committee member. This time Mrs. Fulke drew Marcel, who sighed loudly and gave me a look that could tan leather. Then Donk blew his whistle and off we went.

Even out of his clown outfit, Marcel is not the ideal shopping companion. Anything you pick up to inspect triggers a great display of contemptuous eye rolling. Hey, I wasn't going to buy that rusty calf-castrating tool, I just wanted to see how it worked. Do you suppose they used a similar implement on poor Abelard?

Nor can the Mende market be termed a bargain hunter's paradise. Farm produce and such ilk comprised about a third of the offerings. Yes, you could buy an entire wheel of cheese, but not for *E*10. Another third was apparel related. I spotted an interesting wedding gown that might have fit Reina, but it was priced at a delusional *E*45. Then you had your optimistic displays of rusty tools, odd car parts, musty books (almost all in French), yellowed magazines, old-lady handicrafts, dubious electronic items, obsolete computer components, previously sweated-in shoes, battered toys, and suspect jewelry. I asked Marcel if he thought a rather attractive pair of earrings were real pearls, but he just sighed and rolled his eyes. So I passed on them. I did find a picture frame that seemed the right size for Marcel's drawing. The man was asking *E*5, but I turned Mrs. Fulke's accent up and nailed it for a mere *E*2. Sharp bargaining is to be expected—all Europe knows—when you're confronting a Scot. That left me with *E*8 and less than 15 minutes to go in our one-hour shopping spree. Time to pick up the pace.

A hand-carved oak cradle seemed just the thing to appeal to Reina's maternal side, but the obstinate vendor wouldn't budge from *E*12. A bit bulky for a crowded caravan anyway. For the same reason I had to nix a rusty but repairable Peugeot bicycle in my price range. Then I spotted a glint of gold. An old pocket watch, and yes, it appeared to be ticking. A rather plain dial, but perhaps hand-painted. I pried open the hinged back. An intricate movement with gleaming red things that might be jeweled bearings. Rubies? Sapphires? A tiny hallmark on the case that my eagle eyes deciphered as "18k." I held up the watch and looked inquiringly at the ancient lady vendor. Marcel grudgingly translated.

"She says she is holding it for a mad foreigner accompanied by a giant."

Unquestionably Jiri. I waved my *E*8 and smiled into her cloudy green eyes. Don't be fooled by the wig, I telegraphed, it's a face you remember from your youth. A liverish hand reached out and grabbed the cash. The deed was done. A moment later I spotted Jiri hurrying in our direction. We turned and melted into the crowd. Then Donk's whistle sounded from down the block. Our shopping spree was over.

2:28 p.m. The cargo was laid before Reina at lunchtime in the cookhouse. Mrs. Fulke went first.

"Here is a picture frame for your portrait by Marcel. My guess is it's lime or pear wood. You'll notice the wavy glass is quite old."

"Very nice," said Reina.

"And here's an antique pocket watch. Probably Swiss or French, with an 18-karat solid gold case and jeweled movement. I think it couldn't be any later than early 19th Century. And as you can see, it works fine."

It had lost ten minutes since I had set it, but one could hardly demand precision timekeeping from something that old.

"A beautiful watch!" exclaimed Reina. "Thank you, Morag."

Next up was Jiri, who began by flashing me a look that could bruise exposed flesh. The spendthrift was sucking a large piece of peppermint candy, doubtless purchased in town with funds embezzled from his "judicious thrift" monies.

"Here is old zither, Reina," he said, producing a decrepit stringed instrument. "Not such good condition, but I play you a tune."

He then manipulated the thing to produce a quaint melody and a large cloud of musty mold spores. Jarringly out of tune, but apparently charming to its recipient. Reina thanked him heartily.

"Show her what else you got," prodded Donk.

Jiri reluctantly extracted something from his pocket. It was a distressingly familiar-looking gold watch.

Marcel smiled and offered an explanation. "These fakes are flooding in from Russia. Thin brass-plating over pot metal. Hong Kong movements. They usually sell for two or three euros."

For a change, Mrs. Fulke gave *him* the nasty look. Thanks a pantsful, creep.

"Well, they're very pretty timepieces," said Reina, perceiving our embarrassment. "I'm sure they will come in handy."

For what, I wondered? Target practice? Sock darning? Braining an amorous horn player?

Finally, Tarkan coughed up his baksheesh.

"Dearest Reina, I bought for you this enchanting pair of pearl earrings."

Mrs. Fulke saw red.

"Those things are fake!" she charged.

Ignoring me, the cad smiled at Reina and handed her a formal-looking certificate.

"Anticipating such objections," he said, "Captain Lapo and I had my purchase appraised this morning at Mende's largest jewelers. As you can see, they were declared genuine and valued at *E*480. The settings are 14k gold."

"They are lovely, Tarkan," said Reina, "but I cannot accept them."

"But why not, my darling?" he asked.

"I cannot accept from you your mother's pearl earrings."

A tremendous uproar. Expostulations of outrage from the other contestants. Indignant denials of treachery by the Baturs. Dazed confusion by Captain Lapo when pressed if such a substitution could have been made. More outrage when Mrs. Batur mysteriously unable to produce her own pair of pearl earrings. Then she "recalled" she had left them in Istanbul, but several witnesses testified they had seen her wearing them on this tour. Donk acted decisively. Declared Jiri the winner, Mrs. Fulke second, and Tarkan a fraud. The Turk socked with zero points for the day, and earrings handed back to his mom. She again denied they were hers, but grabbed them in a flash when Mrs. Fulke volunteered to take them. New rankings: Tarkan - 22, Mrs. Fulke - 24, Jiri - 28.

Some satisfaction in seeing Tarkan get his comeuppance, but still smarting from fleecing by elderly Frog sharpie. How can Europe hope to stay united when innocent visitors from UK are prey to such swindles? And why hasn't that old lady been locked away in some luxurious rest home? I thought the socialists were running this country.

11:09 p.m. More outrages. Lovely Reina just spotted sipping wine—in Marcel's caravan! Even more damning, he was in there with her. Both laughing merrily and having a good time.

More buyer's remorse. I should have skipped the watch. And bought the castrating tool.

SUNDAY, August 14 — An interesting development in the "Judicious Thrift" contest. Last night while framing Marcel's picture in his caravan (a likely story), Reina slid out the wooden backing from my frame and discovered an old print. Labeled "Ciconia, Cigogne," it depicted several long-legged birds, possibly storks. It was signed "Nicolas Robert," and appeared to be a hand-colored engraving from some distant century. Madame Poco thought it might be valuable. In any case, it was judged a greater prize than Jiri's moldering zither, so there's been an adjustment in the Tour de Wife standings. New rankings: Tarkan - 22, Mrs. Fulke - 26, Jiri - 26. Mrs. Fulke received a belated lesbianistic kiss, and the storks have gone up on Reina's caravan wall instead of Marcel's art. A very nice gift for a bird lover, even if she is suddenly hobnobbing with despised clowns.

Practiced my juggling this morning after a few days' layoff and found my skills had improved considerably. I believe this is often the case. Just imagine how much better I'll be at sexual intercourse should I ever get a chance to resume that activity. No prospects at the moment though. Many balls are in motion, but not my own.

1:45 p.m. After lunch I called my contortionist pal Violet in Paris. Her mobile phone was answered by an all-too-familiar male voice.

"Hi, Trent," I said. "Where's Violet?"

"She's out talking to the assistant director. We're sharing a trailer on the set. I want to thank you, Nick, for informing my wife of my heinous duplicity."

No detectable sarcasm in that remark. T.P. was nothing if not sincere.

"I hope you guys are working things out, Trent."

"I've made everyone truly wretched, including myself."

Hard to believe a guy that good-looking could be such a depressive. I struggled to maintain an upbeat tone.

"Hey, are you guys working on that movie?"

"Yes, we're in our third day of shooting. Pretty interesting so far. Violet is a marvelous actor."

"She's in the movie too?"

"Yes, they decided to write a contortionist into the plot. I'm not sure the script makes much sense, but the French aren't hung up on such conventions."

No, they wouldn't be.

"How are you doing, Nick?"

"Not bad, Trent. Say, thanks for not ratting on me to the cops."

"That's OK, Nick. I've had a lot of time to think while being soothed by your friends in the wig salon. They all say hello, by the way. I figured out why you tried so hard to get Apurva and me married."

"Oh. You did, huh?"

"I realized that you felt that true love requires commitment. That was always your great strength. You were incredibly committed to Sheeni, whereas I've been a weak and miserable failure with Apurva."

"You'll work through this, Trent. I know you will. You're stronger than you think."

"I appreciate your encouragement, Nick. It means a lot coming from you. Well, they want me on the set. I have to go shoot some more people. My character is quite ruthless and violent. To get into my role, I think about how you blasted Sheeni's father for her passport."

Damn, are there any of my crimes that Sheeni hasn't blabbed to the world?

"She told you that was me, huh?"

"Yes, Nick. It was another magnificent gesture for love. Take care, my good friend."

"Oh, OK, Trent. Keep in touch."

Wow, that guy sure has gone off the deep end. Just goes to show what fame, money, and too much contortionist sex can do to a person. Where do I sign up? All in all, though, I think I preferred our previous arrangement where we just hated each other's guts.

6:28 p.m. Lovely Reina brought one of her many pocket watches to dinner this evening. I must have been blind yesterday. Blatantly crude construction that would appall the most slovenly Swiss artisan. The "jeweled bearings" were obvious simulations daubed on in iridescent red paint. And the "18k" hallmark was in fact "RUS," which must stand for "R U a Sucker?" Just goes to show how the bargain-hungry mind can deceive itself.

Since Mr. G was working nonstop to whip his monkeys back into shape, Mrs. Fulke got to sit next to My Sweet Love at dinner. I love to watch Reina eat. She brings such sensuality to the task of masticating a pork cutlet. What does it mean, I wonder, when you derive so much satisfaction from watching your girlfriend's teeth pulverize meat? And should one be quite so titillated by the mundane act of swallowing? Clearly, Jiri was not the only one with unresolved oral issues.

Yes, he and Marcel were crowded about her too, so you can imagine the competition for her attention. Reina finds us all amusing, but she does seem to laugh more at Marcel's jests. The guy's a real Noel Coward of the Sawdust when he wants to be. Of course, he has an unfair advantage, being a professional entertainer. I mean should any of us be impressed that a clown can be funny?

10:46 p.m. No Tour de Wife contest today. It was Marcel's turn to think of one, but he was too busy chatting up Reina in his new role of witty sophisticate. Somebody should remind that clown he was disqualified from the competition for Reina's affections.

Received another installment of my Dickensian wage today. Such an anemic pile of bills—like something you'd hand to a kid for mowing your lawn. Instead, that's all I get for seven days of hard labor. I wonder how much Marcel makes? Haven't a clue. Seems like a guy would have to be highly paid to paint his face and go out and make a fool of himself in public like that. Wonder what he spends his money on? No visible vices that I can see. And it doesn't cost a dime to sport a miserable personality.

We're on the road to somewhere. Cars behind us are honking away. My guess is Iyad has coaxed it up to a rash 18 mph and is holding steady. Too bad we only travel at night. I'm probably missing some prized scenery. Even so, circus life is quite a rich diet for the senses. The sights, the sounds, the smells are much more vivid than anything I previously encountered. I've been at it just a few weeks, but it seems like I can barely remember a time when I wasn't traveling with the show. Not a bad life if I could upgrade to a better job and get laid more often. The roustabouts, for example, have it pretty good. No shit to shovel, and they earn enough for professional female companionship in every town. Too bad they don't have enough left over for regular dental care. Is the secret to a happy life being a muscle-bound sexist lowlife?

MONDAY, August 15 — We're in Béziers, one of your more historic French towns. The obligatory fortress-like Gothic church plopped down on the highest hill. And two water features: the Orb river and the tree-shaded Canal du Midi. This was dug by hand many centuries ago to connect the Atlantic with the Mediterranean, thus eliminating that bothersome sail around Spain. No doubt somebody got rich treating all those hernias. We're very far south now—nearly to the Mediterranean coast, I'm told. Most pleasant weather. Clear sunny days and not too hot. All around us grapes are ripening on the vines. Lovely views in all directions under a stunning blue sky. Almost makes one happy to be alive, even if countless tons awaiting the touch of my shovel. Laundry backing up too. Mrs. Fulke the smelliest old gal in France?

2:12 p.m. Another excursion into town with Reina in her station wagon to track down a launderette and hair salon. I guarded the tumbling dainties while My Sweet Love submitted to the styling whims of a nearby beautician. Not an unflattering cut if you ask me, and Reina did. We folded our laundry, and Mrs. Fulke attempted to ferret out the reason her companion was so pensive and distracted. Finally, Reina spilled the beans. Early this morning she had spotted a certain horn player exiting the caravan of Madame Poco.

"She's old enough to be his mother!" Reina exclaimed.

"Very true," I said.

Yeah, but so are a lot of attractive chicks, I thought. Who am I to exclude from my masturbatory fantasies our foxy employer?

"I don't understand it," she complained. "Do you men need sex that badly?"

"In my experience, Reina, sex is like water. It's only important when you're not getting any."

"Really?"

"It's the testosterone, Reina. That's what drives the reproductive impulse in both males and females. And we guys have about 20 times more of it firing our boilers than you chicks."

"Oh dear, Morag. That's dreadful. But how do you know all this?"

"Health class. I was paying attention that day."

"Would you sleep with Madame Poco if she asked you? Now be honest."

"Well, I certainly wouldn't if I were married to you."

"Then you would. My goodness, that explains a lot."

"Are you going to disqualify Jiri from the contest?" I asked hopefully.

"If I did that, I'd have to disqualify everyone. Tarkan is always flirting with the townies, and I know he goes out some nights with the roustabouts. And what about those two young girls you were with in Poiters?"

My heart seized.

"How did you know about that?"

"Marcel told me. He saw them leaving your van. He asked me if I thought you were dealing drugs."

"We, we were just talking."

"I always know when you're lying, Morag. You're not as good at it as you suppose. Anyway, it's none of my business whom you sleep with."

"They seduced me, Reina darling. It was quite deliberate on their part. I was feeling lonely and, well, these things happen. But it is you I love!"

Two middle-aged tourists, possibly English, looked up with a start from the backpacks they were stuffing with clean socks and sensible clothes.

"Lesbians," I heard one of them whisper.

"But she's old enough to be the pretty one's grandmother!" hissed the other.

Reina and I gathered up our laundry and flounced out.

On the drive back I asked Reina if she liked Marcel.

"Don't be silly, Morag. He's nearly as old as Mr. Granley."

"He loves you, you know. That's why he agreed to be on the committee. So he can torture the competition."

"Do you really think he loves me?"

"It's as plain as the red plastic nose on his face."

Reina smiled. It was not a smile I found at all comforting.

11:32 p.m. A question posed by Donk in the cookhouse while introducing tonight's Tour de Wife competition: What husbandly virtue is also the title of a Gilbert and Sullivan operetta?

I tried to think. Didn't they write something about pirates? "Rape and pillage"—was that to be the theme of this night's contest? No such luck.

"Patience," explained Donk to our three blank faces. "A good husband must display remarkable patience."

So get on with it, I thought. Let's see what torture Marcel has devised this time.

It was fairly Mephistophelean, even for that fiend. The three contestants were seated on chairs in a circle with our knees nearly touching. Each was handed a glass, only one of which was filled with water. That person was to pour the water into his neighbor's glass, caress his or her cheek, and say "I love you, darling." The water pouring and love declaring would continue around the circle for one hour. The guy judged most sincere in his conduct would be the winner. Anyone who dropped his glass or didn't say exactly the correct words would be out. Any laughter, stressed Donk, would be regarded as evidence of insincerity.

Easy for him to say.

You try caressing Tarkan's leathery puss, calling him darling, and telling him you love him. Not even Reina could do that with a straight face. And why hadn't Mrs. Fulke remembered to shave that morning? I thought Jiri was going to sand off his skin caressing my coarse cheek. Gave him quite a shock the first time and definitely took the edge off his sincerity. Very hard not to giggle with everyone in the company whooping it up—especially Reina. Women are the true sadists, I've decided, even the apparently sweet-natured ones. All in all, I think I preferred her previous mood of pensive melancholy.

Around and around the water went. A very tedious activity, if you haven't tried it. After a while, very hard to do things in proper order and not mess up on the words. Treacherous Jiri inclined to pour sloppily and splash water onto my lap. Fake sincerity difficult to sustain even for Mrs. Fulke. I knew the only way to appear convincing was to look Tarkan directly in his smoldering eyes. Most trying for a person to do that round after round. Psychologically unnerving. The mind doesn't know what to make of this tumult of disquieting data. So the body rebels. The muscles of the face constrict. The voice tries to shut down. The hand holding the glass starts to shake. Would this torture never end?

Donk called out the time. Fifty minutes remaining.

Utter stupefaction. Had we only been going at it for ten minutes? It seemed like an eternity.

At 37 minutes into the torture Tarkan screwed up and said "I love you, dearest." Marcel caught the flub and declared Tarkan out. Violent protests by the Baturs, who said Tarkan was at a disadvantage because he had to declare his love to a man, which was anathema to all Turks. No homosexuals in Turkey? Donk declared them out of order, and Tarkan stomped off in a huff. Now Mrs. Fulke had to express her affections to Jiri, a guy who was sucking the cork from a wine bottle. All my being longed to say, "I loathe you, dickhead," but somehow I squeezed out the correct words time after time. At least now I got to spill water onto *his* lap.

At 49 minutes into the game, Jiri tossed his glass over his shoulder, screamed "You are very disgusting person, Mrs. Fulke," and threw himself whimpering onto the ground. His crackup arrived about 12 seconds before mine was due. Slumping back in my chair, I barely acknowledged the congratulatory kiss from you know who.

Rather amazing results. Nick Twisp, descended from a long line of premature-ejaculating, short-tempered, Type-A heart attack victims, proved the champion in patience. Well, they say juggling can be meditative. New rankings: Tarkan - 23, Jiri - 29, Mrs. Fulke - 31.

Feeling pretty good except for one thing. I may never be able to say "I love you" to another human being for as long as I live.

TUESDAY, August 16 — I rose extra early to snoop. Not only did Jiri exit Madame Poco's caravan this morning, but he gave our negligee-clad employer a kiss and nipple squeeze on his way out. Apparently, he wasn't just crashing on her sofa. This may explain why that nicotine-deprived trumpeter hasn't been fired for incompetence. Too bad my erstwhile landlady Madame Ruzicka hadn't coughed up a spare passport from some deceased male. If I were *Mr.* Fulke, I could have put the moves on Madame Poco myself and been promoted out of the shit pits. By now I might be her pampered houseboy in charge of light snacks and undergarment care. Reina might find this intimate servitude troubling, but at least—like Jiri—I would be appearing to be what she wants but cannot have.

Only one month to go in our circus tour. Yes, there's light at the end of a very stinky tunnel, but what will I do when it comes time to hang up my shovel? I suppose I could camp out across the street from that school in Paris in hopes that Sheeni shows up for class. Or, if I succeed with Reina, perhaps we could sign up for some fall circus tour. I could help her with her birds and show her what she's been missing for the past 17-3/4 years. Speaking of which, I arrived at Reina's caravan this morning before she was entirely dressed. She scurried back to her bedroom to finish, but through a fortuitous confluence of mirrors, I caught a gratifying eyeful. Just as I suspected. Not only beautiful, but a delicious body to boot. Wish English language possessed a better word than "nubile" to describe her pulse-quickening curves. Do you suppose Bill Shakespeare crashed up against this same linguistic dead end while penning his love sonnets?

10:45 a.m. Mrs. Fulke had to excuse herself from the cookhouse tent at breakfast to take a call. It was Connie phoning with an update from Bel Air. Her mother's one-armed factotum Dogo Dimondo secretly videotaped on multiple occasions my father swatting Anna and Vronsky, Mrs. Krusinowski's much-doted-upon chihuahuas. Last night Dogo handed the shocking evidence to his employer, and her reaction was swift and terrible. Out the door went my father, his meager possessions, and his manuscript of the great American chihuahua novel.

"Hitting a little dog with his shoe," exclaimed Connie. "Can you believe it?"

"Doesn't surprise me," I replied. "As I recall, he was always swinging something at me. A shoe would have been a nice change of pace."

"Paulo is thrilled, of course. It's been very tense having to sit down to meals with that creep. I know they kept reminding each other of Lacey, which is the one person I don't want my husband obsessing over. Her and your little bird tootsie."

"How is Lacey?"

"Very affluent, unfortunately. My lawyers continue to insist there's no way to break Father's will. So I'm trying to persuade her to go to Brazil to look after needy slum children."

"Is she interested in that?"

"Not so far, dammit. The bitch appears to have no social conscience at all. Oh, I have some more good news. We put an offer in on a house."

"That's nice, Connie. You found something within your budget, huh?"

"Well, we had to stretch a bit. Not everything we wanted, but the realtor thinks it might have been leased once by Orson Welles."

"In that case, you might want to have the floor joists inspected."

"You're so politically incorrect, Rick. I like that. Nobody in this town would dare touch a fat joke these days."

2:18 p.m. Had a scare this afternoon. Mrs. Poco called me into her caravan on my way to lunch. Her rolling home was quite a lavish affair with a distinctly feminine smell—like pink lacy items nestled in perfumed (bureau) drawers. As usual, she got straight to the point.

"Jiri Mestan seems to think you're not a woman."

Mrs. Fulke colored and looked at her crud-caked shoes.

"Why, why whatever do you mean?" I gulped.

"Your passport identifies you as a female, but to be frank, Morag, your appearance leaves this open to question. As your employer, I have to be concerned that you might not be who you claim to be."

"It's true that my voice is not as bird-like as it once was," I admitted. "But I used to smoke unfiltered Camels—the cigarettes, not the animals."

"It's not just your voice, Mrs. Fulke. Frankly, your mannerisms are rather masculine."

"That's not a very complimentary remark," I said, offended. "What would you like me to do—undress?"

"OK, if you don't mind."

Damn. She would call my bluff. My reeling mind grasped for a Plan B.

"Well, Madame Poco, I must confess there was some, uh, confusion when I was born. My parents made the difficult decision to raise me as a girl."

"I see. And yet you have a son?"

"Actually, Stanley is my nephew. My dear departed sister was much less, uh, ambiguous."

"And Mr. Fulke?"

"He was a very understanding gentleman. He had no complaints in that department, if you must know."

Now it was Madame Poco's turn to blush.

"That's fine, Morag. I understand. We circus people are very welcoming to persons, uh, outside the norms. I'll tell Jiri to mind his own business."

"Thank you, Madame Poco. I appreciate it. Your caravan is very nice. And so spacious."

"Why thank you, Morag."

"Should you ever require the services of a maid, I'd be happy to apply for that position."

"Oh? Well, uh, I'll keep that in mind."

"I wouldn't smell so bad then, you know—not having to associate with animals all the time."

"Yes, I understand, Morag. I know how taxing your current job can be."

She gave me a smile and we shook hands. A very firm grip for a woman. Kissable lips too. Some wrinkles, but not yet at the appalling stage. Yes, no doubt about it. I could do her.

6:12 p.m. "Resourcefulness" has been announced as the theme of tonight's Tour de Wife contest. We are to gather in the cookhouse after the evening performance. As a former Cub Scout, I feel particularly well-equipped in that category. Only two more contests to go after this one, and then dearest Reina will be mine. Though we may not be able to marry for some time, I expect our intimacies will progress immediately to a higher plane (or, as you rigid moralists may fear, to a more horizontal plane).

11:53 p.m. A difficult evening. My poor wrists are rubbed raw. Not surprisingly, the committee's test for "Resourcefulness" was a bit more sadistic than even my scoutmaster's. The three combatants were made to lie down in the cookhouse tent. Then our ankles and knees were tied and our wrists bound behind our backs—all with strong nylon slip ties. We were left on the ground trussed up like turkeys while everyone else exited chuckling. First person to emerge unfettered from the cookhouse would be the winner.

Now it's one thing to wiggle out of ropes. My old pal Lefty and I used to borrow his mom's clothesline and tie each other up occasionally for sport. Even our tightest knots never held for long, because a rope you can work back and forth to loosen. But those nylon ties hold fast no matter how much you squirm. And their narrow edges can cut into your flesh. So we three grubs rolled around on the grass looking for something sharp to rub against. The folding tables and chairs were either aluminum or plastic—too soft to cut tough plastic. And all the sharp-edged cooking implements were locked up tight in the commissary caravan that closed off the open end of the three-walled tent.

Tarkan was the first to get lucky. Under one of the tables he scrounged up an unused kitchen match. Jiri spotted him trying to light it with his teeth.

"Tarkan, no!" he shouted.

I translated Tarkan's mumbled reply as, "Fuck off. It's my match. I found it first."

"Yes, but what you do with it? Match won't burn long enough to help you. I tell you what. I get cigarette butt from ashtray. Then you light my cigarette."

"Jiri, can't you forget about smoking for one minute?" I demanded.

"Shut up, Mrs. Fulke," he replied. "Tarkan, you light my cigarette, I burn off your wrist tie. Then you free me. We cooperate and go out together. We share first place."

Tarkan thought this over.

"OK, Jiri," he mumbled. "Go get a cigarette butt. The longest one you can find."

"Great, Tarkan. We be partners. But you promise to free me too. Right?"

"Sure, I promise."

"Hey, what about me?" I called.

"Mrs. Fulke, go fuck yourself," said Jiri, working himself upright, flopping down on a table, and nosing through an ashtray. "Why these cheap fuckers have to smoke their cigarettes so far?"

He lurched over to another table and located a half-smoked Gauloise. Then the two conspirators got nose-to-nose on the ground, and Tarkan swiped his match against a chair leg. On the third try, it flared into life—nearly setting his moustache on fire—but soon Jiri was puffing away madly on his butt.

"Hey, go easy on that," cried Tarkan, spitting out the match and swiveling around to present his wrists to Jiri's face.

Soon I smelled the acrid aroma of burning plastic.

"Hey, don't burn me!" yelled Tarkan.

"Sorry, I can't see this close up," mumbled Jiri.

In less than a minute, Tarkan's hands were free and he was rubbing his wrists. Then he grabbed the cigarette from Jiri's lips and burned through the ties around his knees and ankles.

"OK, Tarkan, now you do me," said Jiri.

"Oh, right. I almost forgot."

Tarkan bent down, applied the lit cigarette to the back of Jiri's neck, then snuffed it out on the ground with his foot.

Much bellowing from his injured partner as the backstabbing Turk exited the tent.

"Did you really believe you could trust that fink?" I asked, rubbing my wrist tie against the dull steel edge of the commissary bumper. With luck, I thought, I might be free by morning.

"Shut up, Mrs. Fulke!" screamed Jiri, nosing around in the dirt.

Miraculously, he managed to revive the stepped-on butt and soon was inhaling restorative tobacco poisons. He then bent forward and burned through his knee tie. Progress, I suppose, but only Violet could contort far enough to reach the critical ankle and wrists ties. Jiri spat out his butt (it was down to the filter) and rolled over near me. He kicked up on the metal steps that folded out under the commissary door, placed his feet between the steps and their frame, and leaned his knees against the top step. With a startling snap, this leverage action broke his ankle tie. He then maneuvered his wrists into the same position and shoved back against the step. From the intensity of his scream, I gathered that he cut through some skin as well as his wrist constraints. But the resourceful guy was free as a bird. He clutched his bleeding wrists and walked over to me.

"Poor Mrs. Fulke finish last," he taunted. "Now we see if you really a lady."

And then the cad rudely thrust a probing hand down the front of my pink stretch pants. Yes, he found the prize in the Cracker Jacks box. I lunged to bite him, but he pulled away too fast.

"Mrs. Fulke is no lady," he sneered, wiping his blood on my blouse.

"If you tell anyone I'm a hermaphrodite," I hissed, "Madame Poco will never sleep with you again."

"You are very sick person, Mrs. Fulke. I never let any Fulkes touch my Reina. Never! Now I go murder that lying Turk."

Another knockdown fight just outside the tent. Lots of grunting, cursing, and flying fists impacting noses, eyes, mouths, etc. It went on for some time while forgotten Mrs. Fulke lay on the ground in post-molestation wretchedness. At last the fight wound down, and someone remembered the missing third-place finisher.

An unresourceful failure, I never freed myself from a single bond. But where is it written that a good husband should be like Harry Houdini? It seems to me the whole point of marriage is to get yourself thoroughly shackled, not to liberate yourself through unprincipled treachery. Later, I brought up this point with Reina, and she said the committee's original plan had been much more extreme. They were going to truss us up, drive 20 kilometers out into the boondocks, and dump us in some pitch-black field. Very sick, as Jiri would say. The new rankings: Tarkan - 28, Jiri - 32, Mrs. Fulke - 32.

The fistfight turned out much like the first one: Tarkan got a few bruises and rowdy Jiri was beaten to a pulp. Couldn't have happened to a more deserving cretin.

WEDNESDAY, August 17 — Despairing Jiri had to suck his breakfast through a straw today. His swollen lips are too sore for normal eating. Also swollen is his horribly discolored left eye and the knuckles of his right hand. He must have landed some blows on sturdy Tarkan, though you can hardly tell to look at the brute. The renowned Cirque Coco-Poco band may be achieving even more musical lows today. At least Jiri is in solid with his employer, assuming other parts of his body were not similarly ravaged.

More bad news for Jiri. This morning the committee announced the results of their on-going spying effort. It turns out the theme of the secret Tour de Wife contest was "Helpfulness." Lots of groans and boos from the company when Donk divulged this. Yeah, I agree. That's a pretty dull virtue to sneak around in hopes of spotting. I was expecting something more intriguing like "Sophistication of Musical Tastes" or "Ability To Live with Large Cud-chewing Animals."

Believe it or not, Tarkan was named "Most Helpful." The committee cited his assistance to Reina in hitching and unhitching her caravan, leveling said vehicle, hauling birds and props, and running errands in town. He also was observed bringing her home-cooked Turkish snacks and offering her his hand when traversing "difficult terrain." All classic "get-in-your-pants" subterfuges if you ask me.

Mrs. Fulke placed second and was commended for "assisting Reina with her laundry, grocery shopping, and bathroom cleanup." Rude, self-centered Jiri awarded honorable mention for "passing the salt at table when requested." The latest rankings: Tarkan - 33, Jiri - 33, Mrs. Fulke - 35.

Of course, it's a lot easier to be helpful when you have a doting Turkish mother preparing your snacks, and you don't have to spend 12 hours a day cleaning animal cages. Clearly, I was robbed. But I'm still in the lead. And even if I come in second in the final contest tomorrow, I still finish tied for first. Mrs. Fulke is sitting pretty in Fat City. Yes, tomorrow we're playing for all the marbles, as the sports commentators invariably say.

2:47 p.m. I fear Jiri may have spilled the beans about Mrs. Fulke's alleged hermaphroditism. Lots of peculiar sideways glances directed my way from members of the company. I kept having to retreat to the doniker to check if my makeup on correctly. It was. And now receiving frosty reception from other gals encountered therein. Captain Lapo suddenly giving me the cold shoulder too. What's it to him if I am a "chick with a dick"? He was never going to get anywhere near my pants anyway.

4:27 p.m. Ugly incident in the monkey cage just now. Mrs. Fulke was shoveling away when who should appear on the scene but Madame Poco in the company of several elderly Frogs and two gendarmes. I gathered that the old dames were local Béziers animal rights busybodies inspecting conditions at our circus. Not an offensive turd in sight, but they had to dawdle to make faces at the cute baby monkey. Charmed by their attentions, Number 14 decided to demonstrate his developing dexterity by leaping onto Mrs. Fulke's chest. Before I could react, the little pervert pulled down the neckline of my blouse, reached in a hairy paw, and plucked out a great white lump of bra padding. This he carried back to his mother, who chuckled approvingly and gave it an exploratory sniff. Meanwhile, the humans gaped at me in open-mouthed astonishment. I smiled uneasily and pulled up my blouse. Damn, how was it possible I had grown a forest of chest hair overnight? Madame Poco said something in French, the old ladies tittered, the cops peered at me suspiciously, and they all wandered off in the direction of the bear cage.

Paul was right. Once again the littlest monkey had stabbed me in the back.

7:12 p.m. Very quiet around the old folks' table in the cookhouse at dinner tonight. I fear controversial Mrs. Fulke may be making everyone uncomfortable. Most difficult to be an outsider even in circus culture. Madame Poco giving me dirty looks too. I stared at my plate and gobbled down my food in record time. Then I was out of there fast.

Ostracized once again by my peers. And just when I was starting to feel at home.

11:09 p.m. I was holed up in the camel van with the light out when someone knocked on my door.

"Who is it?" I called, fearing the worst.

"It's me, Morag. Reina."

I put down my oranges and let her in.

"What are you doing, Morag?" she inquired.

"Juggling in the dark. Marcel told me it's a good way to practice."

"I talked to Madame Poco, Morag."

"Oh?"

"She said you told her you were a hermaphrodite, but now she doesn't know what to believe."

I sighed, Reina sighed. At a loss for words, I kissed her instead. She didn't seem to mind.

"All we have to do, Reina, is make it through another month with the circus. I'll think of something to tell Madame Poco."

"Like what?"

"I don't know yet. But I'm a resourceful guy."

"Are you? As I recall you came in third."

"Don't worry. And I plan to be way more helpful than Tarkan too."

"Frankly, Rick, so far you haven't been."

"Reina, do you want to marry some guy who burns people with lit cigarettes?"

"Tarkan said that was an accident."

"It was no accident. I watched him do it. It was very deliberate."

"I should never have agreed to this contest, Rick. It's brought out the worst in all of you."

"I think it's been very educational. And don't forget, darling, I'm in the lead."

She didn't pull away when I cupped my hands around her breasts.

"Rick, this has been the strangest summer of my life."

I kissed her hungrily; she pushed her body against mine. Many minutes later, we came up for air. She rested her head on my shoulder and hugged me close.

"What are you doing, Rick?"

"Caressing your nipples through your shirt. How does it feel?"

"Rather dangerous. I advise you to stop."

I was never one to take unsolicited advice.

"Why doesn't it feel like that, Rick, when I do it?"

"I don't know, darling. I think it has to do with the way the brain is wired."

"Very curious, Rick. There seems to be a direct connection between my breasts and . . . and another part of my body."

I made an educated guess and placed a hand on that part. She moaned and nibbled lightly on my ear.

"Remind me again, Rick," she gasped, "how old you'll be when I'm 40."

"An equally ancient 38," I replied, stroking lightly up and down with my middle finger.

"Oh dear," she sighed. "Oh dear, oh dear, oh dear."

And then I felt her body go quite rigid as the cataclysm approached and finally engulfed her. She clung to me as ripples of energy coursed up and down her body.

"My God, Rick," she said at last. "Did you do that to me?"

"Well, it wasn't the camels."

"Are you, uh, equally excited?"

"Oh, you might say that."

"Can I see it?"

"Sure."

I pulled down Mrs. Fulke's stretch pants and displayed the desperately over-stimulated organ. Reina studied it with interest in the dim light.

"I don't see how it could fit."

"It will, take my word for it."

"Shall I touch it?"

"Sure."

"It's very warm and hard."

She gave it a few tentative strokes.

"If you keep that up, darling, you're going to get a nasty surprise."

"I don't mind, Rick. I want to see how it works."

Seconds later I demonstrated the process in its explosive entirety. Reina seemed to find it most fascinating.

"And you propose to do all that inside me someday?" she inquired.

I kissed her and pulled up my pants. "Yes, darling, that is my greatest dream."

THURSDAY, August 18 — I'm writing this in a small café in Bèziers, where I'm enjoying the customary French protein-free breakfast. Decided I better avoid the cookhouse for a few meals since I haven't thought of anything to say to Madame Poco. I'm hoping she'll lose interest in the subject. After all, she's a busy circus manager, and Mrs. Fulke is merely her lowest peon. I'm sure she has more important things to worry about.

The businessmen of Bèziers come in looking sharp in their neat dark suits and stand at the counter, where they drink their *café au laits* and read their newspapers. I envy their orderly, established lives. I wonder what, if anything, they think of the old lady in the corner typing on her laptop. Would they be surprised to learn she is a famous video star on the lam? Do they dread going to the office or do they look forward to their jobs? Do they wish they had more exciting lives in Paris, or are they content with their sedate small town? Hard to tell their states of mind since the French not big on smiling. Would I trade places with them? Sometimes I think I might.

Another anniversary coming up. Tomorrow it will be one year since I met Sheeni Saunders at that trailer park at Clear Lake. One year since that cute stranger whispered "Your robe's open" as I passed her by the men's shower. Three provocative words and my life ran straight off a cliff. What a ride it's been, and how I wish she were here sharing this table with me. She would sip her coffee and read the newspaper—pausing now and again to inform me indignantly of the idiocies going on in the world. I would smile, and admire the passion with which she spoke, and feel again a sense of pride that this marvelous person chose to associate with me. But if I linger on this subject, I'll only depress myself.

Time to go. The last contest of the Tour de Wife starts in less than an hour. Wish me luck, kids.

11:46 a.m. At 10:00 a.m. the three contestants and three committee members assembled for the final showdown in the Plateau des Poètes, a sort of English public garden in Béziers. But we had not come to admire the pretty trees and languid ponds.

Donk began with a surprise announcement. Since the contest was so close and this was the final event, only the first-place finisher would be awarded points. After all, he pointed out, there was only one girl up for grabs. A tie would be pointless. No, in the Game of Love there are no consolation prizes.

The contestants having voiced no objections to this ruling, Donk then requested that we turn over all of our cash and pocket change to Captain Lapo for safekeeping. This I always take as a bad omen, but we meekly complied. The prior events, Donk explained, had evaluated us for those practical, down-to-earth qualities essential in a good husband. But now it was time to delve into those intangible matters of the heart.

Very good, I thought. How about a poetry contest? I, for one, had some burning passions clamoring to get down on paper. But shouldn't they be confiscating our rhyming dictionaries instead of our cash?

Attractiveness, announced Donk, that would be the theme of

today's contest. We participants would have one hour to roam about the town seeing how many people we could persuade to sleep with us. No bribes or any such inducements could be offered. The seducees must come willing of their own volition.

Tarkan was confused. "But where are we supposed to fuck them?"

Such a gentleman of the old school.

"I was coming to that," replied Donk. "Naturally, you won't be expected actually to perform the act. You will be accompanied by a committee member, who will ascertain from each party whether indeed they intended to sleep with you."

Skeptical Jiri raised an objection. "Reina. She has said yes OK to this?"

I could see why he might be apprehensive. He may not have looked exactly like the Creature from the Lost Lagoon, but he certainly resembled its musical brother. Clearly, if he were to have any hope, he would have to locate immediately a ladies' home for the blind and/or insane.

Marcel answered Jiri's question: "The broad general outlines have been cleared with Reina."

"One other thing," said Donk. "The people have to be adults. No little kids or teenagers. And no prostitutes!"

Practical Mrs. Fulke raised her hand. "What if the seducee doesn't speak a language familiar to the committee person—say Turkish, for example?"

Tarkan fired me a dirty look.

"A good point, Mrs. Fulke," replied Donk. "OK, all parties have to speak French or English. That is the rule."

I was glad to see Tarkan drew Marcel instead of the gullible Captain Lapo. But why did I have to get stuck with Donk? Would you confess to some inquisitive giant that you had the hots for a wacky old dame? Clearly, I was starting from a position behind the eight ball. Damn, and I had skipped my morning shower too. Never a sex bomb, Mrs. Fulke was not exactly looking her best. Fortunately, guided by some unseen hand, I had donned a dress this morning. It was that cabbage roses number from Paris. Freshly laundered, so it didn't smell so bad, but all too obviously unironed. I resembled the proverbial unmade bed. Meanwhile, Tarkan was looking pretty sharp in his 'Cowboy from the Bosporus' outfit. He combed his greaseball hair, while Jiri sucked nervously on his wine cork, and Mrs. Fulke performed an emergency tune-up on her makeup.

Then the committee members synchronized their watches and Donk blew his whistle. Operation Alien Seduction had commenced.

Now I've heard that experiments have been conducted where average-looking fellows randomly walk up to women on the street and inquire politely if they wished to screw. Ninety percent of the time the gals screamed, ran away, or called a cop, but a consistent ten percent or so replied, "Sure, your place or mine?" I heard this from my old pal Lefty, but he claimed to have read it in a magazine. Apparently, there is a horny subsection of the populace willing to have impromptu sex with total strangers. And if the figure was ten percent for females, it certainly must be way higher for guys. And even higher still for randy, sexist French guys. It was now Mrs. Fulke's task to root out these libertines. But would those amorous Frogs rise to the bait?

Fortunately, almost all French parks have a few snoozing oldsters leaning on their canes and mentally undressing the passing preschoolers. I sat down on a bench occupied by one such candidate, while Donk loitered discreetly on a nearby path.

"Bonjour," I smiled.

"Bonjour," he croaked, displaying dazzlingly artificial-looking dentures. I guessed his age to be somewhere north of 80.

Damn, how does one say, "Would you like to jump my bones?" in French. Mrs. Fulke would have to resort to pantomime. I made a circle with my thumb and index finger, inserted my other index finger, moved it rapidly in and out, pointed to my breast, then looked inquiringly at my victim. A look of astonishment, followed by incredulity, followed by disgust, followed by skeptical reappraisal.

He whispered something, which even I could translate as "How much?"

Rats. All those working girls in France were spoiling it for us gals who wanted to give it away. I pantomimed opening a purse, then waving no. I drew a heart in the air, smiled coyly, and pointed at him.

He looked dubious, then uncertain. Close enough for rural work. I squeezed his bony knee, grabbed his hand, and led him hopefully toward my companion. Smiling amiably, Donk made the meekest of inquiries, but it was all too much for my prey. He expostulated wildly, yanked free his hand, and tottered off down the lane. Two other solicitations ended just as disastrously. Time to go to Plan B.

Tourists, I need to find tourists. The cathedral! Just as I supposed, the medieval quarter around the church was lousy with camera-dangling Americans. I accosted three likely looking college-aged youths.

"Hiya, boys,"

"Sorry, Granny," one replied. "We're just as lost as you are."

"Say, boys, you see that giant over there?"

"My God!" exclaimed his pal. "Is that Andre?"

"Shhh, not so loud," I cautioned. "He hates it when people ask that. No, that's Donk my son. I have a little bet on with him."

"Is this a scam?" demanded the third youth.

Jesus, Americans are so suspicious these days. It must be all those e-mail solicitations rolling in from Nigeria.

"Not at all," I assured him. "It's just that Donk doesn't think he can get a date. It's got him terribly depressed."

"My sister would probably go for him," remarked the first kid, "but she's back in Cleveland."

"No matter," I assured him. "It's just that I'm trying to convince him that looks aren't that important. That even *I* could get a date."

Rumbles of skepticism from my new pals.

"Come on, boys," I pleaded. "All I'm asking is for you to assure my son that you would sleep with me."

"Are you crazy, lady?" asked the third one. "Or are you some kind of weird old, uh . . ."

"Streetwalker?" suggested his buddy.

"OK, guys," I admitted in my normal voice. "It's a fraternity stunt. I'm really a guy." I gave them a peek at my cloistered chest hair. "But I'll win points if you tell that giant you dig me. You have to pretend like you really mean it though."

Believe it or not, they agreed. Mrs. Fulke scored three Big Ones.

During the balance of the hour I employed variations on this theme with three cute girls from Wayne State, an elderly Irish couple (yes, both the man and his frail white-haired wife assured Donk that they would do me), three insurance salesmen from Colorado on a company-paid barge cruise won in a sales contest, and an English-speaking Béziers taxi driver and his two fares (gay guys from West Hollywood on their honeymoon). I was working on three visiting priests from Fall River when Donk blew his whistle. Still, 15 legitimate scores in 60 minutes is not bad for an old lady well past her prime.

12:36 p.m. NEWS BULLETIN: I think Mrs. Fulke may have won!

Tarkan, Jiri, Marcel, and Captain Lapo did not show up for lunch. The rumor is they are all under arrest in Béziers. Madame Poco most furious. Just peeled out of lot in her truck headed for town.

Taking matters in her own hands, Reina has awarded me a preliminary kiss (and bonus grope) behind the cookhouse tent.

I think we're engaged!

1:06 p.m. The two gendarmes from yesterday are back. I seem to be under arrest. It's all a mistake. Mrs. Fulke was not soliciting anyone. Will write more later.

THIRTEEN YEARS LATER

I found this letter in my inbox at the hotel this afternoon:

Dear Nick:

I read recently of your improbable success in Las Vegas. At least, I suppose it's you. Could there be two Nick Twisps on this planet? I'm assuming not, though I find it astonishing that the Nick Twisp I once knew would take up comedic juggling. Congratulations on your showbiz "triumphs."

I sometimes imagine you must wonder what happened to me. Forgive my presumption if that is not the case. I'm married and living in Lyon. It's not Paris, but Lyon is France's second largest urban region and quite a cosmopolitan place. My husband's wine brokerage business keeps us here (and keeps us very busy). I have two children: Emma, six, and François, nearly four. I try to converse in English with them so they will grow up bilingual, but they insist on replying in French. They are quite a handful, but we have a wonderful nanny (Italian) who shoulders much of the burden. I have 11 more units to go to get my degree (in modern French literature). These days I have to get up shockingly early in the morning to get any reading done. Fortunately, I love the view of the sun rising over the Fourvière hill from our terrace.

Forgive me for disappearing so suddenly all those years ago. Like my brother before me, I had to escape my family. As you may recall, my parents were not to be endured. I went to live with Alfredo Nunez's brother, who had a farm in southern France. I don't know if you remember Alfredo. He was a noted clown who lived down the hall from us. I was quite in love with him for a time, and he helped me with many kindnesses. I believe he now lives in Buenos Aires.

Have you been following the career of Trent Preston? Who could have imagined that my childhood sweetheart would become such a star and marry that odd Brit contortionist? I sometimes wonder if that was your plan all along. Are you still so devious?

Write to me if you get an opportunity. I would enjoy hearing what you're doing. Any marriage prospects? The article I read said you were single. I think of you often with fondness.

Cheers,
Sheeni

No 13-year-old daughter. Well, that clears up that mystery. I wonder if Señor Nunez's brother's farm was anywhere near Albi? Too bad she wasn't more specific about the location. Perhaps his brother was of normal size and drove a green car. I'm annoyed at the short guy's duplicity, but we all know how persuasive Sheeni can be when she tries. So she did love him. Connie's warning turned out to be well-founded.

It surprises me that Sheeni wound up marrying a suit. I thought she had her heart set on some French intellectual-type. Do you suppose little François is named after his papa? In that case, at least one of her presentiments came true. All in all, my old girlfriend's domestic arrangements seem somewhat more conventional than I would have expected. Life is full of surprises.

I sometimes wish I hadn't let my journal-writing lapse. But the unrelenting dreariness of the California juvenile justice system proved more conducive to practicing one's juggling than noting the daily particularities of one's unhappiness.

The irony is that Sheeni escaped her father, but I never could. After I was arrested, he tried to have me brought up on homicide charges. The only Saunders I wanted to see dead was certainly not his daughter. I suppose he thought if I were charged with killing Sheeni, she would have to come forward to save me. Not entirely a valid assumption, I fear. Fortunately, the French magistrate had had more than his fill of the pushy American lawyer. And the absence of a corpse and Rick S. Hunter's high media profile helped forestall a gross miscarriage of justice. But Mr. Saunders made sure I answered to the authorities in California for my many transgressions in my home state.

I notice Sheeni makes no mention of the funds she's been "holding" for me all these years. I don't need them particularly now, but I could have used the money when I was trying to hire lawyers to get her ogre father off my back. Mario and Kimberly lost their shirts on my "mouth jewelry" idea, so there was no help from that quarter. Is it too much to lay the blame for all my years spent in "rehabilitation" at the cinematic feet of Luis Buñuel? Perhaps.

My mother helped a little, but her court case with Lance dragged on for years. In the end he did prevail. For his pain and suffering the jury in San Francisco awarded him one dollar. Perhaps his color photos were too graphic and his demeanor on the stand too insufferable. Last I heard he was working as the head of security for an Indian casino up in the redwoods somewhere.

My mother got her old job back with the Department of Motor Vehicles and still lives in Oakland. Shy trucker Wally Rumpkin is back in the picture as my mother's designated doormat. She was never able to regain custody of my little brother. I think family court judges can sniff out poor parenting prospects. Noel Lance Wescott continues to live with Lance's mother in Winnemucca, and is said to be a bookish teen with an interest in writing. Perhaps one of these days I'll pay his way down to Vegas to catch my act. Though, if he's a real Twisp, he could be trouble in a town full of showgirls.

Last photo of him I saw he bore an unfortunate resemblance to me at that age. No ill effects apparent yet from being dropped on the floor by his careless bro'. These days I could juggle five or six such infants without working up a sweat. That might be something to try: diapering a kid or two in midair.

My father decided to devote full time to alcohol and now lives in a residence hotel near downtown L.A. I send him a check every month to stay away from me. My sister married a nice steady electrician named Bill and they live in the San Fernando Valley. Her son Tyler just passed six feet four inches to become the tallest Twisp in history. He plays sports and is the star of all his junior high school teams.

I was sorry that Trent's marriage didn't work out. Well, it seemed like a good match at the time, but perhaps the cultural differences were too formidable. Apurva gave birth to a healthy son and married one of her college professors. They live in Madison. Todd Amitabh Preston I see occasionally in the summers when he's with his dad. A very bright kid and absurdly well-favored like his parents. His uncle Vijay was admitted back into the U.S. and went to Stanford. I insist on remaining blissfully ignorant of his subsequent activities.

Don't know much about my old pals Lefty or Fuzzy either. I heard Lefty got married, but I think he's divorced now. Fuzzy has entered the family concrete business in Ukiah. His uncle Sal came backstage a few years ago to introduce himself and shake my hand. I thanked him for not bumping me off. He said he was still keeping an eye on me, so I should keep my nose clean. I think he was kidding.

Sonia Klummplatz got her stomach stapled, lost over a hundred pounds, and went into the modeling profession under the name Esqué. You've probably seen some of her ubiquitous cosmetics ads. She always did have the nicest complexion in town and superb bone structure to boot it turns out. I hear she makes over $1,000 an hour and can be quite a handful on the set. Her love life is a favorite topic of supermarket tabloids. For a time she was keeping company with the handsomest Preston of all (Trent's cousin Bruno), but then she dumped him. Once in a drunken moment I confessed to friends that I had nailed her. Needless to say, they called me a dirty liar.

Connie and Paul remain married and have produced three precocious offspring, all allegedly authentic Saunders. Paul has a small record label with an enviable list of highly regarded jazz artists. He also promotes concerts up and down the coast. I see them occasionally when I'm in L.A. They seem quite happy together. It just goes to show that sometimes you can lead a horse to water *and* make him drink. I wonder if the present Mr. Sheeni Saunders had to resort to similar desperate measures to drag her to the altar?

Paul's mother-in-law Rita lives ambiguously with Dogo and their many small dogs outside Phoenix. Lacey married her probate attorney and now runs a string of successful hair salons in the San Fernando Valley. Every year she donates a portion of her profits to an orphanage in Brazil.

As for Reina, years went by before I heard from her. I found out later that she had written numerous times, but Mr. Saunders had instructed that all letters to me from France be sent to him in case they contained coded messages from Sheeni. He was supposed to forward them to me, but he never bothered. No, she didn't settle for second place Jiri or Tarkan. She decided that what she really wanted was another parrot. She named it Rick. I called her a few years ago. She was living in Prague and still touring with circuses. She had married a clown (not Marcel) and they had two daughters. She sounded very happy with her life. I wished her well and told her I would never forget our nights in the camel van. She laughed that same magical laugh. She hasn't changed. So now she's 30 and I'm 28, and it's still not doing us any good. We are lost to each other for good it seems.

I never found out the circumstances behind my arrest in Béziers. I don't know if one of the gendarmes recognized me or if someone betrayed me. For a long time I thought it was Marcel who had gone through my stuff in the van and offered me up to the cops when they nailed Tarkan and him for annoying the good ladies of Béziers. Now I'm not so sure. I suppose it could have been Jiri, or Madame Poco, or one of the Baturs. The gendarmes split Mr. Saunders' reward, but they never said if someone tipped them off. I've thought of going to France and snooping around, but what would that accomplish? You can't turn back the clock. Marcel may have been a bastard, but I can thank him for my profession. I doubt, though, if I could yet weasel a compliment out of the guy for my juggling.

Strange, but of all the people from my youth, the ones I see most frequently these days are Trent and Violet. They always catch my show when they're in town. We pal around and hang out by my pool just like celebrities are supposed to. Trent has loosened up and is quite a pleasant guy to be around. My best friend? Could be.

No, I'm not married, but I have a lady friend I see frequently. Not wildly in love, but we're comfortable together. Las Vegas is a crazy town, but you can have a fairly normal life if you don't let things go to your head. Marriage and children? One of these days I'll have to decide if they're for me. Big responsibility and loads of work from what I can see. Don't know if I'd bring much expertise to either activity. I do know a few things: kids only get one chance at a childhood, and they remember all your screw-ups. I wouldn't want a repeat of my parents' disasters.

I don't suppose I'll reply to Sheeni's letter. Perhaps it's best to let it rest. We live in different worlds now. Our only connection is the past, and I don't think Sheeni is the type of person to look back much. I suspect she wrote to me impulsively and even now is regretting that act. So as the song says, let it be.

So that's it. Enough with this writing. I think I've lost the knack. I'm a firm believer that you can only expect to do one thing really well, and you should stick to that. So I enjoy being an entertainer. I dig the laughs and applause.

Yeah, I still think of Sheeni almost every day. I told her once that when I die hers will be the last name on my lips. So far I haven't had much cause to suppose that will change.

C.D. Payne was born in 1949 in Akron, Ohio, the former "Rubber Capital of the World" famed for its tire factories. He shares a birthday with P.T. Barnum, a fact which has influenced his life profoundly. After graduating from Harvard College in 1971, he moved to California, where he's worked as a newspaper editor, graphic artist, cartoonist, typesetter, photographer, proofreader, carpenter, trailer park handyman, and advertising copywriter. He is married and lives in Sonoma County.